RESURRECTION

SHADOWS OF LONDON

M H AUSTIN

*I would like to dedicate this book to the brilliant scientists and
researchers of the world who daily
seek to improve our health. Their work often goes unrecognized 'til
a great breakthrough is made,
but they are tireless in their determination.*

Serenade Publishing

www.serenadepublishing.com

MORE FROM SERENADE PUBLISHING

Brigadier Station Series

By Sarah Williams:

The Brothers of Brigadier Station

The Sky over Brigadier Station

The Legacies of Brigadier Station

Christmas at Brigadier Station (An Outback Christmas Novella)

The Outback Governess (A Sweet Outback Novella)

Heart of the Hinterland Series

By Sarah Williams:

The Dairy Farmer's Daughter

Their Perfect Blend

Beyond the Barre

A Dying Second Sun

by Peter A. Dowse

Winner Winner Chicken Dinner

by Sarah Jackson

A New Page

by Aimee MacRae

Middle Women

By Jack Garrety

Mim and Wiggy's Grand Adventure

By Jay McKenzie

For more information visit:

www.serenadepublishing.com

PROLOGUE

Prologue – Edinburgh 29th April 1828

Leaning against the tavern doorframe, shadowed by the overhang of the rooms upstairs, he couldn't be sure of her age. When she moved forward into the light, her eyes had a saucy sparkle, older than the rest of her. He slowed his steps; warm-blooded enough to be aroused early on a cold, wet morning. She smiled. He was ensnared.

"Come Sir, comfort and relief for a sixpence." Mary stroked her thigh then brought her hand up slowly towards her crotch, eyes hooded; a sliver of tongue wetly brushed her lips. She arched her back, a small foot braced behind her against the wall. "Nothing barred for a shillun'."

"I'm away to break my fast." His voice was guttural, stern. He tarried for a moment too long. "Mebbe later."

"A poor working girl like me, I canna' eat lest you buy for me." Her target paused. After a moment of careful consideration, in which she rubbed her belly and pouted with great enthusiasm, he conceded.

"You've a way with ye lassie. Come inside then. I'll buy ye a bite."

"And for my friend? We work together real well." She pulled a shorter, thinner girl from out the shadows. Janet thrust her underdeveloped chest forward in a bid to entice him.

"This is Janey. She helps out for fourpence."

Janey smiled; an unskilled wink twitched at her mouth.

"Impudent minx. I'll get ye both a bite but then you treat me in return, eh?"

"And a dram each if we please ye?"

"Aye. Oh aye, I'm sure ye'll both please alright."

1

EDINBURGH 29TH JANUARY 1829

St. Giles' bells chimed eight as I waited, rigid, for the hanging. A mighty cheer broke out, and I closed my eyes. I hadna' meant to. I'd wanted to watch and enjoy seeing him die. I breathed deep the city's damp morning air giving thanks it was over. Burke was dead or would be in a few minutes if he were lucky. Please God, I prayed, dinna' let him be lucky.

I gripped the parapet to steady myself for my head was reeling with the buffeting ice-cold wind. Below me the Water of Leith roared. It wasna' over though, was it? What of Hare? Why should only one of them die? I ached with frustration that after all the public outrage he'd been allowed to walk away. My grief for Mary haunted me. There was no' a thing I could do, I knew that, but I raged inside still, like the city's great river below me, churning and boiling. I looked down at the waves crashing round the bridge's supports through the mist of my tears, and for just a wee fleeting moment I thought to let go of life; slide down into the brown depths to eternal sleep; be carried away from this filthy town and its violence. Oh aye, I could've ended it all then.

Dougal's small hand tugged at my skirt. I turned to look down at his thin, grey face.

"Janey, will ye be coming home?"

"Aye, Dougal." I raised a weak smile and squeezed his chilly fingers. "Don't fret yoursel', I'm alright. Let's get back before we freeze."

"Will he be dead yet? He might be kicking still. Do you no want to go and watch?"

"Let him kick, he can do that without us gawping at him. We should go home. This is no place for you, laddie. Come on, let's away from here."

A cart, heavy with students already drunk this early hour, clattered past across the bridge heading for the square. I pulled Dougal out of their way and called out after them to "Mind who's in your road!" They'd missed the hanging, but their laughter and obscene rhymes floated back to us as they hurtled around the sharp bend into Liberton's Wynd and the mob beyond. The whole of Edinburgh and half the surrounding countryside had turned out for the event, and it seemed to me I must have been the only one to have stayed apart. I'd left home early to get a good place, but as the swell around me thickened and heaved my desire to see it through had seeped away. Sick and giddy, I'd edged myself out of the crowd and down a side street jest minutes before the hangman completed his job, then onto the old post office bridge to breathe the air again.

For weeks the newssheets had been full of the arrest

and trial, the shocked questions, guessed answers. I remember standing in front of the Sheriff giving my own brief statement. I couldn't take my eyes off the dock while I stood there, feeling all the folk were looking at me. My head distant, floating ghost-like above the room. I stammered out my lines.

"Aye, Sir, he's the one. He gave us drink and took Mary into the other room...... aye, the room to the side with the big bed in it."

"You went into this room yourself?"

"No Sir."

"Then how do you know there was a big bed in it?"

He looked real handsome and cocky standing there, Burke. He even smiled. At ease he was, his rakish eyes studying me while he adjusted his cravat, shaking his head, like he was disappointed I'd let him down.

"I saw it through the door when he opened it. I heard the springs in it when they were...." The court-room was noisy with folk laughing. I looked around, angry. But they weren't laughing at me or Mary, just letting their dirty imaginings loose.

"And did you hear your friend, Miss Paterson, cry out? At any time while this alleged murder took place, did she call to you? Shout for assistance?"

What was the man thinking? No, of course not. She was smothered. His great hand pressing on her, stopping her breath. I'd read of it in the newssheets, labouring over the words, trying to hold back my sobs. It was how he'd done it to all his victims. He'd crushed her with his weight to keep her from moving, covered her nose and mouth so she couldn't breathe. And now, in the courtroom, no remorse, no despair at what he'd done. He just stood there, calm, like it was someone else going to hang. But when it came to it, it was his own friend, Hare, as did for him.

Taking Dougal firmly by the arm I steered him past Tanner's Close with its memories and into Cowgate. Uphill all the way, fighting against the wind. I was tiring and breathing heavy by the time we reached the dark brick tenement that was our home. The familiar reek of greasy food, sweat and damp, rotting timbers welcomed us as I opened the door and pushed Dougal into the kitchen.

Ma Lawrie greeted us with wary silence, stirring her great iron cauldron on the range as I unbuttoned my cloak. My hands were that chill my fingers were stiff as sticks when I ran them through my hair. The boy fidgeted, whining his displeasure.

"Can I go see him later then? They're going to take him to the college and show him to the crowd. Hamish will be going, all the students, everyone. The surgeons will cut him and give him a taste of his own medicine, Hamish says. Missus, tell Janey I can go, and she should come with me."

"Whisht boy. Enough! Here have some porridge, Janet. Come, warm yoursel'." She motioned to the rush-bottomed rocker by the fireside, her own chair.

"Thank'ee Ma, I'm frozen through." I took the bowl she proffered and sat down, stirring its contents but with no appetite to eat. Dougal continued his whining for a few minutes more until Ma snapped at him and raised her ladle menacingly. He fled then, fearing her wrath, the echo of his steps fading as he mounted the stairs.

"Bloodthirsty tyke!"

"He's jest a boy, Ma. Men live only for pain and death."

"Aye, when they're not making money or chasing skirts."

"They were baying like dogs out there; savages all of them."

"And the women like as not alongside them." Ma Lawrie was quick to note her own sex's cruelty. "Aren't you glad to see him hang then? You were keen enough to speak against him at the trial. 'Tis only right he swings for Mary."

I stopped my stirring then and let the bowl sit in my lap, food untouched. A warm rush of anger tightened my belly.

"We owe Mary more than that. The other one is still free to walk the streets, and nothing is being done to stop Surgeon Knox and his kind buying more jest like her. The whole sick trade is still as it was. My God, Ma, 'tis a strange world where the dead are used so."

"We can't stop the college folk, Janet. Your Hamish will tell you that. They need the learning from it and there it is."

"There it is! The poor die and those above study us. None of their learning will make a jot o' difference to the likes of us, you'll see."

"Hush now, don't talk daft, girl. They've hanged Burke for his crimes, and they will hang anyone else the same if they kill innocent folk, rich or poor. Eat your porridge and thank God, they caught him and there's an end to his vile business."

"Aye, well, we must be thankful, mustn't we? They can still dig us out of our graves even without murdering us first." I was overcome with the uselessness of my protest and slumped back in the chair, leaning my head on my hand. "No matter what happens, Mary will no' be back with us will she? I miss her, Ma." A tear rolled uncalled for down my cheek, and I rubbed at it angrily.

"No. Poor lass." She picked up her broom. The loss of her best girl had upset her more than she'd admit to. Mary had been with her for years.

Dust swirled with her sweeping and settled about us. It fell on the oaken press and on the great barrel, empty and upended near the door, there to remind folk of her hospitality but which also doubled as a safe place for Ma to keep her takings, hidden inside in a folded shawl. I knew it was there; I guess all us girls did.

"You need to fatten up a bit girl, you're wasting away there. Men like a bit of meat on a woman not a handful of old bones. Get that food inside you and tidy yourself up then you can get out and earn a few shillun'." She hadn't meant to sound as harsh as she did, I'm sure, and mebbe she was sorry when I ducked and bit my lip, wincing as though from a physical blow. Ma Lawrie didn't beat us girls, I'll say that, not like some brothel keepers in West Port. But she was right to worry at me for, God knows, the rent still had to be paid.

"Go on, eat up." Her voice softened and she took herself off to the woodpile in the corner, rattling around with the scuttle, selecting the drier chunks of off-cuts for the fire.

Anything I may have said wouldn't have been heard over the clatter, so I said nothing. After a mouthful or two of rapidly cooling porridge, I went upstairs to the draughty attic room I now had to myself. Once I would have craved the privacy, now I sat on the low truckle bed and stared at the cracked plaster and lath wall. I drew a moth-eaten blanket around my shoulders, my feet curled under me for warmth. Rain pattered against the shutters and in the semi darkness my breath rose in a gentle mist. A well-worn dress hanging from the roof beam gave the shape of its former owner and, reaching across the small divide I drew it to my breast and buried my face in its folds. It still smelt of Mary's treasured lavender water. Sobbing, I rocked gently back and forth. "Mary, oh I'm so sorry. Forgive me for leaving you alone with him." My heart ached and my whispered words were lost in the rough fabric. "He's dead now, Mary. It's alright. The bastard was hanged today so sleep easy now, lassie."

"Mary and I had gone out as usual," I'd told the sheriff. The courtroom was hushed, listening to my cracking voice, and he told me to speak up. "It was then we met William Burke, a stranger 'til that day. We'd had barely a bite to eat afore he pressed us to leave the tavern and go with him to his lodging house in Tanners Close, but a few streets away. There we had a wee bit more drink."

"Was that wise?" The court laughed when the sheriff asked that, like we should have said no to a drink.

"We was grateful, Sir, for a drop of warmth in our bellies." Oh, what fools we were! Looking back, I knew that even as I spoke.

"While Mary and Burke got at, eh, the business part," more roars of laughter then and I had to wait for them to stop before I carried on. "I dozed by the fireside, though it was cooling by then and I thought about throwing on another log but didna' dare lest the man come out and tell me off." There were a few sympathetic murmurs then and I felt I was winning them over. "When I came to, I could hear them moving around still, in the next room, and I called out, 'I'm away home. Are you done there Mary?' and Burke, as I know him now, he said 'Mary's busy. You pour another drink and I'll be out for you in a minute if you want to earn your sixpence.' He sounded out of breath and there was no answer from Mary. I didna' want to stay for I was feeling sick, what with the drink and the lack of solid food, so I decided to forego the sixpence, and make my way home."

The sheriff then asked me about how much sixpence was to me and kept on at me as though he didn't think I should have gone if I cared for my friend. Well, now I know what he did to her, I agree, course I do. Had I known the truth I'd have screamed for help and scratched out his eyes!

"When Mary didna' return, Ma Lawrie became afeared and bid me go back to Tanners Close and bring her home. I took Dougal," the courtroom started laughing again then, though the sheriff looked down at me stern and then over at where young Dougal sat all this time with Ma. The lad was growing fidgety now and when he heard his name and sat up proud, only to be laughed at, my heart sank for his hurt pride. He was no strongarm, but he was a good lad, and with instructions to run like the wind for help should the man turn nasty, we'd walked back to Lough's Lodgings.

"There was no sign of either of them, Sir. Mary or Burke."

"And did you wait for anyone to return, or summon help if you thought there had been foul play?"

"No, Sir." I twisted my kerchief round in my hands and could feel tears pricking my eyes. The sheriff was looking down at me from his seat, high up over the room like an old crow in his nest, and I remembered how I'd been angry rather than alarmed, for I knew no better, and I'd taken myself back to Ma Lawrie's house.

It was only two days later when the medical students saw Mary in Knox's anatomy class and Hamish recognized her at once. Twice Hamish had been to our house to haul his friend Ewan back to their lodgings after he'd fallen for Mary's charms. Hamish had seen Mary and me and would have known her when she lay there in front of Knox with his knife. It makes me shudder even now when I think of it. Ewan had been kind to Mary and keen to learn the art of being a man. He wasn't always such a good student at the college, so Hamish said, and he wasn't at the lecture that day; thank the Lord, for it would have distressed him to see his lively playmate so despoiled.

It was hard to believe I'd never see Mary again. That she was gone and not even buried where I could visit her. Then, another prostitute, old Mary Haldane, died suspiciously later that summer and, like my Mary, ended up in the dissecting room. There followed a simple lad and an old man who sold matches, and the anger of Edinburgh's mob overflowed, for all they were the poorest folk. Knox was already unpopular, so there were violent scenes outside his house. Everyone said he must have known not all his fine fresh corpses had met natural deaths. Why had he asked no questions? I couldna' understand what monsters these surgeons could be that they should cut up the bodies of the dead and not care for either their souls or the families left behind to mourn.

The police arrested Burke and William Hare whose lodging house it was, when another body was found, still warm and hidden in straw under a bed. Eventually they struck a deal with Hare, the polis and the sheriff, so Hamish told me, guaranteeing his freedom if he talked.

I barely remember Hare's face for all he sat there next to Burke in the dock. His friend was much more handsome, and Hare must have had a plain old face for I canna' recall him one way or other. I remember only that he wore a dark coat and had a longish look about him, and him being all sly with the sheriff and then, when the court sat the next day, he wasn't there and only Burke sat quiet and less cocksure.

The police spoke to Knox at his fine house in the New Town, but the sheriff's men were no match for him, with his sharp tongue and wits, and they retreated back to the watch house within the hour, satisfied with the lesser fish they'd caught.

Now, nearly a year after he killed sweet Mary, Burke had been hanged. May God rot his soul!

Morning turned into afternoon, and I dozed on my teary pillow, exhausted for want of a moment's peace from my loss. I had grown thin and was forever tired in those days after the murder, and by the time of the hanging I had little will or strength to do anything, even eat.

Ma Lawrie still gave me a bed and I suppose my not eating was a blessing to her. Though she was a kind enough old soul for a madam, and like a real mother to her girls in many ways, excepting of course that she took as normal the acts no normal mother would ask of a daughter. She herself had no knowledge of a decent family to compare, having grown up in a whorehouse. Not that I could remember much of my early life, in truth, before my real mother died, and I fell to the parish to be raised.

She had just four girls now, Ma Lawrie. She told us if we all got back to working hard, we'd see the winter out safe enough. I didna' want to let her down, but my heart was nae in it. I feared every strange man I met, just as when I first started to earn my keep, a wee lass of twelve. I'd been in the orphanage for two whole years before I'd run away, and Ma found me cowering behind the vegetable stall. I'd gone there for safety, crawling between the stalls pushed for the night against the church wall, and will never forget her face when it came against mine while she hunted a few stray tatties for her 'family's' supper. I went home with her, for the promise of a hot dinner and a cleaner bed than the street.

They were rising now even as I thought of them, the other three. Their voices calling for Dougal; "Hot water and towels," then breaking into laughter as he gave his insolent answers, same as every day.

"Yes, madam just coming, and with your hot chocolate and finest white rolls. And would m'lady like to visit in the coach today only the coachman has died of the clap and the footman is in gaol. Or the sedan chair mebbe, though she may need to lose some weight first afore I can lift her!" There was a sound of a shoe being thrown and roars of laughter. "Or mebbe she would just like to walk as it's such a fine day, barring the sleet and snow?"

Lewd banter filled the house. For all we were poor, and life was grim they were quick to laugh, my fellow whores. There was little to laugh at, but with whisky cheaper than meat, and laughter better than tears they lived a life of feverish merriment much of the time, and when the whisky didn't bring laughter, the laudanum brought peace. I turned over on my pillow and tried to blot out the sounds.

I'd brought home a paying man barely a dozen times since the murder back in April; I couldna' hope Ma would keep me forever and expected every day for her to threaten me with the streets. But she must have had a soft spot for this skinny one, and the last time I came running home in tears without a catch she was quick to reassure me there were enough coins in the rent-box for this week, and with any luck the pastor would visit. She'd let him say a few of his prayers and fumble her breasts if he felt the need. He was easy pleased and always paid without comment and often-times brought a packet of something from his house-keeper. What would she say if she knew what her respected Master was really like? Would she be so free with her shortbreads then? Ah, men! Ma would laugh and say that we would manage a bit longer yet. Somehow.

At just after four in the afternoon, when the house was quiet with the others out working round West Port, I woke from my doze as the street door rattled noisily and I heard Ma's voice talking to someone.

"Ah, come away in, lad. I'm glad as always to see ye."

I got to my feet and splashed some water on my face to wake myself, sure it was Hamish, and I was always happy to see him.

In truth, as a student, he was not likely to bring more than another hungry mouth and a few good stories from the university but, as Ma would say, who knew to what heights he might rise one day. She likely saw in him a future bright and secure. Oh, she could dream! I wouldna' dare to do so myself, but he was always kind and cheery.

"How is the great doctor today?" I heard her ask, while I hovered on the small dark landing outside my door, shivering in my thin dress. Then, "Sit yoursel' down, young Sir, and warm your cold parts by the fire. Have you come to see our beautiful Janet? I'll fetch her down for you if you crave a bit o' company."

"Is she well, Ma?"

"As well as a walking ghost can be, pale as a spirit, fading for want of a strong man's attention. Here, get a wee dram inside you, Sir, and take your boots off if you wish. I'll go and rouse the lazy hussy, she wouldna' want to miss your visit, I'm sure."

"That's all-right Ma, I'll go up and surprise her."

Hamish climbed the two flights to the attic. I heard his boots thudding nearer, carefully avoiding the rotten steps he'd become familiar with over the last year, and I darted back into my room. He tapped on my door before stooping and entering, ever the gentleman.

"Janet, good day to you; I was passing and thought of my sad sparrow. How are you this day? Pleased no doubt with this morning's event?"

"I'm honoured you can spare me your valuable time, Hamish." I lowered my eyes, angry with myself for the sharpness of my tongue when I'd planned to be soft and welcoming. He was a good lad, trying to be kind. Why was I so bitter when none of this was his fault? "Are you not celebrating with your friends?"

"I've had a drink or two to send the wretch to his maker, aye, and you haven't, girl."

"No, I stayed sober to wish him to the devil. He's quite turned me off my liquor."

"Maybe a good thing. Knox says too much alcohol, particularly in females-"

"Knox! Knox! Your precious Lord Knox!"

"No Lord, Janey, but he's a wise teacher for all his ill-fame, and I'm grateful to him for his generosity to me and I'll not say otherwise."

I saw the defensive glint in his eye and steadied my rebel tongue. "Well, is the wise man no' teaching today?"

"No, we're on holiday, but tomorrow we hope to resume our studies with a special subject." Hamish grinned.

"You canna' mean...?"

"Aye! All being well, we'll study the criminal brain using the man himself, Burke. There'll be a goodly turnout for that one anyway." He looked serious then. "Assuming Knox will be able to give the lecture. Things are hard for him since the trial you know; most of the better off students are taking their custom elsewhere, even to Glasgow. Some of the College elders are proposing not to let him teach next term; force him out."

"I weep for him!"

"But Janet, he's the best man they have! I will not attend McCready's pompous lectures just because Knox is out of fashion. They're full of nonsensical speculation and religion, no science at all to speak of. It's a travesty. He uses ancient diagrams and the word of the bible to teach digestion! The man's a fool!"

"You think it makes any difference to our digestion if you pull the guts out of a man rather than read about them?"

"If we are to practice real medicine we must have real guts to study Janey, you know that. It's not sport for me, just practical method."

I studied his earnest expression and knew he was speaking the truth, then ruffled his hair and patted the bed, inviting him to sit. "Well, you're welcome to the guts of Mr Burke, m'dear. If he can teach you which way the porridge goes down good luck to ye," I said.

Hamish laughed and cupped my chin in his hand. "That's better, Janey. To see you smile is a relief to me. Things are improving and soon we'll have you back in full fettle."

"Hmm, we'll see." I was no' so sure, although his being there made the dark clouds lift from me a little.

"You doubt me?"

"I only doubt my future here, Hamish. I'm not sure I can, well.... I really canna' go back to the old ways ye know."

"Pastor Paisley will rejoice; another soul is saved!"

"Jest not, Hamish. I mean I canna' do it. I'm afraid since Mary was killed. I think sometimes I should find another trade. I'm sure I could do something better."

"Yes, surely my lady can become a governess, or maybe a courtesan to the High Sheriff if not." Though he mocked, his eyes were troubled. He squeezed my hand in his. "I will be in a position to take care of you one day, Janey, I promise you. Just not yet. You know I've no money or I would take you away from here today."

I will never know why this strange young man had taken such a fancy to me. Ever since he had first caught sight of me, holding up the head of his friend Ewan while he puked on Mary's bed and mopping his brow with cool water, and she lost in fits of laughter. Hamish had thanked me, as I helped get Ewan down the stairs and away to sober up, and then he visited me on and off to talk of his studies and I listened and made him feel he had a friend to sit with, while Ewan visited Mary for the usual reasons. Then, after the murder, he came more often, even when Ewan wasn't there.

"Yes, I believe you would, silly boy." Then, jumping up and opening the shutters so he wouldna' see the tears in my eyes, I looked out into the rainy early evening. My lamp flickered on the table under the window throwing great shadows on the wall as I turned. "I thank you, really, in all seriousness, Hamish. What would I have done these past months without your visits?"

He shrugged, feigning an off-handed ease I knew he didna' really feel.

"You will survive, Janey, don't worry. With me or without me, I'm sure. Now, I must away. I'm meeting the lads for another drink before we set off for College Square. The night is cold and will be long and loud, I think. There'll be broken heads and windows unless the mob has its' quarry, and they may not wait 'til morning,"

"Be careful, Hamish!" I warned him, worried about the mob wandering the streets with their songs and knives. "Don't get into any fights over a dead man."

"Never you mind; stay safe, Janey and, I mean it, I will do whatever I can to make your life easier." He kissed me fondly then, though as a brother would, and slipped away down the stairs and out into the lane, tossing his sixpence onto Ma's barrel as he passed her, "For the whisky." For he never took anything else from me in all the months he visited, though the girls wouldna' have believed it. Ma knew though, I'm sure of that, and she was glad to have him come.

I watched him from my window as he strode out, an upright shadow dark against the lightly falling snow, cutting a fine figure as he swaggered. A gent in the making he was, to be sure, if a strange one. If only he could hold me close and love me, I thought, and not as a brother; and me to love him in return. But I dare not. One day, but not yet awhile; there was no place for such folly yet. My mother had been foolish once, giving her heart away, and look where it had got her, a bairn in a freezing garret, hunger and sickness. No! I wanted more from the world, no' jest a penniless student. Wait until he is a great surgeon, and he would be soon enough, of that I was sure. And I would wait, and hold my heart back 'til then, for all it ached.

Next morning the crowd waited in vain outside the College, but then on Friday, I learned after, the students had their promised public dissection of William Burke, murderer. His strong, handsome body was barely changed, after three months in prison. Muscled still, and firm, it was laid on the anatomist's table, as fine a specimen of manhood as Edinburgh had to offer, the only blemish the purple band around his neck where the rope had chafed him.

His brain and other organs were sadly much the same as any other man's, so Hamish told me, and there was disappointment among some who had been expecting more. With their bloodthirsty appetites sated for the day, the better folk then departed to make their various ways home, or to the town's taverns as the fancy took them. Burke's remains were, according to law, not buried but fed to the street dogs, less those parts put in jars for future students to study. Knox, the great anatomist retired to his solitary dinner, they say, for he had no wife to join him. But then, what woman would stay with a monster likely to cut her up if she angered him over breakfast? Not I for one!

The night of the dissection the citizens of Edinburgh drank and danced in the streets, rowdy as ever they have been. I heard they tried to burn Knox out of his house and thought, if he is wise, he'll leave town. But, if he does, where would he go? And would my Hamish follow him? He surely would as his apprentice, then what would become of me? These questions tossed around in my mind as I tried to sleep, and though my heart was still full of Mary's loss, the thought of losing Hamish troubled me. He was a living friend, and she a dead one. Her memory would never leave me and would not diminish with his being here. I prayed he would stay, but my head told me he would not, and all the time I told mysel' I should be hating him and all his kind for the work they did and what it cost.

2

TO A NEW LIFE IN LONDON

"London!" I must have looked daft staring at him with my mouth open, for Hamish laughed.

"Aye, Knox promised he would write when he was settled and he hasna' let me down." Hamish was grinning like an excited schoolboy and waving the letter about. "He wants me to join him as soon as possible. This is a rare opportunity Janey, to go to London!"

I felt as though he had punched me in the belly. I went weak, and sat myself down. He came and sat next to me.

"You wanted to leave this place and make a new start, well, here is your chance. Come with me. Knox writes that he has rented a house and will need someone to perform the usual household drudgery, as he puts it. He's asked me to find him a girl when I get down to London, but if you come with me, I won't have to look will I?"

"For a drudge you think of me," I snapped, thinking fast all the while. He wanted me to go with him! I stood and marched away, my mind dizzy with what to do, and how. "I'm grateful Hamish," for in truth I was, "but he is everything I've told myself to hate."

"Put that aside, Janey. Not a drudge, but a new life. Isn't that what you wanted?"

The thought of sharing a house with Hamish sent a shiver up and down my spine. But I wasn't going to tell him so. "But this is the man who was responsible for Mary's death. I might just poison him, Hamish, or in a rage one night mebbe stab him with his own carving knife."

"Scalpel. Not carving knife, Janey, scalpel. He is a good surgeon, and a good man interested only in forwarding the art of medicine. He is not deliberately responsible for anyone's death. It is a sad fact that the gallows and suicides do not provide enough bodies for the colleges. But he is innocent even if he doesn't ask where his subjects come from."

"Innocent you say! He simply doesn't care, Hamish! He is greedy for his own fame and doesn't give a damn for the poor folk he toys with."

"You are too harsh, Janey. Porters find the bodies, and we apprentices prepare them for Knox. Let us hope he has a decent man where he is now, someone who checks his suppliers."

"Who will be in the house, Hamish? Where is it? Is it a fine building like the College here? What does he write?" I made to grab at the letter then, but Hamish raised it high out of my reach.

"He has his man, Hoskins. Miserable swine he is too. He drinks more than he works; no trouble usually but you may do well to keep your distance. Knox doesn't mention anyone else so, well, that's it. Nothing about the house at all other than that it's in Huntley Street. He instructs me to find a suitable girl, and I am to work for him in return for my apprenticeship, as before. He says he can find space for another student or two provided they either work hard for their tuition or pay him fees. I know Ewan would give anything to go to London. He's been out of sorts for months now. I think he misses Mary still."

I chewed a fingernail. They were both going then. Could I really go with them? "Well, I don't know Hamish. It's a terrible long way to go, London...."

"A few days, that's all. We can go on the night mail coach for cheapness. It leaves every midnight from the Old Post Office. Please, say you will come, Janey. I need to see a friendly face each day, other than Ewan's."

I forgot myself then, all anger and restraint gone in the excitement of the moment of hearing him say that, and I held him close, burying my nose in his rough tweed shoulder.

"Thank'ee, Hamish. Let me speak to Ma Lawrie, she'll tell me if I could make a good maidservant."

"Not literally a maid perhaps," he gave an embarrassed smile, "but a very capable young woman certainly. Think on it. This could be a step closer to your wish of running your own household one day. If you impress Knox, well, think, he may make you housekeeper with maids under your command eventually. No-one need ever know you were once...."

"A whore? Yes, I know Hamish, I'm no respectable,

but one day I will be." I felt anger then, the future threatened by my last six years of whoring. It wasn't Hamish I was angry at but life and fate. I tried hard to give him a smile. "I jest fear working with Knox and all his dead bodies. Will they be in the house?"

"There will be an anatomy room, yes. I will be there to take charge of that, and you need never see it. You will deal only with the living apartments. So, I will write back today, and we'll follow the letter by the end of the week? I'll tell Ewan, he'll be greatly pleased. He's a good fellow; you'll like him when you know him better."

"You haven't said how we are to pay for this journey. I could ask Ma but I don't think she has the money, or she would happily pay for me to leave her."

"No need, Knox sent me five guineas. That will pay our fares and enough for victuals for the journey too; oh, and something decent for you to wear perhaps."

"Five guineas!" Suddenly, the idea of working for a man who had five guineas to spare made up my mind. It was more money than I had ever seen. Visions of me dressed in the latest finery came into my mind, wandering down Huntley Street on Hamish's arm like a lady. I asked where Huntley Street was and if it was near where the King lived. He laughed and shook his head.

"I doubt we will get to see the King." I suppose he noted my disappointment then and added, "Well, not in the first week or two, not regularly anyway."

I knew he was making a joke of my ignorance, but seeing his excited face and bursting as I was with the thrill of a new life in London, inside my head I jumped

up and down like a child. I kept a calm face though, not
wishing to show my thoughts too clear. London!

Later that night I lay thinking on what this journey
would mean. I would have a chance of a new life for
sure, but what of my promise of revenge for Mary?
What would I be able to do? To kill Knox would be to
hang myself, and I was fearful of that and jest as much
of losing Hamish as my friend. If I killed his Master, he
would never forgive me. And I had to admit to myself, I
knew nothing of the man really, and it might be wrong
to kill him before I had looked him in the eye. Could I
look a man in the eye and stab his heart? I didna' think
too long on that detail. It angered me, what he did, but
mebbe there were others who would be better held to
account. Hamish had told me that Hare had been
given a new name and sent away on a mail coach to
Carlisle. From there it would be possible for him to
travel on to anywhere, even London, if he should wish
it. He hadna' meant to scare me with those words. But
what if Hare did wish it so and what if I could find him
there and cut out his heart? How would I know where
to look or by what name he called himself now? And
what if he found me and had his revenge for that day
in court?

I must have slept at last for I woke in a tumble of
blanket, tired still but calmer. It was the middle of the
morning, the sun high and there was a fight in the street
below. My eyes were heavy, but my head was clear. This

was a chance I had to take; I coundna' turn it away, for the sake of Mary and for a life closer to Hamish.

As the coach bounced its' way to London, Hamish told me how he and Ewan spent their last evening in Edinburgh in their usual inn at the far end of Cowgate, and over several bottles of ale and a mutton pie, they had planned their futures.

"We worked through all the next ten years of our lives – right up to the level of Surgeon to the Royal Household – much to the merriment of the potboy, I expect." His face flushed as I squeezed his hand. He was such a boy. They had toasted their great benefactor, aye I could just hear them, then swayed their way home no doubt still singing the praises of Robert Knox. Oh, happy students, I thought, so trusting and loyal to their Master; foolish boys to believe in such a man. As he told me all this, I looked away, and out at the passing country and whispered to my dear Mary. I promised I would see Knox dead as soon as I could, that he would pay for what he had done to her. Though as we approached London, I became fearful of meeting him and a large part of me wished I had stayed safe in my attic.

The coach drew into the city in the middle of the afternoon, bringing Hamish and me agog for what lay ahead, but with Ewan snoring contentedly as he had for most of the journey. I ached all over from the bumpy roads, me and the five other passengers inside. They were mainly middling sorts including a man I swear I had seen at Ma Lawrie's but who didna' recognize me at all. I knew nothing of him but that he was a wool merchant. I felt troubled that he had a young woman with him I took to be his wife, and she was large with child. She smiled sweetly at me as we both leant forward at the same time to peer round the flapping canvas at the window, and I held it back the better to take in all the sights.

"Keep that closed, damn it." The voice of an elderly cleric boomed from the far corner of the carriage. "The cold air is not healthy, and neither the stink of the town."

"Your pardon, Sir," I sat back, and my eyes met those of the pregnant wife again. She was a bonny thing and though we'd no' passed more than two words since leaving Edinburgh I felt sorry for her. She might be richer than I, but her husband roamed from her for his comfort. Men are such beasts – though not Hamish. I am sure he would never leave a pregnant wife to take his pleasure with a whore.

The noise that met us as we stepped down onto the cobbles was overpowering and we had to shout at each other to be heard. Our fellow travellers hurried to supervise their trunks' descent from the roof, and I'd barely a chance to wish the grocer's wife well with her delivery. Then, wide-eyed with wonder, innocent that I was, I stood looking about me, shivering, in the chill wind blowing up off the river Thames. My cloak, a thin cast-off of Ma's but longer and smarter than my own, was wrapped around me, and underneath I wore the blue dress that had been Mary's; I wasn't about to leave it behind. The gentle scent of lavender mixed with the smell of home comforted me on the journey and helped a little to cover the sour stink of our fellow passengers.

"Come on Janey, over here, we'll get a cart to Huntley Street." Hamish darted behind the coach and hailed the nearest of a group of carriers waiting there. The elderly driver seemed unaware of the difficulty Hamish was having loading a box of books, bags of clothes for himself and Ewan, and the small trunk and bundle that was all my worldly goods. He just sat gazing at the scraggy rump of his horse until we were aboard, then, with a flick of his whip and a strange guttural sound urged the nag forwards.

The journey was spent in near silence, save the noise in the street. The sights we were passing, greyed by a mist of sleety rain, taking all of our attention. Edinburgh is a great and busy city, but it was as nothing compared to what we saw before us. The horse made slow progress, the road jammed as it was with vehicles of all sizes carrying goods, lords and labourers to who knew where. A cry went up as a driver to our side pitched forward, his wheel caught in a great pothole and his horse brought up sharp. Street hawkers yelled, boys darted between the carts and horsemen wove their way on and off the road, cutting in among those walking on the edges of the bustle thrusting forwards on what must have been urgent business. Above us jutted buildings new and old, rich and ramshackle, and smells both good and bad assaulted our noses. By the time we reached Huntley Street, less than two miles so Hamish said, but nearly an hour later, we were tired but excited still.

"A shillun'." The driver held out a grubby hand and Hamish, looking a mite uncertain that he had heard correctly, handed over the shilling and the cart moved off. Ewan had to jump with the last of the bags to avoid being carried away. He glared after it and shook a fist then turned to us, his expression changing quickly to a grin.

"Well, here we are. Welcome to London Town. Let's away inside."

The house itself was not so grand as I had imagined, midway along a terrace of identical buildings and bore a number over the door, 12 Huntley Street. There were three main floors above ground level, counting the number of windows rising above us, and a basement where the kitchen and servants' workrooms would be, and which was reached by stone steps leading down from the street. The small windows in the roof showed where I would likely sleep. As many stairs as at Ma Lawries, so nothing new there!

The front door was shut fast, and nobody replied to Hamish's banging. Shrugging, and losing none of his good humour, he and Ewan dragged the bags down the steps to the tradesman's entrance below, while I stayed staring up at the house both in wonder and disappointment. It was quite a large house, but not as large as the houses we had passed in the previous street, and it looked run-down and shabby. Yet it was far superior to the streets of West Port, and it was more than I should have hoped for.

A man in shirtsleeves, looking as though he had been

roused from a deep sleep, opened the kitchen door to Hamish's knock.

"About time," he growled. The fellow, clearly the Master of this part of the house, jerked his head to tell us we should enter, and stood back looking at us as though we had great insolence in disturbing him. As I passed, he gave me more than a glance, up and down, but I outstared him, all too aware of what type of man he was likely to be. This must be Hoskins.

"Drop your bags here for now. Your rooms are up above and have no' been prepared as yet." I didn't think he would be offering to do it, and he jerked his head again, now towards a linen press next to a large fireplace. "The doctor is out for now. I waited 'til you arrived but now I have business to attend to, so I'll be away for a wee while. You're all up in the attic; sort yourselves out as you will." With that Hoskins nodded and departed.

We began the journey with our belongings up four flights of stairs to the attic, stopping off at each floor to catch our breath and a quick peek into the rooms we passed. For the most part they were empty, and others had sheets laid out over what furnishings there were. A large room on the first floor, lit by great high windows, had a strange narrow wooden bed in the centre. I caught a glance between Hamish and Ewan, but before I could say a word or enter, they jostled me on to the next stairway.

"Is that...?" I tried to ask, looking back over my shoulder, but they had gone on ahead. I could hear their chatter and the stamp of their boots. The certainty that that room was where their awful work was done unnerved me and I stumbled as I climbed. The floor above housed what must be the doctor's bedroom and a large drawing room with several sofas and a bureau. I assumed it would be my job to clean and look after them, and a small tingle of nerves stirred in me. They were far grander than anywhere I could remember seeing before and I hoped I was equal to the task.

Our final destination, the topmost part of the house, was reached by narrow unlit stairs, and was divided into three rooms, one large and two slightly smaller. The largest room, to the left, housed a bed and a trunk with a pile of soiled clothes on top and was clearly that of Hoskins. I closed the door on it, feeling guilty at having pried. Next to it, the second room had three narrow beds tightly squeezed in and a chair with a pile of blankets. The third and smallest was a brightly lit room. A thin mattress with straw bulging and leaking from it lay on the floor, and next to it an upturned box no doubt intended as a chair or small table.

"Well, this must be your room, Janet." Hamish put his arm around my shoulders and gave me a hug, then turned back to the middle room where Ewan was looking down from the window.

"And this must be for us, laddie. Not so bad I suppose; though I wouldna' care to fall out of here."

"No, indeed, 'tis quite a drop;" Ewan stood back and looked about the bleak room. "We have a choice of beds it seems. I'll take this one by the window."

"I think you'll find I have the advantage of age and seniority, so it'll be my bed. You can have this one by the door then you can be first up in the morning." Hamish quickly dropped down onto his chosen bed and, putting his hands behind his head, grinned at his friend in victory. Ewan advanced on him with fist raised, but lowered it, and laughed good-naturedly.

"Aye, fine. That's mebbe for the best. I hope the window is nay too draughty." He began heaving the bags from the landing and if Hamish regretted his choice, he didn't show it. There was no wind whistling through that day but, come the worst of winter it may be a different matter. I would mebbe keep back some rags to stuff them if needed.

I examined my room carefully and found to my delight it was a good three paces bigger than the one I had shared with Mary in Edinburgh. The ceiling was higher, there was glass in the window and there were no dangerous floorboards. And it appeared to be all my own. My bed at Ma Lawrie's had been a mattress on a frame, a proper bed strong enough for its purpose. Here, I prodded the mattress with my toe and hoped the straw didn't harbour mice or insects, then stashed my bundle in the corner between the bed and the window and checked the strength of the box. It had carried vegetables of some kind; there was a leaf still inside. Cabbage. It was none too sturdy so best I didna' sit down too heavily. All in all, this seemed a good move so far and I was excited at the prospect of having Hamish sleeping so close. I heard the boys laughing next door and my heart smiled. I took myself downstairs to the kitchen to check for a pail, unless I was expected to trail out to the yard for the necessary in the night.

I found what I needed and another for the lads and then a set of sheets for each of us. The blankets were too scratchy without and didn't smell too clean. Beds made up and I wandered downstairs again, content now that I'd made the right decision in moving to London and keen to explore my new world. Hoskins was sitting at the large oak kitchen table. Back from his business already, he looked the worse for drink, more so than earlier, and warily I introduced myself.

"You are the Master's manservant then?" I asked.

"Aye lass, Hoskins. I'm looking after the house for him 'til he comes home. He's away now at the university I think, with his doctor friends anyway. Come and have a wee dram with me if ye like." He held out a bottle, best part drunk already, and indicated the bench by the table.

"Thank you, but no, I jest came to see the lay of the place, the wash house, and everything."

"Ah, yes of course." He didna' seem to mind my rejection, his words slurring as he stood to leave. "I may rest for a while. I trust you'll find all you need."

He clearly wasn't going to show me around, and his stumble on the stairs told me of future trouble. But then, I would have Hamish in the same house, and could deal with whatever arose as it came. Right now, there were more urgent needs like where was the kettle.

3

I MEET THE MASTER

By the time Knox returned in the evening his new household was settling in, with the dust covers off in the drawing room and soup simmering in a pot on the stove. There wasn't much to put in it mind, but turnips and some soft carrots, and a handful of fat bacon that didn't smell too bad. I would need to shop soon if we weren't to starve. The lads ate with me in the kitchen for the doctor had slammed the door shut when he came in and gone direct to work in his study on the ground floor. He preferred his privacy it seemed, and I was mightily relieved I didn't have to deal with him right away. But after Hamish and Ewan had gone out to locate the nearest tavern, I thought I'd best check whether there was anything my Master needed. He'd been very quiet. Hoskins was nowhere to be seen. I tapped at the study door, the hairs on my neck tingling with fear, my feet ready to run.

"Who is it, eh? Who's there?"

"Only me, Sir, Janet," then added, "The new maid.

I brought you a wee bite in case you'd no' had supper." I entered and stumbled forward in the gloom, uncertain of the layout of the room and wondering where to place the tray I was carrying. "Sorry to disturb ye, Sir."

"Ah, a moment. Here." Knox rose to his feet, a tallish man and solid as a bull, and relieved me of my burden. "Thank you, most kind," he said. His eyes travelled up and down my person and he sniffed, shook his head jest very slightly, and gave a wee grunt. I didn't know whether it was an approving grunt or not. He turned to his desk and balanced the tray on a stack of books. I bobbed a quick and clumsy curtsey, then turned, and left abruptly, before he had a chance to say more. In the hallway, my heart pounding, I told myself not to be such a ninny. He was hardly likely to chop me up for bringing him supper.

I went to bed then, tired after the last few days of travel and the excitement of arriving in London and slept soundly. It had taken no more than a few minutes of listening to the strange sounds of the house and street, before I felt myself drifting away. For a mattress on the floor, my bed was as cosy as any I have ever slept in. I wasn't disturbed all night, and never heard Hamish and Ewan return from their drinking, nor the Master settle for the night.

I spent the next day unpacking boxes, getting to know the strength of the pump in the yard, and later wandering the nearby streets where I located a shop selling bread and mealy looking flour, and another with wilted vegetables. I served supper in the dining room - a good sized room off the main hall, with panelling all-round the walls, and heard Hamish mention a new acquaintance to Knox. I watched the Master's face carefully. He seemed to be thinking of something else, his eyes blank and distant, and had I known less I'd have said he was a simpleton. But Hamish had already warned me his mind was as sharp as his knife for all he sometimes seemed unaware of what was going on around him.

"He is a Scot, Sir." Hamish stared at his plate and frowned. I'd got the lamb from a passing meatman and cooked it with an onion and more turnips for dinnertime, and being as there was an awful lot left, I turned it out again for supper. I don't know if it was cooked for too long. "Hoskins introduced us. He claims to have worked as a porter in Edinburgh and knows the university there. Used to supply several of the notables, eh.... He left when he was told there was no more work, when, eh, things were quiet. He's offering his services if you have a position for him, Sir."

I looked at the Master's face as I brought another dish of the meat from the side table, and nodded encouragement to Hamish, though uncertain what he meant. I just knew I would need some help around the house if Hoskins was the only other servant there.

"Well," the Master said, helping himself to a slab of meat. "Hoskins has been a useless rogue of late, disappearing off whenever he gets the chance, and I have less need of a valet and more for a porter. I'm minded to give him his marching orders." Well, the Master had noticed that much, so he was no fool then. "Who is this fellow, does he have a name?"

"Black, Sir. I promised to meet him tomorrow with an answer.... shall I instruct him to call upon you?"

"I'll be busy Hamish. I have a meeting with Sir Astley Cooper and his nephew Bransby Cooper, to discuss his ideas on the best way to remove bladder stones." He laughed then. "He claims to be able to complete the operation in under a minute, but" and here he snorted like a horse, "it'll take him longer than that to select the right brandy and which knife to use! No, you use your judgement lad. Have a word with the fellah, check if he has any testimonials, though I doubt he would have. What they do isn't illegal, but these people are slippery rogues to a man, graverobbers half of them. If you think he's tolerably honest and likely to be reliable I'll take the man on."

"Aye, Sir." I could see Hamish swell with pride at being offered such a responsibility, and he winked at me. I felt uncomfortable then at what they were discussing, and having heard the word graverobbers, I shuddered. Not so much a help about the house, this man Black must be one who delivers bodies. Another man like Burke perhaps. But Hamish had promised not to involve me in their work, so I concentrated on gathering empty dishes and topping up their wineglasses. Knox had a good appetite on him anyway and was soon making a fair go at the stew I'd bought from another street vendor; in case the lamb wasn't enough. It was made with eels and peas and looked disgusting. I curtsied and left them to finish their meal, retreating down to the kitchen to kick off my shoes, thankful Hoskins was asleep in the pantry next door. His snores were loud and regular, and I was pleased we'd passed no more than a dozen words all day. I'd been that busy getting together the dinner and then their supper and surprised at the amount of food it needed to keep a house of men satisfied.

Next day, late in the morning, I was pumping water into a pail in the yard when a cart drew up. I looked up as the driver jumped down and moments later saw a large box as it turned in through the window of the butler's pantry. My eyes were riveted by the sight of an arm swinging loose. The knuckles hit the ledge and though hastily retrieved by Ewan and tucked back under the lid, the sight made me go weak and I slopped my pail and soaked my feet. I stumbled down the basement steps and through the kitchen and sat by the fireside a moment to steady myself with the rhythmic noise of the box being winched up above me.

"Hamish," I cornered him a little later, on his way through the house and asked, "What's to do up there?"

"The Master is about to demonstrate. There will be more students arriving soon, just point them up the stairs and they'll be no bother to you."

A dozen youths attended that morning, and the Master seemed pleased when he came downstairs afterwards.

"All paid their two guineas except one, the pretty lad with freckles; a guinea today and the rest by the end of Saturday," I heard Hamish say. "I trust him, Sir."

Knox waved dismissively.

"Fine, fine. We will eat well enough, provided yon Janet isn't allowed near the stove. Off you go now lad and find me a brace of duck, or pigeons, and a cook who knows what to do with them. That's your final task for this morning. I'll be off now and return for dinner at three."

I retreated then, back down the stairs to the kitchen, reddening with rage. Well, really! The lads were gone some time and returned with Ewan carrying a case on his broad shoulders. They emptied it of six fine plump birds steaming and golden, with only minutes to spare before Knox's declared dinner time. Hamish brought up the rear, carrying a jug of rich sauce for the duck, and a gooseberry tart, which he put on the side table with a flourish.

"The carrots are well cooked, so I mashed them." I banged around with some pans on the stove, angry that I was dismissed as a bad cook before I'd a chance to prove myself. The eel and pea stew was not of my making so not my fault if they didn't like it. They'd eaten it and seemed to enjoy it well enough. The remains I had reheated jest in case but were now burned onto the pan. I'd not buy from that vendor again.

"Well done, Janey, I'll see you are rewarded later." Hamish whispered in my ear. His breath tickled my neck, and I elbowed him gently in the stomach. He'd clearly passed some time drinking in whatever tavern he'd bought the ducks from, but I couldn't be angry with him for long.

The dinner went well and Knox asked to meet the cook. The conversation around the table quieted and I held my breath and stood as still as I could by the side table, ready like a good servant lest my Master need anything, but tense on Hamish's behalf. He boldly explained that he had gone to the Crown to purchase the ducks they had eaten.

"But I'm sure to find a suitable person soon. It may take a day or two. According to the cook at the inn where these beauties came from, a French chef like him would cost you sixty guineas a year at least."

"Outrageous! Forty guineas and not a penny more. Find me a chef for forty guineas a year who can cook as well as this and you will more than earn your keep."

I thought, for forty guineas a year I could learn to cook if they cared to wait awhile, and I plonked the gooseberry tart onto the table and next to it a bowl of custard that I'd made myself, swearing quietly when some slopped over the edge. With luck the lumps would sink to the bottom and not disgrace me further.

Knox eyed the bowl suspiciously before continuing. "We'll find room for him, but the rest of you may have to snuggle up a wee bit." He gave the smallest of smiles and glanced briefly at Hamish before cutting into the tart with all the enthusiasm of a fresh experiment. "There's a third bed in your room isn't there, Hamish?"

"There's no' much chance a proper chef will want to sleep with the students – he'll be demanding his own room." I don't know what possessed me to speak out, and I saw Hamish give a warning glance. It was too late now though, and we were both relieved to see that far from being angry, Knox appeared amused.

It was arranged that Hoskins would move his belongings into the room shared by Hamish and Ewan and the new chef when he came would have his old room. Hoskins was not keen when he was told, and there was much banging about and grumbling on his part. He left the house soon after and returned drunk, stumbling in and waking the household at midnight.

Carlo, not French but an Italian, with a dark complexion and a haughty look about him, joined the household a week later. He stood no nonsense, allowing nobody into the kitchen while he worked. A skivvy called Mab was also taken on, though she stayed only a day before seeing a corpse being manhandled on the first-floor landing while she dusted. She fled the house with ear-splitting screams and didn't return, even though she'd left her hat on the peg behind the door. I hadn't taken to the girl and was glad to see her go. She was a local lass and made out she couldn't understand me. Well, I had no more idea what she said than I did Carlo, though my ear tuned to him after a while and his to me.

And so, our household in Huntley Street was complete and I finally felt free at last to spend some time exploring further the streets around Bloomsbury. My wanderings led me, once or twice, into Seven Dials, a part of London famous it seems as a den of thieves and prostitutes. On seeing what kind of place it was I pulled my cloak around me and didn't linger. I'd no desire to be reminded of life on the streets and now I could watch the wretched girls leaning in doorways and against walls, calling out their wares to any passing man, and think myself apart. I was on the way up and nothing would drag me back down, of that I was determined. 'Tis strange how quick folk seek to move away from their own kind as soon as they have a chance, and I was jest the same.

It was while strolling in a smarter part of Oxford Street, near Hanover Square when I came upon a lad entertaining passers-by. I stopped and watched what he was about. He was a cheery looking boy no more than eight years old, with fair hair and bright grey eyes, and round his neck hung a small cage. Two white mice scuttled about inside, whilst in his hands he held a third.

"'Scusi, Miss, have you ever seen such fine mouse? He will dance for you if I sing." He sang a little then and the mouse sat up on his outstretched hand and waved its wee paws, not quite to time but in a musical way. I laughed and our eyes met for a moment. A man beside me clapped and tossed a coin into the lad's hat which lay beside him, carefully held in place with a foot.

He was an Italian, I guessed, same as Carlo, but not dark. His clothes were old but looked clean, and he had a once fine waistcoat under his coat.

"Signore, my thanks," he bowed and placed the mouse in his waistcoat pocket where a watch would sit on a gentleman. He held up the wee cage and whistled while the two mice within climbed on a wee wheel and ran round and round, to the delight of two small girls standing close by. I smiled, nodding at the lad in farewell before continuing my walk through the square and, in a long and not so direct way, found myself back at Huntley Street.

My outings were a pleasant part of life now, away from the smell of blood and the sound of young men stamping up and down stairs. On leaving the house one morning I came up the steps from the basement and nearly collided at the top with the Master coming down the steps from the front door. He asked me what I was about and, fearful that he would forbid my wanderings resigned myself to return to the kitchen. But he must have been in a good mood for he gave me a shillun' to spend.

"In lieu of some wages, girl. You've worked hard these past weeks and deserve a few hours off."

I clasped the coin tightly in my fist deep inside my pocket. I called at a haberdasher's shop in New Oxford Street, a fine building with a heavy-laden table running down the full length of the room and fingered some of the fine cloth on sale. There were yards of beautiful silk the colour of thick cream, and a roll of pale blue satin that shimmered under my hand. The shopkeeper watched me closely as I fingered it, but I must have looked reasonably respectable as he allowed me to wander about the store. That alone was a step up, I thought. I resisted the urge to lift a fine kerchief from a pile left open to the chance, though it would have been the easiest thing to slip it into my pocket. There was a time when I wouldn't have hesitated, though I was never a real thief. It's true I'd taken a few things when they were left easy like that. Only a few weeks before, the shopkeeper would have thrown me out for clearly being a penniless whore. But I was cleaner, and already plumper than I had been, and though I still wore Ma Lawrie's old cloak, I held myself more like a respectable woman. Some green woollen material, ideal for a cape, lay upon a shelf and I had the man get it down and show it to me. In a while, before next winter, I promised myself to have a few yards, but not yet. A shillun' wouldn't stretch so far. The time would come when I would dress like a real lady. In the meantime, I stepped out in my shabby clothes, and held onto my shillun', saving it for later, and enjoyed my walk in the early spring sunshine.

I strode back into Huntley Street with a new pride, noticing as I went Hoskins, standing on the corner idly chatting with a servant girl from one of the houses further along the street. Having already experienced his attentions on the stairs a few days before, I grinned to myself. I remembered his shock when I paid him for his fumbling kisses with my knee in his crotch. My past had taught me how to look after myself when it came to men like him, and he was more respectful since. I hurried down the steps to the basement, and in through the kitchen door, only then remembering some linen I'd left soaking in Carlo's cauldron and hoping to retrieve it before he started on the dinner.

4

I MAKE MY FIRST ENEMIES

The house was full of students and chatter following another of the Master's demonstrations. Tuesdays seemed to be the day he favoured for these events, and a few weeks had passed regular; the delivery of a body or two on either Monday evening or Tuesday morn, then a lecture and each week busier with students than the one before.

"The heart, Janey, the greatest organ of a man's body," Hamish said, when I asked what the lecture had been about.

"The greatest?" I gave him a look, crude and wrong I ken, and though Hamish turned red before he grinned, young Ewan laughed aloud. There was something so innocent about Hamish and I felt sorry straight away that I'd embarrassed him. But he soon caught on that I was only jesting, and we were all in a fine humour in no time. Only when the new lad came in did we stop our foolishness. A young sprig he was, called O'Rourke, an Irish lad with no sense of humour to save his life. He stood all straight and stiff, and told me to be about my business and gave me a look as though I was some mess he'd stepped in.

"And what business is it of yours?" I asked and turned on my heel. He was a student damn it, not my Master, and I wouldna' be crushed into a miserable slave for the likes of him.

Later, Hoskins told me I should behave with more modesty, so O'Rourke must have reported me, the little shite.

"I ken you're not used to respectable households, girl, but here, you step out of line, and I'll give you a taste of my strap." He fingered his belt and would doubtless enjoy chastising me. "The students are here to learn, not to be led astray by some whore, so mind your manners. If the Master knew where you came from, he'd throw you back out onto the street. So," he pushed his beery face up against mine and I stared back at him without blinking, our noses almost touching. "Don't test me, girl," he growled. I backed down then, fearing he would go through with his threat. I'd made two enemies that day, Hoskins and the Irish boy, O'Rourke.

There were others who were friendlier, in a respectable way, mind. A couple of the regular students were real gents and one, Mr Hargreaves, said "It was a pleasure to be greeted each day by such a pretty young lady." I flushed when he said that. It was meant in a kind way I think, though with Englishmen you never know for sure when they're making a fool of you. Hamish was careful of me, and I thought that even if Hoskins did thrash me he would mebbe take my side. Leastways I hoped he would. His head was in his books so much there was a chance he'd no' notice at all. I was disappointed I didna' see so much of him as I'd hoped for all we lived in the same house.

The next day, I came on Hamish and Ewan in the student's study, next to the Anatomy room. It was a long thin room, full of books and strange models of bits of body on a long bench table that ran down one side. I tidied it by stacking the books that had been left lying around and listened to the two of them talking while I worked. I picked up a plaster model of a tree, leastways that was what it most resembled and noticing my puzzled face Hamish laughed.

"A replica of the inside of a lung, Janey. See how the tubules branch? When we breathe air flows in a tube from our nose through all these branches and refreshes the body."

I replaced the lung on the table and wondered how it had come to be petrified thus. My duster flicked over plaster heads and a heart.

"But how can we be certain Wakley has all his facts correct?" Ewan was flicking through a sheaf of papers.

"He was there and recorded what he saw, but questions it nonetheless," Hamish answered.

"What are you reading, lads?" I asked.

"Some papers handed out at this morning's demonstration at University College. We couldn't get seats but stood crushed by the door so saw nothing and heard little more." Hamish shrugged and added, "Though I can't see why Sir Astley Cooper is so popular. Reading these notes taken by Wakley at a previous operation the patient would have died with certainty."

"How so?" asked Ewan.

"He would have bled to death. Look here," he pointed to the paper, "He omitted to tie off the artery and not only that but there was not enough of the gall bladder left whole to be any use. No, I wouldn't rate the patient's chances...."

I couldna' see what he was surprised about. Not many would survive being cut open surely.

"It's no doubt an omission of the note-taker – it must have been. Who is this Wakley fellah?" Ewan sneered.

"He writes that journal, *The Lancet*; seems a decent man and knowledgeable; He's a surgeon himself," said Hamish. "And I think he wrote the truth about the great man's performance, but see how he ends his report. '*The patient was taken away at this point to recover in an adjacent room, and though we never heard his words ourselves, we are told he awoke some hours later and demanded bacon and eggs for his supper. There was wonder among the onlookers on hearing this, given the gravity of his condition. We trust he enjoyed his meal, if indeed he managed to complete it.*' I have the impression that Wakley doesn't believe he ever had his bacon and eggs. I agree. The patient must have died despite what Cooper claimed."

"Well, I never heard of him. Wakley? He's probably just envious he didn't undertake the procedure himself. Have you read his journal? I hear Cooper forbids it to be brought into Guys."

I suspected Wakley would be popular with Knox

ruffling folk as he did and thought that mebbe he was another man who cut up people in his house and enjoyed it. I decided I'd no' want to meet him in a hurry.

"Yes, Knox showed me a copy he was reading. The fellow writes well, but he harps on about the need for medical reform and seems to upset the top people. A year or two ago he was involved in a court case so Knox told me. The great Abernethy sued him over the right to publish his notes. Wakley lost but the judge was clearly sympathetic and instead of ordering him to pay the two-thousand-pound compensation Abernethy demanded, he granted just one hundred pounds. Wakley can write what he likes now, as long as he doesn't mention the name of the surgeon anywhere." He waved the papers and pointed out that Cooper was not named other than as C---er, and then clattered off down the stairs to show them to the Master.

I must have looked like I had turned to stone for Ewan gave me a gentle prod and nodded to the shelf behind me.

"You've missed some dust there, Janey."

Two thousand pounds! The sums of money these folk talked about were fair dizzying. I slapped at him with my duster, and he grabbed it, pulling me towards him with a face on him like he would kiss me if he could.

"Steady, laddie." I pushed him gently away. "I'm here as a maid now, not for foolery. You have to remember that, or it'll be dangerous."

"I'm only jesting, Janey, and I'll not tell on ye."

"Dangerous for you, mind. The Master won't want ye missing your studies or doing anything daft. You wait for a nice girl to marry and keep your nose clean. Course, there are plenty of places ye can go in the dark if ye must, but not with me mind, and don't let him catch ye." I reckoned him a good lad, jest full of spirit. "And" I said in a low voice, not looking at him direct, "I want to put that business behind me and I'll thank 'ee to remember that."

"Well, of course. I'd never force myself on ye, Janey, and I know Hamish feels the same. Don't worry."

I went about my business then, dusting and tidying around the rest of the house apart from the anatomy room and hoping I'd no' offended the lad. He was probably right about Hamish too. He'd no interest in me, or any other, in that way. He was a strange laddie, Hamish. Kind, handsome in a freckly boyish way and likely he'd never had a girl for all he must be eighteen! It surprised me that I should yearn for him at all, for a fine thing it would be if a man had to be shown what to do by his wife. He'd shown me great kindnesses, but wife! Come on Janey, I scolded myself. Why are you even thinking that way? I was uncertain then just what I felt for him. Comfortable and safe, mebbe that was all. I canna' say cleaning the house was my idea of a fine life, and was I really safe? There was only Hoskins to fear where what might remain of my 'virtue' mattered, and the Master to fear where my life was concerned. For all the lads said in his favour, he was known in the newssheets as a butcher, and I did what I could to avoid going near him.

One morning in March, warm for the time of year I thought, though London is a deal warmer than Edinburgh all the time, Hoskins came into the kitchen and stood looking down on me for a few minutes, quite unnerving me. I'd been trying to sew a rip the Master had made in his shirtsleeve and it wasna' going well. I glared at him, then tried to ignore him, but he wouldna' move off. Carlo was stirring a cauldron hanging in the fireplace, muttering in Italian and sprinkling leaves into the mix. An interesting smell wafted around the room and I for one couldna' wait much longer for my dinner. I cursed under my breath and stabbed my finger when Hoskins sat down so close beside me on the settle, he bumped my arm. Now, with a smudge of blood on the white cloth as well as my crooked stitching, I was wishing I'd left it alone and started on the laundry instead.

I felt his hand on my thigh then, under the table, and paused from my stitching. Staring ahead of me I waited. The hand crept higher, and I started back working my needle and thread, thinking I'd let the man know I wasna' bothered by him. His hand reached the top of my leg. I turned my head to look him in the eyes. He was more drunk than sober, and his breath was foul. I put my own hand on top of his. A little smile played around his mouth, and he shuffled his bulk nearer. The needle I held scored his flesh and he swore and sucked in his breath, then pulled his injured hand up, cradling it in the other.

Blood ran down between his fingers and Hoskins glared at me. Mebbe having Carlo so near he was keen to keep his mauling a secret, for he said nothing save giving a small yelp, but then, when he stood, he lurched sideways and knocked a pot off the edge of the table.

Carlo turned round at the noise, and I ducked my head down to carry on my sewing and hide a grin.

"My spongati. Mama mia, idiot!"

The pot had held some pudding Carlo had been working on and he wasna' pleased to see it a mess on the floor. Hoskins' shrug didna' help things. The two men shouted and swore at each other, Carlo coming out the better of them. Even if I couldna' make out the words I understood the meaning, and Hoskins retreated out of the room.

I was worried what would result, but Hoskins kept clear of me for a few days after that. Then, one evening, nigh on a week later, when the lads were out and Carlo was away visiting a relative he had living down in Somerstown, I'd just done seeing to the Master and a visitor in his study and was on my way up to the attic. I met Hoskins coming down. It was dark on the stairs and I'd no light, so when I ran into him on the bend he took me by surprise.

He shoved me against the wall and held my arms down by my sides while he pushed his face against mine.

"Well, you little whore, I have you now." I could smell the whisky and felt him growing against my belly through the thin cloth of my dress. I wriggled aside but couldna' free my arms. I tried to get away, but he was pushing me down onto the stairs. As I fell back, he thrust his leg between mine and, with my dress hampering him he leant his elbow into my side and crushed me with his weight. He let go my hand for a moment to haul up my dress. I was struggling to breathe, trying to push him off and all the while the stairs were biting into my back.

"You must be missing this, eh?" he panted. "You have na' had a man for weeks now." He was right, I hadna', and I was in no hurry for his kind. I hit at him with my free hand but though I gave it all the strength I could, it wasna' enough. His fingers dug into my right leg as he pulled it further apart from the left and I felt him fumble with his breeches to free himself.

"Get off me," I hissed. I wasna' used to drawers but was pleased to be wearing them now for they slowed his attack. He tried to pull them down but was hindered by the ties and the strong cloth that resisted his tugs. I could feel him shrinking against my leg. The drink and the effort of the struggle too much for him, he lay panting on top of me, scratching and ferreting around. I summoned all my energy to push him off, but this aroused him further and he punched me then, hard in the ribs. He rose, snarling like a dog and with one hand scratching and clawing he worked on my drawers till he freed the ties and dragged them down. I couldna' see him clearly and was choking under his elbow, now resting across my throat. I felt faint and sick and as he thrust into me, I cried out. He clamped a hand over my face, a stray finger scratching the corner of my eye, and my lip was cut against my teeth. He took his time, thrusting again and again, wheezing all the while, and I could feel the wood of the stairs cutting into my buttocks and shoulders. My neck was near breaking, and I tried biting into his hand where it was pushing at my face. He was so far gone in his rutting that I don't think he felt it, but the blood was flowing from his palm and was warm on my cheek. He came eventually and I felt the flow leak down my legs.

Flaccid now and exhausted, I think he'd lost interest and allowed me to crawl from under him, pulling myself up the stairs to the attic. I pushed my mattress against the door, gasping for breath and curled up, bruised and pained. Blood, some mine and some his, ran down my chin and I wiped it away with the back of my hand. A tooth had come loose, and I licked at it.

I'd had violent men before, but not many, and none with the hatred in his face that Hoskins had. My ribs were hurting when I breathed, my lip swelling up and I was sore below. My God, I had hoped to leave such dangers behind me in Edinburgh and yet it was worse here! I pulled off my drawers and examined the torn wet cloth. Well, they'd been some use anyway at slowing him. I threw them away from me and hugged my knees, leaning back against the door. Mebbe I should return to Edinburgh. I might be able to save enough in a few months to pay for the coach fare if I didna' spend elsewhere, though my Master was no' regular in paying my wages. I didna' need for anything, and money for mysel' was something I was growing used to. The clink of a few coppers in my pocket was new to me still and I was likin' the feel o' them. But London was no' the change I'd dreamt of. Men were still takin' advantage of me and I was beginning to wish I'd stayed at Ma Lawrie's.

I heard a noise somewhere in the house and started up; probably the Master's visitor leaving. An hour or more had passed with me huddled there, and it was late. More sounds, naught but the lads back from their outing. I stayed quiet, not wishing to be seen in the state I was in and, after a while, when they'd gone to bed and the house was still, I got up and washed my face. I could feel a bruise spreading across my middle and another around my eye, which was closing. Mebbe after a night's sleep I'd feel better.

The chatter in the dining room stopped as I entered, and I felt all their eyes upon me. I placed the Master's plate of breakfast chops in front of him, shaking a little. He laid down his knife an' reached for my arm as I turned to leave.

"What have ye done there girl?"

"Sir?"

"Ye face. Fighting?"

"I was defending myself, nay fighting."

"Who did that? Come on girl tell me, I'll not have my servants attacked. Was it one of the students?"

I heard Hamish and Ewan gasp.

"Nay, Sir. They're gentlemen," I said.

"Hoskins," he muttered. He didna' wait for me to answer. Mebbe Hoskins had done that sort of thing before to servants. I moved to leave. Knox didna' say anything further and reached for the bread. I left him sawing at it and made my way down to the kitchen, hoping I'd not find myself alone with Hoskins again too soon.

Carlo was cooking already, stirring his cauldron. Hoskins came in behind and startled me but walked on past.

"What are ye boiling there, Carlo? It smells good." He sidled up to the cauldron and looked in.

"Zuppe de funghi."

Hoskins waited until Carlo had turned his back to attend to another dish on the table, and dipped the ladle in, raising it warily to his mouth. Just as he took a sip, Carlo spun round and shouted something in his foreign tongue and Hoskins dropped the ladle into the cauldron with a splash that showered scalding soup onto his breeches. He yelled and swore in return.

I was beginning to enjoy the scene when the Master bawled down the narrow stairway.

"What's that row there? I will not have such a racket in the house."

Hoskins went to the foot of the stairs with Carlo behind him, both of them flushed and angry. Carlo was yelling, and all Hoskins could do was shrug to Knox, who was coming down the stairs now.

"I don't know Sir, the man's upset about something but damned if I can get any sense out of him. What can ye expect though from a Macaroni, eh Sir?" He laughed and winked at Knox, failing to notice Carlo's heavy fist flying towards him. It caught him on the side of the head, knocking him against the wall. The two men looked set to brawl and Knox called for Hamish, Ewan, anyone up there, to come and assist him.

I stood back, smothering my mouth with my apron, trying not to cheer him on as Carlo bested my attacker. Three students having jest arrived for their lecture, hurried to do the Master's bidding, along with Hamish and Ewan. Never shy of taking part in a fight, and mindful who was the more important of the two men, they took up Hoskins and threw him out in the yard behind the house where he fell among piles of firewood. He reached for the axe leaning against the outhouse wall and, fast for a heavy man, stumbled towards the door with a mighty roar. I screamed as he came at us with the weapon held high. Hamish slammed the door in his face. The axe bit into the wood.

Knox crossed the kitchen in six strides and threw open the door. The axe hung there between him and his servant.

"Hoskins, you are the very devil, man. I've had enough of your temper and your drinking. You will pack your things and be gone from this house within the hour. You hear?"

"Aye, and I've had enough of you man, and yon foreigners too. Cooks that canna' speak English, papists, whores and corpses in the house. Damn you all, damn you to Hell!" Hoskins shoved past Hamish and the open-mouthed O'Rourke and stamped off up to the attic. Knox glared at his parting figure before grunting and heading off to his study.

But a few minutes later Hoskins was down from the attic, crashing about and cursing. I tiptoed up to the top of the kitchen stairs and saw him heading towards Knox where he stood in the doorway. Hand outstretched, he thrust his head forward too.

"You owe me my wages. A month."

"I owe you a thrashing you scoundrel. Your wages will pay for the damage to yon door, and the cost to me in inconvenience in getting another man. Be off, before I call the watch and have you thrown in gaol."

Knox retreated then into his study and slammed the door. Hoskins sent out a viscous kick against the lower panel and split the wood, before turning and storming out of the house.

Dinner was a tense affair and Knox, in a foul mood, snapped at the students and drank more than usual, before shutting himself away for the afternoon to work in his study. The students who didna' live in had gone away home, and both Hamish and Ewan set off for the Institute for the evening to another lecture. Carlo was busy in his storeroom counting his sacks of produce, and I was alone.

After I had finished my chores or done enough to pass Knox's not so close inspection, I climbed up quiet as a mouse to my own room. I opened my trunk and reached inside, under a change of clothes, and pulled out my book. It had belonged to my mother and though I hadna' read more than a few pages, I was sure it had something in it that was important for she had treasured it. Inside the cover were a few lines of spidery writing and my finger traced the words.

"For only in the ennoblement of the mind and the freedom of the body lies true liberty. To my dearest Esther; my only daughter."

The signature was hard to read, but I had mastered it long ago and knew it by heart. *Angus Brown.* I remembered my mother telling me the book had been given to her by her father, long dead by then. As for Esther, my mother, she'd taken the freedom of her body and thrown it away on a man. I've often wondered who he was and used to dream at night of all kinds of men, rich and handsome. The church elders and the women who kept me in the orphanage never spoke of her, or of him, and when I asked, they told me she was a foolish and sinful woman I'd best forget and not spend my time worrying about.

I turned the page and read, Mary Wolstencraft, a strange name. I wondered again who this other Mary was, and what life she had led, and struggled to read a few lines of the first page to fall open.

".... it is asserted, in direct terms, that the minds of women are enfeebled by false refinement; that the books of instruction, written by men of genius, have had the same tendency as more frivolous productions; and that, in the true style of Mahomatism, they are treated as a kind of subordinate beings, and not as a part of the human species, when improved reason is allowed to be the dignified distinction which raises men above the brute creation, and puts a natural sceptre in a feeble hand."

I couldna' make any sense of what was written there, no more than I had before, but I did know women were no' different to men in many ways, but generally had more sense. Though my mother had taught me my letters, she died when I was a child and, being so weak and ill herself, had no' got too far with my education. The streets had taught me more, once I was free of the parish orphanage, and I learnt all I knew of life from my poor murdered Mary. I wondered why my grandfather had given his daughter such a thing and what use it might be to me.

I sighed and closed the book. Mebbe I should show it to Hamish and ask him what it meant. The cover was of a fine red cloth, shiny in places where a hand had held it tight. I stroked it and wrapped it again before putting it back in the trunk.

I was sitting dreaming of my mother still, trying to remember the curve of her cheek and the curl of her hair, when the door downstairs closed with a bang. I heard Hamish and Ewan's voices as they came up the stairs and entered their room. I was a little startled when there was a knock on my door.

"Janey?"

"Aye." I hurried to tidy myself up and was still fretting about when he came in.

"At last," Hamish said. "I've been anxious about ye all day. What happened to ye, Janey?" He looked it too, bless the lad, and came towards me with his eyes studying me close.

"I had a bit of a do with Hoskins." I couldna' tell him everything, and I flushed with the memory.

"He hit ye? Why?" Hamish sounded angry as well as puzzled and I took him in my arms, gently.

"Hamish, come, sit down." I pulled him towards the

only seat in the room, the old vegetable box, and pushed him down on it. "Hoskins is a bully. You saw what he was like this morning, and I'm sure you ken him better than me anyway."

"I'm sorry Janey, I should've thought. He was the same with Knox's female servants in Edinburgh, though most of them were too old and ugly for him to bother with. I thought you'd be all right, I'm sorry."

"You mean you thought I'd be ugly enough he'd no' bother, or just used to fighting off men?" I was angry but looking at how upset he was I couldna' be so for long. He hugged me and when I drew my breath with the pain, he loosed his hold and held me at arm's length.

"Knox asked after ye. He was concerned."

"Aye, he asked how I came to look like this and was angry when he'd guessed who'd done it."

"He's a good man. I told you. That was probably why he threw Hoskins out, not for fighting with Carlo."

I wasna' so sure but smiled. The possibility of losing a cook like Carlo was more important than the maid getting knocked about, but it was good of him to say it. Hamish was studying my face and I looked down, all of a sudden shy.

"That's just a bruise, and the lip isn't badly torn. I can put some iodine on it if you wish, but I think it will heal just as well without."

"Thank'ee doctor," I nodded and told him I'd no' be needing his iodine, and he looked at me close.

"Are you well, otherwise?" His eyes seemed to bore into me, and I wondered what he would say if I told him all that had happened.

"Aye," I said. "Nought but a few bruises. Dinna' fret." I pushed him gently out and as he went, I thanked him for thinking about me.

"I care for you Janey," he said, "Really. If any man were to force himself on ye now, when you are trying to be a decent woman, I'd....well..." He blushed and stumbled over his words, and when I moved towards him, he lowered his eyes, retreating to his room. He closed the door, and I closed mine.

That night I couldna' sleep but thought of Hoskins bearing down on me, and of all the men who had used me badly. I thought of Hamish and his kind words, and his innocent and gentle ways, and I thought too of Knox, and how he'd mebbe been angered at my being misused. Were there really men who were good and kind, and enough of them to make the world a better place? Surely more of them were rough and evil than good? Or had I just seen more than my share of them? I lay still, looking at the stars shining in the black sky, little dots of light in the darkness. Mebbe I would stay in London for a while yet. Now Hoskins was gone. Jest to see how things worked out. I could save my shillings and if I had to, I'd be able to go home sometime. But meanwhile I'd give the household on Huntley Street a bit more of a go. Jest for a while anyway.

5

I MEET A GENTLEMAN

The number of students attending the Master's lectures each week was growing, and they came to see him on other days too if they could, though Hamish was no' impressed with all of them. There were at least three of them waiting now to ask him about something, and Knox not yet back from his meeting at the university.

"They want to learn, but they pay nothing extra for his wisdom and take up his valuable time." He snapped shut a book he'd been studying and glared at the door. Voices drifted along the corridor, and it seemed there was a constant clatter of feet about the place.

"The trouble is the Master could be doing with some wealthy patients to bring in more money. The lectures are all very well but the cost of..." Ewan flicked a glance towards me before leaning in towards Hamish. "The last subject cost twelve guineas and was not as fresh as it should have been. Hoskins insisted it was the best Black could get, but I think we should be careful to look around ourselves as well, don't you? Especially now the middleman is gone."

Hamish nodded. If Black was no' the best supplier of bodies, it would be down to Hamish and Ewan as apprentices to find what the Master needed. Though I felt for them, the thought of my lads being involved with such a trade made me queasy. I tried to concentrate on dusting and tidying around them. In the distance down-stairs I heard the doorknocker and hurried down to see what was to do now.

"Good day," the visitor said.

I dipped a curtsey while looking up at the gentleman who stood there. He was tall, jest the right side of plump to be still handsome, maybe as old as thirty and with a pair of blue eyes that sparkled when he smiled at me.

"Is your Master at home, gal? The name is Wakley. If he has a moment I'd be pleased for a few words."

"No, Sir, he's no' home. Was he expecting you?"

"I had merely hoped by chance to find him in. Damn, what a nuisance. I suppose I couldn't come in and wait for him? I am a little tired, I must confess." Mister Wakley smiled, and I decided right away he was the finest man I'd ever seen, then he mopped his brow with a dainty kerchief, and I wondered if he was one of them daft Dandy men. I admitted him with a curtsey and shut the door behind him.

I hadn't had to deal with visitors of such quality before, and none when the Master was out, so I stood for a moment undecided what to do with him. He waited patiently, studying some picture of an old building that was hanging on the wall.

I decided to put him in the study to wait. Then, as I showed him to a chair by the fire, thought that perhaps he should have sat in the room at the front of the house? Knox called that his consulting room, only he wasn't here to consult was he, so mebbe that would be wrong?

"Here Sir, I'm sure he won't be long. The Master always comes home at this time for his dinner. He never misses. Are you warm enough in here?" I prodded the embers of the fire back into life, trying to coax some warmth into the chilly room.

"I'm most comfortable thank you, my dear. Here leave that, girl. We don't want to burn down the house now do we?" He watched me close all the time. I didna' mind, but tucked a strand of hair away, and wiped my hands on my apron.

"Are you new to maiding, m'dear?"

"Does it show that much, Sir?" I was disappointed to have made such a poor impression, but before I could say any more, I heard the front door slam. "I'll let the Master know you are waitin', Sir."

Knox entered the study before I'd a chance to catch him outside, and he looked alarmed when he saw this tall fashionable gentleman had made himself at home in his chair, and he glared at me. I flushed and started to explain, but Mr Wakley stood and spoke up clear for me.

"Please, Sir, do not scold your maid. The girl has been most solicitous in making me comfortable and has stood guard over me, so I don't pilfer any of your books."

I gasped. "Oh, I wouldna' have thought any such thing of you, Sir."

"I don't believe we have been introduced, Mr, Eh?"

"Thomas Wakley, at your service, Sir. I have heard you speak, damnably well too, just the other evening." He gave a bow and Knox looked at him with a raised eyebrow, like he does when he's thinking.

"Ah, *the Lancet*? A pleasure to meet you, Wakley. I've only recently read your article on a proposed unified system of medical qualifications – a sound idea, young man, very sound. Though, of course it will never happen, leastways not with Cooper and his kind running King's College."

"Oh, I don't know. The time will come sooner rather than later when reform will be demanded by parliament, and by the people."

"You attended my lecture you say?"

"Indeed, Doctor Knox. At the Mechanics Institute. Admirable. I met with Birkbeck earlier in the day and he encouraged me to stay. He's always striving to increase the number of his poorer students and I promised to support him. I do what I can. My own coachman is to undertake a number of lectures in engineering, don't ye know!" He laughed but not in a cruel way. "The common man is his crusade you know, to educate and reform 'em, make 'em fit for the new age of enlightenment. We share a great many ideals. As I think you do too, Knox?"

The Master jest grunted and said, "You should read this letter I received only last Tuesday, where is it...." He hunted around on his desktop amongst the clutter of books and rolls of vellum. I stepped forward to offer to help him, but he shooed me away. I couldna' get past him to the door, so I just stood still trying to look like I wasna' there. "Ah, here it is. A letter I had on behalf of a fellah in Suffolk wanting an operation. He has lived for years with what sounds to be a stone, yet he's convinced he's inhabited by the devil. Man's a fool. You wouldn't want to give such a man the vote would you, Wakley? I read your radical reviews on suffrage and I canna' say they sound very practical or even desirable."

"Sir, if the man in Suffolk had access to an education as fine as your own, he would know the devil has no part in his affliction. But as things stand, he is likely to be barely as literate as your maid here." Wakley smiled at me, and I opened my mouth to ask just what that meant, when he continued, "One cannot expect men to know anything if they are taught nothing, or barely enough to read the racing scores."

I jumped in then and told them both, "Nay, Sir. My mam showed me my letters when I was a bairn, afore she died, and she left me a book."

Knox stood there with his mouth open, looking me up and down before roaring with laughter. I flushed more deeply, with anger as much as embarrassment, but before I could say anything more he piped up.

"Leave the lassie be, she knows not what she is talking about. Away girl to the kitchen, and mind you tell no more such nonsense." Knox waved me away and I stamped between the two men towards the door, glaring at my Master as I passed him.

I had mebbe spoken too freely, for I heard Knox apologise to his guest:

"What a preposterous thing. Well, I'm sorry about the girl, Wakley, she ought to know better than to speak out of turn. Did you ever hear anything like it? Ha! I suppose it is possible she can read, but the female brain cannot understand the import of half what it sees. Laundry lists or simple household accounts are a mystery to yon minx, let alone Plato or Pliny!"

"It's refreshing to see a gal that wants to read though, Doctor Knox. Perhaps you should encourage her?"

"What, and have her risk injuring herself? Still, perhaps if I give her a suitable text to read, it would keep her out of mischief. I'll have a look at this book she says she has later, make sure it's decent, not some penny blood."

I was hovering in the hallway by the door still, annoyed to be spoken of in this way, for I heard every word, when the door opened and the Master demanded refreshments. "And be quick about it girl!"

"Aye, Sir." I hurried down the stairs wondering as I went whether Knox would remember to take my book later, and what he would make of it. When I returned with wafers and cordial for them, Knox was looking less cross, all agog at what Mister Wakley was saying.

"I'm in Bedford Square now, since I had the misfortune to lose my house and practice in Argyll Street. The place was burned to the ground. Still, the new house is better appointed, and I have space for entertaining and for my library. Altogether more comfortable and not a stone's throw should you wish to visit tomorrow evening."

"Aye, tomorrow." Knox rubbed his chin. "I doubt this place would burn, 'tis damp enough. What happened, did your servants leave the candles burning all night?"

Wakley's mood sobered then, and he shook his head. "No, I believe it was deliberate. Not the servants, but someone seeking to burn me in my bed. A man with opinions and some small influence always has the danger of annoying someone, I suppose."

I must have gasped at the thought of anyone trying to kill Wakley, and Knox frowned at me.

"Thank yee, Janet. Off you go now."

I left them to it and went about my work upstairs, stripping sheets from the beds to boil next day, if the sun should shine again. They were all in need of a wash, especially as they'd been none too clean when I put them on the beds when we first arrived in Huntley Street. I made up the beds again with fresher linen, though that wasna' as clean as it should have been either. I canna' think how feckless the staff were that were employed before me. Then I tidied the drawing room. According to Hamish, the Master had taken the house furnished with whatever the owner had decided to leave in it. Well, I didna' think much of their linen! The furniture in the drawing room was very grand, with padded settles, not too worn, and with thin carved legs. I sat on them each in turn, still undecided whether the one opposite the window was the softest and most comfortable. I let my mind wander to my mother and the day she gave me the book. She'd been dying then, had I but known at the time, lying pale and delicate in her tumbled bed. "Keep this by you Janey," she had said. "It was a gift from your grandfather to me, and he was a wise man." I had kept it but made little attempt to read or understand it, since the words were crowded on each page and mainly of the sort I'd not understood. Books were a luxury for a working girl and best kept hid, and once out of sight I had in truth forgot about it 'til I packed for London.

The time passed quickly while I day-dreamed, and below me the two men talked on. It was late for dinner-time when I went downstairs and saw Mr Wakley leave. He offered his hand to Knox.

"'Til tomorrow, Doctor"

"Aye, indeed, I'll look forward to it. Good day, Wakley."

Dinner was taken in the dining room, and was a small gathering, since the only students present were those living in, Hamish, Ewan and now O'Rourke. The Irishman had wormed his way into the Master's favours and had got himself the third bed with the lads and a place at the table. I didna' know his first name, for he insisted I call him *Mister* O'Rouke. I made sure I put before him the fattiest piece of meat, and when he called for more wine as I was leaving, I made out I didna' hear him, and shut the door.

The Master called me into his study after supper that evening, and I squirmed under his piercing eye as he lectured me on speaking out of turn and knowing my place. He said he ought to give me a beating for my insolence, but he was busy right then and had to be away. I was thankful for that, but then he remembered to demand my mother's book and thoughts of leaving Huntley Street rose up in me again as I trudged up to the attic to fetch it. I handed it over, fuming at his smug face.

He flicked through the book, snorting at times, and appeared to read parts of it, then he said it wasna' the sort of thing for any girl to read, least of all a servant. He put it in his pocket and silenced my protests with a raised hand.

"Here, I have something more suitable for you." He held out a pamphlet. I took it.

"I felt obliged to purchase it in charity from a street evangelist who called at the house last week. Just the thing for you I think."

I studied the title. "*A Treatise on Humility and Obedience*,"

"Study it carefully girl, I will ask you questions tomorrow after dinner."

It was all I could do not to hurl the pamphlet into the fire there and then, but instead, with as much dignity as I could muster silently curtsied and left the room. I glowered at O'Rourke who was crossing the lower hallway and stamped up to my attic room.

I had thought to do the laundry next morning but when the time came there was a thin drizzle, the grey day matching my mood. I also had no mangle and cursed. I wondered how to ask the Master for one. Deciding to wait 'til the following day I concentrated instead on stitching buttons that had come off shirts, mending tears and polishing the new brass doorknob and letterbox.

When eventually the Master went out, I felt brave enough to hunt in his study for my book. I took with me a duster lest I was disturbed and flicked it around the bookshelves before opening first his desk then his bureau. The desk was full of papers, keys and a purse of money, but there was no sign of my book. I weighed the purse in my hand. It contained a good sum, ten guineas at least. I wondered for a moment about taking it and heading for Edinburgh but decided there was unlikely to be enough to make it worth hanging for. The bureau was locked, and I used one of the keys I had found in the top drawer of the desk to open it. There were dozens of letters, pamphlets and bills, but no book. I shut and re-locked it then quickly started polishing as I heard the door of the room open.

"What are you doing in here?" O'Rourke stood there, his pale hard face sneering at me.

"I'm working, what does it look like? And you?"

"I thought the Master said no-one was to come in here if he wasn't home."

"Aye, well it needed a clean. I'll nay tell him you were here, don't worry." I gave him a confident smile, shook out the duster as I passed him and went down to the kitchen. Who did the little creeper think he was?

I heard him going upwards to the attic as I went downstairs and later saw him leave the house. I couldn't imagine him going drinking, so guessed it must be some less pleasurable entertainment that attracted him. What could he have wanted in Knox's study?

"Do you think he goes to visit loose women?" Ewan asked when I raised O'Rourke's name a while later.

"More likely takes his enjoyment at public hangings," said Hamish and I shuddered. I'd not seen any executions since arriving in London, but I knew Newgate wasna' far away, and Tyburn with its grisly weekly show.

"Still, as long as he brings back a felon for us to work on if that's where he goes, I don't care. We need at least three subjects for this coming week and Knox has told me to go and find them." Hamish bit into a lump of bread greased with butter, his appetite unaffected by such matters.

"Do you use only hanged felons?" I asked quietly.

"Well, people die all the time, Janey. We use whatever we can get our hands on. It would be foolish otherwise. The workhouses and the streets provide a good number of poor wretches, and when we can get a stronger body from the scaffold, we're grateful, especially as most of them go to St. Bartholomews. I know what you think – that we rob graves and murder people, but we don't, not in Edinburgh nor here. Not that we always know exactly where they've come from. Sometimes it's better not to ask."

I nodded and went about my work, sweeping the

kitchen floor and taking the ashes from the hearth to replenish the bucket in the privy.

After dinner the Master tested me on my reading of the pamphlet. I gave a meek and contrite look, biting my tongue.

"It was helpful to me Sir, and I thank 'ee for giving it to me. I shall mind my manners Sir and thank the Lord each night for my position here."

I don't think he believed me. I clasped the pamphlet in my hand, then for greater effect held it to my bosom.

"If I might keep it by me Sir, I can read it each time I feel there be sin calling to me."

His face was a picture but before he could say a word more, I bobbed a curtsey and changed the subject.

"I was meaning to do some laundry Sir but have need of a mangle. If you could spare some money for me to buy one, I'd be most grateful."

"Strong girl like you should be able to manage a bit o' washing." But he took out his purse and gave me two florins in lieu of more wages. "Save them or spend them wisely. Now girl, be off with you."

A couple of florins wouldna' buy a mangle, but I didna' think it wise to linger for he was a shrewd man and if he wanted to question me further on the pamphlet I was doomed. I had a suspicion he knew I'd nay taken the writing to heart. The treatise was short and dull, the paper coarse. The message wasna' what I wanted to read – to know my place and be thankful to God for it. I stared at it with loathing outside his study then, tucking it into my apron, took myself off to the privy in the backyard. There, I carefully tore it in half and attached the pieces of paper to the hook in the wall; much better than the usual rags and no need to wash them. They could go down the pit and good riddance to them. I felt a lot better after that, though my desire to retrieve my mother's book was burning still in my breast.

6

THE INSTITUTE AND A LADDIE IN A YELLOW CRAVAT

The months since we arrived in Huntley Street were passing fast, and winter had become warm spring. I rolled up my sleeves and attacked the crocks in the sink, humming under my breath and thinking of how much colder it would be still in Edinburgh, especially so early in the day. I'd woken soon after dawn with the sun on my face, broken my fast on bread and drunk yesterday's tealeaves revived with hot water and, despite the crossness of the Master over his lumpy porridge, was still in good spirits when Carlo appeared in the kitchen to make his morning coffee.

"What is this?" he asked. "So much dishes so early in the day?"

"Aye, from breakfast. The laddies were eating late last night, and I found some plates and glasses in the Master's study. Men eat a rare amount and make enough mess at it." But I wasna' angry, even when Carlo started grinding his coffee beans and filling the room with foul stink. I dunna' ken his liking for the stuff, nor how it has become so much the fashion. He offered me a cup.

"Nay fear," I said, as I did every morning. "I'll no' drink that foreign muck, 'tis bitter enough to rot the tongue." Carlo jest laughed at my words and took no' offence, for he wasna' a bad fellah for all his moods.

Most days I would have admitted to being thankful for my good fortune, despite living in the house of a man who was my sworn enemy. Indeed, I was lucky to have a roof over my head, good food, and a warm bed in my very own room. On the whole I was ignored by the household, and I amused myself wandering about the area, exploring whenever I could get away. But first, before I could do anything else, the rest of the domestic chores needed done. I sighed and dried my hands. There wasna' a man in the house would notice, mind, but it gave me some pride when the copper shone for my rubbing.

It was no more than a fortnight since Knox had stolen my mother's book, and I was still angry with him if not with anyone else, and chafing for justice. I was determined to get it back, if I had to tear his study apart to find it. I promised myself another look when he went out, but meantime started work on the stairs with my broom. As I swept, I lost mysel' in thoughts of handsome Mr Wakley, when I heard the lifting box start up on the other side of the wall and stopped my sweeping for a while. It was a rare, strange feeling; listening to some poor wretch being hoisted up to the anatomy room. The creaking of it gave me a sick feeling in my stomach. It was mebbe something I'd get used to, leastways that's what I told mysel'. I tried to stop thinking on what they would be doing up there later in the morning and turned my mind back to my earlier thoughts.

Hearing a clatter on the stairs above, I stepped aside, then went down and busied myself sweeping the hallway; carefully brushing the dust into a mound by the front door.

"Ah, Janey, I'd be grateful if you would shake up my bedding a wee bit. Take it outside and give it some fresh air. Something seems to be biting." Hamish was scratching as he came down the stairs and I saw a rash of pink spots on his neckline.

"Aye well, 'tis the time o' year for wee beasties and vermin. The kitchen is invaded with mice and Carlo is threatening to leave unless something is done about it. He says he canna' leave a loaf five minutes afore it has its end chewed off."

"More likely Ewan, do you not think?" He grinned, but then his face turned more serious. "Have ye mentioned it to Knox? You should ask him for some poison, or a cat."

He seemed worried by more than mice, and I leant my broom against the wall. I'd heard the whisperings o' money no' being as plentiful as the Master would like.

"Are you frettin' yersel'? I expect yon Knox is clever enough to get more patients soon, and there's enough students coming in every day to keep him from starvin'." Hamish nodded but his mind was clearly somewhere else. "Are you off out this morning or working up there?" I jerked my head upwards and must have pulled a face for Hamish tutted then gave a wee smile.

"Aye, Janey, I'll be out for a while," he said. "I'm away to the library at the Mechanics Institute. Birkbeck has some fine books there with coloured plates I'd like to take a look at."

"Coloured plates?" But he had turned now for the door. Why go to the Mechanics Institute to look at crocks when we had enough downstairs? He stopped sudden, looking back and I thought for a minute he might be going to say something else about the plates, but it was jest another chore for me.

"If ye want to do something useful, my grey jacket has a button that needs fastening on; if ye have time." Then he was gone.

I glared at the closed front door, picked up my broom again and banged it down.

"Hamish MacDonald. I will no' sew your clothes for you. I am no' your wife or your mother. I am intelligent - Mr Wakley said so!" Fortunately, I'd not said it so loud the whole house could hear, but a gentle cough behind me told me someone had. I turned round sharp and Knox himself, was standing there in his threadbare old dissecting coat with a stained apron tied around his middle.

"Janet, would you fetch me a bucket of warm water and when Hamish gets back tell him his arm is ready and in the student's study upstairs. Thank'ee."

I didna' dare think too much on what he'd been doing up there, and jest nodded and went to get his bucket of water. What must he have thought about what I'd said? I flushed as I filled the bucket and carried it upstairs. I was dreading having to go into their workroom, with the thought of arms lying about the place, but the Master came and took the pail from me at the top of the stairs, and when his eyes met mine, he had a look about him that was kindly enough. He was getting' more and more difficult to hate.

Later in the day I asked Hamish how he had found the Mechanics Institute Library. "Is it as grand as the Master's?"

He laughed and said, "Aye, and ten times bigger, Janey. There are hundreds of books there and all free for the reading. I'll be going back tonight."

"Could I go too?" I don't know why I asked; it jest came out in a rush.

"Eh, well... I suppose it would be alright." He didna' look too happy at the thought, and then said, "of course tonight I'll be going to a lecture first, so I'll not have time to show you around."

"What's the lecture about, Hamish? Could I go to it? I saw a notice in the Master's study about these lectures being free to attend, so mebbe I....."

"Free for men of all ranks. That doesn't mean for women. They will be discussing things not suitable for your ears!" He grinned then when he saw my frown. "Though I doubt you would be as shocked as some ladies."

"Aye, well then, if I'm no' like other ladies, mebbe I should attend!"

Just then, Ewan passed through the hallway. He'd

have overheard most of our conversation and added his penneth.

"Women are allowed into the debating rooms upstairs, to listen, and the library, if you are so keen to learn. I doubt you would appreciate tonight's lecture though, it's on the subject of applied geometry, and to be frank I'm surprised that you would want to attend, Hamish. You have a sudden interest in engineering?"

"That lecture has been cancelled. Guthrie is speaking instead on the digestive juices and the workings of the bowel." He frowned at me. "A subject Janet is not particularly interested in, I'm sure; and anyway she disapproves of dissection."

I blushed. "Aye, well I'm not sure I want to know my innards so closely. I would like to go to the library though, so if it's alright, that's what I will do." I continued then with my sweeping, and the two of them went off to attend to their affairs.

***

Compared to Knox's library, the one on the first floor of the Institute was huge. Bookcases twice the height of a man covered all four walls, with ladders to climb to the top. As Hamish had said there were hundreds of books, and all in neat rows and not a speck of dust. I ran my finger along a shelf and marvelled. The doors were covered with books too, so they looked like more shelving, and every now and then they opened to admit another visitor. One, a tall young man with a bright yellow cravat, entered as I was studying a row of small green books with golden writing running lengthways along their spines. His entrance startled me, and I stood up straight, feeling guilty though I hadna' any reason to be.

"Grand, isn't it?" he said. "No space wasted here on Chinese paper or portraits of our illustrious forebears."

I shook my head, uncertain what he meant, and turned back to the titles on the shelf. Many were in a foreign language, Latin mebbe? Others might as well have been for all the sense they made. Slowly I moved along until, all of a sudden, I saw it! I must have gasped, such was my surprise, and I took hold of the slim book, pulling it from its resting place. I read the title page, amazed and turned to the young man at my elbow.

"This is my book! The same as my book, I mean. I have one just like it at home. Or I did have, 'til he stole it."

"Well, I'll be blowed." The young man was clearly shocked at my outburst. "Who is this thief?"

I couldna' say the truth of it without admitting my lowly position and was thinking on how to explain, but the young man had leant forward to peer over my shoulder at the book I held; "*A vindication of the rights of woman*". Ah, Mary Wollstoncraft. Don't know her well myself, but I hear she's an interesting read." He looked me up and down then, as though he wasn't sure what to make of me.

"A woman with political ideas, eh?" He shook his head; "Your pa disapproves I suppose?"

I didn't know whether he would have or not, or indeed whether this young sprig did, but told him it was the same as the book my ma had given me. "I didna' realize there was more than one copy."

He laughed loud then, and I felt foolish.

"Most books have many copies Miss, such is the demand. I expect there are more outraged young ladies in this city than our librarian could satisfy if he did but realize." Smiling then, he turned away to his own searches along the shelves leaving me puzzled by his words. Outraged? But how did he know?

He turned back after a few moments, scratching his ear and looking at me like he was a cat sizing up a mouse for dinner.

"If it's of interest to you, the debating room will be hosting Mr Henry Hunt on Thursday, talking about the reform of Parliament." Then in a quiet voice as if to himself, he muttered, "I don't doubt my sister will be attending..."

"Oh, aye? Thank 'ee, Mr?"

"Chagford. Charlie Chagford. Well, if you approve of Miss Wollstonecraft, you'll want to hear Hunt's ideas on the way the world should be run." He gave me a little bow and moved away, and I wondered who this Mr Chagford was, and what to expect of this Henry Hunt.

I took the book and sat down on a bench to study it. I had an hour or so before Hamish would be ready to leave and decided to spend the time making a proper start on Miss Wollstonecraft's writings. I could continue at home when I found where the Master had hidden *my* copy of the book, but at least now I knew where I could come to read if I wanted to.

I didna' notice Mr Wakley come into the room. With

my head bent over the book and concentrating on the small tightly packed words, it was only when I heard his voice that I looked up. There was a woman with him, well, a young lassie really, all yellow curls and dimples smiling up at him dewy eyed and gormless. He saw me too and looked pleased then turned sharp back to his woman when she prodded him in the ribs with her elbow.

"Your pardon, m'dear. What was that?"

"Mr Wakley, I cannot think there is anything here to amuse us." She had a scratchy high voice like a lot of the richer English seem to have, and there was a whine in it too. "Why do we not go to the debating room and see who is there, or take some wine at Miss Engleby's soiree? She lives not far from here after all." She looked around like there was a bad smell under her nose then ran a thin white finger along his forearm. Not his wife, surely? I was horrified at the thought. "Perhaps we could slip out and stroll there; it's such a fine evening." Well, she was trying hard, I'll grant her.

Wakley didna' look too eager for that and unhooked her arm from his and told her, "I had hoped, m'dear, for a word or two with Doctor Birkbeck, if you would excuse me. I'll join you in a moment or two, er...." He looked across the room at me and I saw the flash of a smile before he made a line for me steering the girl forwards. What was he doing?

"My dear, let me introduce you to an acquaintance of mine." He couldna' mean me! Startled at being hustled across the room, the gal didna' look too pleased to meet me but, being a well raised girl, she gave the smallest smile she could without it reaching her eyes. She was dressed in a beautiful pale green gown and was staring at me with an expression that I'd seen on the street when two whores meet over one culley. She was no street whore though, but neither was she his wife. Mebbe she had plans to take the job if she got the chance, and I didna' rate his chances of holding out. I got to my feet and bobbed a curtsey. That seemed to please her.

"Mr Wakley, good evening Sir. How do you do M'am?" I tried to look demure.

"Miss Astley Cooper, this is Miss, eh?"

"Janet Brown, Sir." A fine acquaintance if he didna' know my name!

"Ah, of course. Doctor Knox's eh, ward, isn't it?"

"Sir?" I wasna' sure what he meant. Ward? But he was standing there behind her back winking and nodding like a fool, and I thought I'd play along with him. "Aye, his ward. Yes, Sir."

"Delighted." Miss Astley Cooper didna' return my curtsey. I'm no' so sure she was taken in. I was pleased my best dress was clean and I'd left ma's old cloak off as it was warmer now. At least I looked respectable if poor. She looked uncomfortable and scowled at Wakley when he suggested we amuse ourselves with a cup of tea while he went to see Doctor Birkbeck.

"I am sure Miss Brown would not wish to be disturbed from her reading."

"Oh, that's alright." I'd got into the spirit now and was enjoying seeing her put out, though only because Mister Wakley had set it up and he was clearly trying to get away from her. "You might find something here yourself, Miss Cooper." I pointed at the bookshelves, and she raised big grey eyes to the heavens.

"Please, I think not."

"Miss Cooper does not read a great deal," Wakley said. "But I'm sure she could still discuss books at great length nonetheless." He bowed to hide his grin from her, but I saw it and knew he was being rude about her. "I must go now. Ladies." He turned away, leaving Miss Cooper open-mouthed and scowling after him.

"Well, really! Do ignore the rogue Miss Brown. I cannot think what he meant by that. Of course, I read. But the sort of writing they have here, as far as I can tell, is not for young ladies at all. Your pardon," she added quickly; mebbe thinking she shouldna' insult me before she knew who I really was. I'd no need to worry she'd hold back once she did know, mind. "I'm sure you have found a most charming book there, but it would be one of the few I assure you." She fanned herself and looked around as though seeking an escape and I found myself feeling both amused and embarrassed on Miss Cooper's behalf. Whoever you are, beauty or no, there was no way Mister Wakley could possibly marry you, Missy. Him with his love of books and her looking so, well, simple... A lot of upper class women look vacant on purpose, to prove they are too rich to be thinking of anything, I suppose. So, why was he here with her at all? And did he really disapprove of Miss Cooper, or was that jest my hoping? Maybe this was a lover's game they play?

"Well, Miss Cooper. Shall we find something to

drink? I'm sure I saw a sign pointing to some refreshments before I came up the stairs." I put Miss Wollstonecraft's writings back on the shelf and headed off towards the door, and waited there a minute while Miss folded her fan primly and nodded. The girl had clearly realized I was not of her own class, even in my best clothes that much was clear, but she was struggling to place me exactly. As we descended the ornate staircase she walked apart and looked anywhere but at me. I headed for the glasses of lemonade on sale for a ha'penny, pushing my way through the dense crowd of workmen standing around the doorway. They were roughly dressed, though on the whole clean, and I noticed how Miss Cooper blushed and looked away from their smiles and bows. Poor dear, to be so discomforted. I didna' know what Mr Wakley expected me to say, and Miss Cooper wasna' helping just staring ahead and fiddling with her glass. Perhaps he would come back soon. I hoped so.

A few minutes later, though it seemed longer, there was a familiar cry as Hamish entered the room with Ewan at his elbow, and I turned to greet them, raising an arm to return their waves. I felt rather than saw Miss Cooper shudder then make an excuse to leave, though she apologised politely enough. It must have been awkward for her to be talking to me at all.

"I'm sorry," she said, "but I really must be leaving now. I promised to meet my father and Mr Guthrie after his lecture, and it seems it has concluded. You have some friends coming over and so I will wish you good night. Perhaps we will meet again." And with a swift nod, she hurried towards the door without giving the young men she passed so much as a glance.

"Who was that?" asked Hamish.

"Miss Astley Cooper, a friend of Mr Wakley. He introduced us."

Hamish stood open-mouthed and stared at me. "How did you meet Wakley?"

I smiled, sipped my lemonade, and let him wonder. I said nothing of Wakley's visit to Huntley Street, or how he had abandoned Miss Cooper or the secret smile he had given me. Or indeed, how my heart had given a strange beat afterwards. Hamish preferred to talk on the subject of bile and had quickly moved on to that and how certain foods induced its manufacture in the liver. Ewan argued then about something to do with blood and I sighed, slipped one arm into his and the other into Hamish' and together the three of us made our way home.

7

MISTER HUNT AND SOME POLITICAL LADIES

Thursday evening came after a long wait, and I fear my impatience made me cross with everyone during the last days. I was looking forward to hearing this man Henry Hunt speak after what Charlie Chagford, the lad with the yellow cravat, had said.

The Debating Society met in an upstairs room at the Mechanics Institute, he'd told me, next to the library, and I hurried there hoping not to be late, annoyed at having been delayed polishing the Master's few bits of silverware. I was surprised Hamish had decided to go drinking with the other students rather than attend with me, but mebbe it was for the best after the things he'd said. Charlie would be there, and he was good company. I ran up the wide staircase and arrived panting to a tightly packed room.

"Hello; glad you decided to come," Charlie's voice, to my right somewhere, was bright and friendly. The young fellah had a shocking mess of dark hair, and was still wearing the same article, the yellow cravat. He grinned at me over the bald head of a short dumpy man standing between us and pointed to a group gathered around the fireplace. Why they should want a fire on such a mild night I couldna' imagine.

"Come and meet some interesting people," he said, and turned towards them. I followed his tall trim shape pushing his way through the crowds and tried to fight down the nerves rising in me. Nearly all the folk in the room were men, and some clearly the worse for drink. I was relieved when I saw some women in the group to which we were heading, though they were mostly well-dressed ladies. What would they say to my being there, and what would I think to say to them?

I didn't need to be worried as a gloved hand was thrust towards me.

"Good evening. Maisie Baldwin. Pleased to meet ye, sister."

"Eh, good evenin' Miss." I touched her silk-covered finger ends with my bare ones. Mebbe I should curtsey? But she grabbed my hand and pumped my arm up and down like she was drawing water.

"Goodness me, no formality now. We are all sisters together here – apart from young Charlie of course." She laughed like a horse. The men in the group didna' seem to mind her but turned away to have their own conversation to the side.

"Janet Brown, Mi...." I murmured. "Pleased to meet ye."

"You here for Hunt's talk, I suppose?"

"Yes, Charlie invited me. Is it allowed?"

Maisie looked at me open-mouthed for a moment

then burst out laughing again. The other women around her set off too, and it was like being in a farmyard with all their squawks and noise. I felt myself flushing and was getting ready to run for the doors when one of them stopped and took me by the arm, anxious.

"Don't mind us, sorry." She was slim and fair, with soft blue eyes and a gentle smile. "We're not laughing at you. Of course, it's alright for you to stay. We welcome all women, no matter how poor or.... oh, dear that sounds rude... all women, rich or poor, from any walk in life. We are all sisters; we are all slaves."

They all cheered then and a few of the men turned their heads. Charlie raised his eyes to the ceiling but was grinning.

"I'll leave you with your sisters then, 'til the talk starts. I'm just here." He pointed to a group of young men in a huddle nearby and briefly our fingers touched. I felt safer and turned back to the odd womenfolk.

"Esther, but no surnames," the fair one said. She kept her voice low now. Bit late for secrecy, I thought, now they know mine and Maisie hadna' minded giving hers. I shook hands with half a dozen of em, Mabel, Jenny, and Winifred – who seemed to be more of my own walk of life – and a few others I canna' recall. All seemed friendly and most talked at the same time. Esther was the quietest, and had most sense I'd bet, and she kept a firm grip of my arm.

"Sisters, we are here to listen to a great man speak. But later, an even greater orator will speak, and I do so hope you will stay and listen to her." Esther gave my arm a squeeze and I nodded, unsure what Hamish or indeed young Charlie would say to that. A woman orator, well!

We didna' have long to wait before the noise dropped and bodies moved back to clear the middle of the room. I couldna' see much over the crowd but got the feeling someone had come into the room. A voice, clear and strong sounded out and I felt the hairs on the back of my neck rise.

"Hunt," whispered Charlie in my ear.

"Gentlemen, and eh, our few Ladies of course." There was some polite laughter from near the speaker and hearty clapping from the ladies around me. "It is a great honour for me to be present here, in the halls of a man dedicated to learning, no indeed, the education of the vast multitude of working men. By so inspiring them to better their minds, hone their thoughts, Mister Birkbeck is preparing our nation for government." There was a great cheer and I looked around me, startled. "Only by education and debate will the people be rendered fit to govern themselves, and 'tis my aim to win the right to universal suffrage for all tax-paying men within the year!"

"And women!" shouted Esther. There were laughs and someone called out for her to pipe down. A few men around us muttered under their breath, but the rest of the room went wild. I think it was most likely at Hunt's words, not Esther's. A lassie standing to the side of her gave me a look as though to apologize for her.

Hunt spoke for what must have been an hour, but the time passed so fast I canna' say for sure. I didna' follow all he said, but it was stirring stuff and made me feel he cared for folk less well off than himself, though for sure he was a gent himself even if an odd one. I lifted myself up onto my toes and every now and then I caught a glimpse of him. A red-faced hearty man and sweating some too. He must have been fifty or more but had plenty of energy.

"Great man, eh?" Charlie was at my elbow. "He's standing for Parliament. Not for anywhere here in London, too difficult to get elected with all the toffs voting, but Preston up in the north country."

"Do they no have toffs up there then?" I asked.

"Oh yes, but plenty of self-made men too, some who believe in giving common folk a chance. Leastways, we hope so. Once Hunt is elected, he can bring great changes in the House. There are already some good men there, like your friend Wakley, so 'tis only a matter of time before there's change." He turned away and left me staring. Wakley, in Parliament, well!

"So, what will he do when he gets there?" I asked and wondered about Wakley. But Charlie couldna' hear me over more cheers. Mister Hunt was speaking again.

"Remember Peterloo? Aye, fifteen good citizens died that day. For what? For freedom!" More cheers. "And there are men, aye and women too, here in London ready to die for the cause." I gasped. Die?

There was an even greater cheer and caps were thrown in the air. At the front of the crowd, I saw a sword raised high and waved about. This was turning nasty! The ladies around me were still cheering though, so I bit my lip and looked at the sword as it came down gentle enough.

"But tonight is not the night for bloodshed. No. Our battle is not one to be fought on the field but at the ballot box. With an end to Rotten Boroughs and the enfranchisement of the new towns and cities of our industrious land, a new breed of politician is being born. A new future dawns. A future that is ours!"

There was cheering and stamping then, clapping and hooting and I put my hands over my ears. The ladies were jumping about, and I was in Bedlam. But then, after a long time, the noise died down and another voice called out.

"Birkbeck," Charlie said, but he didna' whisper this time or I wouldna' have heard him. "Good man."

"Ladies, Gentlemen, pray silence. We are indeed indebted to Mister Hunt for his words of encouragement. Let us hope those with the power to vote will exercise their right in his favour." A few more cheers. "But now, we have a rare treat. We have a Lady here tonight to bring a few words of womanly wisdom to our excited blood. Lady Eversholt...." Polite clapping now; some of the men turned to leave. Well, really, I thought. They coulda' waited to hear what she had to say. I looked around half expecting Charlie to be heading out the door, but he was there still, eyes laughing but paying attention. Good. The ladies took a breath and stood straight and keen as a tall, stout, grey-haired woman stepped forward and took a small stately bow.

"Good evening. I am greatly honoured to be asked to speak tonight, and I echo Mr Hunt's desire for greater suffrage for all the people of this great land. However, firstly we must ensure that the working people are educated and to this end this fine building in which we stand has been dedicated. It is a great shame I think, that so many of its classes are only for men, and women are excluded, but...." and here her Ladyship held up a black-laced hand, "I appreciate that space is limited. It is my hope to open a school for girls in Spitalfields, and I ask that you support me in this endeavour. Once our girls are able to read and write, and to join their brothers in their offices and in the service of our banks and Temples of the law, then, and only then, will there be true enfranchisement. Why, the ladies here will attest that...."

"What about men being put off, eh?" a voice cried out. "Where will the men work if the womenfolk are employed?"

"And who will keep the family, raise the child?" cried another.

"These are matters concerning both husbands and wives surely," her reasonable voice rose up but was drowned out, and despite shrill calls for silence from the ladies around me the men were booing and stamping.

"Oafs!" Esther shouted. "What do they think women are for, brood mares!"

"Aye, most likely," I said. "I never met one yet as thought we were worth schooling. My ma gave me a book and...."

But Esther was joining with her friends, arms linked, crowding in on their leader and providing a fence around her. Together they called out for books for the girls and rights for the daughters of Eve. The lassie I'd noted before came and stood with me.

"She means well, the Mistress." I nodded, and then she held out a hand, "Verity," she said. "I'm her maid, and..." But there was a noise from the crowd and men were shaking their heads and growling. Some were shouting and shaking their fists, but a few took the women's side. Charlie strode up and spoke out loud.

"Gentlemen, come, do not be churlish. The ladies should be given what they ask for, education. The hand that rocks the cradle rocks the world, is that not, right? A mother can better raise her sons, and daughters, if she has some learning, surely? We can have no objection to that!"

But more men were leaving now, muttering about what they'd give girls if they took their jobs, and such, and I watched as Charlie lowered his arms and shrugged.

"I tried. Still, most of them are rightly scared of losing their jobs. The workhouse hangs over us all like a threatening raincloud." He asked me if I'd finished my book.

"I didna' get far," I confessed. "I couldna' make head nor tail of it to be truthful. Have you read it?"

He blushed and said, "I found it hard work too. But Esther has read it from cover to cover and back again, so she'll explain. Oh, by the way, she's my sister for her sins." He grinned as Esther joined us her furious face relaxing a little when she saw him.

"What's the young scoundrel saying? She asked.

"Only what a clever, scholarly sister I have." He bowed and I saw the likeness in their eyes. Otherwise, the two were as different as is possible, the one dark and the other fair.

"If I only believed him with all his praise," Esther laughed. "But Charlie tells me you are reading Miss Wollstonecraft? How wonderful! What do you think of her? Do say you agree with her. We are a downtrodden race, we women, and there is no justification for it!"

"Now then sis, don't bully the girl. She's had trouble with the lady's writing, just as I have. Some of us have fewer hours in the day to struggle over her wanderings than you."

Verity and I exchanged glances. The grey lady, Lady Eversholt, joined our small group and having overheard our conversation smiled at me.

"Her wanderings, indeed! Fine writing by a fine mind, let me tell you. But my dear, Charlie is right, she does take some study. You are a working girl, are you not, rather than one of us idle rich? Slaving in some man's house? Some brute that beats and bullies you?"

"Well, he's no' so bad.... He did take my book though and I had to come here to find another."

"Hah! Just as I thought! Well, we'll see about that. There are plenty of fine books here that you are most welcome to read, and if there's anything you particularly want to read, and it's not here, well you must let me know. I may have it at home and would be delighted to lend it to you." She smiled again, before walking away to join a party of gentry on the other side of the room.

Esther put her arm through mine.

"Took your book indeed! I could have our sisters

march on his house and demand he return it to you, how about that!"

I must have paled at the thought, for she laughed and slapped her thigh with her fan.

"Never fear, we wouldn't want to get you into trouble, but such men should be shamed and made to feel the monsters they are. Our time will come, Janet, and soon!" She swirled away then, Verity in her wake, back to her sisters, all crowding round Lady Eversholt. That tall stiff lady bowed her head graciously to her friends and I wondered whether she knew Mr Wakley and whether he'd approve of her school for girls. Yes, surely, he would!

The room was emptying, and Charlie was occupied with some of his male friends over by the bookcase near the door. I wandered that way to say goodnight before leaving, but they were all busy congratulating each other and joking and I crept away, down the stairs and out onto the street. I'd not gone far when Charlie panted up by my side.

"Going so soon?"

"Aye, I have to be home. Some of us have to rise early and work."

"Ah, yes." He took my hand and raised it to his lips. I looked around embarrassed. "Such fine, small hands to be working at scrubbing and cleaning. 'Tis a crying shame." He kissed my fingers then and when he lifted his head his eyes wandered over my face. He touched my head, my chin, my neck and I fancy he would've kissed me if I hadna' gone cold on him.

"I should get home," I said, sharper than needed.

Then more softly, "Thank'ee for inviting me. One day mebbe yon ladies will get their school, but it'll no' be for the likes of me. I didna' see many working girls tonight."

"They can't help being who they are either." He went to touch my face again, but I stepped back.

"No. But folk will likely listen more to them."

"Let's hope so, eh? And what of you? Do you want to read that book of yours and understand it properly?"

"Yes, when I get it back I will."

"And in the meantime? Will you come back to the library and let me read Birkbeck's copy with you? Who knows but two heads may be better than one at mastering the unfathomable Miss Wollstonecraft!"

I laughed then, and he laughed too. We parted in good spirits, and I walked home in the gloom of the evening, a mite more confident my future could be bright. The damp air was grey, and swirls of mist hid figures walking on the other side of the road, but then their shapes grew suddenly large as the clouds lifted and they reappeared. I pulled my cloak around me and hurried onwards, not fearful, but keen to be at my own fireside. It was chilly now and my feet and hands were cold.

It was when I reached the end of Southampton Row that I saw Hoskins, not alone but with a shadowy shape at his side which put a hand up and pulled his hat further down.

"Well, well, the little whore is out and about. Does the Master know you're back to your old ways?" Hoskins stumbled forward and breathed in my face. He was drunk and Black grasped him by the elbow to steady him, stepping back only when Hoskins shook him off.

"What old ways? I'm on my way home. And you?"

"Aye, I too am on my way home. But this is no' a night for decent wee girls to be out alone. Ye should be safe indoors, or folk will assume you are looking for trouble, or to earn a few shillun, eh? You wouldna' want to earn a few shillun?"

"No, I would not! And if I were, it would be none of your business!" I sounded braver than I felt, and I saw his eyes glint. He moved closer and I took a step back. Behind me the road stretched away, and beside me the solid wall of a house scraped my knuckles. I stepped to the side, away from the wall, but he was quicker. He blocked my path, and I had the choice of running back to the Institute or standing my ground. I stood. He put a hand out and grasped my shoulder, pulling me towards him. I stared into his eyes then brought my heel down as hard as I could onto the toe of his boot. It made little impact but caused him to grip me harder.

"Now then; no call for that!" His fingers dug into my shoulder making me wince. "I was going to offer to walk ye home, friendly, that's all. No reason to stamp on my foot. If you'd rather walk alone...."

"I would, thank'ee."

"Then walk alone, and take care no man stops ye and has ye in a dark place on the way, eh?" I broke free. Black stood aside then, and I darted past him, trying hard not to run but walking fast and with my head down. They both laughed then, loud and mocking. I could feel them behind me, steps in tune with mine. No' more than a few feet away, Hoskins breathing loud, though my heartbeats were louder still in my ears.

I started to run when I got to Bedford Square, crossing the open ground at full tilt, and I heard them laugh again. They stopped following me then. Either Hoskins knew he couldna' keep up or he'd lost the will now he'd made me run and thought he'd won the battle. I didna' stop. I glimpsed Black supportin' him on a corner but didna' slow. All the way to Huntley Street I ran and arrived puffing at the tradesmen's door.

"Where the blazes have you been, girl?" Knox roared, when I'd let myself in and climbed the stairs to the ground floor. He was standing, hand on hip, in the doorway of his consulting room, a stained apron tied around him. "I've been calling out for hot water for ten minutes now, and I'll have it before ye take yeself off to ye bed; hear me?" He was angry, and when a thin voice called from behind him, I realised he had a patient with him.

"Aye, Sir, sorry, I didna' hear you call." I hadna' lied but felt foolish remembering I was still wearing my outdoor clothes. I reached up and untied my cloak, and lowered my head as I turned and went downstairs again to the kitchen. His eyes were burning into my back. Knox was angry still when I returned with a bowl of warm water and placed it on the table at his side. He grunted then, with one hand holding a knife over the candle beside him he used the other to pick a small square of rag from a pile and dip it into the water. He started dabbing at a great boil before slicing it open. I shouldha' left earlier for I felt my belly rise. The man on the table hollered. A spurt of pus had covered his chest, and the Master made a go at clearing it up. I didna' think but quickly took up a second square of cloth and wet it for him. He stared at me for a moment then took the rag. I gave a hasty curtsey and fled the room. As I pulled the door to I heard my Master tell his patient I was a difficult lass but on the whole not the worst servant a man could have. Nothing a firm hand couldn't......

In the morning I took Knox a cup of chocolate to his study, nervous of what he might say about my absence last evening. It was a relief to see he was in a bright mood.

"Well, Janet. Here's good news." He held up a sheet of paper and waved it about. "Sir Henry was pleased with my service last evening and has written a note to say as much."

"That's good, Sir." I stood quiet, wondering when he'd start lecturing me on my lateness.

"A few more patients of his stature wouldn't go amiss." He folded the letter and put it in a drawer of his desk. "I want you to wash my green wool coat, Janet. Have it clean and fresh for Saturday, and my lace edged shirt. I'm going to a soiree at Lord and Lady Eversholt's, and I'd better be looking my best. She's raising money for something and wants as many of the better sort there as possible. It'll be a good opportunity...."

"That'll be for the school, mebbe?" I said.

"What? School? She's raising money for unemployed weavers in Spitalfields.... but what's it to you girl?"

I said nothing, gathered together the plates from his desk where he'd broken his fast among his papers, and dusted crumbs off the books around him.

"If I gave you a hiding, do you think it would make a damn bit of difference?"

I stopped still, frozen with my hands full of crocks, trapped by his desk. What should I say? I grappled with the problem, and he watched my face intent on flummoxing me.

"Hah! Well, I'll let ye think on it and in the meantime ye can tell me where ye were last night. If it is something I'd approve of ye may be spared."

"I, eh..." Would he approve? "I was with Lady Eversholt, Sir."

"Eh?"

"She was giving a talk Sir, and I went to listen to her Sir and give her my support."

"A talk? Where?"

"At the Institute, Sir. She was very interestin', and she thanked us all for going and, well, she said as how it's good for girls to have an education and read books, Sir, and so would ye give me my book back now Sir so I can read it and do as the Lady said, Sir?"

He was quiet for a moment then stood slowly. I backed off. Damn, that was too much for him. I tensed, watching him move to a cabinet behind him and open a drawer. I guessed it was where he kept a cane or... no, he was holding my book! I took a sharp breath and moved forward.

"If this is the sort of nonsense Lady Eversholt recommends, then I'm a Chinaman. This is not for your eye's girl, or for any respectable woman. Lady Eversholt is a good woman. She cares for those less fortunate than herself and collects for good causes like her husband collects fine wine. This book remains locked in my cabinet for as long as I say. If I find you have been reading any such thing as this, I will not only give you a sound thrashing, but I will dismiss you from my service. Ye hear me!"

I stared at him, his face red and angry, and felt a rage growing in my chest. It was all I could do to bite back a rich curse. He seemed such a good man in so many ways, yet when it came to my book.... I licked dry lips and nodded.

"Aye, Sir. I hear." I curtseyed and silently left the room, but when I got down to the kitchen and put the crocks down, I gripped the edge of the sink so hard it hurt. I will have my book back, I will! I swore under my breath. On the memory of my ma and by all the saints, I will have my book!

8

AFFAIRS OF THE HEART AND GREED

It was warm on Friday morning and I was glad to have the back door wide open. May has always been my favourite month of the year. Back home in Edinburgh we'd not see too much green 'less we walked along the river out of town, and that meant following the stink of folk's waste, but in the house on Huntley Street we had things growing in every bright space the Master could find, including in tubs out in the back yard. I watered the 'herbs' as he called them, enjoyed the scent of some of them, and spent a few minutes with my face turned towards the sun, eyes closed, thinking of how my life had changed so much. Mainly for the better, in truth, though the Master's taking my book rankled still like a rotten tooth. There were things about Edinburgh I missed, and sadness hit me when I thought of Ma Lawrie and young Dougal, some of the lassies and the laughter we'd sometimes shared. But no' the cold, the often hungry nights, I nae missed them. And remembering Mary; the tears welled up still. She didna' deserve to be murdered and cut up. My morning was no' so bright then, and when the sun moved behind a cloud I went back inside the house.

My hatred for Knox had eased over the months in his employ, yet still I yearned for some kinda' vengeance for Mary. Hoskins was my sworn enemy now, and many a night my sleep was filled with the remembering of his rape of me. Knox had defended me, thrown Hoskins out and he had been in many ways kinder than I'd expected. My feelings tumbled in my head.

I'd heard the lads chatter up above me, coming from their study room, and wondered what they might be working on. It wasna' often they had the window open. I climbed the stairs to see, trying to cheer mysel', taking with me some shirts I'd mended lest I had to explain my business to anyone. Not that Knox would notice if I was working or no', but if O'Rourke was about he was always testin' me.

"What's to do, Hamish?" I asked. As he turned to face me, I took a step back. "Oh, Hamish!"

"'Tis a leg, that's all. Don't be alarmed."

"But it's, oh...." I felt a wee bit foolish, for what else would they be doing but cutting up some poor soul? Ewan stood there with a book in his hand while Hamish, with a knife in his, was part way through some grisly work. They'd pushed the desk up to the window and had a single leg there, all alone without its mate the skin stripped off so it looked like a lump of meat. I put a hand over my mouth but couldna' take my eyes from what they were about. Before I could say anything more, Hamish wiped the blade on his apron.

"Come and take a look, Janey," he said. I wasna' keen but came up to his side, drawn to him against my will. "See how the muscle is made? And this, connecting matter that joins it to the bone." He prodded at some portion of the thing.

"Come Hamish, Janey won't be wantin' to see that. She has no interest in anatomy." Ewan was right, but the way he said it made me feel cross, as so many things did, and too easily at times, I know that now.

"I am interested," I lied, and leant forward. Hamish smiled gently at me.

"Sorry, Janey, Ewan is right. I shouldna' be showing you things like this. I just get carried away sometimes with what wonders are held within our bodies."

Is there anything so wondrous about a leg? I thought they were going daft. I nodded and looked from one to the other.

"The pair of you will make fine doctors some time. If my leg complains of sickness I will bring it along to ye for a cure." I took a final look at the limb, noticed a big fly had landed on it, and watched as it was joined by another. They wandered over it, feasting on the blood. I shuddered and turned away. "Will ye no' be having a lecture today from the Master?"

"Not today. Tomorrow if all goes well." Hamish was concentrating on pulling some threads of meat apart and didna' look up. "He is away to visit the wife of a dead patient after dinner, to ask if he can have the body."

I must have gasped for Ewan turned to me. He didna' say anything but looked at the floor.

"He had a very interesting heart," Hamish said. "It was the death of the man, and we hope to see in more detail what caused his suffering. He'd been sick for some time, years most likely. There would be a good audience for the occasion, so you may be needed to help Carlo with some refreshments afterwards."

I was surprised by Hamish's words. The students usually went off home after their lectures, not stopping for feasting.

"Special guests," Ewan explained when he saw my puzzlement. "Doctor Birkbeck is invited and Wakley, and some of the worthies from University College. We don't want to spread the word too far just yet though, in case Cooper gets to hear."

"Cooper?"

"Aye, Sir Astley Cooper." Hamish stood upright again, stretching and arching his back, for no doubt it was stiff from his labours. He lowered his voice and made a show of peering around as though surrounded by listening enemies. "Cooper has been hovering like a fly around Master Jakes, waiting for him to die so he could get his body first, but the old man promised it to Knox. So when our Master got word this morning that he was dead, he arranged to visit the widow this very afternoon."

"Who told him about it so soon?" I asked

"His man came round. He was keen to have Knox win, he...." Hamish stopped and I gave him a questioning look. "He'd wagered with the other servants that

Knox would win over Cooper, and rather than risk losing his money he sneaked out to tell him himself."

"He admitted that to you?"

"Aye. He thinks he's made two guineas on the bet."

"Well!" I was too taken aback to speak. For the man's own servants to be gambling on what would happen to his body! My expression must have shown how I felt. At least the two lads had the decency to blush. I didna' say a word more but took myself up to their bedroom to put away the linen.

I remembered then, I was to wash the Master's green wool coat. Heavy it was, and far too warm for the time of year, but if he wanted to wear it next day it had best be ready. I pummelled and punched it in the tub, anger and tears rushing out o' me, then squeezed as much of the hot water out of it as I could before laying it over the bush by the privy wall, in the strongest sunlight I could find. I watched as the mist rose from it. Good, the job done, and with the day's heat it should dry in time. I wiped my eyes and blew my nose afore going back into the house.

The Master was in a hurry to visit Mistress Jakes and gobbled his dinner down. Serve him right if he got the bellyache, I thought. When I cleared the table he hardly gave me a look. I supposed his head was full of Master Jakes and his heart. I took the plates and other crocks to the kitchen sink and left them soaking, and while he was upstairs checking on the lads I went to check whether his study door was locked, determined to get to my book. It wasn't, but O'Rourke came down the staircase and I quickly moved on and spent my frustration shining the knob and knocker on the front door. The brass plate bearing the name of Doctor Knox, 'General Surgeon and Practitioner of Medicine', had a rubbing too, before I came back inside and finished the crocks. At last the doctor went out and I stole into the study to 'dust'.

The drawer of his bureau was locked fast. I hunted for the key in every place I could get to, and cursed the man under my breath for hiding it somewhere. He must have had it on his person. I flicked my duster around the bookshelves and read some of the sideways writing on what Hamish calls the 'spines'. None of them were very interesting, and several were not even in English. I knew some words were in Latin for they were the same as the papist's bible I came across upstairs by O'Rourke's bed. I gave up my search, for the while only, and went about my other chores.

Doctor Knox was in a good mood when he returned, and called for Hamish to attend him immediately. I was helping him off with his coat when the lad arrived, wiping hands still bloody from his studies.

"Here boy, run to Doctor Wakley at once, then on to Birkbeck. Tell them both I will be opening the heart at nine o' clock tomorrow morning, here, and they are to come and bring open minds with them. All will be revealed but they are to keep their lips tight on the matter."

It was barely an hour later when the Master had a visit from Mister Black, calling by appointment I heard him tell Ewan.

"You shouldn't come to the front door Black. We're to be mindful of what the neighbours might say."

Black laughed as he was taken along the hallway, and I heard the Master then coming out of his study, giving orders.

"Here's the address," he said. I listened, head cocked, from the bottom of the kitchen stairs. "Take a couple of students to help you. Collect the body immediately it's dark, and bring it here with all haste. Tell Mistress Jakes' servant that their Master's body will be returned tomorrow afternoon, quite complete, and we will show it the utmost respect throughout the procedure. Mind, handle him carefully and watch your manners. We canna' afford to upset the good woman, or her household; she's been most accommodating in this affair." I wondered at his tone and couldna' catch what the man Black said in reply. Doctor Knox told him "She has him in a locked coffin, so be sure to have the key from her...."

I kept mysel' downstairs in the kitchen with a cup of strong tea – or as strong as tea leaves twice used could brew.

I watched the arrival of Master Jakes that evening from a distance, standing well back against the landing wall. The coffin was carried into the house, a student sweating at each corner and Black walking at the head, backwards, balancing it. He was still wearing his black greatcoat and wide hat, for all the weather was fine

"It was so heavy," Hamish told me later while I was working in the kitchen. He'd been one of those helping to get it off the cart and into the lift. "The old woman was reluctant to let it out of her sight. The lead coffin cost her nearly a hundred pounds and she wasn't keen to entrust it to a gang of students and ruffians - her words exactly. O'Rourke told me she had to be held back from coming along too, to make sure we don't lose him, or lose the coffin. I don't know which was more important to her."

"Why Hamish, you are hard. I don't blame the poor soul. It's awful sad to lose one you love." I looked down at the dough I was working on and told him, quiet, "I wouldna' want you to be taken away and cut up I'm sure." He mebbe didna' hear.

"Well, I'm sure the sixty guineas Knox paid her will make up for the heartache. Dammit, just think. She gets to have her man back tomorrow and her fine funeral, and his name in the newspapers and the medical journals too. How can she be anything but relieved that he's dead, especially after his suffering?"

I was so shocked by his words I forgot myself and banged down the bread I was kneading and slapped it hard. I took Hamish in my floury hands and shook him.

"Hamish Macdonald, you are a heartless beast and

when you die I will sell you to the butcher's boy, see if I don't! How can you mock the poor woman in her grief? What of the man's soul, and its' journey to heaven? Have ye no' thought of that?"

"He hasn't been delayed on his journey, not if his soul flew free of his mortal body, as I'm sure it would have done." He pushed me off and then brushed his white-dusted sleeves. He stepped away from me, then, and when he was happy I was no' going to attack him again he said, "The man himself wanted to be of service to science. He left instructions for the Master to have his body and make good use of it. You know, maybe I'd have done better to have left you in Edinburgh and found a woman with more sense. God doesna' care whether you arrive at the gates of heaven with your body intact or not. 'Tis your soul he wants girl, not your earthly remains. Why do people think otherwise, eh?"

I stood staring at Hamish. He stared back, face set and angry, and with his hair wild from where he'd pushed his hands through it. His shoulders were broad and stronger now than jest a year ago, I was sure. His boy frame was gone and he was become more man than when we had first met. I felt foolish, shaking him like that when I was but a servant and with no right to raise my voice let alone my hands to him.

"Sixty guineas?" I said, quiet now and trembling. "But that's a mighty big sum of money for a dead man. Doctor Knox must have wanted him real bad."

"Aye, well that is the cost of scientific enlightenment.

I've no doubt Sir Astley Cooper would have paid twice that for the man if he'd the chance to."

I was taken by surprise when he kissed me very gently on the end of my nose and felt a strange relief when his hands went around my waist and he pulled me close. He could have been angrier with me and rightly so, but he was a kind lad and understood I was not so wise about his world and its ways yet awhile. He stopped his squeezing as sudden as he'd started it, and turned to go upstairs. He was gone 'til after supper, preparing Master Jakes for the next day probably, and I went back to my work in the kitchen. Carlo had been busy too, and when he returned from the pantry, he had me help him make fancy things for the morning. Tarts and biscuits, and little sponge cakes iced in bright colours, and all in the shape of hearts.

When I went to bed I tossed about and couldna' sleep. What with the body of Master Jakes below me, and my book calling out to me from the Master's study, I was restless. It was a warm night, and I threw back my blanket and got out of bed. I stood by the open window for a few minutes looking out at the blackness of the night. The stars were bright and a cooling breeze made rustlings in the eaves, else it was the rats. The house was quiet otherwise, and I wondered.....Why not? I decided to try the study once again.

I crept out of my attic room, bare feet making no sound on the stairs, down past the Master's bedroom, from which came deep and regular snores, and past the anatomy room with its' newest lodger. I held my breath, moving like a ghost down the servant's stairs and along to the study, feeling my way in the darkness. I tried the door handle and it opened with the smallest of creaks. Inside, I pushed the door almost closed and let my eyes adjust to the dim light of the moon.

The sash window was open. I stood and stared at it for a minute. The Master was very firm about locking doors and windows, and he wouldna' have left this one open. I went to it and pulled the window down. The wood shrieked and I froze. There were no shouts, no sound from upstairs. I moved slowly over to the bureau and tried the drawer. It was locked, jest as it had been before.

As I passed behind the desk, I brushed against the Master's silk coat, thrown over the back of his chair when he'd got home. Leaning over, I felt in all the pockets. There was a key! I was about to try it on the bureau drawer when I heard the creak of a stair, and I ducked down to hide behind the desk, the key still grasped in my hand. Nobody entered the room and I ran quickly to the door and listened through the panel. Nothing. Gently I eased the door open, pleased I hadna' closed it fully when I'd come into the room, and looked out into the hall. A shadowy figure was at the top of the main staircase, though who it was I couldna' tell, seeing jest his legs passing over my head.

I stayed at the foot of the stairs peering into the darkness above. Over the sound of creaking floorboards, I heard the snores of the Master rumbling on. I decided to retreat to my bed; the house was no' as quiet as I'd been hoping. But I was fearful lest I'd meet whoever it was. Could it be a burglar, or one of the lads coming home late from the tavern?

Slowly, I climbed the stairs, and walked on the tips of my toes along the landing. The door of the Anatomy room was ajar. Noises came from within. I felt my heart jumping inside me and ran, past and up the attic stairs to my room. Master Jakes must be abroad, that's what it was! His ghost had come to haunt us all for what was planned! His spirit couldna' rest! I threw myself into my bed and pulled the blanket up above my head, teeth chattering in fear.

Time passed and Master Jakes didna' come into my room to avenge himself. The noises directly below me in the Anatomy room were muffled but still there. I heard the sound of a window opening, squealing wood like in the study, but nearer. I got out of bed and went to the small window of my room. Looking down, I could make out the side and back of a cart in the street, the rump of a horse. A hoof stamped on the road, but soft, muffled in sacking, and I could hear the harness as the horse shook his head. He was getting restless. There was a creaking sound, a few whispered curses but, though I strained, I couldna' hear what was said. A few minutes later the cart moved off, the horse gently, slowly clopping away.

Next day when I woke, I knew straightaway I'd overslept. I scrambled out of bed and hurried to dress. When I got downstairs it was to an angry Carlo.

"At last!" he cried. "I was about to come and drag you from your bed. We have much to do. The Master will want to eat very soon, and the day students and the guests will be arriving. Already I hear the doctor above us. Take his hot water up, now."

I did as I was bid and the Master, with a blue and gold gown wrapped about him, was waiting impatiently to shave. I bobbed a curtsey and left him to his toilette as he called it. I took water up to the lads after, and I could sense their excitement when they came down to break their fast. No sooner had they laid down their spoons and they were off up the stairs to the Anatomy room, with Knox on their heels, to make sure all was ready for their guests. It was no' more than a moment when I heard a cry and confusion above, and came up from the kitchen to stand at the bottom of the main staircase. The Master was swearing loudly.

I felt Carlo's presence behind me, and he whispered, "What is it? What has happened?"

I shrugged, but my mouth felt dry as I remembered the noises in the night.

"The body is gone!" Hamish came down the stairs, pale and his voice was shaking. "Jakes has up and vanished in the night. He was left on the dissecting table, and now he's gone." He stood dazed with horror as the full meaning of his own words sank in. Knox came down next, grey as a dead man himself, and in a dangerously quiet voice he asked where Black was.

"Well if that rogue shows his face I shall have him arrested, thrown into gaol, hung if possible! It must have been him that has taken Jakes. He was the only one outside the household who knew he was here."

This wasna' quite true, after all he'd sent messages out hadn't he, but I wasna' about to remind him. Knox raged and fumed. How was he to explain to his visitors when they arrived that Master Jakes had gone? And Mistress Jakes – how could he explain the missing husband?

It was Hamish who stepped forward and suggested Black couldn't have been working alone, "If indeed he was involved?"

"I...I saw, eh..." I'd been silent until then, but had to say something afore I'd burst. "I heard some noises, Sir, and when I looked outside I saw a cart waiting. I heard Master Jakes moving about too..."

"Damn! This will be our undoing if the body isn't found. I'll wager the subject has been sold on, almost certainly to Cooper." The Master was pacing up and down now, wringing his hands and huffin' and puffin'.

Hamish, still upset, was always one to add a hopeful suggestion. "Sir, the demonstration of the heart could still go ahead, without the rest of the body. I removed it last night, thinking to save time and..."

"What!" I thought the Master would burst for he had gone from grey to scarlet. He took a deep breath and said again, but not so loud, "What? You took the heart out already?"

"Aye, Sir. You said the demonstration was to be of the heart itself, to see the faults in it. I thought you wouldna' need the rest of the body, leastways not straight away, mebbe later, and so I took out the heart and put it in a jar ready. I packed some straw in the chest cavity to stop it collapsing in, and......"

Doctor Knox looked like he didna' know whether to laugh or cry, his expression kept changing and his mouth was working but not making any sound. For a minute I thought he might take a fit and die too. I squeezed my hands together in my apron and felt the key there still, and fumbled with it to calm my nerves.

After a while, the Master composed himself and looked up to the ceiling. "Well, for once boy you may have saved the situation. Thank'ee. We will examine the heart as planned. Though it would have been useful to see how such a defective organ had affected the other parts, we will have to forego the pleasure until we can get Master Jakes back. Now, our guests are about to arrive. Make haste and pour some glasses of sherry ready for them, Janet. Not for the students, just the gentlemen. Now...."

He went off then, once more becalmed, to change into his operating coat, and I felt a weight had lifted from me. It was no' the ghost of Master Jakes I had seen the night before, but jest a thief; a thief who stole bodies rather than silver plate. I busied myself in the kitchen with the sherry glasses and then remembered the Master's best coat was still outside in the yard. No' time to fetch it then, but after I had served the sherry to a dozen gentlemen, including Mr Wakley who gave me a smile, and denied it to as many cheeky laddies, I collected the article from the bush by the privy. As I snatched it up, I was pleased to feel it was warm and dry. I hurried upstairs best I could through the crowd of students on the landing, and laid it on the bed, then returned to the hall downstairs where yet more folk were arriving.

When everyone was settled up there and a hush fell upon the house, I sighed and leant back on the wall at the top of the kitchen stairs. The last of the sherry warmed my mouth and throat, and I closed my eyes for jest a moment to enjoy its glow. I heard the Master's voice above me, for the door was open, and the appreciative murmurs of his audience were gentle and soothed me near to sleep.

"The chambers are arranged thus to allow the blood to flow between them, but only in an ordered manner. These mitral valves are designed to prevent any irregular return of the blood, forcing it to travel in one direction," he was saying. "The muscle is strong and in a healthy heart contracts and relaxes with every breath a man takes." I frowned and wondered whether a woman's heart works any different. I thought I would ask Hamish later.

Down in the kitchen I helped Carlo arrange plates and trays of fancy cakes and 'canapes' as he called them, and puffed up and down to the dining room with them. When every surface was covered, and Carlo set himself in charge of the wine table, I went downstairs for a few minutes rest. The demonstration would be over soon and they'd all descend to feed like flies. Mebbe Master Jakes would not be missed too much after all, and the mystery of his going would pass.

"Sir, surely instead of burying Master Jakes himself, the coffin could be filled with stones – I hear that is the practice of some graverobbers, is it not?" Hamish glanced at me where I waited behind the Master, for I must have been standing open-mouthed.

"Tush, Mistress Jakes would be expecting to see her man before having the box sealed up. The idea is good but it wouldna' work." Knox dismissed the idea out of hand and, no doubt a wee deflated, Hamish leant against the doorframe.

"He has a point, Sir," Ewan said. "We could say that during the examination of his heart, the gentleman was disfigured in such a way that his wife would not wish to see him, so we could wrap him up and keep him hidden."

Hamish groaned and shook his head.

"Where is the sense in that? How could removing his heart disfigure his face? No, we could say, oh, perhaps he has deteriorated in the heat – it is warm is it not, Sir? Or, he had a contagious disease we didna' notice before and it would be safer to keep him wrapped up."

The Master seemed to consider this idea for a moment and nodded slowly.

"You may have something. Not the nonsense of a contagion, his wife would know he had none when he died. No, simple deterioration should do it. We could tell her that he had to be wrapped and put in the lead casket as soon as possible before he was sent home. Perhaps if we delay a day or two that would be the more convincing; and it would give us a bit more time to mebbe find Jakes and get him back..."

Not expecting to be taken seriously, I cleared my throat.

"Sir, there's a cat outside in the street; I fear he's been dead a couple of days and is a mite smelly now. Ye could put him in the casket to add some stench if ye will."

"Just in case Mistress Jakes is tempted to open the shroud and take a last look at her husband you mean." Ewan gave a nervous laugh then the others, looking aghast for a moment only, started to laugh like schoolboys at the cleverness of the idea. I smiled but was shocked at mysel' for suggesting such a thing.

Doctor Knox waved a hand to silence the lads and reminded us that this was a serious matter and Jakes should properly be found and returned to his wife.

"And Black, he must be found and made to pay for his greed. He, and likely Hoskins with him, has overstepped the mark of decency and likely forced us into this fraud. It is not something that respectable members of my profession will stand for and, should word get out that I had behaved thus, well, it would be my undoing. I trust I can rely on the discretion of you all in this matter?"

"Aye, Sir." We all agreed, for what else could we do, and this cheered him.

The rest of the afternoon was spent wrapping a number of large stones and sacks of soil, which we laid out in the rough shape of a man, on the oilskin sheet inside the coffin. The dead cat was collected from the gutter and carried, at arm's length, into the house at the last moment, and neatly arranged in the area of the 'corpse's' chest, before closing the oilskin over the whole and fitting the lid. It added a smell of death, but it was one we couldna' possibly live with for a moment longer than necessary. 'Master Jakes' would have to be returned to his wife, and before the end of the day.

Fortunately for the purpose of the plan, the day was warm again. Indeed the sun burned down. The cart, driven by Ewan, with the other students ready to run along beside it, set off. Later Ewan told what had happened and how he had dealt with Mistress Jakes' butler.

"Best not to disturb Mistress Jakes if possible, I told him." Ewan couldna' help but laugh. "And then I said as how Master Jakes had started to turn. "He is not the man he was...."

"And did the Mistress see you arrive?" I asked.

"Aye, and wept over the coffin. As she stood by the hall table, on which the coffin had been laid, she said how her husband would be happy to have been of such service. Then she said, 'Make certain the bolts are fully closed. No one is going to have my man out of his resting place.' Well he chose the coffin himself you know, for its security. The burial is due Friday, and the Master is invited....."

The casket was certainly a beauty and the straps of solid steel that wrapped around it would keep the contents safe forever. The household was content again, now knowing Mistress Jakes was satisfied. The day had gone well. The Master went upstairs to change his clothes for the soiree he was to attend at Lord and Lady Eversholt's.

I was pleased with myself for having got all ready for him when I heard him cry out and ran to the bottom of the stairs.

"Janet! Come here girl and explain what in the name of God you have done to my best coat!"

9

I MAKE A FRIEND IN VERITY AND ASSIST THE MASTER

From the way he looked at me, I knew I was in for a beating. Doctor Knox was a big man but I was lighter on my feet, so I ran. I was down the stairs, along the hall, then down the servants stairs to the kitchen like the devil himself was after me. I could hear him, his feet like thunder on the stairs, and all the while shouting.

"Come here you.....I'll have ye!"

I bolted through the kitchen. Where to hide? Through the door, out into the yard, past Hamish filling a pail at the pump; he looked up startled. No time to talk, I ran into the privy, slamming the door shut behind me and pushing the bolt across. I shrank back into the darkness, my heart fair pounding and part of me wishing I'd stayed at home with Ma Lawrie. She didna' beat us, and I didna' have to wash clothes for a man either.

The Master had been angry on and off all day, firstly with the loss of his 'subject', as he called Master Jakes, and then when some of his visitors were no' as impressed with his heart as they should ha' been. Then, when he saw how his coat was shrunk to half its former size, he was livid.

"Out of there girl, now!" The Master thumped on the door. "I'm going to give you a hiding you'll remember!" I knew it well enough, and I wasna' going to take it if I could help it. I stayed where I was, in the dark stink of the privy, praying he would soon tire of waiting and go on his way to his soiree. He ranted for a few minutes then it went quiet. Jest when I thought it was safe to come out he banged again, making me jump. Then, when he spoke, I reckoned his voice wasna' quite so harsh.

"Come out wench. I promise that this time I'll not lay a hand on you, but don't ever wash anything of mine that other folk will see. Stick to sheets, shirts and drawers, ye hear me? Now come out, there's others have need of that privy."

Despite his promise, he stood there slapping the carpet beater against his leg and growling low when I slid out, and I was careful to keep the door between us 'til I could hop past. The lads were hovering nearby, half a dozen of the visiting students too, smirking at me. I glared at them. O'Rourke was licking his lips at the chance of seeing me punished. Hamish was there too, with his worried face, and when our eyes met he gave me the smallest of smiles, reassuring me. I gave the Master a wide berth lest he change his mind and hurried indoors to the safety of the attic.

The lads went that evening with the Master, to Lord and Lady Eversholt's for their soiree, but I had a few minutes alone with Hamish first. He was in a lather with his dressing up and came to me for help. As I buttoned him up in his best coat he said,

"You never know who will prove influential in the future, Janey. These occasions are all about making an impression."

"Oh aye? You mean they might get sick one day and remember to call on you?"

"Maybe, one day. No, leave the top buttons Janey, I want to show my new cravat. They could help ensure positions for us. Doctor Wakley will be there and he's looking for help with his patients. He has less time now he's in Parliament. Of course I would need to finish my time with Knox first, get my examinations done, but I want to talk to the man."

Inside myself I wished him success, but I couldna' help thinking all the same, would that I could find an influential person to ensure my future. I squeezed his arm and straightened the cravat. Hamish tutted and ruffled it again.

"Not too tidy. The fashion is to be a touch wild, ye know." Well his hair would be the most fashionable, for it never saw a comb that I knew of.

Doctor Knox was wearing his black coat. Aye, I thought, much better than the green wool one, cooler and lighter for the warm evening. He gave me a look, but I curtseyed as he passed me, head down, careful to keep still and play the good servant. I hope it was a good glimmer I saw in his eye, but most likely he was planning on having me still when I least expected it. I shut the door after them and went down to the kitchen where I made myself some tea with what was left in the Master's pot. The leaves were still lively enough to give off some taste and with some freshly boiled water the scalding drink refreshed me. I closed my eyes for a moment or two and remembered my mother in our happier times, and the way she stirred the pot before she poured her tea. To the left then to the right, round and round, then left again. I rinsed the pot and straightened my apron.

I was pleased to have the house to mysel' when at last Carlo went out to visit a woman he'd met, though he liked to think I didna' know about her. A man is open as a babe when his feelings are raised and I think he was mebbe smitten with her. Else it was the exotic spices she sold.

When he was gone, I took mysel' to the Master's study and tried the door. It was open, and fishing in my apron pocket I tried the small brass key I'd taken the other night, in one lock after another 'til I found the drawer it opened in his desk. There was no sign of my book. Some stubs of pencil, broken quills, papers and ugh, a long curved bone. I pushed the drawer shut, sharp. The bureau, where I'd seen him put the book when first he stole it, was locked and there was no way into it. Mebbe I should break the lock? No, that would be too plain an act of folly. Even the Master would notice that. I sat down on his chair and stared at the piles of paper and books spread before me on the desk, and the shelves around the room stuffed with more besides. How could a man read so many books in one lifetime? I sighed, despairing at ever having my mother's book back. I would have to go to the Institute again if I was to read Miss Wollstonecraft's words. But even as I thought on it, I remembered Charlie and his friends and how mebbe that would not be too hard a thing to make do with 'til I got back what was properly mine. The evening was still light, being not long past seven o'clock, and I decided to waste no more time. I went upstairs and fetched my coat, then set off for Southampton Row.

When I arrived, the entrance hallway was crowded. I knew the way to go, and as no one stepped out to stop me, I climbed the great staircase, looking out for any faces I knew. There were only a few visitors making use of the library when I got there, so mebbe the rest were waiting to attend a lecture in the drawing room downstairs. I found Miss Wollstonecraft's book and a seat by the unlit fire, and settled myself to try again to understand her writing.

I had not been long at it when I heard voices I recognized, and Charlie Chagford and his sister Esther entered the room. A few paces behind them was the girl Verity, but it was she who saw me first and came over to speak, the other two being taken up with their talking.

"Good evening, Miss." Verity bobbed a brief curtsey to me and I nodded back. I motioned for her to sit by my side on the couch.

"Good evening, Verity. How do you fare? Are you here for another meeting of the debating society?"

She gave a little shrug and smiled. "Where the Mistress goes, I go." Then, perched on the edge of the seat, her eyes followed Esther as she walked slowly with her brother. I was puzzled.

"I thought Esther and the others believed all women to be equal. Yet she treats you as her servant. Are you not here to learn yourself?"

"Gracious, no. I can read but I haven't any need for more education. I'm too busy looking after the young Mistress and seeing she keeps safe. Her father'd never forgive me if owt happened to 'er. Between you and me, he doesn't trust 'er brother to keep her out of mischief. Not that he's a bad lad."

I was disappointed. I'd thought mebbe Verity was her own woman, but of course, how could that really be? Esther and Charlie were still talking, in whispers now, over on the other side of the room and I thought how serious they looked. Charlie was shaking his head and his sister was getting het up about something. I looked back at Verity.

"She's a trouble to ye? She looks like a woman with a strong mind. When I was here before she seemed kindly enough, though mebbe she didna' realise I was only a maid too."

"She's no bother, not really. Some daft ideas mind, but...." she gave me a look, working out in her mind, I suppose, whether she could speak freely. She must have decided I was trustworthy, and carried on. "She plans on helping out at some school for girls, and there might be a job for me there too though I don't know I could take to it, mind. Where do ye work?"

"At the house of a surgeon. Doctor Knox, in Huntley Street. Ye mebbe have heard of him?" I hoped not.

Verity shook her head frowning. "No, but then the Master, Miss Chagford's father, he's a clergyman and doesn't hold with doctors. He's a praying man not a bleedin' one."

"Well, better for you I dare say." I thought to myself how she wouldna' come across limbs and hearts all over the house while she worked. The worst she would have to bear would be praying on her knees every day for her supper and breakfast too. Though mebbe they didna' get so worked up about their religion here as in Scotland.

"It must surely be a busy household?" Verity was saying, "With patients arriving to see the doctor every day. You help him with them?"

"Oh, aye. He has a good number of patients and students besides. They come to watch him with his, eh, experiments and practising." Should I tell her? Well, why not? "He has bodies delivered to the house to cut up for them to study. Ye'd never believe the things they do there in the name o' learning!"

Verity shrank back from me, a small white hand over her mouth and eyes wide with horror.

"No! Lor', 'ow terrible! You don't have to clean up after 'em do you?"

"No, fear not. There are a couple of students who live in the house and earn their keep by dealing with that sort of thing. I run the household, cleaning the living rooms and other chores. I admit his patients and wait on the more important ones 'til the Master is ready to see them. There are so many visitors. He had a Lordship the other day...." I grew under her gaze, the near-lies swelling inside me, and hoped Hamish wouldna' arrive and give away my exaggeratin'. He might approve though, making Knox out to be even bigger than he was.

"That must be a very responsible job." Verity was warming to me and I to her, and by the time Esther and Charlie came over we were friends.

"Good evening, Miss Brown." Esther, or Miss Chagford as I now answered her, was smiling bright as before and no sign now of what might have been worrying her. Charlie too seemed cheery enough and the three of us spent a minute or two talking of the weather and what Hamish called 'pleasantries', and all the while I was trying hard not to stare. She was a lady, or close enough, and a real beauty. The strange thing was she clearly didna' know it and carried her looks off without using them at all. She didna' stay long but moved on to greet another group of visitors, leaving Charlie standing by my side. He ignored Verity. She took herself off to stand behind the sofa and her eyes followed her mistress dutifully. Charlie looked down at me for a minute, thoughtful, then turned and stared down into the grate. He kicked gently at a half burnt log left cold in the fireplace since last it was lit.

"How goes Miss Wollstonecraft?"

"Slow," I answered. "I havena' got my own copy back yet, so I came here to read this one." I showed him the book I still held in my lap.

"A strange woman," he said. "She held that boys and girls should be educated together, to both learn rationality and be better able to live together as sensible adults. As I recall, she didn't hold with the classics. Rather unlike the education I endured I must say. Did you have any schooling, Miss Brown?"

I didna' want to look a fool, but what could I say?

"I learned how to read at home, with my ma....my mama." I smoothed my dress with a hand that was damp with sweat, thinking of how he was ignorant of my lowly station. Should I admit it or carry on with my pretence? "She died though, when I was still very young and I....." I looked up at his clean-shaved young face, his grey-blue eyes turned to me with polite interest. He was very handsome, like his sister, but more aware of it p'haps. "I was taught at home by the village clergyman." Well, so I was. He used to come and give us our lessons at the orphanage, teaching us gratitude for the food in our bellies. I remember how he'd call us girls up one by one to sit on his knee and recite bits o' the bible. He was a big man, grey haired and fat, and he'd squeeze us close and breathe on the necks of the girls who pleased him, and spank those who didna, holding them down and praying while he hit them, all pink faced and sweating. As for his family, I met Mistress Bull only the once, at Hogmanay when she brought us sweets.

"He was a very learned gentleman," I lied, "but I turned my hand to working for a woman on the other side of town when I had the chance."

"Ah, and what did you do there? My sister has ambitions to teach."

I stared at him, my mouth dry all of a sudden. How could I say to this fine young gent what I'd done at Ma Lawrie's? I was saved from having to think of any fresh lies, by a commotion starting off by the door and working across the library. The man Hunt was back, and with him Doctor Birkbeck himself, the man Hamish had pointed out to me when I first came here. A gaggle of followers all talking at once at the top of their voices, hung onto their coat tails and both men were enjoying their popularity. Charlie stood up sharpish to gaze after them.

"Pray, forgive me," he turned back briefly and I sighed with relief when he said, "I must speak with Hunt if I can. I will ask my sister to come and join you if I may. Perhaps you would care to take some cocoa with us later?"

He didna' wait for an answer, and I'm not so sure he would have his sister take cocoa or be anywhere near me if he'd known what my profession had been, but I answered his back nice as anything.

"Thank'ee Sir, I'll look forward to that."

I had given up struggling with Miss Wollstonecraft and chatted instead with Verity for a while longer. She was a bright, cheerful girl as it turned out, and it seemed her household lived not so very far from Huntley Street.

"I know of St. Giles. Indeed I passed it only a few days ago on the way to Covent Garden."

"Just take care," Verity warned. "The market is well enough itself, but the area is not a good one. The Master is very keen to preach to the locals and goes out nearly every night. He says they all have souls, every last man jack of them, and he's determined to save them all whether they like it or not. One day I reckon someone will slit his throat."

"What's that, Verity?" Mistress Chagford had arrived without us noticing, and we both wiped the smiles from our faces as best we could.

"I was just saying as how the area around Covent Garden isn't one for wandering in, Miss, leastways not after dark."

"Very true. Though when the school is up and running things will change. Of course, it will take time. Once the children are taught their letters, and as many parents as can be encouraged too, they will seek out better work than thievery and prostitution." Miss wasn't one for mincing her words. "All this is so close, Miss Brown, so close! Do you not share our passion?" She was bursting with it so I couldna' let her down.

"Aye, very good. A school sounds a grand thing to build for them. Are these boys or girls ye's thinking of teaching, Miss?"

"Both. It is Lady Eversholt's intention to educate them together, though I am not sure that is altogether wise." She raised her hands, flustered then. "But of course, if she says it is for the best, who am I to criticise. What do you think, Miss Brown?"

"Well, Miss Wollstonecraft has writ the same, and if she agrees with her Ladyship, then so do I. She thinks both will be more rational for it." I wasna' sure what that meant but hoped it sounded like I was.

"Ah, rational, yes. But is it healthy?"

"Healthy?" I didna' think her brother had

mentioned their health. "That I wouldna' ken, Miss." I would have to ask him about that, or mebbe Hamish would have views on it. If Miss Wollstonecraft had anything to say on the subject I'd not yet fathomed what. I closed the book as Esther sat down by my side. She reached over and patted my hand, her brows twitching very slightly in a frown. She was wearing silk gloves and my bare fingers curled in embarrassment. Mebbe she sensed it and was quick to make good.

"Miss Wollstonecraft is most sincere, and I agree with so much of what she writes. But when it comes to the very poor, base instincts tend to overcome our best efforts. Why, keeping the sexes apart is the kindest thing sometimes and the only hope for the girls. They can so much easier be trained when they are not hampered by the bestial attentions of men. I have known girls as young as nine or ten who are more worldly in areas of ..... but there, I should not wish to shock you. You would not believe what I have seen with my own eyes when I have been out with my papa."

I shook my head politely.

"You help your papa often?"

"Whenever I can. But where he preaches to their souls, I wish to take a more practical stance with Lady Eversholt and teach them skills they can use straight away. These girls can earn a penny or two from sewing, and better yet, once they can read a little they would appreciate some simple receipts perhaps and make far more capable wives and mothers in the kitchen, or in service. Papa is not so keen on them reading. He thinks they may develop ideas of their own that would question his words. I think that most unlikely myself, don't you?"

I glanced at Verity and our eyes met.

"I'm sure they are most grateful for your attentions, Miss. Now, your brother mentioned cocoa might be found here. I know they sell lemonade, but...."

"Yes, indeed. We shall go and find some downstairs. You must allow me to play hostess though." Esther led the way to the refectory, and I was pleased to let her buy cocoa for us all. Even Verity was allowed a cup, and we sipped the warm brew as the room filled up around us. I drained my cup and licked my lips.

Those who had been attending the evening lecture were talking loudly, discussing what they had learnt, and I realised it must be after nine o'clock.

"I had best be heading home, Miss Chagford." I made to stand up but Esther bid me sit down again.

"We will all go together. The carriage will be here shortly. Now where is Charlie?" She peered around then had Verity run and find him. They returned together with a group of several dashing young men and another young lady who turned out to be the sister of one of them. There was a deal of conversation about the lecture and the merits of the speaker, a man who knew all about ancient Egypt and had shown them several pots. Then the subject of going home was raised again.

"Now, Charlie and myself, Elizabeth and ah.... did you say you had let your brougham go already James?" Esther asked.

"I had Henry take it with his party. Not to worry Esther, we can go with you. Just drop us off at Adelaide

Place, there's a dear thing." James placed an arm around Esther's shoulders and hugged her. He wasna' completely drunk but had been drinking a wee bit of something stronger than cocoa.

It seemed there wouldna' be room for all of us after all. Verity and I were happy to walk together.

"But do be sure and keep clear of shadows and not to stop on the way." Miss Esther was clearly concerned, but the one she called James, who looked at me close through slitted eyes, assured her that we would be safe enough on the short walk. I didna' want to linger, so Verity and I set off arm in arm into the evening, grateful for the street lamps, but pleased to be excused the company of our betters.

"She means well, like all those women," Verity said. "But really, what can they know of the poor however much they visit them?"

I nodded, and gave her arm a squeeze.

"Where were you born Verity? Are you a London girl?"

"No, I was born in the country, out past 'ampstead. But my family moved to the City when I was a littl'un."

I wasna' familiar with where that was, but she told me she was sure it was a good ten miles away.

"And yourself?"

"Edinburgh. Hundreds of miles for sure."

"My! Our coachman is from Ireland and Charity, the other maid, is from Reigate. What a mix London is, ain't it?"

"Aye, so it is. Most of our household came down together with the Doctor, but we have a foreign cook, an

Italian, and Lord knows where some of the students are from. We had a local girl for a short while, employed to assist me, but she took fright at the Master's work and wouldna' stay. Silly chit."

We strode out together and when we reached the Church of St. Giles, Verity took my hands in hers.

"Now we must separate. Are you sure you'll be safe the rest of the way? It's really quite dark now. I do worry, when I think of what goes on. Why only a few nights ago," she looked around into the gloom and pulled me closer, "some men were seen in the church-yard. They was diggin', just think! It was only the quick thinkin' of the curate who was walkin' by and called a constable, that they was stopped in their beastly work."

"Grave-robbers ye mean?" I shuddered. Even though Hamish had told me it was a necessary evil, I didna' relish being so close to it. The graveyard was jest across the road from where we were standing, and we held tight to each other.

"And they do say," Verity continued, her eyes bright and wide, "some men will knock a person down and sell 'em to the surgeons and, oh, forgive me. I'm sure your Master would never.... I mean."

"Oh, I believe Doctor Knox is most particular. He has his bodies from the gallows, in the main, good and fresh. Them and others as have interesting illnesses. Don't fret now, I'm sure 'tis too early yet for murderers to be about."

"Will you walk with me, just to the other side of the church?" Verity whispered. "You can walk back along the other side of the road, without crossing in front of the churchyard. Will you?" She was pleading, really frightened, and I gave her hands a squeeze and agreed. The night held no terrors for me, I told myself. Once we were safe past the churchyard, where no lights showed and no sounds of digging came, and then St. Giles itself, and come to the gate of the rectory, we both felt safer.

"There, hurry indoors," I told her. "I'll away as quick as I can. Mebbe we will meet again soon?"

"Oh, yes, let's. Per'aps when you're going to the market next, you could knock at the servant's door and take some tea with me?"

"Your Master would allow it?"

"Oh yes, especially if he's not at home! He's out visiting his parishioners most mornings or taking tea somewhere in the afternoons. Don't worry, we'll be unlikely to be disturbed, or if we are it'll be the young mistress and I'm sure she wouldn't mind."

I was excited at the chance of going out to take some tea, and it gave me some comfort on my walk home that evening. My footsteps were not loud, but they echoed to me in the stillness, and I couldna' stop my thoughts going back to the streets of Edinburgh, and Mary, and how we had worked each night. We were so young and foolish and for the most part had little fear. Besides, it had been morning time when we were took, and it was not by a man in the dark but by trickery that she was killed. I was startled out of my thoughts and my heart jumped when a cart rushed past me so close I fell aside and cursed. From my place lying by the roadside, I watched as it drove on, swerving back into the middle of the road. The dark bulk of the driver turned in his seat and spat. I cursed under my breath and raised my fist then, when he was away out of sight I gathered myself and carried on home, sore and with jangled nerves. I turned into Huntley Street, and crossed the road to the house.

I was halfway down the area steps when I saw a shadowy figure out of the corner of my eye, hurrying up to the front door, our front door. There it halted and banged the brass knocker. I turned, peering up to see who was calling so late. The door opened and I could see Carlo, lit up by the hallway behind him.

"Please, is the doctor at home?" I heard the woman's voice, then Carlo's answer,

"No, he is not 'ome."

I climbed back up the steps to the street, turned to the front door, and called out,

"He's no' expecting you is he?"

The woman turned to me. She was young, mebbe about my own age, not grandly dressed, but a respectable lassie. Carlo looked pleased to see me.

"Ah, here is the Doctor's maid. She will speak with you. I will go back downstairs." He mumbled something and left the visitor to me. I wasna' sure what I should do, but I know I was pleased the Master wasna' there to see me standing in his doorway bold as brass and talking to a patient, Well, I thought, that's what she must be if she was asking for him.

"No, I have no appointment," she told me. "But this is a matter of urgency. My father is a patient of his and he's very ill. Oh dear, where will I find a doctor at this hour?" The woman raised a handkerchief to her face and patted her forehead and cheeks. She was close to tears I could tell, and I felt sorry for her.

"Where do you live, ma'm? If you give me directions I will run for the Master and ask him to visit you. He is out but I know where."

"I'd be most grateful. We are not far, Tavistock Place. Doctor Knox has served my father before on another matter. Here," she thrust a calling card into my hand. "When you find him, please ask him to come, as quickly as he can. Please!" She put her handkerchief to her face again, sniffed and hurried away, back down the steps and along the road, half running. I looked down and read the name, "Samuel Willows," and went inside the house, calling out for Carlo as I closed the door. He stood at the top of the servant's stairs.

"Carlo, I'm away out to fetch the Master."

"You are back 'ome, now you are out! Where have you been, eh? The Master he will be angry if he knows you been out all evening. What you doing? Drinking?"

"No! Honestly Carlo, would I go out drinking? Indeed, I've been to the Institute, where the young gentlemen go, and where I was taken by Master Hamish last week. But I've no' time to stand here gossiping with you, I must away."

I picked up the Master's bag from where he kept it ready in his study, and left the house, running all the way to the Eversholt residence and up the steps to the front door. I panted as I reached up and banged hard with the knocker. A tall thin footman opened and glared down at me.

"What do you think you're about? The servant's

stairs are there," he jerked his head towards the area steps and was about to close the door when I jammed the bag in the gap.

"Not so hasty, mon. Wait. I need a word with Doctor Knox as is visitin' here. He's my Master and is needed right now, this minute!"

"Then you had best step inside, but wait by the door and don't show yourself past the pot. And don't touch it," he added, "It's from China." The servant stood me by a tall monster of a pot moulded in alabaster with a curved neck and handles and with blue and red patterning all over. It was set back by the front door and surely served no purpose at all other than to take up a great deal of space and keep lowly folk like me from view. From China was it, indeed. Well, the things rich folk had in their homes.

"Janet? Whatever are you doing here, girl?" Doctor Knox looked down and must ha' seen the bag by my feet, and when he spoke again his voice was softer. "What is it?"

"'Tis a Mistress Willows has called, Sir. She says her father is real sickly and would ye come, quick as ye can." I held out the card. He took it and read the name.

"Willows, well, and I thought his stone was safely gone. Still, these things can recur. Come we will attend him straight away, and thank'ee for bringing the bag, Janet."

The Master picked up his bag and headed off into the evening and I hurried in his wake, surprised he'd want me there.

"We, Sir? Ye said we. Am I to come too?"

"Eh? Oh aye, hurry along girl. I've no idea where the lads are or whether they'd be sober enough to be of use. You'll have to do. Ye can keep the daughter out of the way at least, and that will help. I can't be dealing with weeping females." Knox spoke harshly but yet he smiled at me. I wasna' used to such a face, especially after that morning with the coat, and I welcomed it. "I'm glad you came for me, Janet, if you want the truth. I was being forced into a corner by an overbearing female with three unwed daughters, all of them insisting on displaying their glowing health. The mother said it was down to eating spinach – did you ever hear anything so daft? I canna' bear spinach! And I've no desire to be wed right now."

Aye, Carlo had complained a deal too much about the household not eating green things. Myself, I was with the Master on this and grinned back at him.

The house in Tavistock Place was a solid gentleman's residence, with its own yard at the front and a gate in the fence. The Doctor had told me he'd been there before and as soon as Mistress Willows saw us approaching, she opened the door wide for him to enter.

"Now then, Mistress, do not worry. Has the attack lasted long? You know a stone, though painful is unlikely to kill. A little...."

"I'm afraid this is not his stone returning, Doctor I fear this is much worse. Please do come up; he is in his bed." Mistress Willows was already mounting the stairs, and Knox climbed after her, panting a little from his rushed journey. I waited a moment in the hallway then, after taking a last mouthful of clean air, for the smell of the sickroom was bad even downstairs and closed the front door. Not knowing what I was supposed to do, I followed them up the staircase.

The stink grew stronger as I turned the bend in the stairs. I put my apron over my nose and mouth. The memory of my mother's last days returned to me and made me pause a moment, for I knew the man up there was in a bad way. There is a smell to death, I'm sure, and the Master must've known it too. My ma had been but a week dying, and there was no doctor for her. By the time she was really sick all her money was gone. She had naught but her own mother's wedding ring and two fine dresses to pawn when she died. I fought back a tear that came uncalled for to my eye, took a moment, and climbed the last few steps.

Master Willows lay propped up in his bed and his thin worn face had the greyness about it that warns of death. Ye don't need to be a doctor to know that, for it's a face we've all seen. I waited in the doorway, lest the Master need me for anything. The old man may not have been as ancient as he looked, with his hands like claws, feebly clutching at the sheet. He groaned but recognised the Doctor

"Ah, Knox, I'm pleased you've come...." his voice was cracked and weak, and his yellow eyes peered up at the man he mebbe saw as his saviour.

Mistress Willows looked down at her father, wringing a handkerchief in her hands, fretting. She was a tall woman, thin like her name, and now in the candle light you could see the dark rings under her eyes where she'd no' slept for days.

"It is, isn't it, doctor? The cholera? I'm not mistaken?"

I jumped at her calm voice, and stared first at her then at the Master, horror freezing me to the spot. The old man in the bed groaned again and made to sit up. He vomited, his spew flying forth, and though his daughter darted forward with a rag to staunch the flow, it dribbled down the side of the bed and onto the floor. A wave of stench came from the bed as he moved and I felt the bile rising in my throat. Gagging, I backed out of the room and stood on the landing where, though further from the patient, the air was still foul with the sickness.

'Cholera!' I was in a house with cholera! I tried not to breathe, and was about to flee down the stairs when the Master called out.

"Janet, some water; a bowl of warm water and a jug of the same; away downstairs, and Mistress, where are your servants at this time?"

I didna' hear her answer, for Mistress Willows spoke in low tones, but I was relieved to be sent down to the kitchen and didna' linger. There was a kettle ready filled by the fire and I waited while it boiled, pleased to be in the kitchen for as long as possible. I poured some of the hot water into a jug and, standing it in a bowl, carried it carefully upstairs.

The Master filled a beaker from the jug and added to it the contents of a small glass jar he took from his bag. Holding his patient's head steady he put the potion to his lips and, when the old man had swallowed it, he laid Mr Willows back on the pillow.

"There, now. Mistress, Janet here will assist us to wash your father. We must try to keep him clean and dry – a difficult task given the state of his condition I know, but all we can do is our best. He must have plenty to drink to counter the loss of fluid he has incurred. That's it, nothing much more we can do. Here, another beaker of water. I will mix him another potion and if you have some milk? He may be able to keep that down. Janet, stay with Mistress Willows, she needs some help here." With that he left the room in quest of milk and, alarmed at the thought of staying, I was tempted to run after him to the safety of the kitchen.

"I'm so grateful," Mistress Willows was close to tears and gently dabbing her father's face with a damp cloth. "Come, help me with him."

The bed was wet when we pulled back the sheet, and a thin foul matter escaped from the old man as quickly as we mopped it up, and every now and then Mr Willows would raise his legs as a cramp took him, and empty more of himself either upwards in vomit, or downwards in a stinking blast.

The Master returned with milk in a goblet, all the while stirring it.

"I've added some powders, a little something to ease the cramps. Here, help hold his head up. There, that's it."

I was fair shocked at the calmness and the kindness of Doctor Knox as he tended to his patient, soothing his brow and feeding him with as much fluid as he'd hold. I was trying to breathe as little as possible, and kept my eyes from the old man's shrivelled form as much as I could. I spent the next three hours running back and forth for more towels, more water, and doses of brandy. The servants, we learned, had fled the house earlier in the day when they knew their Master was sick enough to die. I prayed quiet to myself that I wouldna' catch my own death that night.

Master Willows died despite our work, two hours after midnight, with a slow, weak sigh. His daughter had continued to mop his brow and whisper to him, and it was some time before she collapsed onto him, weeping. I gently coaxed her off and held her as tears racked her body then, when she was calmer, helped her give the old man his final wash. We took the linen from the bed down into the kitchen, and there in the great fireplace burnt it all, as Doctor Knox instructed us and as we knew we should. Though they were fine cotton and would have fetched a good amount if they were sold. Exhausted she was, the young Mistress, and me too. She finally laid herself down on her own bed and fell asleep.

It was near dawn when the Master and I left the Willows' house and returned slowly home. Both of us were tired out, and walked slowly, breathing deeply the fresh air of a new day, leastways as fresh as the air ever is in London. The mists were clearing and the sound of carts moving reminded us we'd had no sleep.

Back at Huntley Street, the Master let us in with his key. The household were still abed, and I turned to the Master as, candle in hand, we approached the stairs.

"Sir, Doctor Knox, Sir," I sniffed and I could feel a tear trickle down my cheek.

"What is it Janet?" Knox turned a sleepy eye on me

and asked, "What are you sniffling for? He had a good life and though his end was not the way he would have chosen to go, at least he didn't linger for too long. That's the blessing of cholera; it's generally over in a day or two." He had begun to mount the stairs but turned back and smiled gently. "You did well there, lassie. Thank ee for your help."

"Will I get it, Sir?"

"Eh? I wouldna' think so. You cleaned the sickroom and burnt the linen, and you should make sure you wash yourself now, Janet. I'm sure you'll be safe enough."

"How did he get it do you think, Sir?"

"Well, who can tell? We medical men canna' make up our minds whether it is breathing the night air that passes it on, or being too close to a person already sick with the disease. Some think it comes from rotten food, or from drink – though there is no reason to suppose that – others think it is in the miasma of the air. I hold with the miasma theory, but then, ah...." He shrugged. But seeing me still concerned he said, "Mistress Willows has the look of a strong young woman, so we will hope she doesn't succumb." He paused and looked up at the heavens. "Of course if I were a religious man, which I am not, I would suggest you could pray."

Despite his being easy about it, and my being so tired I could barely stand, I washed myself from top to toe before I crawled into bed, and lived in fear for days, queasy with the certain knowledge that I was going to die. Then the news came that Mistress Willows herself had fallen prey to the sickness, and had died before help could be sought.

"The servants who returned after her father's death found her body, and the swine lingered only long enough to loot the house before they finally left." Doctor Knox was angry but his voice wasna' the loud bark he normally had. He was bitter sounding, and he looked in his eyes like he was far away. I stood his cup in front of him and he didna' stir. "You know, Janet, sometimes I despair of mankind and how foul the creatures can be." He turned his sad eyes on me. "But you, the other night, you showed a kindness there, Janet. You made me feel proud and it restored my faith in my fellows. I'd been thinking of letting you go as your housekeeping is damn bad, but no, you can stay. Aye, you're a good lassie. Well done."

I walked slowly down to the kitchen and sat by the fire. I felt warm, without the glow of the coals, and my eyes were damp. I rubbed at them. The Master was a strange one, to be sure. One minute tyrant, next a kindly soul. There was more to him than I'd reckoned. When first I'd come to Huntley Street I was no jest afeared of him, I'd wanted him dead for what he'd done to Mary. But now? How could a man as gentle as the one I'd seen with Master Willows be a monster? No, mebbe I had him all wrong. I stared into the coals and sighed. How could I have vengeance for my Mary if he was no' a monster, and who could I direct my anger at when my memories of her death kept me awake at night? My poor Mary. You were treated badly and I would have someone pay for that, or leastways, something should be done to stop such foul deeds being done to others. I leant forward and pushed the poker in among the glowing coals. Hoskins was more than jest a bully I was sure. The likelihood was he had killed too. And the man Hare still lived, somewhere. What right had they to breathe God's air when good folk died? Where are you now, Master Hare? Where are you? If in London, could I ever find you and make you pay for the pain you had caused? Was I mad to dream such dreams? A chunk of coal rolled down out of the fire, across the floor and Carlo must have seen it jest as he came into the room. He took up the broom and swept it quickly back to the hearth, then using the tongs put it safely among its fellows.

With a swipe at my leg he said, "What are you dreaming of, Janet? You try to burn down the house?"

"No, Carlo. I was lost in my thoughts." I gave him my best servant smile, with jest my face for my heart was no' so happy. "Away with ye, I'll put the screen across the fire." I did so, then went to the scullery to help him with the preparations for dinner.

10

A MANGLE AND TEA WITH VERITY

Morning broke bright and fresh. It had rained and the world seemed to me washed clean of sickness and dirt. The road below steamed in the sunlight, and buildings all along the street shone. I splashed my face with cold water then adjusted my mobcap, pushing my hair up inside. It was an item I hated at first, preferring my hair free and loose, but Carlo had bought it for me and liked to have me wear it in the kitchen. I was growing to tolerate it, and today I had particular need to be tidy and give a neat account of myself. The sight made Hamish laugh when he saw me.

"Oh that cap, Janet. You are the respectable house-wife today?"

"We are shopping, Hamish. It wouldna' do to look a whore for the shopkeeper, would it now?"

"Shopping?" He frowned.

"Aye, for a mangle. I mean to get on and do the washing today. The sun is out, see. The Master gave me a guinea for it yesterday even' and I need you and Ewan to help carry it back here." Then I checked myself for I didna' want to seem too demanding. "If ye would, please?" He smiled. I carried on. "I don't want a wee thing mind, it needs to be strong enough to cope with yon sheets." I nodded towards the greying soiled pile in the basket next to the table.

"Well, I can't disagree, they need a good wash."

"Aye. Well then, as soon as you've broken your fast, if ye'd be so kind." My conversations with Hamish and Ewan were a mite lacking in formality, true enough, for they had been good to me and easy like brothers sometimes, but the look O'Rourke gave me showed what he thought of that. I ignored him, serving the others their bread and small ale first, and then gave a wee curtsey to Hamish, to show what a respectful servant I was. The smile he gave me back encouraged me, for he was no friend of O'Rourke either. I put the smaller stub end of bread in front of the Irishman but didn't deliberately slop his beer over his cuff; he made me nervous. But as I turned away from him I caught Hamish' chuckle behind his hand, and then I too was grinning when I hurried away to collect up the rest of the laundry I could be trusted with.

Seven Dials, in the parish of St. Giles in the Fields, is a warren of houses and businesses, with no fields at all from what I could see. That nature showed hersel' anywhere in that dark place was a wonder but, even with the lack of light, colourful flowers grew tall on window ledges, for all they struggled to reach up to the sun.

"Do you know where you are going, Janey?" Ewan sounded doubtful. I didna' want to admit I wasna' real sure. The area was packed with poor and villainous looking Londoners, but there were decent folk too, and we were safe enough together. 'Twas no worse than West Port on a morning, and had more shops for sure.

"Aye, I saw a wee shop round here somewhere when I was wandering ...." Then I recognised the great column with the six roads leading off, like spokes on a wheel, and over there, yes, a big corner building where I'd turned left. I headed off, dodging between two carts, the lads behind me.

The narrow lanes housed many foreigners, and the signs outside their doorways were crudely drawn with pictures of their trades if they had no English letters to write them. As we walked down Great Earl Street, Hamish stopped and moved to peer into a house. The window was made up of small rounded pieces of glass, like the bottoms of beer bottles. He squinted; I stopped to see what was so interesting inside.

"An anatomical model maker, see!" Hamish was excited and Ewan pushed past me and joined him. I was impatient to get on with my business but squeezed closer to see what had distracted them.

"What is it? What are you looking at there?" The window was too small for us all to stand in front of, and I could make out nothing inside but a few large white shapes high up in the gloom. The lads disappeared into the shop and left me standing outside. I tapped my foot for a moment or two, and had jest decided to join them inside when my eye was taken with the wee laddie sitting on the pavement no' so many feet away. He was dirtier now, his wee waistcoat torn, a blue cap on the back of his head. He was thinner too, but it was the same Italian laddie I'd seen a few weeks before. He'd lost his shoes, or mebbe sold them, and his feet were grimy. He lifted his face up at me when he noticed me looking his way, and I was drawn towards him by the sadness in his eyes. At that moment, though, the lads were back out of the shop and chattering like monkeys at a fair, and I turned my attention to them.

"So fast? Did he no' have anything ye wanted?"

"Oh, aye. We'll tell the Master of this place. There were too many folk inside to wait now but as soon as we have sorted out yon mangle, we'll come back, eh Ewan?" Hamish hurried me along then, eager to be done with me. I didna' mind for we were only a few yards away now from the little store I'd seen the week before. I did take a look over my shoulder though, and the boy was sitting there still, staring after me like a wee doggy. My heart lurched, but I told myself we are all become hardened with such sights day after day, and I canna' do anything about it. I pulled my face to the front and walked on. I'd work to do.

One half of the building was a shop selling second-hand clothes, 'kerchiefs and shoes, ribbons and hats; the other side was an ironmongers. Piles of household things were stacked against the outside walls. Saucepans and cauldrons hung from hooks along with graters, mincers, tin baths and chamber pots and, jest by the door a mangle almost the height of a man, the tracery of the cast iron a beauty to behold, and with a box front where the water could be collected. I gasped when I saw it and Hamish, hearing me gripped my hand.

"Steady, Janet, you have a guinea. Yon mangle is more than that for sure. We will ask if they have anything cheaper inside the shop."

I kept silent. Nothing could compare. Inside, the air was thick with the smell of oil, tallow and dust. It took a moment for our eyes to work in the dimness.

"Good day." A quiet voice from the shadows made me jump and I backed into Hamish. His reassuring hand on my waist calmed me.

"I would look at your mangles, if you please. A sturdy machine; not too costly." I glanced over at the beauty outside then back at the shopkeeper. He nodded. He was a short man, with long hair tied back with twine and his stout body wrapped in a huge oilskin apron with a pocket sewn to the front.

"Ah, well the Grimley-Haynes is four guineas. Is that too expensive for you?"

"Yes! Something less ornate, perhaps." Hamish spoke up now.

"There is this machine, imported from Hamburg, solid and reliable at two guineas ninepence." It was a squat affair and looked ugly and heavy. "And this," he waved to his left where a smaller mangle stood, festooned with dusters and a selection of lampwicks tied on a string. He brushed them aside. "This is a sad case, a requisition from a widow across the way. She took in laundry; had it six months, no longer. Very sad."

I examined the mangle rubbing the rollers to test how smooth they were. They were wooden, on metal axles, and seemed sound enough. It was a neat machine and the handle was smooth with use. It turned easy without stretching my arm.

"Why did she give it back?" I asked.

"She died, Miss. The cholera took her. She lost her children too, three boys and a girl all inside a month. Terrible it was."

I withdrew my hand. More cholera!

"Oh, poor woman. And she had to sell her mangle?"

"Her husband did. He couldn't pay for the funeral otherwise. He wanted to bury her deep and safe, away from the snatchers. But then the littl'uns was took. Ruined him I should think." The man shook his head and wiped his hands down his apron. "I could let you have that one for a pound and six shillun'. A bargain and I'm a soft fool and takin' the bread out of my own babe's mouth to sell it so cheap, but there," he sighed heavily but I ken'd his game.

We all of us stood silent for a minute, Hamish shaking his head and Ewan examining some tins stacked high, looking bored. The shopkeeper didna' give up easy.

"I will see my family starve, I know it, but you are as fine a young couple as have been in this store for a long while. I can't see your good lady struggle with heavy washing when she has a lifetime of it ahead of her, young squire. You need this mangle my dear, you do indeed. A pound and five shillun' then? What do you say, young Sir? Would you say no to your good lady wife?"

A better deal was done at last, and Doctor Knox' guinea plus three shillings from Hamish' own purse were spent. The mangle hadna' looked heavy but the lads struggled with it out of the door and across the street. Steadying it, Hamish lifted his eyes from the kerbstone to meet mine.

"Come 'wife', best be getting this home."

I flushed at his grin, but was soon laughing with him and Ewan. What a thought! By the time we had got it to Huntley Street, the lads were sweating and glad to set it down. As they stood there panting at the top of the area steps, debating how to get it down, I noticed the wee Italian bairn had followed us all the way home. He stood now, one hand on the railings of number six, watching us warily from under the dirty blue cap. I gave him a nod, in friendship, but left him be.

I had them take the mangle through the kitchen and out the back of the scullery to the yard. It took half an hour afore we were satisfied with its position, for the handle needed room to turn and the water to drain away from the house, across the small yard, without wetting my feet every time I used it. I didna' dwell on the fact the first one I'd seen had a box to collect the water in....

"Will it not run into the privy from here?"

"Well if it does so Hamish, it would be a useful thing. To wash it through."

"Hmm, I'm not sure Janet. Do you want to paddle each time you visit? No, if we turn it just so, or dig a small trench running to the wall there, it will divert the flow to safety." And so, with no regard for the time or for his studies, or the call of the model shop, Hamish dug a channel across the yard. It went round in a curve to where the Master had planted more of his herbs and, next to them, a small patch with some vegetables Carlo was growing from seeds saved from the kitchen. They were jest poking through the mud now and looking a wee bit thirsty.

"There," he straightened up, rubbing his back. "The Master won't need to water his herbs now, you will do it for him each time you wash his clothes; an efficient use of both water and time, eh Janet?"

"Oh, Hamish, you shouldha' been an engineer not spend years training as a Doctor You could fill that cauldron for me my 'husband', then mebbe you should attend to your books." I gave Hamish a peck on the cheek then, for nobody was watching, and after our working together I felt a foolish bravery come over me. He didna' seem to mind. Then I hitched up my skirts and hurried to fetch the laundry, keen to get on with the washing in earnest.

The next day I saw the wee laddie again, from the upstairs window of the Master's drawing room. He was sitting opposite the house, leaning back on the wall, at his feet the cage with white mice in it. He poked his finger in, and I saw his aged young face was smiling. He was so thin, and when I smelt Carlo's baking I went down to the kitchen and, carefully, took a couple of cakes and slipped them, still warm, into my apron. As soon as I could, I opened the front door and caught the laddie's eye.

I didna' want to act fast lest I scare him, so timid he seemed, so I made out I was polishing the sign outside the house. The laddie sat up. A familiar figure had entered the street. Hoskins, bold as the brass plate, here in Huntley Street. He walked past the first few houses and stopped by the boy. I couldna' hear what was said, but I saw Hoskins pat the lad's head and give him something, a small coin perhaps, before walking on again. He didna' look my way and I wondered why he was in the street at all. Then he crossed over and ran down the steps to the servant's entrance at number twenty. Ah, a certain serving wench lived there and I knew Hoskins was friendly with her, for hadn't I seen them wrapped in each other in the sideway the first week I'd arrived in London. I looked back at the boy and saw he had risen to his feet. He slowly made his way back to the corner with Gower Street, the cage hanging from his hand, his bare feet and grubby legs stiff and crooked. I reached into my pocket to the warm cakes. Too late, he was gone. Well, I couldna' put them back in the kitchen, so I ate them there and then. I turned to see the Master watching me from his window.

I swallowed the cake, nearly choking, and carried on polishing, not wanting to go back into the house jest yet. After a few minutes I took the stairs down to the area below, to busy myself around the kitchen. Carlo was standing by the table scratching his head and counting his cakes, so I slipped out to the yard to check on my mangle.

———

The little lad became a regular visitor to Huntley Street and I noticed Hoskins there more often too, on his way to woo his woman. He would talk to the boy and pass him something, a coin or a pastry, each time he saw him. This was a puzzle to me, for the Hoskins I remembered would give nothing away unless he had to. I stood in the window watching him, and when Hamish came up beside me I pointed out the pair across the way.

"What's Hoskins doing, eh?" Hamish must ha' thought his behaviour strange too.

"Mebbe he has become a kindly gen'leman all of a sudden? He said he was away to make some money didn't he? Mebbe he has and he's rich and generous now...."

I knew it was unlikely.

"Well, if so it can't be by doing anything honest." Hamish spoke sharp and moved back into the room to his books. He'd no' forgotten the stealing of Mister Jakes, and how the Master had more or less blamed Black. But there was no proof, other than his absence, that he'd had anything to do with it. Hamish likely suspected Hoskins was guilty, but now the lad was in trouble with Doctor Knox over something else. "Move out of the light would 'ee Janet, you cast a shadow on my book."

"What are ye reading, Hamish?"

"'Tis a study of boils and cysts. Ye know they can be dangerous things if they're not removed properly. The King had a cyst...."

"Oh aye?"

"Astley Cooper removed it for him. It was one of his more successful operations."

"The King lived then?"

"Aye, and was suitably grateful. That was a shrewd move of Cooper's and he did well out of it." Hamish stretched and yawned, then closed the book. "You know Janet, sometimes I think it's not so much what he does makes a man successful, but who it is he pleases. Cooper was made a baronet, and everyone must call him "Sir" for the sake of that cyst. To think, if the King had not had a blocked sweat gland on top of his head that had turned bad, the fortunes of Cooper would mebbe have been different.... "

"Aye, well there's no justice in life as we all know." I shook my duster out of the window and watched the wee laddie with his cage wandering down the road with Hoskins at his side, the man's arm resting on his skinny shoulders. They turned the corner into Gower Street. "Will ye be reading more today or is that it?" He'd not gone more than a few pages while I was in the room.

"The Master wants me to sharpen all his knives and then prepare the Anatomy Room for a demonstration in the morning. He wants it scrubbed out with lime. There aren't too many more lectures left of the season. The weather grows too warm and it's becoming foul in there. I may yet redeem myself if I can find a good pair of kidneys."

"The Master is angry with you. Why, Hamish? Is he still frettin' over Master Jakes?"

"No, well not just that. I ... Never mind. I wasn't to know the last subject had a tumour in the very place Knox wanted to demonstrate. He is sometimes unreasonable, but then it must frustrate him when he canna' rely on a cadaver being good and sound." He drew out the Master's case of scalpels from the drawer to sharpen them on a grey stone he had for the purpose. The light glinted on the blades, sharp and true. I left him to it and went downstairs.

Hamish went out towards dusk, after he had finished scrubbing the Anatomy Room. He was probably planning a night of drinking with Ewan for all he was meant to be seeking offal. I watched them go and I couldna' help wondering where they would look for the kidneys they sought or whether Black would turn up and save them the trouble, producing them from some horde of parts he had somewhere. It was late when they returned, and I heard them winching up the lift. It had been a successful evening then....

I attended the Institute again with Hamish, on a warm evening at the very end of May and, while he listened to a lecture on poisons, I read in the library. I hadna' had time or opportunity to have tea with Verity yet, and I was pleased when she arrived and waved to me from across the room.

"The young Mistress not with ye?" I asked.

"No, she's away with her father walking the streets of Silvertown spreading the gospel. I came to return a book for 'er and pay 'er dues. Are you still reading the same item?" She quizzed me and peered at the page I had open.

"Aye. I've got to a piece here that makes more sense than some of it. What do you make o' this?" I read a section aloud.

'It would be an endless task to trace the variety of meannesses, cares and sorrows, into which women are plunged by the prevailing opinion, that they were created rather to feel than reason, and that all the power they obtain, must be obtained by their charms and weaknesses.'

"Well, too right there, no? The things women have to do to make ends meet." I didna' dwell on the things that came to my mind that I'd had to do. Verity nodded but I'm no' sure how well she understood. I asked her, "Why do men never want a woman to be clever as them? Daft women, like a certain Missy I've seen in here, she has Doctor Wakley and all the gen'lemen hanging around her like bees, but a well-read woman is laughed at and has no chance of a husband, or so the Master would have me believe. He told me I'd be better reading books concerning cooking or household management than the ones here at the Institute. Just think!"

"Did you box 'is ears, Janet? You're brave enough to!"

"Not this time." I smiled and shook my head. "But it does make me angry sometimes when men are so greedy with their learning."

"Have you managed to get back your book? 'Tis weeks now and you still 'ave to come 'ere to read. Do you know where the Master 'as it 'idden?"

"Aye, I'm sure it'll be in the bureau in his study. I tried to open it but had the wrong key. I'll have to try some trickery...." I couldna' think what though.

"Wouldn't your young friend Hamish 'elp you? He may be able to get it back for you if 'e has Doctor Knox's trust."

"I wouldna' ask him now. He's trying to stay out of trouble with the Master. I think he's disgraced himself a few times too often. He told me it was because of a man with bad kidneys he brought in to be cut up, but I think it was more likely the mess he made gettin' rid of him. That, and there's mebbe not much money coming in right now. Some of the students are saying they will go to Guys Hospital for the autumn term, or to Mister Webb's School. Mebbe he's cheaper?"

"I expect it's hard to find bodies. Oh, what a business." Verity shuddered and I was surprised to find myself feeling easier with what went on in Huntley Street than I had but a few short months ago. The idea of bodies coming and going was still hard to bear sometimes, but the talk at home was all of the clever work they did, of sickness and cures, and the students were not shocking me now as they had. Was I grown hard?

"If the weather gets hotter they will stop. Hamish says they'll use models made of paper or clay, so the smell won't be so bad. If there are any students left to teach, that is." I found myself worrying for the Master, and hoping he had enough living patients to work with, the sort who would pay him.

Verity and I walked together part of the way home, leaving Hamish talking with some of his student friends, then when our paths split we waved good night. I promised to take tea with her the very next day.

"And no excuses!" said Verity.

The next day I saw our man Black at the top of the road talking with Hoskins, both of them standing with their backs to me, heads bent together. Black had his big hat and long coat on, for all it was warm, and when Hoskins briefly turned, I noticed he wore a bright red cravat with his tight breeches and couldna' help thinkin' he was a fool if he thought he looked the fine dandy.

After a few minutes more of scrubbing the doorstep, with my knuckles and my knees sore, I looked up and noticed the two still there, with Hoskins looking at me direct, and from the way he nodded and leant into Black I felt mysel' to be the subject of their discussion. I heard a cough behind me and looked up.

"Janet, that's the cleanest top step in London. I think ye can come in now, and make yourself useful to Carlo, he has need of another pair of hands in the kitchen." Doctor Knox squeezed past me, carefully stepping over my bucket and down to the street. He strode off towards University College, and I stood up slowly, rubbing my knees. I picked up the bucket and threw the contents down the steps, took my broom and brushed the water away. A few minutes later I went down to the kitchen and a huge pile of tatties Carlo had set aside for me to peel. I sighed. My new life in London wasna' all what I'd dreamed it might be.

As promised, in the afternoon I walked over to the priest's house by St. Giles' church to take tea with Verity. She had spent the morning baking. She reckoned she enjoyed it more than their old cook did whose liking was more for meat. Mistress Jennings, the cook, was away somewhere so the kitchen was ours alone.

"There were cakes and tarts to make for the family, so I did enough for us too. The Mistress has 'er friends 'ere. Listen, you can 'ear the chatter." Verity passed me a slice of cake the colour of mud, but when I bit into it the taste of warm spices filled my mouth. I raised my eyes in surprise.

"Oh, that's made wiv ginger and molasses. Do you like it?"

"Mmmmm, that's good. If you have the receipt, I'm sure Carlo could make it."

"And you yourself could. Or aint you allowed into the kitchen?"

I shrugged. "Well, the Master would have no mind if I baked, but Carlo is a man who guards his hearth. I'll speak to him; tell him I have a ginger cake I could share with him. He's always curious for new tastes."

"If it'll win you favour in his eyes, I'll try and write it

down for you!" Verity poured more tea and sat down. She put her feet up on a stool, hitching her skirts up and leaning back with a sigh. "Men always like to be the masters, whatever it is they do, like you was saying yesterday. Carlo will tell everyone it's his newest invention and Doctor Knox will thank 'im for it. But never mind, we'll know different. Now, 'ow is that young man o' yours? Hamish." Has 'e been 'elping you with your studies?" This was a saucier Verity than I was used to. Being at her own fireside seemed to make her braver.

"He has little enough time for his own, but he helps when he can. I was thinking of what you said, about having him help me get back my book. It seems that tonight the doctor is away to a dinner at the hospital, so he'll be home late. If Hamish is in a good mood, and that nosey pest O'Rourke doesna' interfere, I'll ask him. Mebbe he has a key and can open the bureau...."

"Good, then you can read all you want in the warmth of your kitchen. Though why you would want to bother if it's that book you 'ad the other day, I don't know." She shook her head and put down her cup and saucer on the table at her side. "Why don't you read something more interesting? Miss Esther 'as some books wot she took off her niece and hides from 'er father. She calls 'em Penny Dreadfuls... 'Romantic nonsense and cheap thrills,' she says they are, but she loves 'em! She reads 'em aloud sometimes, when I'm doing 'er 'air or dressing 'er. I think you'd find 'em 'diverting' as she'd say. Would you like me to fetch you one?"

"Would she mind?"

"No! She wouldn't notice one gone, and if she did

I'd tell 'er I'd lent it to you. Don't worry, she's the kindest person when it comes to things that don't matter any. Now, more tea?"

While I drank, Verity ran upstairs and brought back a thin book with a drawing on the cover in black of a woman in a big hat with a finger held against her lips. "*Tell not the reason.....*" was written underneath. I looked at Verity innocently.

"What do ye suppose she's up to?" She winked at me as she asked.

"I'll read it, but I think from the picture she's in trouble by now!" Laughing, I slipped the book into my pocket.

"Hmm, maybe. I can't remember that particular one." Verity shrugged and turned to other matters, more sombre now. "Wot do you think of our young Master, Charlie 'ere? Not the sort of boy to get in trouble with the peelers?"

"No, he seems a good lad. Why?"

"They were 'ere, last night, quizzing 'is reverend. An hour they was. Then when they'd gone, ol' Reverend Chagford had Charlie in 'is study and was yellin' at 'im and I don' know what. Right quiet the lad is today an' all. Gone off now to 'is uncle to visit. I didn't like to listen too close, but I reckon the boy 'as been in with them revolutionaries again."

"Revolutionaries?" Startled, I slopped my tea and had to put down my cup.

"Oh yes, them what 'e's mixed up with lately, at the school. 'E's bin warned. There's a group of 'em they talk 'alf the night and 'e comes home all full of daft ideas. 'Is father tries to talk 'im round, but they've both got fiery tempers on 'em...." Verity sipped her tea then shook her head like a wise ol' woman. "Still, 'e's a good lad, and meself, I don't reckon 'e'd do anything too wrong. Just the 'hot blood of youth' as the mistress's ma says."

I didna' know him well, but I couldn't believe that Charlie would do anything criminal either, and dismissed the idea from my mind. We drank more tea, freshly brewed with new leaves – no shortage of money here, I thought – then chatted about the house and garden.

"The mistress calls it an 'island of peace, in a sea of eh, something.' Anyway, it is too. Would you like to walk in the garden?'"

"Would we be allowed?"

"Oh, yes. The Master is awight about that, as long as we don't disturb 'im. 'E's in his study writin' some sermon for Sunday. Probably about dutiful sons, I wouldn't be surprised!"

We walked in the grounds at the back of the house, and I admired the flowers blooming there, the neat lawns and the quietness. The usual roar of London was now a murmur, shielded as we were by high walls and thick borders. I could hear birds singing.

"The other side of that wall is the burial ground," Verity reminded me, speaking in a low voice. "We can't see from 'ere, but Samuel, 'e's the Master's coachman and has 'is bed up there;" she pointed up over our heads to where I saw a small window, high in the eaves above the stable block. "He says that at night sometimes 'e's seen 'em, the snatchers. They come with lights and move about in the graveyard, but they've gone so quick, 'e says, by the time 'e'd got his britches on and down the stairs they'd be away."

"So he lets them dig in peace? That's like to be the safest thing to do. Hamish has told me that sometimes the snatchers are armed. To challenge them would be dangerous."

The way Verity had looked up quick to Samuel's window, and the worried look that crossed her face fleeting so fast as to nearly be missed, had me thinking. Before I could ask her whether Samuel was of particular interest to her, she gave a little laugh.

"Of course, Samuel has more sense than to go gettin' involved with snatchers, but 'e told the Master and 'e, the Master, 'as told the peelers."

"Is there anything they can do?"

"No, nothing. The burial ground has its own watchman, and the peelers don't want to get mixed up in what 'appens in there. The old watchman though, 'e's eighty years old if 'e's a day! Still, 'e has a blunderbuss what's as old as 'imself, so 'e can shoot 'em if they attack 'im."

That brought a smile to her lips, though it worried me for a moment whether Hamish could ever be lured into robbing graves. If he was going out at night with Black, might he be tempted to help with his digging? Black looked the sort of man who wouldna' stop at such a thing. But Hamish? Surely no? Of course not! He wouldn't be likely to be shot then! I must ha' frowned at my thinking such a thing, for Verity took me by the hand.

"Awright? You looked worried."

"No, nothing really. I think mebbe I'd better be going home though. The Master might be wantin' me for something and it's getting on. Thank'ee for the tea, and for the book." I went with her back into the house, and waited patiently while Verity wrote out her receipt for ginger cake. The scrap of paper was so covered with crossings and smudges I wondered if Carlo would be able to make out what was writ. I had her read the instructions aloud in case I'd have to help him.

As I was leaving, Verity said, "Now the light is lasting longer in the evening, the Gardens at Vauxhall will be open for strollin'. Samuel 'as asked me if I'll walk out with 'im this night or next." She blushed. "I don't think I ought to go alone, but...." She looked at me, head on one side, sizing up my answer afore she asked me. "If you was to ask your Hamish, would 'e likely come with us, make it four and proper?"

I was right then. Seeing the Master was to be out that very night, I promised to ask Hamish the minute I got home.

11

A TRIP TO THE GARDENS AT VAUXHALL

As I made my way back to Huntley Street, I thought on what Verity had said about Charlie and the revolutionaries, about how he was a good lad and couldna' be involved in anything dangerous or criminal. I thought about Black and the body snatchers and my Hamish. Could good men like Charlie and Hamish be tempted into doing such wicked things? But then, could my mother ever have believed I would be as I had become? Of course, all of us are like to do what we believe we must. Oh, such a world. No matter our hopes and desires, are we jest what we must be? Is there no hope of better things? I hurried my steps. Mebbe we needed a visit to this Vauxhall, to cheer us if nought else. It would keep Hamish away from seeking out Black for the night and I could mebbe quiz him on where he got his 'subjects' as he called them.

The house was quiet when I arrived home and with Hamish out I busied myself with some chores until he and Doctor Knox came back. Knox was looking pleased with himsel', so that was a good thing. Another patient made well and content, mebbe? I was about to try and catch Hamish' eye, when he signed that I should slip outside with him. The Master didna' notice, and I wondered what was so secret.

"Knox is away out to visit Wakley tonight, and with Miss Cooper attending and Lady Eversholt they will likely make a night of it." He took my hand and I saw a dewy softness in his eye. He whispered, "While they are enjoying themselves, perhaps we should take a turn about town ourselves? We still have the fine warm evening and it would be a shame to waste it indoors."

I perked up on hearing this.

"Aye," I said, "I think I've earned a night of entertainment. If ye have no other plans, I hear there are some Pleasure Gardens at Vauxhall. But if the Master comes home early and misses us....."

"Ah, don't worry. If he's away playing cards and drinking he won't be home early. I heard him when he came back from Bedford Square last time, the sun was rising. He woke me from my sleep with his stumbling about. I think Doctor Wakley is a bad influence on the Master."

I wondered what the fair Miss Cooper would think of Wakley gambling, even if it was what many gen'lemen did; but I couldna' see the Master playing cards.

"Knowing the Master he'll be up all night discussing real hearts, no' those on cards," I said. Hamish smiled at that.

I didna' mention then that we wouldna' be jest two

on our evening out. I wasna' sure how he would take to Verity, or if he was planning for us to be alone together as sweethearts? But if that had been his idea, it was quickly forgotten when Ewan came into the kitchen after dinner and Hamish invited him to join us.

I went into all the downstairs rooms to make sure the windows were tight shut, and when I was in the Master's consulting room I saw the wee laddie across the street again. He was sitting on the step opposite our house and I waved and signalled for him to come over. By the time I'd picked up a scrap of paper and stub of pencil and had opened the front door he was still in the same place but had stood up. He was looking over at me, nervous, but slowly made his way across the road. I promised him a penny if he would deliver a message, and quickly wrote a note to Verity telling her we would be at the Gardens tonight, and asked her to pay the laddie another penny when he reached her.

"So, tuppence for ye, if ye run fast." The boy scuttled away, though I knew he'd likely be worn out half way there. His wee bandy legs were no' meant for running.

When it was announced that O'Rourke was to come as well, my heart sank. He was always sour company, though at least he would even up the numbers, and I was still feeling pleased that the idea of me going along with them wasna' out of the question for the lads. I rushed upstairs to change my clothes before they changed their minds. For this special occasion I would wear Mary's dress, though the seams strained with the meat I'd put on since coming to London. But it laced up most of the way at the front and I wore a shift underneath so it was decent enough. I combed my hair with my fingers and tied a piece of ribbon in it, then hurried down to the hallway.

It was minutes later when the Master left, his eye lingering on me for no' more than a moment, then we young folk set off south to the river, to take a boat to Vauxhall.

The waterman was a squint eyed fellah, short legs but powerful built, and a head as bald and shiny as an egg. The water looked like slate, and a breeze had picked up. I pulled my cloak round me.

"Wait 'til I find out how much it will cost," Hamish told us in a low voice, pulling Ewan back from stepping into the boat. "How much to Vauxhall Stairs?"

"From 'ere, that'll be two shillun'."

Hamish gasped and stepped back. The bald man held up a hand to halt him.

"As a special favour to you son, and don't go shouting this about the place, I'll take you and your party for one shillun' eightpence. How's that? Otherwise, you can walk down to the London Bridge, won't take but half hour, then cross the river on foot. Couple o' hours up t'other side and you'll be at Vauxhall."

Put like that, two shillun' didna' seem so bad, one and eightpence even better. The wherry should have had plenty of space for six passengers, but with the ferryman's piles of boxes and trunks, and with a vicious looking hound atop them, the four of us squeezed into what space was left. The vessel sank deep into the water, with small waves threatening to lap over the sides. Once seated, and with Hamish clutching the side and his bench seat, and looking like his heart was in his mouth, the ferryman nodded and pushed off into the fast flowing current of the Thames.

The boat shot along, and the roaring voice of the ferryman cleared slower vessels out of the way. I fancied Ewan had taken on a greenish look, though it could have been the light reflected off the water, and O'Rourke had his eyes closed, his lips moving in silent prayer. Only I was completely at ease, and I gazed around taking in the sights and sounds of the river, my body swaying to the movement of the vessel.

"Look over there, Hamish!" I cried, and "Why Hamish, see that! Well..." Boats of all sizes, some with sails and others with oars, laden with goods and with people, made their way up and down the river, mixing and barely missing others crossing from one shore to the other. A huge dark hulk of a boat, moored half way across the river, creaked as it moved on its chains. A stink came from it and, as we passed, I heard the moaning of those on board. Our boatman spat over the side, leaned on his oars for a moment and looked up at the ship.

"They'll be away to Van Dieman's land. Just waiting for the tide to rise. Prison hulk that be. Good riddance."

I looked back as we made our way further along the

river, to the huge dark shadow on the water, packed with poor wretches. It wasna' easy to bring myself back to what was meant to be an evening of fun, 'specially when our boat lurched as it did and the wind whipped my hair round my face and chilled me so. The sun had shone warm on the shore and I hoped it would again when we got to the gardens.

Once across the river and after climbing the steep steps up to the bank, we took a few minutes to get our legs back to knowing they were on dry land. The wind had dropped; the air was again warm and still. We moved among the crowds at Vauxhall, seeming hundreds of folk. I had a feeling I'd be crushed or swept away if I let go of Hamish's arm. How would I find Verity in this great sea of faces, I wondered, and me not even knowing what her Samuel looked like? But Hamish had his hand on my arm, and we approached the Pleasure Ground steadily, all staying up close, the four of us. The whole mob was heading that way, and I was amazed by the size of the crowds. Ladies and gen'lemen too, judging from their fine clothes, as well as common folk dressed up in their best and all of us happy, laughing and joshing.

The gateway into the Gardens was built like the entrance to a castle, a huge place with great iron doors. Inside the archway, the crowds had thinned and formed a line, and there was Verity in a yellow hat waving to me. At her side a thin man in a grey coat and, as they came towards us, I saw he was attached to her. He had a loping walk, like that of a simpleton. His eyes were shaded by a felt hat and tufts of hair stuck out from under it, like straw. A big grin split his face.

"This is Samuel," Verity said, pushing into the queue with him. We made our introductions as we moved along, and finally reached a turnstile and a wooden booth. A sign painted there told us the prices of tickets, and there was a lot of fumbling in purses and then muttering behind us as we counted out our coins. The regulars had their money ready so it was us slowing things down, but nobody was really angry and we moved through the turnstile.

"We are in luck tonight," said Verity, pointing at a notice, "there is a big celebration of some kind and there will be fireworks later. Shall we stay?"

"Aye, indeed," Ewan and even O'Rourke seemed happy enough, and Hamish nodded. This was to be a special night out, though the prospect of what it might cost by the time we had done was worrying me. I had two shillun' and ninepence when I'd left home, and already a good part of it was gone. I'd been hoarding my wages whenever the Master remembered to give me any, and I could see they weren't going to last long.

There was music to distract us, and the sound of pipes and drums ahead and the splash of fountains, and the cries of stallholders selling food of all kinds, and drink. We stopped for a cup of punch; according to the man selling it, made from Arrack and the grains of the Benjamin flower laced with rum. This heady mixture warmed the heart, and as the mob surged around us I felt a little giddy and held onto Verity with one arm and Hamish with the other.

"Stay close," I said. "If we are split we may never find each other again."

"You folk go on if you want to see the tumbling," Ewan shouted. "O'Rourke and I have a fancy for the tables over the other side." I turned to Hamish. He nodded and the lads disappeared into a sea of people. I worried lest they be lost forever.

"Aye, they have acrobats and a tightrope walker in the main arena. You want to see them ladies?" Hamish and Samuel led us, pushing their way through the press, and we stopped only once more along the avenue that cut through the park to buy slices of some strange fruit Samuel said was called pineapple.

"Our gardener tried to grow some in the glass house a few years back, but he only got one or two fruits, and they too small to eat. The tree wants more sun than we get here. They come from overseas where it's a deal warmer." Samuel had a funny twang to his voice that was neither the same as Verity nor Hamish, and I heard all kinds of other tongues around me, town and country both.

Fine ladies and gentlemen walked, swinging canes and parasols, and children who should have been in bed raced around getting in everyone's way. It was growing dim now and some lights were being lit in the trees.

"This is grand!" I gazed about, taking in the sights around me, and Verity gave me a squeeze.

"Samuel and me, we came last summer. It woz less crowded mind, not so warm, and there woz fireworks then too."

What went on in the quieter corners and shaded

groves we passed, nobody asked, but I saw signs enough I knew. There were prostitutes, petty thieves and pickpockets all plying their trades unhindered. There'd been a warning notice on the gateway as we entered the Gardens, telling us to take care of our pockets and purses. I loosened my hand from Hamish's arm and made sure I had my pocket buttoned tight.

The "World famous Juan Bellinck" would walk the tightrope tonight and, tomorrow, fly in a balloon through a fiery display, with fireworks all around him – or so the sign claimed. We went into the main arena and down the steps to where rows of benches were set out in a great arc.

"Shall we sit and watch?"

"Aye, this should be a sight worth seeing," said Hamish.

"Where will the tightrope walker be?" I peered around, not clear what I was looking for.

"Up there, over the stage," Verity pointed and I saw a rope stretching across the sky from one tower to another built around the sunken theatre.

As we took our seats, the music struck up and the crowd quieted. Hamish encircled my waist with a protective arm, pulling me tight, and we waited for the performance. He smelt warm and spicy and I pressed closer against him.

Master Bellinck stepped out onto the rope, his body taut. He held himself erect and steady, carrying a long cane level in front of himself.

"That is to assist his balance," Hamish whispered in my ear. The crowd drew in their breaths as one, and silence fell. As he approached the halfway point, a few catcalls from the rougher sort encouraged him to hurry, and a lout not far from where we were sitting, threw an empty bottle through the air to see if he could dislodge him. Disapproving voices called out. Master Bellinck seemed not to hear, and continued on his way. He was dressed in tight leggings and a short cape hanging from his shoulders took up the breeze, flowing out behind him. At the end of the rope, he turned and somersaulted, straddled the rope and swung back again to the starting point. Cheers went up from the crowd and the band, silenced for the spectacle, struck up once again. I loosed my hand from Hamish's and it was sweating where I'd gripped him tight.

A fat woman came out onto the stage and started to sing, her voice cutting through the air like a blade. The crowd didna' seem taken to her, and our little party decided to move on. By now the sky was darkening proper, but the lanterns were shining bright enough for day and being lined with coloured paper, or painted glass, they lit the trees and statues around them in all the colours of the rainbow.

We walked on along what Verity called a 'colonnade' of trees with more statues and fountains. In little arbours we could see private parties dining, hear the chink of their crocks and their laughter. Surely, there was nowhere on earth as fine as this. A squeal of laughter went up from a woman in a very low cut dress sitting at a table under a tree in full view of the path. A man she was with patted her, then kissed her full on the mouth and plunged his hand down her dress, fondlin' her breast and rubbin' himself against her.

"Old enough to be her father," muttered Samuel, and Verity lowered her head to hide a smile.

The old man shifted in his seat and rubbed his leg between the whore's, while feeding her titbits from his plate. I knew what she was, but she was of a kind I'd no' seen before. The dress was mighty fine looking, and the jewels around the woman's neck must be worth a fortune, if they were real. No common streetwalker, but a rich man's mistress mebbe. Her art was the same as any others though, and I saw her hand slide down to pleasure him. The risks she took were no different from other whores. No different from what Mary and I had faced. Though this whore didna' look so hungry. I turned away. Mary once said she wouldna' want to be one man's property when she had the choice of all of Edinburgh. She had a way with her of always soundin' like she was in control of her life; though of course she was not. None of us are. Hamish pulled me then, to a stall of apples piled high, and I forced myself to smile when inside my heart was breaking again when I thought of Mary. She would have loved this place.

The evening passed quickly then, and at eleven there was the firework display in the main arena. It sounded to me as if a hundred guns were firing and the flashes and bangs were enough to terrify anyone who, like me, had never before seen such a spectacle. Verity and Samuel had 'ooed and aahed all the while and seemed at ease with the noise, and I tried to put on a brave face. The clouds of smoke left behind dimmed the light and people coughed and spluttered their way back to the colonnades. It was like walking through fog.

A man in a light coloured coat pressed against me and as I turned to shove him away I saw, in the shadows, a figure I knew. Leastways, he looked uncannily like Hoskins. But even as I looked again to be sure, my watering eyes clouded my vision and he faded into the crowd. Mebbe I was wrong and it wasna' him at all. Then the smoke cleared a little and there he was, the wee laddie by his side, pulling away from him but held firm. An older man was with them, smart in a fine topcoat and hat, and Black dressed in his dark cape and big hat as usual. Then they were gone, hidden behind a group of revellers, dark shadows and smoke.

It was after midnight, and still the numbers of people didna' grow any less. The music played on and Hamish and I walked, with Verity and Samuel jest ahead of us, arm in arm. Then the bells of the clock on the Prince's Gallery, by the main pavilion, struck one in the morning.

"Do you not think we should be getting home?" Hamish's lips tickled my ear as he bend down close.

He sighed when I answered him. "Must we?"

"It will take us some time to get there and Knox may have missed us already if he is home."

I knew I was a little drunk, and mebbe so was Hamish, but I had enjoyed the most wonderful evening of my life. The summer breeze was soft against my cheek, and I was with Hamish. I clung to him, not wanting to let go or the night to end. His steps slowed and he turned to me and pulled me close. He kissed me then, soft and gentle, his hand pressing on my back. I was losing mysel' in his arms, our mouths working together, when he pulled back, sudden, and looked at the retreating backs of Verity and Samuel.

"Come, we must hurry to catch them up so we can share a boat with them."

12

O'ROURKE FINDS HIS HEART AND VERITY
LOSES HER CHARGES

Ewan came into the student's study with a face as miserable as any I'd seen, and when I asked him what was to do he said he'd been instructed to write a report on the function of the appendix. I had nae idea what that was but made some soothing sounds and wished him well with it, then continued my cleaning of the first of the big windows.

"Where am I to begin?" he muttered to himself.

O'Rourke was sitting, legs drawn up under his chin, on the second window seat. I was hoping he might move so I'd be able to get to it next. They were a grand pair, good glass, tall as a man but smudgy with smoke outside and in, and the devil to clean. His brow was furrowed, his fingers drumming on the ledge, and I wondered what he was to write on and if he was struggling too.

"Ah, good morning, O'Rourke. Your forgiveness if I disturb your thoughts," Ewan dragged a chair out from behind the desk. "I have this piece of work to complete in extremis, before I adjourn to the College Arms." He opened a reference book. The text was in a small script and he screwed up his eyes to make it out. Hamish had told him he should ask Knox about getting some spectacles, but I doubt he had done aught about it. Compared to the others, Ewan had less of a grasp of medicine so mebbe thought it safest to avoid drawing attention to himself.

"How much do you know of man's appendix, O'Rourke? I cannot see a use for it myself."

O'Rourke gave a hint of a smile then, after a sigh, his frown returned. He asked in a quiet voice, "Have you ever lost somebody for whom you had great love and admiration?"

Ewan looked up, taken by surprise at such a question. "Well," he drew a long breath and leant back in his chair. "There was a young woman, back in Edinburgh." He looked up uncertain how this would go down with the prim and proper O'Rourke. He didna' look my way and notice my hand stayed in its' work. He continued. "She was a close friend of Janet. A lovely girl, long dark hair, the sweetest of smiles; dimples I remember." He sighed. I found myself frozen and breathing shallow though my heart was beating fast. Mary. He had loved her then.

O'Rourke grunted. "I mean, somebody of importance to you, a brother, father a close friend, not some dalliance."

"Not really. Nobody other than her. I had a dog when I was a lad. He was a bonnie little thing, but grew ill and died when he swallowed a bone. That was one of the reasons I wanted to become a surgeon....."

O'Rourke said, quietly, "I was raised by my mother in Ireland, along with half a dozen sisters, all of them younger than I. They took it bad when my father died." O'Rourke stroked his hand down his thigh, his face set serious like he was lost in distant thought.

"With six sisters you must have been well looked after?" Ewan smirked, the idea of a spoilt little O'Rourke, pampered as the only son seemed to amuse him.

"My mother and sisters were right proud when I was accepted to study at medical school. That I might become a physician, or at least a surgeon, well, I was the talk of the village. I determined to do well for their sakes. But, more than anything, I wanted to do it for my father."

"Ah, he was a learned man? A physician himself, was he?"

O'Rourke laughed aloud at that. "Physician! No, alas. Far more humble. He was a militiaman at home, and a tenant farmer, 'til the rents became impossible. Life is hard in Ireland, especially for us Catholics. He moved about looking for work and the next we heard was nought but a report in a newspaper a year ago, that he was dead."

Ewan glanced my way, mebbe feeling as awkward as I did. What had brought on this maudlin O'Rourke? He was a strange one. He must ha' forgotten I was there else he'd no' have said so much I'm sure. Ewan put down his pen and coughed before saying,

"My own father is a tenant farmer. He's still chasing sheep around the hillsides of Perthshire as far as I know.

Well, tis a brave man who leaves home to win his fortune. Your father tried and, eh, maybe he succeeded, before he eh, died? What was the manner of his death?"

O'Rourke looked up sharply. Then, ignoring the question and with his eyes distant again, he said, "I last saw him when I was a lad, nine, ten maybe. I remember him, when he was about, as a great strong man with a loud laugh. My mother said he was a fine catch. She cried herself to an early grave. I came here after I buried her. I heard of Doctor Knox and wanted to meet him, learn and honour my father's memory."

"Ah, looking back, we see a child's eye's view of our parents. Mine was a hearty man with a rage on him as strong as any Knox has shown, but still, I think he is proud of me." Ewan smiled and turned to concentrate on his book. We'd never known O'Rourke speak for so long and I for one was wondering why was he talking about his dead father after all these months?

"Be of cheer, O'Rourke," Ewan slammed his book shut a moment later and stood up; "the day is bright and the future lays before us for the taking. The College Arms is close by and, I swear, I can smell their mutton pies baking. Come, let us away and refresh ourselves." O'Rourke seemed to like that idea and raised a smile, and both made for the door with Ewan clapping the Irish lad on the back. The appendix could wait 'til later it seemed.

Hamish came home with the other two, a couple of hours later, for he had found them at the College Arms.

"Well, they were sat on a bench in the sun, two rogues together," he told me later. I was cleaning the great cauldron for Carlo while he was away to visit the spice woman. "They seem to have become great friends of a sudden. They did well at the tables at Vauxhall last night they said, and bought the pies and ale out of their winnings without me having to ask." His humour changed then when he said, "Hoskins was there, seated on a bench in the shadows in the far corner. 'Twas too dark to see properly, but Black was with him and they looked as though they were arguing, growling like dogs over a bone."

"Perhaps it was bones they were fighting over," I said, setting the cauldron down and resting my arm for a moment.

"I'm surprised he has the cheek to show himself in these parts. Black must have had help to remove Master Jakes, at least one other, to drive the cart or keep watch for the Runners," Hamish said. "A cadaver is no easy thing to handle alone. It would have had to be Hoskins to know the easiest way to break in." He frowned then and ran a finger round the edge of the table in front of him. "When we'd finished our ale I went outside in order to er.... and I saw the pair of them. They seemed in better mood than half an hour before, and they went off together somewhere, thick as thieves. They're up to something. I fear 'twas a bad choice I made to accept Hoskin's recommendation of Black. I don't like to think

I am responsible for the Master being robbed by the rogues...."

He was a good lad, and I could see the thought worried him. I didna' tell him I'd seen the rogues at Vauxhall. I gave him a peck on the cheek. He was cheered a little and, after a moment's thinking, said

"I will see if I can manoeuvre Black into confessing to his crime and get him to repay us with another body.... That might save him from the Master's wrath."

"Well, the Master has been in a good mood today," I told him, "Though his head is a wee sore after last night. He got in later than us; I heard him. Mebbe he and Mister Wakley had a good night on their tables too."

Hamish gave me a hug and returned the kiss, then set off to Covent Garden and the shop of the maker of papier-mache models; I suppose the one he'd been so taken with the day we bought the mangle. Mebbe he would be lucky enough to come across Black on his travels.

The item he was to collect from the model maker was a head, and when he brought it home he showed it to me. It was hinged along the back and opening downwards through the centre of the nose. Inside, it was layered like a shell, with a hole for each eyeball, a larger one for the brain, and a hollow tube running down the back into the neck where it joined the backbone. Nothing very interesting but less bloody than the real thing, and he seemed pleased with it.

"Very good, let's hope the Master likes it," I said. The lad dropped it back into its box and carried it away upstairs.

I was curious to hear what was said and, unusually for me, thought to listen at the door. But as I went to take the stairs up to the landing, I was overtook. I stood back as Knox hurried ahead of me with a group of students at his heels, and with a ball of twine in his hand.

"Janet, fetch me the wool from my study," he called back over his shoulder, "there are two balls there in red and blue," and I hurried to do his bidding. Whatever was the Master to do with wool? I couldna' see him knitting. When I panted upstairs with them he was already in the anatomy room and I settled myself a moment before tapping on the open door and entering. He was standing in the midst of a group with the model head held before him, and barely gave me a glance as he took the wool from me. He threaded a cord of each colour down through the hole in its base, leaving the balls in place of the brain. He held the thing aloft and said,

"The brain is a complex mass of material, and alas little is known of its function. But the nerves, ah, here is an area of great interest, gentlemen." I lingered for a moment, 'til his steely eye settled on me and he paused. "Thank'ee Janet, you may go now."

From outside on the landing I heard more of the lecture, fascinated though I couldna' grasp all of it or see what he was about. But it seems if he broke the wool it could mean a man wouldna' walk any more, no matter the state of his legs.

"Here we have the real thing. Pass down that specimen jar," I heard him say; "Saved from yesterday's subject, where you remember we discussed the jaw and the teeth. The brain..." There was some sound of commotion then, "Are you feeling unwell, Ewan?" The Master asked.

"Aye, I think so, tis just ....." But then a noise of retching, and I held my broom tight against me. A few curses and gasps from the students, then Hamish helped Ewan from the room. I stepped forward and took the poor lad's arm.

"That was never lamb," Ewan muttered. "More like the hoof of an ox, or dog-meat." He groaned and Hamish helped him upstairs to the attic. I followed and between us we cleaned him up and put him to bed. I asked where O'Rourke was, as I'd not seen him since shortly after their return from the inn.

"Is he at the lecture?"

"No, indeed." Hamish looked up from straightening the blanket over his friend.

"You all ate the mutton pies?" I asked.

"I thought mine wasn't so fresh and didn't finish it." He realised then what had made Ewan ill. Ewan vomited again, mostly into the bucket at his side, and Hamish nodded his approval. "Just as well, my friend. Better to rid the body of it completely. I will ask Knox for an emetic for you and one for O'Rourke too if he is as sick. Meanwhile I will fetch some castor oil."

As it happened, O'Rourke was sick, and when I went downstairs he was jest coming from the privy, weakened and shaky. The pair of students were duly dosed by Knox and given a lecture on the perils of eating pies in public inns. I washed out their buckets and set them clean by their beds again, then left them to rest.

Their absence made the house seem unusually quiet for the rest of the afternoon.

As Hamish hadn't eaten more than a wee bite at the College Arms, he had no ill effects, and was happy enough to dine at three o'clock with his Master and several of the other students who were about to take examinations, partaking of kidneys and chops with a large helping of baked custard to follow. Carlo had made it with cream and called it a panacot. The atmosphere was a wee tense, but I was absorbed in my own thoughts so didna' hear straight away what Hamish said.

"O'Rourke was most talkative after a few drinks, Sir. He was boasting of how he would avenge his father when he gets his hands on his father's murderer. He named him as Hare. You remember, Sir, the man released after Burke's execution?" He helped himself then to more wine while I stood silent and stared at the pair o' them. "It would seem he, Hare, is in London. O'Rourke had been to see the police at Scotland Yard to ask where he is, as they have him on some sort of licence, but they wouldn't tell him. O'Rourke more or less admitted the only reason he came here to join you, Sir, was in the hope of coming across Hare. As if you would have any dealings with such a man!"

I was shaking, the crocks in my hand at risk of falling, but I steadied mysel' and leant against the side table where the brandy bottle stood. My eyes darted between Hamish and the Master and I ignored a pair of the other students present signalling to me, til they got up and marched down to take the bowl of panacot from under the Master's nose and move it to their own end of the table. I stirred then, mumbling an apology and serving them with the fruit platter whilst listening to the Master.

"I'd not heard anything about where Hare went after the trial. I never met the man but I do believe some of our subjects quite likely passed through his hands." He shook his head, murmuring "Sorry business....." while he cut into a pear.

I banged about clearing some of the table, stacking things on the side table. The Master barely raised an eye to me but bit into his fruit. Sorry business indeed!

"Be careful to avoid the area around Tyburn if you are walking that way," the Master told Hamish. "The mob will still be celebrating today's hanging." Then he added, "And I don't doubt there's another useful specimen we've missed out on." He cursed Black then, for his disappearance lately, for mebbe he should ha' brought the dead felon home. Now someone else was to have it. Hamish kept quiet, gave me a hint of a wink then excused himsel' from the table and headed off. Later over supper he said he'd been down to the river, to watch the boats and crowds, before returning in the early evening.

The house had been quiet without Ewan or O'Rourke crashing about, but it seemed they were none the worse for purging. They came downstairs in the evening and joined us for supper, hungrier than usual. It was their habit to eat in the kitchen, informal, and Carlo had prepared a thin soup for them with bread, on the Master's orders. Hamish had no' noticed how quiet I was, or how I made more effort to see O'Rourke was fed and better for his rest.

"If Carlo food not good enough, you say so. Why you eat this foul pie at inns?" The cook was clearly hurt they'd decided to eat elsewhere the previous day, but he didn't let his feelings mask his concern for the lads. They all ate well enough and made it up to him by finishing all trace of the saffron cakes baked that morning.

I tried to give him a smile but excused mysel' and went to my room saying I had a headache. There I sat and thought on what I'd heard that day, worrying over Hare like a dog with a bone. Where was he, and would he be about his old work? Would he know I was in London and seek to avenge himself' on me, as a witness at the trial? How could I find him? As the hours passed and night grew heavy, I determined that I would hunt him out. He would pay for Mary. If it was the last thing I ever did, I would have my revenge.

The next morning, it being a Sunday, the whole household slept a little later than usual. When I entered the kitchen, Carlo was beating eggs into a coddle. I was careful with him for his feelings were still a mite sore from the day before and thought to distract him remembering the scrap of paper Verity had given me with the receipt for ginger cake. He took it grudging, but I knew he'd be baking before the day was out, for he couldna' keep from trying something new. I was not let off from his mood altogether, and he had me scouring and polishing and fetching more logs to heat water.

The lads came for their breakfast, arranging themselves at the kitchen table, instead of in the dining room, and I put a pan on the fire as Carlo heaved the cauldron out of the way. I added a knob of butter. The yellow fat sizzled. I added the beaten eggs to the butter in the pan and stirred, sprinkling some salt and ground peppercorns onto them. Carlo nodded and I stirred with more vigour. Before they set too much, I tipped the eggs out onto plates and took then steaming to the table. Nods of approval from all o' them, and a squeeze from Hamish, filled me with pride. I was learning. Even though I would never be allowed to do anything to equal what Carlo could do, at least I was progressing enough to cook eggs. So it was in a happier mood I set out to the Vicarage later that morning.

When I arrived at the Vicarage, all there was chaos. A young housemaid let me in through the servant's door and I found Verity pacing about the kitchen. Above me I could hear doors slamming and the good Reverend shouting at someone.

"Verity, what is it?" I asked.

"'Tis the young mistress, she was.... oh dear, wherever can she be?" Then, seeing my puzzled face, she explained. "She was supposed to go to her uncle's 'ouse, but 'es turned up this morning and tells the Master and Mistress 'e's not set eyes on 'er. Well! Where can she 'ave gone? And why would she 'ave gone without me?" Verity raised her hands to heaven for answer, for I could give her none.

I looked at her, blank, not knowing what to say. I had come ready to tell her my news from Huntley Street, of how Hamish's feelings for me seemed to be growing, how strange a man O'Rourke was, and how I had seen the wee Italian laddie with Hoskins and was afeared for him. I had thought how I would tell her the most important news, about Hare, but knew not how. That I wanted more than anything else to find where in London he was lurking and put a knife into his heart. But now, here was Verity, her world turned upside down. She continued her tale, ushering me into the wee room off the kitchen where the cook kept her jars and sacks of produce.

"And young Master Charles, 'e's gone too. The Master and Mistress are that put out they don't know where to turn, and 'im supposed to be in church ministering. The 'ousehold is in uproar and Lord knows what's to become of the pair of 'em. Or me neither, for 'tis all my fault!" She wailed then, pulling her apron over her face. I reached out and gave her a hug, for all the difference it made.

"How is it your fault?" I asked. "Could they not be with friends? Mebbe someone from the Institute? Could they have gone there? Or be away with some of the students, up to innocent mischief?"

"I don't know, Janet." Verity was shaking her head and her eyes were wet with tears. "I should've stopped 'er," she sniffed. I don't know how she could have, having met the girl. Her love of her young mistress was touching, though mebbe Verity feared more for herself, having failed her charge. I know how Esther would be more than able to look after herself, wherever she was, and tried to cheer Verity.

"'Tis likely they are away on some jape," I said. "Did they go together?" I was trying hard to sound light hearted.

"No sooner as Miss Esther come 'ome yesterday but she raced off again without even stopping to tell me. Just grabbed 'er bonnet and a shawl and out the door like a scalded cat. Oh, the pair of 'em are mad as monkeys, but they don't mean no 'arm. She said she was going to Parliament with 'er brother. The Mistress is for sending out to the police, but the Master, 'e won't 'ear of it...." Verity dabbed at her eyes with a grubby kerchief, and I felt helpless to be of any service to her.

I stared hard at the jars behind her on the shelf, racking my brain for any idea of who might have led Charlie astray; and did his sister follow him? I didna' know many of the students at the Institute, but likely it was some Radical from there.

I gave her a hug and said, "All will be well, Verity. Don't 'ee worry, lassie. If they're anywhere it'll be with friends and they forgot the time with all their talk." It came to me then that the one place Esther would go if she were in danger would surely be to Lady Eversholt, for she was her guiding light. I asked Verity and she frowned.

"I'd thought of that meself, but her Ladyship's gone to the country. Miss Esther would know that, for they talked of it last week. Lady Eversholt said Miss Esther was more than welcome to come join 'er there, in Suffolk, and said 'ow they could go riding out and fings. Miss Esther weren't so keen. She 'ad a fall from an 'orse when she was little and ain't never got over it."

Well, I thought, mebbe there was someone in Lady Eversholt's household who would know where Miss Esther was. We could do worse than ask. And if that failed, I would go to the Institute and see what I could learn.

"Come on Verity," I said, reaching for her bonnet off the door; "We canna stay here frettin'. Let's away and find yon lassie and set the matter to rights."

The wee Italian laddie, still with his mice in a cage, sat on the corner of Adelaide Place and Bedford Square and looked up at us as we passed. I gave him a small nod and moved along, pleased to see him but with my mind full still with Verity's news. I felt her falter on my arm, and she looked back.

"Wait," she said. "'Ere, Aldo, come 'ere lad."

Aldo? She knew the laddie's name then. He got to his feet and limped over to us. Verity took his shoulder and put her face close to his.

"Do yer know if Miss Esther, the young lady as lives at the Vicarage, 'as passed this way? She might 'ave been in an 'urry, maybe wiv 'er brother, running up 'ere yesterday?"

Aldo shook his head, and I thought 'twas a waste of

breath asking him, but he spoke then, the first words I'd heard him utter.

"I'll look out for 'er, Missy. I'll tell 'er you was looking for 'er if I see 'er."

We were about to walk on, when I thought to ask the laddie something more.

"Tell me eh, Aldo, do ye know where yon man Hoskins lives these days? You see him about don't ye laddie?"

A look of what, fear, crossed his face but then he shook his head and he mumbled,

"I dunno' Missy. He tell me not to talk to nobody. I dunno where he lives."

He moved off then, almost at a run, and I knew he was lying. I glanced at Verity out of the corner of my eye.

"I've bin giving the lad some small jobs to do, shining shoes and sweeping the yard, and payin' 'im in food and the like. Don't you say a word though! Poor little beggar." She had a heart of gold. I knew that for sure now.

We came to the road where the Eversholt house stood and I was torn. Should I ask there, jest in case anyone could help? And should I ring on the doorbell, or go and knock on the tradesman's door? If the household was away, it wouldna' matter would it? I quickly ran up the steps and pulled the bell. Verity came and stood by my side. I felt her shiver and gave her hand a squeeze.

"Who's there?" A thin old voice asked as the door opened, jest a crack. Not the stuffy servant who'd defended the house the night of the soiree. I was relieved.

"'Tis only me Walker, Miss Esther's maid, Verity." She pushed past me then, recognizing the old wizened man behind the door.

"Ah, oh. Well, what is it you want?" The old man opened the door a little wider but didna' let us in. His face was fearful and his gaze flickered past us, up and down the street. "Nobody is home."

"Are you sure, Walker? Only the young Mistress is gone from 'ome and I thought to find 'er 'ere."

He paused for a moment too long before shaking his head and pushing the door to. I knew the old buzzard was lying then.

"Wait," I said, putting my hand to the door. "If by chance you should see Miss Esther, tell her that her family is worried and would like to hear from her. And if she needs her maid, Verity here is ready to come and see her quick as she wants."

He gave a small sharp nod his eye lingering for a moment on Verity, then shut the door fast.

"I told yer they're all away." Verity sniffed and pulled her shawl around her shoulders.

"Oh, I reckon she's here alright." I looked up at the high windows, the ornate carved stonework. "Aye, she's in there and yon old fellah knows it too. I can always tell when a man's lying. He's been sworn to secrecy."

"But why?"

She asked a sensible question. I couldna' give an answer. I shrugged and we moved down the steps to the street.

"Mebbe Miss Esther doesna' want to be found jest yet," I said. "We can try again somehow. Or send a message in." I thought for a moment. "Do you know any of the other servants here?"

"Samuel knows the coachman a bit. 'Bald man wot's got a thing for one of the 'ousemaids. 'E's from the same part of Salisbury as my Samuel."

Well, that was useful, I thought. I wouldna' say anything jest then, but mebbe there was a way we could get Samuel to find out from the girl if Esther was there.

The following morning Hamish was in a hurry to leave the house.

"I have business to attend to, Janey. I can't believe Charlie would do anything to endanger his sister, or indeed himself. Not that I know him that well, but he seems a decent lad."

I hovered around him as he stood in the hallway and, keeping my voice low lest anyone be listening, I told him that I thought Esther was safe at Lady Eversholt's.

"But I need to know for sure, to put Verity's mind at rest – and the lassie's parents."

"Well, what do you want me to do?" he sounded a wee bit short. "I can ask at the Institute if anyone knows where Charlie is, but if he is hiding somewhere he may not thank us for interfering."

I understood what he meant. Perhaps it would be better not to stir things up. But there'd be no harm in Samuel making some enquiries.

"Are you still there, boy?" The Master's voice boomed down the stairs and made me jump. "If you're not back within the hour it'll be you on the dissecting table!"

Hamish lingered only to give me a quick peck on the cheek then he was away. I tried to do a bit o' housework for an hour, fretting about the kitchen and tidying things away, but gave up and hurried to the Vicarage to see Verity.

Samuel was sitting with Verity in the kitchen of the Vicarage, a hunk of bread and cheese in front of him. The cook was still out and not expected for a while.

"She likes to stretch 'er legs of a morning, and then will stop off to 'ave chocolate with 'er friends. I wouldn't expect 'er before noon then it'll be all panic to get the dinner done!" Verity poured tea for us all and put a lump of sugar in Samuel's cup. "At least 'tis just cold cuts today, and a tart of some sort."

"Well, I been to see after the lass as you said," Samuel slowly stirred his tea and took a bite of cheese. After chewing for an age, he carried on with his tale. "She has charge of the visitor as the lady's maid has gone off with her Ladyship to their country house. The coachman, 'e be away there too, having driven them all to Suffolk." He took another bite and slurped some tea. "Pretty little thing she be, but so excited at her rise in position she couldn't keep from telling me all about it." He chuckled and added, "Although she swore me to keep it secret, for the lass Esther, for she don't want anyone to know she's there."

"Well done, Samuel." Verity kissed the top of his head. I was relieved that at least Esther was safe and Verity was reassured. Her feelings were hurt though, her young mistress not thinking to take her too, and to see her every so often wiping away a tear was heart-breaking.

"She jest doesna' want to put you in any danger," I told her. Though more likely it was herself she was protecting. It wouldna' do to have Verity going back and forth to her and bringing the Peelers in her wake. "And what if you were followed there? You could lead trouble straight to her door."

"Oh, my! I'd never do such a thing!"

"Well then. Jest be mindful of her feelings and let her have her way on this. You should take the opportunity to have a few days holiday."

She smiled at that, 'til she remembered young Charlie Chagford.

"And what of 'im? I do 'ope 'e's not in any trouble. What if e's bin arrested?"

"Well, if he has been, the household would know by now. If he's in any trouble let's hope he has the sense to keep out of sight for a while."

We sat quiet then and drank more tea. I hoped Charlie hadna' got himself involved in revolution. But why else would he ha' gone to the Parliament building?

13

REVOLUTION COMES TO HUNTLEY STREET

That evening the Master went to Bedford Square to dine with Mister Wakley and another surgeon, one with a sight too much interest in women's parts from what Hamish told me. The house was quiet with Carlo also out, and I was reading the novelette Verity had leant me, the one that was Esther's. I could not concentrate on its silliness. I had tried the Master's study door, but finding it locked and my own book still beyond my reach, this nonsense would have to do. It was better than polishing the silverware, and I was no' in the mood for working.

I had made up my mind to question O'Rourke about Hare. If he had found out where the man lived perhaps I could get him to tell me. I poked the kitchen fire and wondered as I had done so many times whether, if I could find Hare, would I have the courage to kill him? Would I really put my new life here at risk for such a thing? I needed to see him, to look him in the eye, and I needed to stop his murderous work. I leant the poker against the chimney and settled back down in Carlo's rocking chair and it was no' long before I felt a warm drowsiness coming over me. It didna' last long, for there was a banging at the front door and not a soul but me would answer it I was sure. I climbed the stairs and raised the wick on the lamp in the hall before opening the door. You couldna' be too careful and I wasna' wanting to be murdered on my own doorstep in the darkness.

"Master Chagford!" I gasped when I saw him, propped against the doorframe white as a ghost and his clothes wet with rain. "Come in laddie. What's to do?" But enough time to talk when I had him inside and safe. I took his arm, gentle as I could, for he didna' look too steady; and he came into the hall with a stumble. He leant against the wall and raised a pair of exhausted eyes to me.

"Miss Brown. Good evening." His voice was low and he was trying to act the same polite gentleman as ever, but he was no' fooling me. He was about to fall down where he stood from the look of him and I knew I'd need some help.

"Hamish!" I called up the stairs and, when I had no answer, I put a hand on Charlie's shoulder and looked him close in the eye. "Stay quite still laddie, lean here against the wall and do ye no' move. I'll away to fetch some help to ye." He didna' protest, so I left him and ran as fast as I could up the stairs, along the landing, then into the student's study. Hamish was snoozing over his books, a hand lying on the table by his side with the skin cut back off three fingers and the saw marks clear at the wrist. Ewan was playing cards with nobody but himself, spreading them out on the table in front of him in neat rows, and O'Rourke was so deep in his books he didna' raise his eyes from them.

I gave Hamish a light shake and he came to with a jolt.

"What's the matter, Janey?"

"Young Charlie Chagford is downstairs. He looks like he's been running for he's tired enough to drop and I dinna' like the look of him. He has a wound some-where Hamish, I'm sure of it."

Ewan and O'Rourke looked up in interest but no' enough to stir, but Hamish was wide awake before I finished and, putting aside the hand, he went with me down the stairs to where Charlie was slumped now, half on the floor under the picture of the Tower of London.

"Come on laddie," I knelt beside him. Hamish slipped his arm under Charlie's shoulders and together we hauled him to his feet and into the Master's consulting room. I hurried over to the shutters and pulled them close, then raised the lights so we could see what was to do.

"I'd be obliged...." Charlie stopped talking and gasped as we sat him on the chaise longue then raised his legs to make him more comfortable. I put a cushion under his head, and he closed his eyes for a moment only, then, resisting peace, he opened them wide and asked for the Master. "Is Doctor Knox at home? I would crave a few minutes of his time. I...." His hand hovered over his side just above the belt, and I lifted his jacket to see what was amiss. Blood had soaked into his shirt and dried, but the whole area was wet again with a more recent bleed. He groaned and laid his head back. I raised my eyes to Hamish.

"The Master is out this evening, but fear not." Hamish laid a reassuring hand on his arm and Charlie moved, restless on hearing this. "He has left us with the key to his dispensary and I will find some dressings for you. Janey here will help me and we'll have ye right again in no time."

The lad on the couch groaned as, biting my lip I pulled his shirt aside from the wound. It was a ragged gaping hole, blackened around the edge and oozing blood. I was no' sure what we should do, but Hamish, bearing down on us now with armfuls of bandages, jars of ointment and with the Master's bag under his arm, took charge of the patient with a confidence I'm no' sure he really felt. He paled a little when he saw the wound and sent me away to fetch hot water and Ewan, so I knew Charlie was in for a hard time. Hamish was talking to him in a low voice as I left the room.

"Seems to me a bullet has entered you here, Charlie, is that so? Who shot you lad?"

It took a deal of time and laudanum to get the bullet out, and Hamish was blooded to the wrists in his work. Ewan, quiet and serious, helped him and I ran back and forth for swabs and more hot water, all the time praying the Master would come and take charge. The students were no' yet surgeons and while they might be practised at working on corpses, here was a patient who writhed and babbled while they worked. Sweat ran from his forehead and his teeth clenched the wooden peg Ewan had put across his mouth. When the bullet was found and pulled forth he fainted, and Hamish patched up the wound and dabbed his own sweating brow.

"Well," he wiped his hands on his britches and when he saw me frown, he used the towel I'd brought him for the purpose. "This bullet was not from a duel, 'tis meant for business." Charlie stirred, awake enough to mebbe hear all that was said.

"Who has shot you, Charlie?" Then, anxious, Hamish asked "Did anyone see you come here tonight?"

"I don't know. I was with the students....Saturday. Just gathering. The police...I slept in the graveyard then, after the service, hid in Pa's church up at St. Giles for a while....made my way here after dark. I've been walking. Didn't dare show myself at home, though that's where my feet first took me. I'm ashamed to bring trouble on the house. I thought Knox..... might patch me up, maybe give me a bed for the night; but if he's away from home..." His troubled face made me speak rash.

"Whisht, you can stay here Charlie. Nae fear, I'll make up a bed for ye in the Master's study. Wait here and I'll see to it."

And so, the hunted lad spent the night in safety and it was after he had breakfasted and was sitting up sipping tea, wrapped in a gown of the Master's and looking a deal brighter, when there was a fearsome banging on the door.

"Open the door! Open up in there!" The four peelers who burst into the house the minute I pulled the latch were a fearsome rabble. They all of them stood more than six feet high and were made another foot taller by the high black hats they wore. Tight four-inch collars gripped their necks and it was as if their heads were floating loose above their dark blue bodies. They clattered into the hallway like a single monster with many heads.

I stepped backwards and let out a scream of surprise, bringing the man in the front of the pack up short.

"All right lads, hold up there. Miss, don't be afeared. Where is the Master of the house?"

My heart was pounding and I felt I would be sick, but even so my brain was thinking fast how to get out of this danger. I pointed towards the consulting room, but before the men could move towards it the study door at the other end of the hall opened and Hamish, surprised and angry, stepped forward.

"What is the meaning of this intrusion?"

"We're here to arrest a criminal," said the lead man, no' impressed any by Hamish. "We have reason to suppose a radical agitator is sheltering here and, if you are wise Sir, you should hand him over to us straight away."

I noticed he had something written in silver on his collar, the letter A and number 21, and thought it strange. This was the closest I'd been to a polisman and despite remembering all my wee sins, I barred the passageway to the study while Hamish ushered them all into the consulting room.

"Please, take a seat in here, gentlemen, and I will fetch the Master to attend you. Janet, would ye make our visitors comfortable if ye please."

I didna' know what he was about, for the Master was

still abed as far as I knew, if he was home at all. I hadna' heard him come in.

I poured the officers drinks from a decanter the Master kept on his desk and when they had downed them they seemed less harsh.

"Another?" I asked A21, and he gave me nigh on a smile. My hand shook slightly as I poured.

"We're here to arrest a man, Miss, not drink. You shouldn't lead us astray." But I noticed he didna' say no and his hand touched mine as he took the glass. His fellows seemed not to mind the wait either and in no time emptied the Master's Madeira wine. I was beginning to wonder what to give them next. Should I open a bottle of the laudanum mebbe, or was that too risky a thing to do?

"What nonsense is this?" barked the Master, when he was barely in the room. Hamish had fetched him from his bed and he was wrapped in a bright red dressing gown with a nightcap still upon his head. "This is an Anatomy School, man. I have a few students present and the girl here, other than them, my cook and myself. Search the house if you wish, you will find no agitators here!"

I tried to catch his eye for he obviously didna' know who was in his study or he would've been less keen to make the offer. But, taking up his invitation, the men searched the ground floor and kitchen then moved up the stairs to the first landing. I ran into the study and looked around to find it bare of fugitives. What? Where was Charlie? It was no' possible he could have gone far in so short a time and with his wound to slow him. I chased up the stairs, then made to follow the two men who clumped up higher to check the second floor attics, for I'd no fancy to have them prying in my room. I paused on the first step. The other two had halted and pointed to the closed door ahead of them on the first landing then ordered the Master to open it.

"Well, I hope you have strong stomachs gentlemen, this is the Anatomy Room and my students are even now preparing for a dissection I am due to perform this morning." He pushed open the door slowly and continued in a voice loud even for him. "The students have need to dispose of the skin and unwanted parts, and the smell is merely that resulting from a demonstration on the bowel we carried out yesterday – no worse than the stench of the gaolhouse though I suspect, if you are used to that?"

A21 put his hand over his mouth and nose as he entered the room, while his colleague waited in the doorway, horror written on his face. I couldna' help myself as my feet took me forwards. Ewan and another student were standing by the dissecting table, a pair of coffins stacked, one on top of the other, beside them. Sawdust and wood shavings had spilled onto the floor and were now absorbing the blood, of which great globs splashed about the lad's feet. Blood had also soaked into the sheet which covered the cadaver on the table, though mercifully it was pulled up and the face hidden. Not so another that lay naked on the side bench, with a rope mark vivid on his neck. From the table where the lads worked, a leg hung loose, and an arm and, as A21 approached, Ewan picked up the leg's partner and went to throw it in the box. I looked at the gory stump, ragged where it had been hacked off, felt my breakfast move along with the ground under me, and turned away.

"Good morning, gentlemen," I heard Ewan greet them, but I didna' wait to see what happened after that.

"Jesus, Mary and Joseph," the polisman in the doorway crossed himself, and his face was white as he gripped the doorframe.

The two men, who had been searching up above, banged down again, calling out that all the rooms were empty and then, seeing their fellow stepping back out of the Anatomy Room, came to see what was afoot.

Constable A21, who must ha' had the stronger stomach of the group, demanded to see what was under the sheet and Ewan, shrugging, pulled it back with a flourish. I couldna' look but cried out and ran down the stairs. There was no need to fear, as no hidden rebel was laid out for the taking. The polis came down a few minutes later looking angry and made stiff apologies to the Master. They left the house and Hamish shut the door after them with a triumphant gesture.

"Would you like to check in the coffins, while you're here?" Ewan acted out the way he'd asked the polismen, and with his face the picture of innocence all the while. Hamish roared with laughter and even the Master smiled. "When I pulled back the sheet and they saw the cadaver that was spilled out there, well they turned as one and fled along the landing!"

Doctor Knox and the other students were gathered in the kitchen, grinning like schoolboys while, covered still with wood shavings, Charlie sat at the table and helped himself to another of Carlo's fruit buns. It seems he had been hid in one of the coffins all along and looked none the worse for it.

"Well, gentlemen, enough foolery." The Master had given Charlie a brief examination and seemed happy enough with Hamish's work. He became serious then and the patient lost his smile too.

"We've done naught wrong, Sir. We were defending our God given rights, nothing more. There was a meeting, up by Westminster, and the Peelers tried to break it up. We weren't even marching, just gathering ready, to demand our rights.... We had done naught to be ashamed of. They had no call to open fire, but one of them took aim at me here and," he pointed at his belly and paled. "He deliberately raised his pistol and fired. Why Sir, why would he do that?"

"Why indeed? They were part of this new Metropolitan Police, eh? Damn menace they are too. They're supposed to carry only staves, or at most swords, but pistols? No, these were not your normal Peelers I suspect." Doctor Knox stroked his chin and we all waited nervous as to what he would say.

"Let ye rest, lad." He said after a tense minute or two. "You are safe enough here, for the while. What happened to your friends? Did anyone see you enter here?"

Charlie shook his head. "I think not Sir. You need not endanger yourself by knowing any more about who was there. It is good of you to risk housing me, and as soon as night falls again, I will leave you in peace."

Knox frowned. "I thought most Chartists to be artisans, older men. You look barely out of school, and better bred than most revolutionaries if I may say so. How do you come to be mixed up in protesting?" He didna' push fierce with his questions but gave the lad almost a smile. "But at least you are resurrected, and the danger would appear to be gone. The Peelers will assume they missed your departure this morning and have gone elsewhere no doubt to seek their pleasure. In a day or two it'll be time to think of getting you home laddie, or somewhere else that's safe – out of town maybe? As for the School, back to work; and no doubt Carlo and Janet are wanting to get on with preparing dinner. Ewan, tidy up the Anatomy Room and give the floor a good scrub, and you Hamish, attend me if you would in my study."

Sighing, the students did as they were bid and Carlo, no' keen himself on the polis, was still in a happy mood when he produced four chickens from his store for me to pluck. I sat down and began my work before I realized I'd no' seen O'Rourke since last night when Charlie had arrived.

Hamish was in Doctor Knox's study for some while, but there were no raised voices and when he came out he was no' the worse for it.

"There's a man at the front door as won't go away til he speaks to someone," I called to Hamish from the doorway of the student's study. He put down his book with an unhappy sigh so it must have been a real good one.

"What, he asks for me? Should ye not call the Master?"

"He's gone out to visit a patient, so will ye come and see to him? It seems mighty important for he won't go."

Hamish followed me down the stairs. The man wasn't anyone we knew, and I must say I didna' like the look of him when I opened the door again and saw his scowling face pressed up close to it.

"Yes, what can I do for you, Sir?" Hamish has a way of raising one brow, copied from his Master like as no', when he talks to folk he doesn't welcome, so I knew he felt the same way as me.

"If you are the Master of the house?"

"Doctor Knox is away from home I'm afraid, but if you would care to come in and wait for him in his consulting room? Are you a patient, Sir? You have an ailment perhaps?"

The man laughed then, low in his throat, but his eyes lit up a wee bit so he didna' look so fierce.

"No, I'm as well as I can be thank'ee. I have a friend I believe many be staying with you here, someone who might welcome my visit."

My breath froze in my throat. I shot Hamish a look and could see he was thinking fast what to do. The man was no' a polisman, I'd wager that, but who was he? He had a heavy look, all jowls and shoulders like an ox, and his hands were rough with callouses when he rubbed his grizzly face. He was wearing a red coat, torn on the sleeve and sewn again, old but tidy, and from the colour and the cut of it I guessed he'd been a soldier once.

"Wait, no, that was foolish of me," he said. "You neither of you have any knowledge of who I am, nor reason to trust me, but if you would kindly tell your guest that Nathaniel Brushwood is here at his service, I would be obliged."

I bid him wait again, then shut the door and without stopping to hear what Hamish might say, I hurried to tell Charlie about the caller.

"Brushwood! Well, I'm honoured. I'd be greatly heartened to see him." Charlie knew him then.

I showed Mister Brushwood into the Master's study where Charlie had been resting in an armchair by the unlit fire. He jumped up when the visitor entered, as keen as his wound would let him anyway, and the two men embraced like the greatest of comrades. I went back down to the kitchen relieved, to carry on with my chores, and found Hamish there already, staring out of the window at my mangle, though likely he was lost in his thoughts in that way he has and not admiring the domestics.

"Well," he said. "Charlie's visitor is likely another Chartist and I hope he doesn't bring more trouble. We need to get them both out of the house as soon as possible before we all end up behind bars. I've been wondering Janey, how the police knew to come here yesterday.... and now this latest visitor..."

"What did the Master say to ye about all this,

Hamish, when he had ye in his study? Was he no' put out to have a revolutionary in his home?"

Hamish frowned, thoughtful, and shook his head.

"No, but he was sure as I am that yon Charlie was betrayed by someone, else the police wouldn't have known to find him here." I thought to mysel' that O'Rourke may be the one, for he had no' been for his breakfast.

Hamish was still speaking and said, "Knox relishes the chance to make fools of the police I think, so he was happy enough to hide the lad. I think he has a soft spot anyway for the Cause."

"What Cause?"

"Why the Chartists, Janey, the Radicals who mutter together in clubs around the town and meet in dark corners everywhere. He talks enough about the subject of their politics with Wakley and Mister Birkbeck when they get together, setting out between them how to educate the common folk and civilize them, let them vote and run their own affairs." There was no bitterness in his voice, but a sadness I think. I remembered the day Wakley had visited. "I'm grateful for what he has done for me though, Janey, and I know the Master is a good man and sincere. I hope he is not led into folly with all this business, for I fear his dreams will never come to pass."

This was true enough, and the thought of the country being run by some of the common folk I'd met made my blood run cold. But he was certainly not the Doctor Knox I'd thought I knew jest six months before, a murdering monster who cut up bodies for his own amusement. No, the man was daily becoming more noble, and I was worried I'd no' be able to hate him at all soon. But then I remembered he had my book still and my spine stiffened. I banged about with the crocks in the sink and when I looked up again, Hamish had left me to it. I'd no' had a chance to tell him my fears that I'd no' seen O'Rourke around since Charlie had turned up covered in blood, and he wasna' generally someone who'd avoid causing trouble to folk if he could help it. I dried off the crocks and was hanging the cups up on their hooks when I heard the Master return. I hurried upstairs and waylaid him in the hallway to tell him about Mister Brushwood's arrival.

"In my study?" He was a mite put out I thought, but interested too to see who this man was. He strode to his study door and opened it right away. I could hear them then, the two revolutionaries still at their talking, but then the Master closed the door behind him and I couldna' make out all they said. I fetched a tray of hot chocolate, and some of Carlo's batch of saffron cakes, and knocked. They mebbe didna' hear me, so I let myself in.

The Master looked up sharp from where he sat at his desk, and the other two gentl'men turned, afeared at being caught out in something from their faces, but they relaxed when they saw it was only me. I expected a reprimand but the Master said, "Thank'ee Janet", and gave me a small smile. "Just put the tray there, that's it." He shifted some books and I set down my tray. I hovered there waiting to hear anything else, but as nobody was about to talk in my presence, I bobbed a small curtsey and left them to it.

"Who can this Brushwood be, I wonder? Looks a rough rogue and not anyone I've seen at the Institute." Hamish fingered the edge of his book but had clearly lost the interest he'd had in it before.

I shrugged, but his question was on my mind too. I told him my thoughts about O'Rourke. "Where has he gone to? If he has acted as informer on Charlie and on the Master, well he won't be coming back here, will he?" I so wanted to talk to him on the matter of Hare as well, and how I wanted to find him, but when I tried he said nothing but chewed on his lip, his mind away with other worries.

They came out of the study after a while and there were low voices in the hall. It was grown quite dark outside now, in the street, and I saw Charlie was wearing an old coat of the Master's, the green woollen one. It looked a mite tight, even on his thin frame. I was glad I hadna' thrown it out like the Master had wanted, and it had found a good set of shoulders to rest on after all.

Charlie and the Brushwood man set off into the darkness, slipping along by the railings to the end of the houses, visible for a moment when they stepped into the light of a lantern hung above a doorway then disappearing again into the shadows between. At the end of the road I saw them turn right, towards the University. The Master stood watching from the doorway and when he turned he saw me hovering by his elbow.

"Ah, Janet." He shut the door and pulled the bolt

across. "What has taken place here is best kept to ourselves ye understand girl?"

"Oh, aye Sir. I'll no' tell a soul." I waited for a minute, no more, then taking a breath I said, "Though it would be more certain forgotten, Sir, if I had my book to read so as to take my mind off it." Was I mad? I watched his face turn stiff, and I thought he'd go into one of his rages, but then he changed and sighed. He nodded slow and motioned me to follow him and I think he was chuckling to his self when we went into his study.

He gave me the book, and with it a short, tight kind of smile.

"Janet, I ask ye pardon lass for treating you badly over this. It's a wee bit unsettling to have womenfolk reading this kind of stuff, but if it pleases ye then do. It'll come to naught, though. You have to remember folk are set in their ways and a well-read servant isn't likely to get on, ye ken."

I wasna' sure what he meant, but then he added, "It'll be a marvel if this Parliament gives men the vote, but women will have to wait many a year I dare say."

I had no special need to vote, whatever that meant, but I was pleased to have my property back and hurried upstairs to hide it lest he changed his mind.

14

I VISIT OXFORD CIRCUS AND BEDFORD SQUARE

The next morning I made a special hard effort not to upset the Master or Carlo. I'd cleaned the grate and laid the wood out jest as Carlo liked it, and got a smile from him, and the floor was swept, the spoons and knives laid, and all in order by the time the household stirred. The Master had his porridge, his coddled eggs and his bread and cheese and was looking content over his book of bodies when I thought it safe to ask him for the afternoon off.

"Verity says she has an afternoon off once a fortnight, and I've no recollection of havin' such an arrangement discussed here, Sir, not since I got here....." He scowled but I carried on. "I was jest thinking, tis a fine day and if ye have no special need for me to be here, with youself being busy upstairs, I thought I'd go for a walk to take the air, for the sake of my lungs." I looked across at Hamish, hoping I had the right bit of my body in mind. He nodded discreet so the Master didna' see, and hid a smile behind his cuff.

"Aye, Janet. It'll no doubt give ye a bit more colour in your cheeks. I'd feared you're looking pale lately, so it will do you good. Mind you are back here in time to help Carlo with the supper, and don't get into any mischief with that minx from the vicarage."

Verity is less like a minx than anyone I've ever met, but I knew he was jesting. I was thrilled, and after the midday dinner, served early that day on account of a special lesson upstairs on more kidneys and innards, I hurried and washed the plates so I could get away.

I saw the wee Italian boy, Aldo, at the top of Bedford Square, and watched him and his mice for a minute or two, thinking he looked tidier and with his waistcoat neatly patched. I waited for the little crowd around him to leave, throwing a few pennies in the cap at his feet as they left. While he was gathering them up I asked him again whether he knew where I might find Hoskins.

"I've seen you with him a few times laddie, mebbe working for him? If ye do odd jobs for him I understand"

"If he want an errand run, something to deliver, he ask me. Once I follow someone and tell Mister where he go. He give me some small thing or a coin."

I was right then. I nodded to reassure the laddie all was well, then sent him on ahead to rouse Verity and have her ready to meet me. It was the second Wednesday of the month and her afternoon off, I was sure that's what she'd told me, and it was a great joy to me when, as I approached the Vicarage, I saw her coming down the path tying on her bonnet as she walked, looking up the road towards me.

"Well met, Verity! Are ye free for enough time to walk about the town?"

"Where would you like to go? If you 'aven't seen them already we could go to the shops and see the sights of Piccadilly Circus? Or would you rather take a turn around the Regent's Park?"

"Shopping mebbe, but a circus, that sounds fun indeed!"

She laughed at my ignorance and tucked my hand under her arm.

"That settles it then."

In no time we were walking around the Circus, though it wasna' what I had imagined. I was left staring open-mouthed at the grand buildings. There were no strange animals but the jostling crowds, and shops much finer than those of Seven Dials, with clear glass panes in the windows and high, tidy piles of goods behind them, and dozens of servants tended to well-dressed customers. The folk going in and out of the shops were careful to avoid seeing us even though we moved amongst them under their very noses, with quite a few pickpockets about nae doubt. A woman in a green silk coat nearly knocked me off my feet when she turned round and didna' give me more than a sneering glance. She smelt of cologne and I swear she had real rubies hanging from her ears.

We walked on, coming upon Regent Street, named after the Prince Regent himself, Verity said.

"Fancy, having a whole street to himself," I said, and she laughed. She had a fine laugh, Verity, and a face that gave nothing but warmth.

"Do you want to see where the rich folk live?" she asked. I nodded, keen as ever, and we crossed the top of Regent Street and carried on to Piccadilly itself, a wide road that led straight out from the Circus. We had to jump careful and watch our step for the traffic was giddying, coming at us from all directions, and not a one of them would stop and give way to another. When we were safe upon the paved walkway we looked up at houses like palaces, great fortresses with flunkies standing by the doors to stop common folk even knocking should they dare to think on it. Eyes followed us down the street, I could feel them burning in my back, like we were housebreakers indeed!

"I'm thinking we're not welcome here, Verity."

"Oh, don't mind them. We have every right to walk 'ere, just let 'em stare!"

We walked to Green Park, then back again on the other side of the road. I stopped a moment to look at a house, new built and still with a painter working on the window frames, and with a gaggle of carriages and wagons outside. Boxes, crates and baskets littered the pavement and men in oilskin aprons and rolled up sleeves struggled, carrying furniture up the steps to the front door. Grand stuff too, by the look of it.

"All these houses are new, or built in the last ten years anyway. I see'd 'em go up, one by one. Was a time when it was all fields," Verity sniffed and waved her hand vaguely. "All the way up there to Mayfair and 'yde

Park, folk with more money than you could ever dream of, Janet. More money than you or I could carry in an 'andcart, and they're taking over all the land around London, so there won't be nowhere left for our sort to live soon enough, lest we're servants to 'em of course." We stopped and looked up at a fine brick front, glass windows glinting in the sunlight. Upstairs a maid was leaning out of one shaking a duster, but she caught sight of us and ducked inside, pulling the window to. "Just think though, Janet, being a servant in an 'ouse like that one there. I 'spect the lowest maid 'as 'er own room, with a proper bed and a velvet footstool too....."

I doubted that, but when I went to say so I saw the glimmer of laughter in her eye and we locked arms and rolled up the street laughing loud enough to cause a horse to bolt.

We had done a fair distance by the time we found ourselves back at the Circus, and I noticed Verity had quieted as she looked up at the front of one 'specially tall and decorated building.

"What is it, Verity?"

"Nuffink."

I squeezed her arm and she turned.

"This was one of the young Master's favourites. 'E said they 'ad stone brought up special from somewhere, and 'e....e'd a great passion for fine buildings; used to draw 'em on bits o' paper all round the place. Oh, I do 'ope 'e's safe and not come to 'arm. I walked many a time around 'ere wiv 'im and the young Mistress, and them two talking about fings and windows and columns and stuff. 'E was 'appy, 'e was, and talking about going to Rome and places, and of 'ow 'e'd build 'imself somefing like this, one day...." She rubbed a tear away then, and I couldna' help telling her what had come to pass.

"Charlie is safe, Verity. Don't ye fret yoursel', I've seen him on his way with my own eyes. Now then, let's away to find a teahouse and a big fat bun, then I can kick off these shoes for a few minutes and tell ye more."

We took our rest jest off the main road, in a side street, a not so grand place with mebbe twenty small tables filling a big room as was a stable recently from the smell of it and the straw still on the floor. Most of those folk around us were working men, or mebbe poorer middling sorts. Not so many maids on their day off, but shabby clerks and their wives, or elderly ladies fallen on hard times. They were like us, enjoying a penny tea and a gossip. It seemed to me that the streets of London were full of servants and working men, teeming around like rats. Verity had cheered somewhat after hearing Charlie was safe, and she offered to pay for the tea herself, in gratitude for my kindness towards him.

Our tea was served in a pot with a pair of sturdy beakers, not the dainty pieces Verity used at home, and the stuff was so weak it barely stained the cup.

"They make a quarter of tea go a long way 'ere don't they?" she said, and stirred the pot hard to get some more from the leaves. "I know it's expensive to start but you can only re-use it a couple of times before it ain't tea anymore. But the bun is fresh anyway." She bit into it and chewed slowly.

I picked out the couple of sultanas I could find,

saving them for the end, and thought what Carlo would say about these buns compared to his. I must be getting grand, I thought to meself, for I had become used to much better.

"Well, we canna' sit here like the idle rich all day," I said, after we'd drained the pot and rested ourselves. "I've to help Carlo with supper later and there's fish to gut. I think he'll be making that ginger cake again this afternoon. Your receipt went down well with him you'll be pleased to hear, and the lads finished off the first attempt in one go."

Verity popped the last of her bun into her mouth, chewed and washed it down with the dregs of her tea. She seemed to have shaken off her sadness of earlier and my mentioning her ginger cake pleased her.

"We would 'ave a better tea at 'ome, but this makes a change I s'pose," she said.

Leaving the shop, we passed the door of the kitchen where two great ovens where being emptied of bread and more fruit buns. A ginger headed lad leant for a moment on his paddle and gave me a wink, but then received a cuff round his head from his Master. I grinned back, linked arms with Verity and we walked as far as the Vicarage together and there I parted company with her and headed home to Huntley Street.

Talk of tea was not done, for no sooner had I got my bonnet off than the Master called to me.

"Janet, would ye make sure the drawing room is

clean and tidy; we're to have guests for tea tomorrow. You'd best tell Carlo, and help him make some dainty things for the ladies." He was about to shut his door but stopped. "On second thoughts Janet, leave the cooking to him, you could run and deliver a note to Bedford Square for me, soon as ye can."

While the Master wrote his note I hurried downstairs to instruct Carlo and then left him banging his pots about, no' pleased that the fish was still waiting to be gutted for supper.

The moment I entered the house on Bedford Square I knew I could endure almost anything to live in such a place. Larger than the house in Huntley Street, though not a shadow of the ones in Regent Street, it was a real grand home. The high ceilings were beautiful, with great swirls of plaster; flowers and fat cherubs sat tucked in the corners. The walls were painted in pale tones, soft to my eye. The only things tucked in the corners of the house in Huntley Street were cobwebs which, though I tried to remove them regularly, crept back again overnight to taunt me. Bright, clean light streamed in here, through windows tall as most houses, and reflected off the polished floors. A wide, sweeping staircase rose before me, covered in a rich blue carpet, and I couldna' resist the urge to bend forward and feel the soft depth of it. This house would involve a deal of cleaning to keep it so spotless, but I fancied there would be a lot more staff than jest me to do it.

While waiting in the hallway for the butler to carry the Master's message to MrWakley, my eye was caught by the bust of some fine fellah who stared from an alcove opposite the front door, and portraits of well-dressed gentlemen and their ladies hung from the walls; all of them watching me, probably waiting for me to touch something and leave dirty marks.

"Ah, m'dear. Thank you for the message."

Startled, I turned round to see Mister Wakley heading towards me across the hall; such a fine, handsome man.

"Come into the drawing room for a moment or two while I finish what I'm about, and I'll compose a short reply." He waved me into the room and bid me take a seat. Uncertain of which chair to sit in, there were so many to choose from, I opted for a rather severe, upright one, and when Wakley laughed aloud I blushed and went to stand again.

"Heavens girl, take the opportunity of a comfortable seat for goodness sake. The chaise longue there, that's it, much softer. Won't be a tick." He disappeared across the hallway and left me sitting perched on the edge of the seat, uncomfortable despite the horsehair padding. What if the butler came back? He would be sure to shoo me out of the drawing room, for he'd looked down his nose at me when I arrived and kept me waiting in the hallway for long enough.

A tall clock stood between the two windows and, as I looked at it, the minute hand clicked onto the twelve. The six o' clock chime made me jump, even though I should have expected it. I'd seen a clock inside a house for the first time when I came to London, standing in Doctor Knox's study. He was prone to swear at, and hit it from time to time when it stopped working and it certainly didna' make a chime loud as like this one. I fiddled with the braiding on the edge of a cushion, and studied the painted faces looking down at me from the walls. One, jest like Mister Wakely, had pride of place over the fireplace. It couldn't be him though, the clothes were all wrong and he was much older; likely his father.

"Ah, here we are, now then..." Wakely came in again, and sat himself down at a tiny bureau in the corner and picked up a pen. Scratching away there, I had time to study him, and was thinking what a fine jaw he had when the doorbell rang out. The butler appeared so quickly he must have been ready and waiting only feet away. There was something about him that reminded me of Hoskins, the way he looked at me and sneered. It was an expression alien to Mister Wakely who only ever looked kindly upon me.

A female voice loudly demanded to see the Master of the house, and in a flurry of silk and taffeta Miss Astley Cooper strode into the room, stopping suddenly, clearly taken aback by my sorry figure sitting on the chaise-longue.

"Well, when you invited me to take a glass of wine and supper I had a fancy it was for a tete a tete, Thomas. Then I had thought, just possibly, that Lady Eversholt and the usual parties might be present, but I see we are joined by, eh, Miss Knox, is it?"

"Brown, Miss. Janet Brown," I reminded her quietly enough but with my eyes fixed firmly on her pointy, hard little face. "I live with Doctor Knox."

"Ah yes, his 'ward'. I do remember."

I told mysel' she clearly hadna' been fooled by that

lie. Mister Wakely greeted her with a formal bow. She touched the side of her nose with her folded fan and gave a high laugh. The humour did not reach her eyes, not when she looked at me, but they were soft as a doe's when she spoke to Mister Wakely.

"You are a rogue, Thomas, really." This delivered to him in an undertone, but still loud enough for me to hear. What she could mean, I wasn't sure, but I saw him look up from kissing her limp hand and frown slightly. Why did she think Mister Wakely a rogue?

"Do not be cruel, my dear. You embarrass Miss Brown".

Why should he think that? I watched the two of them, flirting together but with watchful eyes, as though they didna' trust the other. She was very young and mebbe had yet to conquer a man's heart. She'd have to learn to be a wee less obvious in her charms, but it wasna' my role to point out the female arts to one so clearly above my station.

Mister Wakely, Thomas, then turned to me, holding out a neatly folded sheet of paper. He instructed me, in the softest of voices.

"Take my answer do; a few ideas to put before Doctor Knox. I'd be delighted to join him tomorrow afternoon, and he mustn't worry, I'm sure we can spike the guns of our opponents."

Puzzled at this remark, I took the note and remembered before I left them to give a brief curtsey.

"Thank ye Sir, Ma'm," I said quietly, keeping my eyes firmly on the patterned rug before me, then turned and hurried from the room. I could feel the eyes of Miss

Astley-Cooper on my back, burning through my rough brown dress, searing my skin.

———————

The tea party went very well, I think, though with all the coming and going up to the first floor I had to ask myself why the drawing room was up there rather than downstairs where it'd be a site more convenient. Mister Wakley came as promised, and had been joined a few minutes later by Lady Eversholt who was fanning herself with black ostrich feathers, near swooning in the warmth of the afternoon. Her skin was still pale so she hadna' spent long away in the country, I was thinking.

"Good day, gentlemen. I do hope there is a good reason for me to have to rush here, Knox. To what do we owe this pleasure?" her Ladyship asked. I hovered to take her shawl and my instructions from the Master. I'm no' sure she recognized me.

Mister Guthrie was also there, coming early and bringing with him what the Master called a summer cold, and he sniffed and snuffled like a pig.

"Why madam, Mister Wakley has just begun telling us of his latest doings in Parliament." Guthrie sniffed again. "There is to be a Bill presented to the House shortly and Doctor Knox seems in something of a lather about it."

Lady Eversholt lowered her bulk onto a chair, and Mister Wakley bowed and sat down too.

"I would not bore you with the details, save to say that momentous times are with us. The medical profession has for some years bemoaned the fact it cannot satisfy its requirements with the limited supplies it has to study, and now Mister Warburton has come up with a very sensible sounding additional source. Yet there are those among our profession, including myself I may add, who are horrified at his suggestions. His Bill would cause the devil of an upset in the country if it was passed into law, and yet it would seem on the face of it foolish to reject it." Wakley threw his hands up in a display of hopelessness.

Doctor Birkbeck arrived, and I rushed down to admit him and show him upstairs. I was jest taking his hat and cane when I noticed Hamish in the hallway by the student's study. He would no doubt be listening to the conversation too.

The Master had been shaking hands and fidgeting about, not so easy in his manner in a group like this, being more comfortable with his bodies and jest a few students. He bowed to the guests and waved towards the tray of sweet cakes and pastries on a small side table.

"Come; let us eat up Carlo's dainties. He's been busying himself in the kitchens all morning and would be most aggrieved if any of them go back down."

"Doctor Knox, how can you allow Mister Wakley to arouse our interests with such great passion and then talk of eating?" Lady Eversholt leant forward and picked up a beautiful wee pastry, and bit into it. "What supplies are you so short of that only Mister Warburton can satisfy, and why are his ideas so terrible?"

"We speak of the supply of dead bodies, ma'm. Without 'em the medical students have nothing on which to practise, and their masters nothing to show 'em." The Master was mebbe a bit blunt, but hadna' noticed how folk took it, leaning forward and helping himself to a piece of ginger cake.

Lady Eversholt stopped her chewing, and sat even more uprightly in her chair

"Why Doctor Knox, you wicked, wicked, man!" she exclaimed. "How could you speak of such monstrous things! And you, Wakely, to say you cannot decide on how to vote! Why, you should vote to stop them doing such awful things, and at once!"

Having recovered her composure, and having laid the remains of her pastry carefully onto a beautiful blue and white plate from Mister Wedgewood's factory, Lady Eversholt dabbed her mouth with a damask napkin.

I stepped forward to pour more tea for her, our eyes met, and her Ladyship winked at me. Taken aback mysel'for she clearly did recognize me, I fidgeted the plates of pastries, fussing about our guests, no' wanting to leave the room and miss out on the talk.

"But we must not be foolish." Lady Eversholt regained her composure. "Mister Wakley is a scoundrel and no doubt knows exactly how he plans to vote. I suspect he wishes to enlist our assistance in some way else he wouldn't have raised such an inappropriate subject at teatime. Am I right, Sir?"

"Indeed, ma'm, your sharpness has undone me. I cannot hide my true intentions?"

There was yet another visitor, for a loud rap sounded on the door. I hurried down and returned with Lady Harewood, dressed in a peacock blue gown with matching bonnet. She was a tall lady, very severe, and looked down on the Master when he stood and bowed his greeting.

"Good afternoon Doctor Knox, Mister Wakely, and Lady Eversholt. How time flies. It seems only a matter of days ago since we were all together at your establishment in Bedford Square, Mister Wakely. To what do I owe this invitation to tea today, Doctor Knox?"

"Our host is feeding us cakes in order to win our approval for something, and delicious they are too." Lady Eversholt, her hand hovering over the plate, finally decided on a tiny marzipan confection and transferred it to her mouth in a swift and graceful movement.

"Ah, and no doubt he wants me to win over my husband before the week is out?" Lady Harewood dismissed the proffered dish and sat down. "I am not averse to being helpful to you, Sir, but I will not get fat for you." Then, with an eye on Lady Eversholt, added, "A woman should be careful how much she eats or, I firmly believe, she will do herself no favours whatsoever. Now then, what is it you wish us to do Doctor Knox?"

Lady Eversholt stayed her hand, but only for a fleeting moment, before a tart dusted with cocoa and almond flakes got the better of her judgement.

I was a wee overawed when I heard amid their chatter that not only was Lady Harewood's husband a Lord who sat in an Upper House somewhere, but so did Lady Eversholt's and he was a friend of the Lord Chief Justice too. I had shaken so much when serving the Master his tea that some had slopped onto his breeches.

"Here, never mind girl," he had waved away my

hand and used his own lace kerchief to dab his thigh. "Good thing it isn't wine. I had six bottles from a grateful patient the other day, excellent claret, best keep that safe, and a pound of tobacco." His guests were impressed at that I'm sure. "Pity I don't smoke a pipe." He laughed but fixed a severe eye on me so I hurried to gather up the empty platters and leave the party to their discussions.

"'Tis good of you all to come at such short notice," I saw Doctor Knox nod his gratitude just as I pulled the door to, careful not to close it completely. "But I believe we are united in our outrage over Warburton's Bill?"

There was a murmur of agreement from around the room.

As I let go the door handle, a knife tipped from my tray and, stooping to pick it up, another tumbled forth with a clatter.

"Here, have a care Janet." Hamish, crossing the landing, stopped and knelt at my side. Returning the cutlery to the tray he took in the assortment of fine china and napkins heaped upon it and raised an eyebrow. "Who is the Master entertaining? I saw Birkbeck go up, but he doesn't normally trouble with the best silverware for him."

"Tush, two Lady's no less, Mister Guthrie and Mister Wakely. They're talking about uniting to stop Mister Warburton getting his way. I couldna' make out what they meant but the Master was in a rare excited state. I think Mister Wakely is calming him some, but there's mischief stirring for sure.."

Hamish stepped over to the door and leant his ear to

the stout panelling. He nearly jumped out of his skin when I tapped his shoulder and he spun round to face me, standing hands on hips.

Before I could say a word Hamish clamped his hand over my mouth and hissed,

"Be still. This could be important, Janey." Then he returned his attention to the door and the dull whispering behind it. I leant in beside him and held my breath.

"If, as we think likely, the Anatomy Schools close altogether, medical training will be solely in the remit of certain favoured universities," Knox's voice was angry. "That would leave too much power in too few hands – why already there are naught but half a dozen men of significance in the Royal College of Surgeons and most of them buy and sell positions as though they are their personal property."

"We all want to stamp out the robbing of graves and, God forbid, the murder of innocent citizens, but taking the unclaimed dead from workhouses makes victims of the poorest of our community," that was Birkbeck. "They have dread enough of poverty forcing them into the workhouse, now they will fear dying there even more than they already do. Why, I heard one fellow say he expected the inmates to be murdered where they slept and their remains sold to profit the parish, and no amount of reasoning would dissuade him of the notion."

Guthrie, quiet until now, joined in. "The stigma of dissection, associated as it is with punishment for the most heinous crimes, will be laid upon the poor. To make it the prescribed end for breaking the social rather than the criminal code is to make poverty itself a crime."

"There is considerable discord in the lower classes already, with the refusal of the government to grant all working men the vote. This will outrage them further. This Bill must be halted, for the sake of the poor and also the safety of our society." Birkbeck was right, I thought.

I heard a chink of a cup being put down as Lady Eversholt spoke. "Well, I know how my husband will vote, gentlemen, should this reach the Lords. And I beg you Lady Harewood to apprise your good husband of the necessary action and vote against it."

"In the meantime," Mister Wakley said, "If I have any influence at all with my colleagues, we'll crush this Anatomy Bill and it'll go no further. On another matter, the much needed Reform Bill and extending voting rights. I doubt any immediate revolution if it fails, but folk will not be happy. Parliament don't want to risk going the way of the Froggies across the water. I fear they will block it and just fall back on their heavy handed tactics if any step out of line."

The Master spoke then, loud and clear.

"Gentlemen, I think the new powers of law and order will have their work cut out to control the streets if there is any truth in what Parliament fears. They would have us believe the students intend to join the Chartists in a march upon Parliament and enough hotheads amongst them planning to arm themselves in response to the new Peelers. One of their number was certainly shot the other day by a policeman, damn near killed him. I won't be surprised if the marchers turn ugly if there's much more of that, and if that happened, retribution will be swift as you suggest, and not just on them, on their colleges too. No doubt there would be calls to have offending institutions closed down."

Gasps from Guthrie and Birkbeck, and from Hamish at my side. When they asked where these students came from and how Knox knew this, there was silence for a moment.

"I cannot give away my sources good sirs, but suffice to say, there are students we ourselves may have met who could be implicated, if not directly involved. I think we should take firm action with them as soon as possible, or God help us all. Seems we are under attack from every quarter."

The tread of footsteps towards the door had Hamish and I jerking backwards, then I was away, skittering down the landing towards the servant's stairs, and he up to the attic.

15

THE LASSIE FROM BETHNAL GREEN

My mind was still troubled by how the polis had known where to look for Charlie, and why he would be of such interest to O'Rourke, if it was he who had informed on our household. It worried at me all night that Charlie might be involved with revolution and I woke tired and tetchy. Breakfast was a quiet affair. Hamish was clearly tired after a late night out drinking, and Ewan crumbled a piece of bread on his platter, sighing and holding his head up with difficulty. O'Rourke had still not returned home, which made me doubly sure he was the traitor responsible for the polis raid.

"I think this morning some quiet study is in order." Knox looked across the table under heavy brows. He'd mebbe not slept so well either. "Ewan, the essay on the appendix, how goes it?"

"Eh, it goes very well Sir," Ewan's face suggested he lied. "'Tis not yet quite complete, but nearly there, Sir."

"Well, complete it this morning and bring it to me at noon, I have to go out for a short time later and want to see it before I go. Hamish, have you had any success in finding that rogue Black? No? We need a cadaver for tomorrow afternoon; a female, for the uterus and reproductive organs. She must be above fifteen or so, and young enough still to be of childbearing age. No old harridans, hear?"

"Aye Sir. At once."

"Ideally a virgin, but that'll be difficult....what is it Janet?" Knox frowned.

I had no words, but quickly finished loading my tray with their dishes and fled to the kitchen.

"Foolish girl." I heard Knox say as I left. Foolish! Mebbe I was, but the thought of some wee, innocent lassie being cut up was too much for me right then.

———

Ewan would no' be budged from his books for the rest of the morning, though Hamish pled with him to help in his task of finding a body.

"Sorry Hamish, not until this appendix is complete. What can I say about it though? There is nothing here remotely interesting and the only complaint it can have is to grow large and burst. Where is the point to it?" There was a hint of desperation in his voice, and Hamish sat down next to him and reached for the topmost book on the pile.

"Look under peritonitis – you could elaborate on that. But it would do no harm to point out in your essay that the organ is largely redundant in man, as we are not grazing animals such as sheep."

"Knox would think me missing the point, or insolent."

"No, really, that is the point. Write it, you'll see."

"Not much of an essay."

"Not much of an organ. Take ten minutes to write it and then come and help me find a cadaver." Hamish slapped Ewan on the back and hurried downstairs to wait in the kitchen. I gave Ewan a reassuring smile, finished dusting around the student's study and after straightening piles of books and papers, followed Hamish down.

I saw young Aldo outside. He was with Hoskins, standing by a cart. When Hoskins went inside to visit his servant girl, I stepped across the way to speak to the laddie, slippin' a coin into his hand.

"How goes it, Aldo? You are about to help your Master this morn'?"

He looked up at me, standing proud, and answered that they were off to Bethnal Green. It took but a few minutes to learn it was Mister Black they were visiting. Trying not to look like I was too interested, I asked if he knew Bethal Green well.

"Is it a country place?" I asked.

He laughed at that and said "'tis a dull place with a big workhouse, nothing much else there indeed, but 'tis favoured by Mister Black and easy for us to visit."

"So, where will ye go for a young woman?" I asked when I was alone with Hamish and drying dishes.

"I can ask around; maybe at the Fortune of War; there may be someone there who can supply one." Then, when he saw my questioning look he said, "'Tis a public house much favoured by resurrectionists, down in Smithfield. I know, Janey, not respectable, but what choice do I have with Black lying low and no sign even of Hoskins. It's either that or begging at the workhouse."

"At least young women are common enough at a workhouse, and dying there besides. Where else would we go if we're hungry or sick, or mebbe carrying a child we shouldna'." I couldn't believe this conversation, especially after what the Master had said the day before, about poor folk likely to be given away when they died.

Hamish went out after that and I spent the rest of the morning flicking a duster around and fretting over so many thoughts tumbling in my head, about Charlie and O'Rourke, and what the Master and his guests had talked about, with the Anatomy Schools mebbe closing, and the miserable lives of ordinary folk and workhouses and all sorts. By the early afternoon I was fidgeting to get out o' the house for some air. Ewan came out of the Master's office looking relieved, so his appendix essay must ha' been a success. I watched as he went outside to join Hamish in tending a cart and a slow looking nag he'd hired from somewhere.

They were deep in whispering together when I went out to shake my duster and give the brass plate on the front door a bit o' a rub.

"Are ye away on a wee outing?" I asked.

"Aye, Janet. Would ye care to join us?" Ewan looked nervous after such a hasty offer.

Hamish didna' look so keen and from his shifty look they were up to mischief o' some sort.

"Where to?" I wasna' wanting to seem too eager.

"We're going on a tour of the area" Hamish said. "Just to make some enquiries. Maybe visit a few of the local hospitals."

I shuffled a stone into the road, looking at my feet with my mind racing. They were after a body or two.

"Bethnal Green is no' so far, and there's sure to be a grand big workhouse there," I suggested, brazen for sure. With the day being hot and the air inside the house close and dusty, I was tempted at the idea of joining them for an excursion.

Hamish waved to the seat next to him, and with his bonnie smile I'd no' the heart to refuse though all the while knowing I'd mebbe regret the trip if it were to mean haggling over the dead.

So, sitting high up on the cart, we trotted away, down Hackney Road, out to the east, though the green fields of Cambridge Heath which were no' so pretty and said to be the hunting ground of highwaymen. Bethnal Green was a dismal looking place, neither town nor country. Aldo had been right. A few hovels here and there, scrubby patches of small trees and shrubs all surrounding a brick works. There were piles of lime and dirt and baked bricks seemed heaped at random. The air was jest as full of dust as the house.

We stopped outside a big building, the workhouse Ewan said, as he jumped down. Hamish draped the reins over one knee, content the puffing old horse was going nowhere further for a while, and asked me to give the nag a nose-bag.

I carefully got down, keen to stretch my legs and took the sack of hay. I fondled the nag's ears looking into his old rheumy eyes. "Poor ol' fellah…" I whispered. He chomped away, and I pulled him gently along to drink from a water trough. While the horse refreshed himself, I looked about me determined to make the most of my outing. It was a few minutes before I noticed, among the few folk on the street, the familiar figure of O'Rourke.

"Look," I hissed up to Hamish, "what's he doing hereabouts?"

He must ha' come in a hackney, for one was pulling away from the roadside jest behind him. Without looking in our direction, the Irishman turned into a lane and I saw jest the top of his head above the wall as he walked along.

I set off up the road, ignoring Hamish calling me back, jest to see where O'Rourke was going. He hadna' gone far, striding along, and was already half through a low gate when I slipped behind a broken tree on the corner of the lane, from where I could watch unseen. He approached a run-down cottage; outside the same cart I had seen Hoskins with that morning. Before he reached the door it had opened and in the shadows the form of a man, though I couldna' tell who it was. The two men stood in the doorway for several minutes, and even from a distance I heard their raised voices, though couldna' make out any words. Eventually, O'Rouke went inside and the door closed behind him.

I waited, no'sure what to do, but eventually moved from my hiding place behind the tree and crept like a thief til I was close enough to see Aldo sleeping in the footwell of the cart. From the path at the side of the cottage, I squinted through a window and could see Hoskins standing, large as life, but no' who he was talking to. The two men picked up a great hamper and carried it through to the back o' the house somewhere. I walked on tiptoe down the path and from the cover of a pile o' bulging sacks was able to see them when they came out into the back yard, an area of junk with a dripping water pump and pieces o' wood and broken furniture all about.

It was Black helping Hoskins carry the hamper. It looked awkward and heavy, and there was a deal of cussing. While Black tied the straps around it Hoskins went back through the house, and I heard him say he'd bring the nag round and they could load up.

I ducked down and sped back up the pathway to the road, fearful o' being seen and was jest in time to avoid the cart running me down. I looked up at its passing and into the eyes o' the laddie, Aldo. His surprise was clear in his open mouth, but when I put my fingers to my lips he gave a smile like he knew not to say anything.

I hurried back to Hamish who was pleased enough to see me, though I was panting and more than a mite pleased to be back with him.

"Janey, what are you thinking of? We're here on

business, not gadding about. Ewan won't be long, he's inside."

"You don't want to hear who O'Rourke is visiting then?" I climbed up and joined Hamish on the driving seat, trying to stop mysel' from grinning now I was safe.

"Well, I doubt it would be anyone respectable round here."

"Mister Black!"

"What!" Hamish near startled the old nag with his cry. "Black, living out here? Well! The Master will be interested to know we've found the rogue."

I started to remind him it was I who had found Black, but Hamish was distracted by Ewan's return, and got down to talk to him. The two of them stood huddled on the far side of the cart, and a few minutes later came round to the side where I was sitting.

"Janey," Hamish looked serious. "We need your help. There's a young woman in there," he nodded towards the workhouse behind us, "with no family to collect her body. She died yesterday. If you and I go in and tell the matron we are come to claim her, she will be...."

"What!" It was my turn to be shocked. I'd known why they'd brought the cart, I'm no' a fool, and I'd half expected a purchase at some time. "You came here to get a subject for the Master, I know, but to use me...to have me lie for you!" I was angry now.

"Please Janey. Don't be angry. The lass has a pauper's grave ahead of her. There is nobody here to mourn her. Ewan has established her name, and that she died in childbirth. If we take her home at least she will have had purpose at the end of her life, and it will be easier to convince the warders we are family if there is a grieving sister come for her not just a strange man alone. I could play your husband again..... like we did for the man who sold us the mangle.." He gave a small smile then, to win me over, and though it did, I gave him a wee thump on the arm as I climbed down.

Hamish reached up and banged on the iron knocker. The grille slid open and the beadle unlatched the gate for us to enter.

"Wait here," he pointed to a narrow bench in a small side room and turned to go and fetch the matron.

We waited, some long minutes, mebbe half an hour, and Hamish was getting annoyed. We heard the outer door open and close several times, mebbe desperate folk arriving seeking help; footsteps on stone floors. There were fewer folk about than I'd expected and the inner corridors seemed fairly quiet.

"Busier in the winter," Hamish whispered.

The matron came at last, out of breath from rushing, and looked a wee bit disappointed when she saw us. Mebbe she was hoping for someone rich who would give a big donation.

"Madam, we are here seeking information about my wife's sister. I understand she came to you to have her child, and would have been due around now. Her name is Eliza Waller. Do you have her here?"

"She's gorn."

"Gone? Gone where?" Hamish was aghast. "She would be in no state to go anywhere." He stood and stared at the woman, any previously held fear of her evaporating fast. "We came to take her home to her family, right away. Where did she go? Has someone else taken her?"

"I mean she died, young Sir. She was in difficulty with the baby coming and 'aving a bit o' a fever. I dosed 'er but the poor lass didna' live through it. She was very weak when she presented herself here. Poor girl, when will they learn?"

Hamish, could not hide his relief from me, but put on a grief stricken face for Mistress Blunt.

"We'd no knowledge of where she'd gone 'til a few hours ago. And to have learnt there was a child on the way....Coming here, I had hoped to be an uncle, to find dear Eliza well." Hamish was acting fit for the stage, and I remembered at last that I was a grief-stricken sister.

"This is such a shock, Mistress Blunt. My poor sister." I shed a few tears then, snuffing into my kerchief. "And what of the bairn?"

"Didn't last but one night, poor little'un. Oh, young Sir, she said her parents had thrown 'er out, keen to get shot of 'er... brought disgrace, she did." But then her face hardened. "If you take 'er, what of all our expense of looking after 'er? Besides, we can't release our charges to just anyone. How do I know you are kin?"

But Hamish had come prepared it seemed.

"Madam, we are most grateful for the care you have shown her. We will of course make full reparation for your costs." He pulled a heavy purse from his pocket.

She brightened then, and took us along a few corridors to a small ward where a couple of old women stitched, slowing only to study us passing. A tiny room stood off to one side. It was bright enough, but was bare of all but the most essential furniture or any homely touch. A thin bed stood alone against the wall, under a high window, and on it a thin young lassie was neatly laid. Her long dark hair was tied into a bunch each side of her face and laid across her shoulders. Her eyes were closed like she was sleeping, her hands crossed on her breast and a grubby sheet covering her lower half. She was wearing a faded shift of some rough stuff and in a basket by the side of the bed her wee baby, swaddled in a dirty rag, nameless, silent and uncomforted. I had no need to act for the tears came to me of their own making.

Mistress Blunt left us alone for a few minutes before returning with her ledger.

"Three guineas for vittals and the midwife, the tending of 'em both and the laying out. If you're wanting a box for 'em that'll be another guinea."

I gasped, but Hamish was no' arguing, paying her what she asked.

"Thank you, madam, I'm obliged."

Two surly looking inmates arrived to assist and Hamish supervised her removal, cursing under his breath as the box banged against doorframes and nearly jammed in the passageway.

We joined Ewan outside with our purchase, dumped on the back of the cart, and covered over with a tarpaulin, then set off at a trot back towards Huntley Street before news of us having a cart ready reached the Matron and aroused any suspicion in her.

"Come, 'tis nearly three already, we must get the girl back and ready her for the lecture tomorrow."

"And the bairn?" I asked. The tiny body had been placed in the coffin with his mother, arranged to one side so the lid would lie flat.

"Eh? Oh, yes of course. I imagine the Master might have a use for it, poor mite.

"So did you get her for a fair price?" Ewan asked

"Indeed. Four guineas with the box included, so the little one was free....." Hamish's voice tailed off when he saw my face. But as we set off my head was as full o' my own plans as much as of the poor lassie behind us, and I was grateful for the silence as we made our way home.

I had never known such ingratitude! The Master, far from being pleased with our lassie complained that the uterus wouldna' be any good since she had jest given birth. I stood in the doorway of his study while he berated poor Hamish.

"I specifically said I needed a uterus and female organs, and these will be mis-shaped from her quickening." He mopped his brow. The day was warm, and he tossed his kerchief onto his desk in frustration, but after a minute he calmed and sat down. "It might be a useful comparison should we be fortunate enough to have a more suitable subject alongside her. You still have time Hamish, else we will need to use her for something else entirely. See what you can do."

Hamish was rarely angry but having thought he'd

done so well with his outing, he was disappointed at the Master's rebuke. An hour later we were sitting in the kitchen no' sure where to turn when a cart drew into the yard outside.

A short man, with a tall thin companion climbed down and walked unsteadily towards the kitchen door, but instead of knocking they peered through the window to the side, tapping gently on the glass.

Hamish opened the door and greeted them like ol' friends.

"Ye wanted a gal; a gal we've brought ye." The short man bowed and the tall one grinned. They were both drunk, and stank of beer and sweat.

Ewan dashed outside with Hamish to see what was supplied, and I was left in the kitchen open mouthed at the thought of them haggling outside over another lassie. I moved to the doorway, and saw the body lifted onto a board and carried towards the house. The two men put down their burden outside the door and stood back to await their reward.

Hamish crouched and turned back the edge of the blanket which covered her. I couldna' resist stepping forward to look. She was a slight girl, probably not much older than fifteen or sixteen, and as she lay there, she could have been stone, stiff with the rigour of death. Her hair was matted with filth and moved at the roots with lice. He withdrew his hand. In a few hours she'd be easier to handle, and the lice would have crawled off in search of a living meal.

"Fine, thank 'ee. Wait here and I will get the money and...." he shooed me back into the house then, and hurried up to the Master's study. When he returned I made a great play of rattling pots in the sink, but I froze as I saw what he handed over along with a bag of money. The wee babe from Bethnal Green passed hands quickly.

"Fair trade, thank'ee Sir," his round head nodded on his shoulders. "Pleasure to do business wiv you. The small will be most welcome at Guys. Good day to ee."

The dirty corpse was hoisted up to the Anatomy room and I was up and down with hot water for the next hour while the lads cleaned her up ready. I was left wondering what would become of the bairn, or his mother, spoiled so by having him and now separated from him forever.

It seems the two men had been at the public house Hamish had visited in the morning and they had come across the river with the new lassie and a number of other bodies for use at the university, enough to make the journey worth while. I went to bed that night knowing she was below me, wondering how she had died and how many poor souls were being bought and sold each day for these learned men to work on. But most o' my thoughts were taken up by the house in Bethnal Green and how I could mebbe find out from O'Rourke, Hoskins or Black if they had perchance come across Hare in the course of their business and, if so, could they tell me where he might be.

It was still only nine in the morning when Hamish went to refresh himself in the College Arms and find Ewan to give him a hand with the 'subject'. I walked with him as the inn was on my way to the market at Covent Garden, for we were in need of food as well as bodies. I stayed for a small beer, and sat in the shade outside for a few minutes, for the sun was already shining bright and warm. Hamish swallowed the last mouthful of his flagon.

"Ah, that's better." He wiped his mouth with his sleeve. The stink of the Anatomy Room had filled the house this past week but was now finally gone from my nose and I was likin' the freedom of sittin' out in the sun. "It's too far into the summer for many more days of cutting," Hamish said. The mother will have to be used by tomorrow too or she'll be near a week old. Here, Ewan, drink up and we must be back to work." They made their way back to Huntley Street while I walked to the market, and tried to turn my mind to Carlo's shopping list. I strode out, enjoying the warm sun, ignoring a cart that pulled abreast of me, and the driver who called lewdly to me.

Later, after returning and helping Carlo with dinner, seeing everyone fed and set up in the Anatomy room, I washed the dishes and settled down for a rest in the privacy of my room. A dark mood came over me.

I sat huddled on the bed and couldna' help but berate mysel'. How could I have become so comfortable and at ease here, working with the lads as I had been? I was guilty as them in their sordid trade, when I had come to London with every intention of avenging my dear friend, Mary. But though I was angry with mysel', and horrified at what was proposed for the wretched girl below me, I settled at last with the knowledge that my revenge was now assured. All I had to do was to confront Hare, then slit his throat. I felt sure Black and Hoskins would know where he might be; for those involved in this business of bodysnatching seemed a tight band.

I ignored Hamish's call at first.

"'Tis perfectly safe to come down Janet, do not be foolish. The lecture is over and I must away now, and you should be about your business. Come, open the door."

Eventually, I opened the door, but the the sight of his anxious face upset me.

"You certainly don't think Knox would harm you do you?" Hamish asked, after I mumbled my fears for the lassie below. I didna' want to tell him all my thoughts for he would surely no' approve of me planning murder.

"No, of course not. It's jest I was a wee taken aback by what he said, about the – well, inside parts." I was no' used to lying to Hamish, but carried on. "'Tisn't decent, a man seeing those things."

Hamish tried not to laugh, jest keeping his face under control enough for a small smile, and ruffled my hair.

"For a former prostitute you have some strange notions about decency. Janey my dear girl, to a doctor there is nothing indecent. They see all, even our most private parts, and feel nothing but wonder at nature."

"Not lust at all?"

"No! Well, not for most. Not Knox. The idea would not occur to him."

"Then I will come down and sweep the yard, and there's the kitchen grate to do." I smiled and squeezed his arm, and went down to busy mysel' and be the dutiful servant.

I was done sweeping and stood on the front steps taking the sun for a few minutes when I saw Hoskins walk past the School cool as ice, off to his servant girl at the end of the road, and wondered how his business was faring, and whether the lassie there knew what he did for a living. He'd not looked towards the School, so we were clear gone from his thoughts. I sighed and shook out my broom before heading indoors.

16

MURDER, SUSPICION AND THE STINK OF
DEATH

Dinner was served late owing to the lads having to write up their notes then dispose of the waste from upstairs. The house was still full of the smell of the lassie they'd cut and the other one still left behind who was growing riper every day. Carlo had supplied what ice he could, and the windows were all wide open, but even with the Master's herbs to help, the sickly smell flowing through most of the house was too much. It was a wee bit less overpowering down in the kitchen, with the benefit of cooked meat and onions to mask it, but my stomach heaved as I crossed the hall to the dining room.

Hamish was shoving his food about the plate and they'd clearly been drinking more than usual. Ewan was nearly asleep in his dish, and the silence was enough to fill the room.

"Tomorrow's practical lecture will be the last of the summer, unless we have a change in this weather." The sudden bark of the Master's voice startled me as I served another plate of bread. "After that you'll have to rely on the models for the rest of your preparations. We will take a look at the lungs. It'll be of help to you with the coming examinations Hamish. "

I hovered at table, ready to hear what else might be said, and busied myself topping up the Master's glass.

"I have a gentleman I need to visit this evening, nasty case of syphilis, and when I return we can perhaps discuss likely subjects the board will question you with. I have every confidence in you laddie."

I saw the smallest smile from Hamish then, and he murmured his thanks. The laddie was looking nervous, and I cursed mysel' for I hadna' realised how these examinations must ha' been playing on his mind o' late.

That evening, when the Master returned from his visit, he and Hamish were locked away in the study for at least two hours. Ewan had gone out. He wasna' ready for the examinations it seemed, but I think he was happy enough for another year of grace. By the time he came home I was abed mysel', and the house was quiet.

In the morning there were callers to the house. Breakfast was barely over and the Master had given his instructions for the day, when the knocker sounded. I ran up the stairs quick enough from the kitchen, but the front door was already open. Ewan was there showing two smartly dressed and sombre gen'lemen towards the Master's study.

We couldna' hear what was said behind the door though we strained. They were no' patients, but who they were I didna' have a clue for they had no' introduced themselves loud enough for me to hear. After but a few minutes, they and the Master left together. Hamish had been in with the Master having been practicing his answers and stayed during the visit, so he was left standing pale-faced in the hallway when they'd gone. I hurried to ask him what was to do.

"That was a policeman from the new detecting branch, and a doctor from University College. They have a body over at Bow Street needing an autopsy. They want the Master to help out."

"So why are ye so pale laddie?"

"They said he might be able to identify him. I just wondered who...."

He went upstairs then, and was quiet for the rest of the morning, he and Ewan being tasked to work on their books, but when I called in they were whispering together and no' doing much studying.

I went about my chores, my mind also wondering whose was this body and why did the polis think the Master might know him. Our questions were finally answered when the Master returned and called the lads into his study.

"'Tis O'Rourke," Hamish said when I questioned him later. "That's why he didn't come home."

His voice was so quiet I could barely catch what he said, and he rubbed his palms against his breeches. I was about to ask him more of what the Master had told him, when the man himsel' came out of his study and saw us, locked together in the hallway. From our faces he must have known what we were talking about.

"The police have him at Bow Street. He's dead and laid in the mortuary, poor lad. Someone has cut his throat and I was summoned to look this morning and give him a name so they know for sure who they have. Fortunately he was carrying a receipt for a list of books I'd recommended and had my name on it, so they knew he must be a student of mine.... " He frowned and shook his head.

Murdered! But who would....? I gasped and allowed mysel' the comfort of Hamish holding me clasped against his chest, where his heart beat hard and fast against my cheek. He was shaken by this, and so was I and I didna' even like O'Rourke. Who could hate him so much to kill him? We had seen him but days before so 'twas strange to think of him now dead and cold.

"Aye, 'tis a shocking thing. From what you told me laddie, 'tis likely O'Rourke was killed for betraying yon plotting Radicals. That's what the police are thinking, too. There'll be a bounty on Chagford's head for this. He's already a wanted man, and now both he and Brushwood are clearly suspect for this murder. The law will not rest 'til they have 'em in gaol."

"But no!" I cried. "Charlie would nae hurt a fly, I know that." They looked at me with sad faces, then turned away and went about their business. I was left standing there, in the hallway, wringing my apron before me in disbelief. I knew nothing of Brushwood, but Charlie? Never was he a murderer! What could I do? I had to stop this nonsense and have him home safe where he belonged. I couldna' easily say to the Master that I'd seen O'Rourke in Bethnal Green, for to do so would be to admit my being there with the lads and I'd no' want to get any of us in trouble. My heart was racing and then, without stopping to wash the dishes or even tell

Carlo where I was going, I was away out of the house and running towards the Vicarage. I must tell Verity! Mebbe the family would know what to do. Would they know by now where he was? I didna' know what I was about, but only that I had to find Charlie and make him safe!

I ran half the distance before reason came upon me and I slowed my steps. What good would it do to cause heartache to the family, and to poor Verity? The lad wouldna' be at home hiding, and they wouldna' be able to help any. I'd go to the Institute and ask there, for mebbe someone would know of Brushwood and where the runaways may have gone to. I hurried along Shaftesbury Avenue and when I came to the grey building of the Institute took the steps two at a time, holding my skirts high.

All was quiet in the great hallway, and only a few folk passed me on the stairs. I opened the door to the debating room and looked in. Maisie Baldwin's voice drew me forward. She was the woman who sounded like a horse and today she looked even more like one than I remembered from the night Hunt came to speak, propped against the fireplace with her foreleg planted on the grate and her shoulders back. Her long face was bright with passion. I dinna' ken what she was talking about, but she slapped her thigh and broke out in a neigh when her companion said something to her. They both turned as I approached.

"Ah, it's Janet. Welcome to ye, Sister." Maisie's face faltered and I thought, sudden, what a sight I must look. I put my hand to my hair, for without a bonnet it was blown about and untidy with the run I'd had. I bobbed a wee curtsey, and felt a tear come to my eye when she reached out and pulled me to her.

"What's this Janet? What has happened, m'dear? Anything we can do? This is Georgina Trott by the way. That Master of yours cutting up rough, eh?"

"No ma'am, er Maisie. He's right as can be, but he's upset too. One of our students has been killed and, oh Maisie!" I stopped, hoping I wasna' about to give anything away that I shouldna'. "I'm looking for Mister Brushwood, eh, to give him the news, and I'm hoping someone here might know where he can be found....."

Maisie frowned, her eyes darting to her friend, Georgina, who stood quiet the other side of the fireplace. Georgina gave a little nod and Maisie took my arm in hers and we walked all three together to the far corner of the room to sit on an ornate chaise longue against the wall. There were more people coming in and I suppose she'd decided it was time to be less loud.

"This is a difficult time for men and women of spirit, Janet. Mister Brushwood is visiting London from Birmingham to put his views before the Commons Select Committee." Here Maisie lowered her voice even more, her eyes searching the room behind me for government informers. "He was to have come here tonight for a speech to the Debating Society, but has sent word that as he is at the House tomorrow it may be best not to risk arrest beforehand. He will come to us on Thursday perhaps, before returning home. A disappointing delay for our members, but there we are."

"Is he no' likely in danger at the House, Miss?" It

seemed a strange thing to walk into the very mouth of the lion if he was to talk against it.

"There are privileges to the place. The government is honour-bound to protect those who speak before its' Committees. It's the only way they ever get to hear anything about the people's plight and what's going on. Those on the Committee are in the main sympathetic and we have our own Mister Wakley there, so Brushwood will be able to talk away as much as he pleases."

"Mister Wakley! So he would mebbe know where Mister Brushwood is now, and if he has seen... if he has heard anything. Mebbe I'll call on him on the way home..." I turned to leave but Maisie put a gloved hand on my arm to slow me.

"Hmm, I think he may be rather busy this evening, m'dear, entertaining. Some of his guests may be a tad modest and not wish to be disturbed..."

Georgina nodded at what Maisie had said, but I was no' going to be put off. I bid my farewells and didna' argue, but as soon as I was out o' the building I hurried back the way I'd come, then turned into Bedford Square.

I was running still when I crossed the Square and there, stepping up to his carriage was Mister Wakley himsel'. He must ha' been surprised to see me, leastways the speed I was going, and stopped in his tracks and walked up to me with his face a picture of concern.

"Why, Miss Brown!" He looked a mite taken aback. I was panting and I put my hand to my head, a sickly feeling of panic held me in its grip. There was no sign of

Charlie, or Mister Brushwood, and Mister Wakley was looking very calm for someone involved in revolution.

"Oh, Mister Wakley, Sir....He didna' do it, I know he didna'." Tears threatened to come then, and I know my voice was high. He took my elbow, firm, gave a sharp order to his footman, and walked me fast into his house. I remember being sat upon a chair, a glass pressed into my hand and the burn of the brandy in my throat. The footman stood like a statue by the door, a blank look on his face, but his eyes bore into me. Mister Wakley ordered him to leave us then paced back and forth for a few moments by the fireplace. I could hear the distant sound of men's voices, mebbe upstairs, but not a word of what they said.

"Now child, slowly. What distresses you so?" He was a kindly man, Mister Wakley, and I found mysel' telling him all about Charlie and Mister Brushwood, their visit to us and slipping away after in the dark.

"And they never could ha' killed O'Rourke for all he was mebbe a traitor. They wouldna' have known anyway. How could they? There's naught to say it wasna' someone else gave them away. I must find Charlie, Sir, and make sure he's safe. And Mister Brushwood of course."

"Well, there's naught to fear," he said. I swear he was smiling then, not in the least alarmed by my tale. "Brushwood is safe and will be appearing tomorrow afternoon before a Select Committee of Members. He has the protection of Lord Leverbridge himself. Young Chagford is with him, and so he is safe too, helping him prepare his speech maybe. Now, compose yourself do, dear girl. The police invariably go after the wrong people when a deed like this is done, but never fear, we'll put 'em straight, eh?"

"Oh, Sir, do you think so? Are they really safe?"

"If they stay within the House tomorrow, yes, and they don't go wandering about the streets in the meantime. I will be there myself and will ensure they are discreet." He scratched his chin. There were quiet voices from somewhere but no sign of his guests and I wondered whether he had Charlie and Brushwood there, hiding in cupboards or under the beds 'til I was gone. From the blankness of his face, Mister Wakley was giving naught away and no' so much as a look passed between him and the maid who came to speak to him and who took my glass. I studied her face and her eyes wouldna' meet mine, though I swear her face flushed as she turned aside.

"They couldn't have murdered O'Rourke, Sir. I know it! And mebbe someone else had known about Charlie and Mister Brushwood being at Huntley Street. But who?"

"Never mind about that right now m'dear. We'd best get you home before you're missed, eh? What would old Knox say if he knew you were running about the town in your apron? He'll be expecting his dinner won't he?" He smiled kindly and had a servant show me out. I walked home, tired and cold for all the sun was warm.

The Master was indeed waitin' for his dinner. He was walking around the kitchen growling at Carlo and snapping like an angry dog at Hamish and Ewan. There was an uncomfortable feel in the place and I hurried to lay out plates and knives. I was expecting him to question where I'd been, but he seemed to soften his growls when he spoke to me.

"When dinner is finished, Janet, I'll be taking my Madeira in my study. I have a visitor or two coming in a wee while, and we won't want to be disturbed. As we're a student down now, perhaps you would help the lads here with cleaning upstairs in the Anatomy Room. The windows are a disgrace in there. I can barely see to cut and we've a visiting lecturer tomorrow. See if you can get some of the summer dust and grime off the panes."

I served his Madeira wine in the study. He nae even looked up from the letter he was reading when I put his glass by him, wi' the decanter too for one glass was rarely enough to satisfy. Then I went to fill a bucket with water and, at Carlo's suggestion, added a splash o' vinegar. As I climbed the stairs, I could feel my guts tighten and prayed I'd no' see anything too bad when I went into the room.

All was well. Ewan was setting up a ladder by the tall windows overlooking the street, and Hamish was scrubbing the table in the middle of the room, the odd shaped item stained too dark for all the scrubbing in the world to shift. The floor around was marked too. I felt queasy and turned away to the window.

"It's all right Janey, there's not a cadaver in the place right now." Hamish had noticed my discomfort at being there, and though he was in low spirits he gave me a kindly smile. "We had but a quick look at the lassie's lungs and the Master decided she wasn't worth spending too much time over. She's gone now."

I was saddened by the way he spoke of her, as if she were a piece of rubbish, but the main part of me was pleased she was no longer there. Ewan was quiet, and as I rolled up my sleeves I thought it would be a monstrous thing if O'Rourke was the subject of a dissection in the next few days. But no, surely they wouldna' do such a thing? I shook my head and climbed the ladder, then started the job of scouring the filthy windows 'til we could see out and the sun could shine in.

I'd barely finished one window when a carriage drew up outside and lo, there was Mister Wakley himself coming up our steps. There was another gen'leman with him, tall and thin with a face like a hawk. I nearly tripped on my skirt as I climbed down from the ladder, but gathered mysel' together and ran down the stairs to open the front door. He was looking same as I'd left him, a gentle smile and no sign of frettin'. The other man didna' say a word. I tapped on the Master's door and showed them through.

"Mister Wakley, Sir, and eh....."

"Ah, thank'ee Janet. Wakley, Lord Leverbridge, good day. Bring some clean glasses will ye, Janet. A drop of Madeira wine gentlemen?"

I scuttled down to the kitchen and had the glasses and a plate of crackers up with them in no' more than a minute, but already they were seated, either side of the fireplace, deep in talk. They quieted when I walked in and their faces gave away naught of what they'd been saying. I bobbed a curtsey and hovered outside the door.

"Windows, Janet!" The Master hollered. I don't ken

how he knew I was still there, but I thought I'd best move mysel'.

Up the ladder again I sloshed my rag in and out o' the bucket, wringing it and soaking it, and wringing it again. No' getting much cleaning done, but thinking what the gen'lemen were about. Who was this Lord Leverbridge? He was supposed to be looking after Mister Brushwood and Charlie, so why was he no' in the Parliament House? Hamish had been up and down a couple of times then came and stood by the window and peered out. He gave the glass a quick wipe with his own rag and left a pinkish smear.

"I've no' done that bit yet," I said, and started on the pane above.

"Janey, is that laddie looking up here?"

Down in the street stood young Aldo, staring up at us, and when he saw me look his way, his wee stick of an arm waved. I waved back and he gave a great smile, turned and walked the few doors down to where Hoskins' sluttish servant girl lover was making a great play of cleaning the letterbox. I watched her as she watched me, each of us polishing hard, and she only stopped when none other than Hoskins himself came up the steps to her and gave her a hug and a doggish kiss on her mouth. I nudged Hamish with my toe.

"Look'ee who's come calling across the way."

Hamish gave a low curse and moved away from the window.

"He's no good, that man," he said. "I saw him outside Kings College a few days ago with Black and a great hamper. The two are in cahoots but they'll have to be careful. There's a bigger man than either of them, Bishop his name is, who regularly supplies Kings, and I hear he's expanding his business over this way. It wouldn't do to step on his toes."

"The Master has never forgiven that pair for stealing away with Mister Jakes," I reminded him. "Remember all the trouble we had next day sorting things out. All the upset he caused. And the poor ol' widow lady....I wonder how Mistress Jakes is now...?" None of us were like to forget that night, nor how the Master had sworn to have naught to do with either of the rogues again.

"No surprise with such men," said Hamish. "They're all the same, steal bodies and sell then to whoever will pay the most, no matter who'd prior rights to them."

"You talk of the poor souls as chattels. I canna' get used to that. Are you cutting up anyone tomorrow?"

"We were supposed to have a lecture on anaesthesia and no more dissections til the weather cools. But the Master must change his plans. His visiting doctor is delayed, it seems. Just as well I've arranged a delivery in the morning, same man as brought the last lassie. At least he was reliable."

"Who...?" I wasna' sure I wanted to know, but asked anyway.

"He's a felon, nobody to feel pity for. He's due to hang for murder no less; drops at eight then, if my man is first to the hatch, the cadaver will be with us before nine."

I shuddered.

"And if he's no' first to the hatch?"

"I gave him a florin for the hangman, so he'd better be."

I stared in disbelief, as Hamish grinned and turned to gather up knives and saws and laid them out in neat rows. But the man was a murderer I told mysel'. He deserved no pity. Even so.... My eye cast over the knives laid out. When there were sure to be no more dissections due then mebbe I could borrow one and use it on Hare.

Down below the sound of a carriage door closing broke into my thoughts, and I saw a hand wave from the window. The coachman gave jest a flick of his whip and the sleek black horse stepped out.

"Mister Wakley is at the House tomorrow," I told Hamish. Then deciding to share my news I told the lads what I'd found out earlier. "He's at a special meeting there and Charlie and Mister Brushwood will be with him and safe, so long as Mister Wakley and Lord Leverbridge protect them."

"Wakley? Lord Leverbridge? Well..." Hamish was impressed and Ewan, who'd been mighty quiet for the last half hour, whistled.

"So, I thought he was a fly one, Wakley. He'll have to watch out for the police on the way there and back if he has Charlie with him."

"You mean they might go there together?" I hadna' really thought about how they would travel there. If they were all staying at Mister Wakley's house, mebbe they would use separate coaches. "We'd best not say a word more," I said and hushed them both with my finger against my lips.

The felon's body came next morning on a cart, covered in a grey sheet and laid upon a board. He was a strange one, the delivery man, looking like a country farmhand in his smock and straw hat. He didna' make much conversation with the lads when they helped him down with his load and no' even a curse getting it into the lift. The Master wouldna' allow that contraption to be used for aught else, no matter how heavy a pile of laundry I might have to carry upstairs. I folded the last of the clean sheets and left the pile to take up later and put away.

The house was quiet while the menfolk were busy with their work, and I worried mysel' thinking on what was happening to Charlie and the revolutionaries. Was he safe at the Houses of Parliament yet awhile? I would have talked with Carlo, but he was busy making some fancy mess of egg whites and sugar – no' big enough for the household so it must ha' been to impress his sweetheart.

I took mysel' out for some air and to work off my anxiety and my feet took me to Bedford Square. I saw a carriage outside the house of Mister Wakley. So, they hadna' gone yet. My heart beat faster. I hovered, on the far side of the Square, in the shadow of a big spiky shrub, and watched, jest needing to see that Charlie was with them and well. Through the new railings jest recently put up around the open green space, I saw Hoskins and Black drive up in a covered wagon and stop some distance from the carriage. Young Aldo was with them, up on the driving seat. What were they about?

The door of Wakley's house opened at last, and a group of half a dozen folk trooped out and headed for the carriage. As they did so I heard a shout go up. Young Aldo had jumped down and was running towards them, with Hoskins giving chase. Black stood on the cart cursing loudly. All was commotion for a minute and I could see naught of the crowd for the carriage blocked my view. Wakley's party must ha' boarded safely, for the carriage took off at a great lick with nobody left on the pavement. Hoskins had reached Aldo by now, and was shouting and cuffing him. I was too slow, for had I hurried from my stupor I'd have got to him and put a stop to the bullying. I cursed mysel' as I saw Hoskins bundle the lad into the cart, thrashing at him with a cane as he did so, and then drove off, away from the Square in the same direction as Mister Wakley's carriage.

17

I MEET A CORPSE AND SEE CHARLIE SAFE

"So I saw Charlie away and Mister Brushwood with him," I stirred my tea and took a piece of rich fruit cake. Verity put the plate down and shook her head.

"Oh, Janet, I can't believe the young Master would get into such mischief. What can 'e be thinking of? 'Is Reverend is beside 'imself. We 'ad the police 'ere agin last night. Questions, questions, 'alf the evening. Madam went to bed with a megrim and even then they didn't stop. Agh," she growled. "They want to go and find some real villains, not chase after innocent young boys as don't know what they're doing!"

"Oh, I think Charlie knows what he's about," I said. "He's brave enough to want to change the world and it needs a deal o' changin'. We should be proud of him, Verity." I don't know why I was so sure, but he seemed such a sensible lad and the sight of him with Mister Wakley and Lord Leverbridge in Bedford Square, looking every inch a gent well, I jest knew he was going to do great things.

Verity was giving me a strange look and I stopped my tea cup half way to my lips and set it down again.

"Anyway, they should be in their important meeting now. So, Charlie will be safe, and Miss Esther is safe with her Ladyship, Lady Eversholt, and we have a fine afternoon. The only thing to spoil it is thinking about young Aldo...."

"You say your ol' manservant, 'Oskins, was laying into 'im?"

"Aye. The man's a monster. The way he was beating the laddie, well, he must ha' done something real bad to have riled him so. I canna' think why they were in the Square jest then either, except mebbe to attack Charlie or Mister Wakley, and why would they do such a thing? And why had the laddie hitched up with him and Black? Mebbe he'd been promised some work, for I canna think Hoskins would give him any charity. But he's a bit wee for body snatching."

"'E's not been 'ere, not for more than a week. I give 'im bits o' work, cleaning shoes and sweeping the yard and the like. I've 'ad to spend 'alf my mornings skivvying since he's not bin comin', like I 'aven't got enough to do. Still, I don't like to think of 'im being knocked about, even if 'e is a lazy little beggar."

But I knew Verity wasna' so much angry as fearful for him, and sweeping the yard hadna' been taking much of her time for I could see Samuel through the window hard at work with a broom. She was a kind hearted soul and if she wasna' worrying for her charges upstairs she was frettin' over a street boy. I squeezed her hand. I was hoping to see the laddie soon and ask him about his trip to Bethnal Green and whether he had heard of Mister Hare or met him.

"He'll be back, don't worry. Lads like Aldo know how to take care of themselves." I hoped I was right and was pleased to see a shadow of a smile cross her face.

I stayed with her for another half an hour. We talked of nothing more important than the paper arrived that week for the Reverend's wife, full of drawings of clothes and bonnets, shoes and reticules, all the way from Paris.

"And her a parson's wife too!" I shook my head disapproving that she should have such fancies and wondered at the price of some of the things drawn there. I turned over a page and pointed to a hat. "Five shillun'! Why look at that! Nothing but a few feathers and a bit o' silk." It did look beautiful though, with the pale swirl of the feathers against the darker blue..... "It would go with this dress o' mine don't ye think?"

Verity and I laughed at the idea of course, but my mouth watered at having a bonnet like that and the chance to wear it. We couldna' agree on a silver grey dress, and the wee bag to carry with it.

"What would ye carry in such a tiny thing?" she asked. "It'd not hold anything bigger than a shillun' and costs four. And look at the neckline on the dress; it's a year out of date being that low."

There was a tiny frill of lace above the scooping neckline, and I saw mysel' wearing it, instead of the pencilled girl in the picture. In my mind's eye, I was climbing the steps of the Institute, and Charlie was coming towards me with Mister Wakley and Miss Astley

Cooper. She nearly tripped when she saw me, her mouth open in surprise and there was envy all over her face. She had a nice enough gown, but she couldna' take her eyes off me in mine for all that. I tossed my head and felt the light movement of the feathers, and gripped the wee little bag in my hand. Her eyes lowered to the pair of dainty blue pumps on my feet at a guinea the pair. I gave a curtsey and there was Hamish, stepping down past the others, his face all smiles and his hands bloody..... I came back to the kitchen with a start.

"She don't buy these papers for 'erself," said Verity, her voice cutting through my dreams. "She likes to know Miss Esther is up with the times though, so she can get 'er a good match. She's set 'er eye on every unmarried gen'leman this side of the River and is marking 'em off one by one." She laughed then and said, "Make sure you keep your 'Amish close by or she'll be looking for a young doctor for 'er!"

I laughed too, but felt my heart miss a beat. I realized I'd been thinking more of Charlie these past few days than of my Hamish who was safe at home with his books and his bones. I told mysel' it was because Charlie was in danger and had need of me. With a sigh, I looked upon the bonnet once more then folded the paper and gave it back to Verity.

"I must to be getting back home, Verity. I'm sure Esther won't have any trouble finding a nice young man, and my Hamish will not be the one for her. He has far too much to do setting himself up as a doctor, and he needs first to pass his examinations before a board." I gave her a peck on the cheek and made my departure, all thoughts of fine dresses and feather hats banished from my mind.

Doctor Knox was jest closing his study door when I came up from the kitchen, and I saw Hamish heading off up the stairs to his books. He didna' notice me.

I thought to check upstairs for my bucket. I must ha' left it in the Anatomy room after cleaning the windows, though what it might have been used for since then I dreaded to think. I determined to keep my eyes away from any occupants as I pushed open the door and moved towards the windows. It was still bright, the glass gleaming for the most part and only a few streaks not easy to see when I was cleaning it.

I picked up my bucket and turned to leave. I don't know why I looked. It was the same as the way we pick at a scab, mebbe, or wiggle a loose tooth. I *had* to glance at the table and the hump that lay there under a greying sheet. Naught was showing but a foot, and I tweaked the cloth to see if its partner was there too. It was, and thin legs gave way to flaccid thighs, young but not well fed this one. He was covered with a rag over his manhood, and his belly was flat. The sheet slipped to the ground and my eyes fell on the face.

I screamed then, for all he was not a man I knew or had any feelings for. But the rope had cut deep into his neck and the eyes were bulging near to bursting, the tongue hanging long and slack from his mouth. The face was rigid with the fear he must ha' felt as the trapdoor fell open under him and the rope pulled tight around his throat. I screamed for him, and for the shock of seeing him frozen in his last minute of life. A fleeting vision of Charlie being there turned into one of mysel', a murderess, hanged and lifeless. My soul in Hell's fire, my body sold to be cut.

Hamish was the first into the room to grab me and pull me out. His face was angry and he shook me. I gasped for breath.

"Oh, Hamish. Do all folk look this way at the end, when the hangman leaves them swinging? What if it were Charlie? Oh God, Hamish, he must get away safe. He must!"

He let me go then, dropping my arms as fast as he'd taken them. His face lost its anger and in its place there was blankness, a distant coldness. He went back to his books and I followed him out, and went down to the kitchen, parting without a word.

The felon's remains were dispatched to the common grave later that afternoon once he'd served the class, his lungs having been cut and studied, for the Master was at least no' so hard-hearted as to throw them to the street dogs. I approached Hamish slow, not sure how to be with him. He turned his head at my footstep and gave me a wee smile. Could he have any real doubts about his place in my heart?

"Ah, Janey." He fiddled about with some small thing on his desk, and when he looked at me proper, his eyes were sad. "A good heart and lungs this morning, but the liver was rotten. I'm afraid I upset the Master for pointing out that there was evidence of what too much wine or spirits can do to that organ."

I shared a small laugh with him then, for the Master was a great one for his bottle.

"I've no worry for him," I said. "The Master seems to know what he's about. Ye canna' smell the drink on him like with some folk."

"Aye." Hamish paused. "He'll be fine too, yon Charlie. Don't ye fret. Wakley will have him out of the country by nightfall if there's any danger to him still. I heard him talking to the Master about sailings from Ramsgate and Dover, though I don't know which they'd use."

I'd no' thought of his having to flee the country and my heart gave a lurch.

"Will he be able to come home sometime?"

"Oh, aye. Sometime. Not for a while maybe. If he goes at all, that is. He may not..."

Hamish may have seen my feelings writ across my face, for he was quiet then and moved back to what he was doing. His papers were strewn across the desk and he started tidying them into piles. A few sheets fell to the floor and I bent to gather them. I gave them into his hand and our fingers touched.

"You'll excuse me, Janey. I've to work now. I'm to take the first of my final examinations in a few days, and must put in some extra study I fear."

"Well! You'll be a real doctor then, after these examinations?" I tried to sound excited and wondered why it came out flat. I *was* excited for him and knew he would do well in any test he was given. "If I can be a help to ye in any way, Hamish, by asking ye things or acting the part of a patient, well," and here I touched his arm gently, "I'm jest here. Remember."

He stood and gave me a wee hug then, and I went about my chores with a lighter spirit. There was no' a sign of him then 'til the middle of the evenin' when he was called to the Master's study and came out with a pile more books. He shrugged and turned his eyes to the Heavens, and I gave him a wink.

"No' an early night for ye tonight, Hamish?"

But before he could mount another step or answer there was the clatter of a carriage arriving with a gen'leman to see the Doctor He'd a poorly wife with a screeching voice and a fit of the vapours, and Hamish took them in to practice his kind words with her while I sought out the Master.

After the patient had gone, the doctor was in a bad mood, muttering about screeching hysterical females. He took the bottle of brandy from me, put an empty one aside and settled back in his chair.

"Janet. Yon man earlier, he was hanged for the greatest felony and he has no business looking anything other than afeared to meet his end." He must ha' heard me then, talking with Hamish. His voice was a wee bit slurred, but he was far from drunk. "Let it be a lesson to ye. If you kill or commit sufficient crime to warrant hanging, ye hang. And if ye hang ye end up on the table there to be cut and buried in a common grave if you're lucky. 'Tis not a pretty ending."

I fled upstairs then, and sat for a long while on my bed in the growing darkness, fretting over the cruelty of the world, and over Charlie and my tangled thoughts for him and for Hamish. I sighed for the look on Hamish's face when he came to my aid and found me where I'd no business to be, and for wondering myself why I was there at all. I cried then for Mary, yet to be avenged, for my weakness and the fear I couldna' carry out my promise to her, and I cried for my guilt at that. Then I curled up on the bed and watched the stars come out through my attic window.

I may have slept a little, but I think not long. The house was abed and I was more composed now, and lay listening to my heart beat gently. The world was dark and silent but for a dog barking somewhere not far away. I rose and lit the tallow candle in its holder by the bed, and by the light of it and the moon I picked up my mother's book from where it was hidden in my trunk. I'd not read much of it since it had been returned to me, being busy and knowing I had it safe, and now my eye lit upon a chapter entitled "*Some instances of the folly which the ignorance of women generates.*" I sighed. I knew I was ignorant and yearned for learning, but no' sure what knowledge I wanted. From what I knew already of the world it is a cruel place, but I was sure there's better to be had. I wanted to be a lady, and learning might get me least part way there. Yet would I throw it all away and swing for killing Hare? Would I ever find him? And if I did, was there some way of getting my revenge without getting mysel' hanged? He might be here somewhere in London, but it's a vast great city. Hoping for Hoskins or Black to tell me if they knew him and where he was living was no' likely. And which of them killed O'Rourke? I read a little, found my eyes grow heavy, and lay down once more. I held the book to my chest and wondered what kind of man my grandfather had been, and why he'd given this book to my ma before he died. I tried to remember what I'd heard of him, and of my mother, and realised I knew very little save he loved her and had writ as much inside the cover of the book. I fell asleep at last and as I sank my mind travelled off to distant child-hood memories. I kept the book hugged to me, that in the night it might pass some of its wisdom straightway to my heart.

When the Master returned from the university at dinner time, I was sleepy but composed after my disturbed night and served his rabbit stew with a steady hand. The pinkish white meat fell from the bones as it landed on his plate and he set about eating it with his usual great energy. Hamish was quiet and both he and Ewan looked tired, one from reading half the night, the other from being out late at the College Arms. I'd no' seen much of Hamish all morning and there was still a cool distance between us and our eyes didna' meet but briefly.

"Have you finished with the book on diseases of the mouth and tongue, Hamish?" The Master asked. "I've a feeling there might be a question on the subject at yon first examination."

"Aye Sir. Can I ask what makes you think that?"

"Well, the questions are set by a panel of worthies at Kings College, as you know. I happen to have met with some of 'em just yesterday. I'm told the Honourable Sir Astley Cooper, spared for the moment from ministering to His Majesty the fourth English George, is in a raging pain and canna' touch his food. He reckons he has a disease of the nerves, a neuralgia, rather than a toothache. If that's so, you can expect a question on the subject next week." Then, looking a wee bit troubled that he'd said more than he should, he quickly added, "though I could be completely wrong and he'll ask about a bowel complaint instead. He believes himself a great expert on bowels."

I felt myself colour and turned sharp, slopping some of the stew on my apron as I moved away to the sideboard. There was a tray with Carlo's latest dainty tartlets, and I carefully rearranged them on the plate and licked my fingers.

"Janet, if you're not busy there, will ye be so good as to bring me the blue bound book from off my desk." The Master's voice made me jump. "There's a list of complaints you might find useful to study – both of you lads. It was compiled by a country doctor from his notebooks. The most presented cases in his lifetime, or some such."

I hurried away to fetch the book, hoping it might be of help to Hamish and not make him fret even more with how much he'd to learn. He would make a fine doctor, and the professors on the board would see that, but I'd a feeling he didna' quite believe it himsel'.

On the desk in the Master's study was no' a few books so much as a great pile, tumbled over each other in a mighty mess. I started to gather them up, all the while looking for blue ones. There were two. One had a title in Latin and was full of bright coloured pictures of feet and hands. The other was plain and dull, and was probably the one the Master was after. As I made my choice, I couldn't help but notice a note lying on the blotter, only two lines long and signed by Mister Wakley. I turned it round so I could read it.

"Knox, a Happy outcome! Take tea with us tomorrow before my guests depart and we will talk further."

I was much relieved. So, the Master would be going to take tea with Mister Wakley and Charlie and Mister Brushwood would be there, surely, full of their success with the Committee. But wait! Was "tomorrow" this day or tomorrow? I knew not when the note had been delivered for I'd no' taken it in mysel'. I was burning with the question when I carried the blue book to the dining room. Despite waiting patiently at his elbow, it seemed I was no' needed for anything else and the Master shooed me away. The menfolk were chattering so much, I couldna' interrupt to ask whether the Master was going out later, so I left them to their talk and carried the tray of dishes to the kitchen.

Looking out of the kitchen window the rain was falling steadily and the sky was grey. He'd be wantin' his umberella if he was going out this afternoon and mebbe he'd need someone to carry it for him, if he had bags or anything to take? But no, I was being too hopeful for he'd no' want me to go along with him. Most likely Mister Wakley would send his carriage. I wanted to go, for a last word with Charlie, and racked my brains for a reason he'd ask me. Carlo prodded me gently in the back.

"Is the big dish finish? The chicken he waits to cook now. If you would dry please?"

I dried the dish and he took it, muttering something in that foreign tongue, and I put away the rest of the crocks. By the time I'd finished my chores it was near time for the Master to leave if he was going, and I went up to the hallway to be ready on hand should he call.

"Janey come, a moment please. Would you sit and let us listen to your heart and measure the beats?" Hamish pulled me into the consulting room and sat me down, before I'd the chance to say no. Ewan had the Master's stethoscope tube in his hand and Hamish pushed me back in the chair when I started to resist.

"Be still, aye, that's right." One end of the wooden tube he held against my chest, looking at the far wall so as not to embarrass me, the other end he listened to. I felt my heart racing and held my breath.

"Breathe out. Aye. And in. Good. You have a strong and powerful heart there Janey." Hamish looked about to say something more.

"Janet!" Ah, the Master, at last. "Where are you girl?"

"In here, Sir.

The Master came in and shooed the lads off me.

"Go on, you two can practice your skills on each other. Leave the lassie alone. Run ahead to Wakley's girl, and tell him I'll be along in a wee while. I've a few things to finish off here which will delay me a short time, and then I will join him."

I ran all the way to Bedford Square, my heart full of joy. He didna' know how much I wanted this errand, but I quietly blessed the grizzly ol' physic jest the same.

"Right Miss, I'll let 'im know." The butler started to close the door. No, this wasna' right! I bravely put my hand out to hold the door open and cleared my throat.

"I need to speak to Mister Wakley mysel' if ye don't mind. 'Tis a private message."

He didna' like it any, but the butler recognized me and must ha' remembered that his Master had shown some kindness towards me before, so he let me in. As he showed me into the drawing room, I passed him with a short nod.

Charlie and Mister Brushwood were both there, sitting far back from the light of the window, while a serious looking man I didna' know sat on the padded windowseat. Mister Wakley stood with his back to the fireplace. They all turned to look towards the door at its' opening, and I bobbed a curtsey to the room.

"Afternoon, m'dear. You have a message from Doctor Knox?" Wakley stepped forward, and I pulled mysel' together.

"Aye, Sir. He sends his apologies. He'll be a wee bit late. No more than an hour, mind. I'm to let ye know."

"Thank'ee. We'll save him some fancies." Wakley

smiled. I stood there. He raised an eyebrow and tilted his head, like he does. I gave a little cough and rubbed my hands together.

"Eh, I jest thought to say, eh.....Well, I hope it all went well with the Committee, Sir?" I turned my attention to Charlie then, and he smiled back and nodded. Mister Brushwood made a humphing noise in his throat. The other man stared, silent. Mister Wakley answered.

"Oh, yes. Admirable. Mister Brushwood here gave a stirring speech and will do so again this evening, will ye not Sir, to the good members of the Mechanics Institute?"

"Indeed, Sir." Brushwood gave a little bow to Wakley and then frowned at me. "Not that I'd have been able to leave London with the damned rabble outside the other day. They've been protests left, right and centre til they saw me and started cheering me as we stepped outside. Good thing the Home Secretary is a reasonable man on a good day else he'd have clapped me in irons."

He'd been talking to Wakley rather than to me, and seemed startled when I spoke.

"So they don't think you killed him then?" I heard mysel' ask the question but I don't recall meaning to.

"What? Killed who?" He was startled and more so when Wakley laughed.

"She has in mind you two killed one of Knox's students, or at least the police are under that illusion. Still, a word with the Chief Constable and all is well. It was no doubt some street fight or a footpad got him."

"You mean they are safe and free now?" I was so

happy, so relieved. I ran over to where Charlie sat, in a great stuffed chair, and hugged him to me. He flushed with surprise and looked over at Brushwood. The ol' soldier lost his shock and gave a hint of a smile.

"Well, well. I do believe the only danger we have is from over exuberance." Mister Brushwood was looking at me then with a serious face. "The Cause is not a welcome one with government and we must tread carefully. Mister Chagford here is safe enough if he keeps out of sight for a while. It would be no good to be arrested for any breach of the peace, such as last week's activities. No a trip away is just what's called for; as you suggested Wakley." He paused for a moment then directed his stare to me again. "What is your name girl?"

"Janet Brown, Sir."

"Brown.... hmm. The less you say of our being here today the better. In fact, I think it'd be wise if you forgot all about us, and all about the Cause we fight for. Nothing good would come of making it widely known at this point. The lives of us all could be made somewhat uncomfortable if some in government took too much interest." He squinted at me. "I'm damned if you don't look familiar to me..... Where would we have met Miss Brown?"

"I don't believe I ever saw ye before this week, Sir." I stared hard at him and shook my head. He'd no' been in Edinburgh as far as I could recall. He scratched his chin and shrugged, turning his attention to a slice of cake and crumbling it on his plate.

All this time Charlie sat, quiet and sombre, watching

the others in the room. I placed my hand on his arm, looking hard into his face.

"If ye are going away, Charlie, stay safe, please."

He flushed a little, brushed a crumb from his trouser leg and seemed about to say something. He changed his mind and lowered his eyes from mine. A knock on the front door roused us all, and a moment later we heard the voice of Doctor Knox in the hallway. He came into the room and strode up to Wakley.

"Well done, Wakley," he said. "You had a good hearing in the Committee? Well, now we can divert our efforts into something more important – saving your feelings, gentlemen – there's the Anatomy Bill to be discussed this very week and the government wanting to close down all our Anatomy Schools. I'd like your support Wakley against this damned bill. You can give me that, can't you?"

"My dear Knox, of course I understand your view of the affair. Trouble is, people are worried about being snatched off the street, or dragged out of their graves to supply you and your kind, and a safer measure might well be to use those unfortunates from the workhouse. I think it's appalling myself, and support you entirely, of course I do...."

The Master was looking at me now, though I tried to disappear behind a tall plant stand next to Charlie's chair.

"Why don't ye away back home, Janet? Ye have things to do don't ye?"

"Aye, Sir." I bobbed a curtsey to them all, and out of sight I felt Charlie give my hand a squeeze. I smiled at him but already he was turning away, and I dropped my eyes to the carpet and hurried from the room.

Rather than making my way home, as I knew I should, I made my way to the Vicarage and the comfort of Verity's kitchen, where I knew we could share a pot of tea and rejoice at Charlie's safety.

18

MUCH STUDY AND QUESTIONING

Hamish moved to gather up the book before him, but I gently took it from him and replaced it with my platter of bread and cheese.

"You need some food inside ye, laddie. Once that's gone down you'll feel much better."

"Aye, you are no doubt right, Janey." He stretched his arms above his head and I heard his bones crack. I winced and turned to place Ewan's food by his sleeping form.

"Thank'ee, lass," Hamish said. "What would I do without you?"

I flushed a little and rather than leave and return to my duties downstairs, I lingered. While he ate I watched him, with his fine form and that serious face, and while I did so I glanced through the book, careful with turning the pages lest I cause them to break. There were beautiful pictures, plants so like the real thing I could near smell and feel them. Lavender and marigold, peppermint, rosemary and sage. The names were writ below each plant, in Latin and in common English, which was as well because I knew almost nothing of such things. There'd been nowhere to grow flowers in West Port and no doctors there to use them. I screwed up my eyes to read the small writing describing the merits of each plant.

"This looks more a store cupboard for Carlo than for a physic," I said. "I know there are many plants for healing but nothing of what they can do. Must you learn all of these?"

"Where should I start? Here, ask me about one of them. A test. Choose a plant and I will try to answer, just as if I was in the examination."

I perched on the edge of the table, proud to be asked to help Hamish in this way, and chose the marigold. "'Tis a bonny looking plant and I'd like to know why the Master grows it. I've seen it in the yard here."

"Ah, it has many uses, but the doctor likes it for its antisepsis properties, for the skin. 'Tis good for spotty youth, or it can be mixed with sage and er, raspberry leaves and other things, to assist women when they er, in their middle years they er, when they flush and burn and," his own face was doing likewise and I laughed. He had a fine face. "What other plants have ye there?" he asked.

"What are the uses for this, lemon balm?"

"To soothe and calm. To promote a refreshing sleep."

"Hmm, mebbe we should grow lemons..."

"In London! I think we would have to join Charlie in the sun of Italy...." He flushed again and I lowered my eyes.

"I feel naught for Charlie," I said, to fill the quiet that had grown between us. "You know that laddie. Other than as a friend, like Ewan here." I glanced at the snoring heap leaning on the other end of the table. "I worry when aught happens to the folk I care for. But my strongest feelings are for you, laddie. Ye know that, don't ye?"

At that moment there was a loud snore and Ewan twitched and grunted. My eyes met Hamish's and we both smiled.

"Aye, well...that's kind of ye...." said Hamish.

"Kind! Oh ye daft lummock! I do love ye, in a way. We're different, I mean, our station in life, at birth, I mean...." I stumbled over my words. He was staring at me. I didna' mean to flummox the lad, but he must ha' known how I felt! His closeness with me had grown so, especially since Vauxhall.

"Shh, Janey." He put a finger to his lips. "Don't wake Ewan. I feel so much more for you." He rose from his chair, stepped forward and took the book from my clenched hands. He put an arm round me. Drawing me to his lips he kissed me and I felt his warm breath. I moved in his arms, my heart beating violent in my chest.

"I don't doubt ye really. But it will no' do, laddie. What would happen in the future? When ye finish with ye examinations and are a real doctor, I mean. Will ye want to stay here with the Master, and me, or will ye be looking to move away? To marry mebbe? The Master will advise ye to. A fine lady like yon Mistress Cooper might suit ye?"

"What! Astley Cooper's daughter? God, no! Wakley is welcome to her! And she'd no' look at the likes of me. No, I am in no hurry to marry, but when I do, it'll be to a helpmate, not some beauty in a silk dress with no' a grain of sense." He kissed me again, lightly and then opened his book. "There's no need to rush things, at least not til I'm established and able to support a wife properly. Now, where were we?"

So, that was it? He passed me the book, expecting another question, and I quickly turned a few pages.

"What can ye do with nettles?" I asked. He loved me, but that his mind could turn so quickly from the subject in hand to his plants, told me of his youth and he was no really ready for marriage.

"They are a great restorative," he said. He carried on, listing the benefits of nettles and I studied him. He was a sensible lad, thinking of his examinations and I had no business to distract him. I loved him dearly, but I had no thoughts I'd make a doctor's wife, or any wife. I had too many things to do yet awhile, with a situation to improve upon and a murderer to find.

"You're not listening," Hamish broke into my thoughts. "Am I right?"

"Oh, aye, of course," I said. Our eyes met. "What would ye do with that other plant, the foxglove ye were looking at when ye fell asleep over your book?"

"That's a more powerful thing," he said. "A careful

hand is needed when measuring out a dose of digitalis. A little will calm the heart, but too much will kill a man. We grow it but the Master is skilled enough to ken what he's doing. Ye can fool about with nettles if ye will, and make some broth maybe to keep away the winter chills, but don't touch the foxgloves, Janey."

I nodded, wondering if the foxgloves be easier than a knife to kill Hare when we should meet.

———

Early next afternoon I was darning a sock of the Master's when a hammering on the front door disturbed me and I pricked my finger. Sucking on it, and cursing under my breath, I ran upstairs and opened the door to a thin young man with a large nose and pointed ears. He gave a few small bows, like a boat bobbing on the river, while he said his name.

"William Fossett, and apologies for being a day late."

"I'll let the Master know you are here." I showed him into the consulting room and hurried to find Doctor Knox. I'd no' been told we were expecting a Fossett.

"What? Oh, aye! The Master hurried from his study and I left him pumping the man's arm up and down and fussing around him, and went to make tea. When I took the tray into the room a few minutes later they were at the desk with a collection of glass jars, tubes and a funnel and the Fossett man had a handful of papers. I left them to their work, fearing a lot of washing up would be coming to me, but at least no blood was being spilt in there yet.

I didna' hear any more from them for an hour or more and by then Hamish was home from his examination and seemed happy enough. He and Ewan were away out again in minutes, before I'd a chance to ask how the morning had gone, and when the Master called for them I braced mysel' for one of his rages.

"Out? They just came home didn't they? I heard them on the stairs."

"Aye Sir, but they've been working hard on their studies and I think Hamish wanted to tell Ewan about the examination, to let him know what he'll be facing himsel' next year. I doubt they'll be away long."

"Hmm, not 'til the beer runs out at the College Arms, I think. But should they return before supper, tell Hamish we have a visitor who could help with his next examination, on Friday – and it wouldn't do any harm for Ewan to learn about this as well. That should hold their attention. Master Fossett will be eating with us, and will be staying tonight. Thank you, Janet."

I went downstairs to tell Carlo, and left him counting chops into a pan when I hurried upstairs to make ready the only spare bed we had in the house fit for a gentleman. The Master's bedroom had a smaller room off it, a mess of clothes and cravats, and under it all a narrow bed. I cleared off the pile and hung what I could of the clothes, folding the rest into the trunk in the main bedroom. I own I should ha' been better at tidying up for him. I spread sheets on the bed, plumped up a pillow and found a blanket with no' too much of the moth about it. Master Fossett didna' look like he was too fussy about such things. I'd noted his well-worn coat. We'd do.

I turned down the edge of the sheet so he'd get in easy, and laid a towel next to the basin on the side table. I'd bring up warm water when it was needed.

The lads were home in time for supper, and not so drunk to raise the Master's temper. I was relieved they were all chattering away happy enough all through the meal, though why they always had to talk about boils and warts or some such over dinner I don't know. There was some talk of plants and poultices and I was pleased when Hamish named several we'd discussed the day before. Our visitor was drinking port with the Master for the last part of the meal. The lads stuck to their ale. I took away the plates and stacked them on the dresser, then put out fresh crocks for the final course. I was getting used to this idea of different dishes for every-thing now, something the Master insisted on when he had folk to stay for meals, and Hamish gave me a wink as I passed him to take up my place by the Master's chair again, ready should I be needed.

"Try some of this cheese, Fossett?" The Master cut himself a hefty wedge and Fossett nodded and took a piece as large. Whoever he was he had a good appetite for a skinny fellah. I moved the dish down the table after he'd helped himself, and let the lads have a bit. Carlo came in behind me carrying a tray of cut fruit to the table. Slices of pear and apple he'd been stewing in cider that afternoon, and a tart made with rhubarb. I hoped there'd be some left for us afterwards.

"Now lads," the Master belched into his napkin and took a swig from his glass. Fossett refilled it for him and topped up his own. "Master Fossett here has made a study of anaesthesia, and he has brought some of his equipment along to demonstrate. I know it isn't something approved of by the whole medical establishment, but we feel there's a growing argument for reducing pain if at all possible when operating on delicate patients."

I closed my eyes and took a deep breath. No, I'm sure the patients were happy to be cut up alive!

"Ah, we've heard, Sir, of the properties of nitrous oxide, though the effects are not long lasting." Hamish earned a nod from the Master for his comment, and my heart filled with pride. Fossett was speaking then, and my opinion of him grew as I listened, all the while carefully spooning fruit into a bowl for the Master.

"Indeed. But there are some operations lasting several minutes as you know gentlemen. Rather than rushing them and failing, and far better than being distracted by any distress in our patients, I prefer to render them still and as silent as possible. There is the method you suggest, called 'laughing gas' for the effects it has, but I prefer to use a formula of a different kind. It has been much lauded by Matthew Turner. You may recall his paper of 1788, 'An account of the extraordinary medicinal fluid, called aether.'

"Aye, Sir." Ewan produced a notebook from his pocket and quickly turned the pages. "Was he not successful in setting a dislocated shoulder with never a murmur from his patient? Yes, here it is, eh, Master Jerome. He practised for a long time on dogs first."

"Indeed. Dogs and horses, birds and any other crea-

ture that came to hand. He has a vast collection of spec-
imens, though none of course to rival that of Doctor
Hunter. I believe he operated on his wife too – though
the poor woman died in the end."

I spilt a little of the juice as I put the bowl down in
front of the Master, and he tutted and flapped me away.
I left them then, worried about a doctor who cut up his
wife. I took the dirty crocks down to the kitchen and a
few minutes later heard them all heading for the
consulting room.

"How would you like to be operated on without
anything to dull the pain, Carlo?" I asked, through a
mouthful of rhubarb tart.

"Ha, I would not let them near me. Mad men with
knives and not any idea of what they do – I see them
with small boy in Gracechurch Street, I know!"

"What did you see, Carlo?"

"Small boy, he is run down with cart. His leg is
under wheel and doctor comes from hospital. Poor boy!
His mother she is scream and crowd comes too. Doctor
he cut off leg and boy is awake and crying, and mother
is crying and crowd is crying and ten minutes doctor is
sewing and stops only when man tells him boy is died.
He is angry, this doctor, and say he would not waste his
time if boy is dead and why did the mother not tell him?
He wanted to be paid but the crowd, they want to hang
doctor from lamp post and policeman he take him away
to keep safe."

"When was this Carlo? You didn't say before."

"No, I remember well this thing. When I first come

to London, three, no four, years ago. I remember Doctor He was crazy man. I think if cart was move the boy would be free and he might have walk away. I not have good English then, or I would tell them. I think he, doctor, want to cut boy just to show what sharp knife he has." He lifted his own knife then, a massive cleaver like thing, and sliced clean through the head of a pig he'd been saving for the doctor's special dinner next night with some important folk from the university. "I know sharp knife and his was no sharp enough!"

I'd never heard Carlo talk so much and with such passion, and realised the cider he'd poached the fruit in had all gone from the pan. I hoped whoever the doctor was who had upset him so didna' come to dinner at Huntley Street.

Later that evening, Hamish was buried once again amongst his books and I took myself out to have a breath of air. I picked some of the nettles by the house, thinking to make some soup, then cursed for the pain of it. I shook my hand, then hugged it under my armpit and, wondering if there was too much smell of dog around the nettle patch to make it wholesome anyway. I was about to return indoors when I caught sight of the wee laddie, Aldo, across the road with Hoskins' woman and they were deep in talk.

I watched them enter the house by the servant's stairs, and I wondered again where he was sleeping at night. Surely they wouldna' allow him to stay there? As far as I knew, the folk whose house it was, weren't the friendliest sort, and they'd no' be likely to let a stranger off the streets into their home. Ah, I was right. He came out again a few minutes later and crossed the road not far from our house.

"Hello, Aldo!" He came to a halt, his head up like a startled pony then, once he'd recognized me in the fading light, he was easier. "Are ye alright, laddie? I've nay seen ye lately and I know Verity was asking after ye."

"I'm alright," he said, but he had a wary look and kept his eyes down on the pavement. "I've got to go, it's late and I got things to do."

"For Mister Hoskins is it? Or Mister Black?" He didna' answer. "Where are ye staying, laddie? Have ye a bed for the night?"

"I got a grand bed, and all me own too." His face was proud as a peacock and I had to smile.

"Are ye staying with Mister Hoskins? Or are ye bedding down in Bethnal Green? Did ye enjoy ye wee outing the other day?"

"I ain't allowed to say nuffink 'bout that." I don't know why I cared so much, except that Hoskins wouldna' give a lad a bed for doing nowt.

"If ye have any fears, if ye're in danger lad, you run to me or to Verity, ye hear?"

He looked at me like I was crazed and then, taking a grubby yellow kerchief from his pocket, he flapped it open like a gent, and dabbed his nose. There was a dark stain on the edge and a long tear mended with ragged stitches.

"I's got a good life now Miss, so long as I do as 'e says. 'E give me a penny today to get meself a pie. I ain't in no danger."

I watched him walk away, limping still but now with a cockier air. My heart was pounding though as I turned back to the house, for the kerchief he was holding was one I'd washed often enough. And those stitches.... I remember thrusting the needle through with anger, stabbing the cloth rather than the owner, and that poor lad who'd angered me so much now lay dead and rotting in Bow Street even as I thought o' him.

"Don't be daft, Janey, " said Hamish. He frowned over some green weedy thing on his desk, its long thin roots hanging over the edge and covered in dirt. He shook it over the floor and then, with a small knife began cutting at it. I took a deep breath and stood my ground, looking at the mess but in no frame of mind to sweep again.

"But if Hoskins killed him, think laddie, 'twould explain Aldo having the kerchief. And the hamper I saw at the cottage that day, there was mebbe the laddie's body in there all along!"

"No, Janey, it would explain nothing. How do we know Aldo didn't steal the kerchief from O'Rourke or indeed, from Hoskins? He's a street urchin and...."

"And not a thief!" I had no reason to be so sure, but I

wasna' winning him over so stomped off and left Hamish to his work. I didna' dare interrupt the Master to tell him, not with the Fossett man still with him. I had no choice. I hurried to put on my bonnet and, taking my cloak from the back of the kitchen door, I left the house and ran to the Vicarage. Verity would hear me out, I was sure. And if there was murder done, the Vicar himself might hear me out!

19

MY SUSPICIONS ARE WELL FOUNDED

"Janet, 'amish is right, you've no call to think it's 'oskins; 'ave you?" Verity looked at me with her head cocked on one side, eyes narrowed but no' yet ready to disbelieve me.

"He's the sort of man wouldna' think twice about cutting someone's throat. And more, I swear there was a stain on the kerchief. Blood. It was blood!" I told her about the heavy hamper being carried out, and that I'd no seen O'Rourke again after his visit to Black's cottage.

Verity closed her eyes for a moment, shook her head, and took up her flatiron. She flicked water onto some dainty piece laid on a folded towel on the table and pressed down hard. There was a sizzling. The smoothness of the thing was grand to see after, but she folded it sharp and put it on a pile beside her. She put the iron back on its stand in the hearth and turned to me, looking firm like she'd stand no nonsense. My back stiffened.

"Now then, *if* what you say is true," she laid heavy

on the 'if', "what do ye think we're going to do about it?"

"I could challenge him; have him deny it!" then quickly added, "aye, dunna say it, and get my own throat cut....I know, 'twould be foolish....That's why I came here to you Verity. He would mebbe deny it or say it was Black."

Her eyes widened at my words, and with hands on hips she took a deep breath.

"Am I to fight 'em both then, hold 'em off you?" She was always so sensible. I looked down at my hands and cursed their weakness. "Look, ducks," she said in a softer voice, "best thing is we tell the police or," she waved me down when I made to interrupt her, "maybe the Reverend could 'elp. 'E's good at going an' praying over sinners an' fings. Maybe we could all go together and 'ave 'im out. Where does 'e live, 'oskins?"

I stared at her then, my head suddenly reeling. Where did he live? I flushed and felt my back lose its' stiffness. But I couldn't be defeated as easy as that!

"We can find out. Mebbe Hamish would know," though I thought that unlikely. "Or Aldo? I've seen 'em together...He won't tell me, but he might answer to you if you ask him."

"And where is Aldo I'd like to know." Verity picked up her pile of linen and moved it to the dresser, plonking it down and straightening her apron.

My heart sank even lower. "Aye, you're right. I've no idea how to find Hoskins. If Hamish knows he won't tell me for he thinks the same as you, that I'm acting foolish. Mebbe I am, but 'til I see Hoskins, or his lodgings I'll no' rest easy." I pulled my shawl around my shoulders and stood up. "I'll away home now and leave ye in peace." I was more than a wee bit hurt that even Verity had dismissed my worries so easy, and was much relieved when she put her arms around me and squeezed me.

"Never mind, we'll find 'im," she said. "If it's so important I'll 'elp ye. Mind, you're as daft as 'amish says, but best fing is to find out proper, ain't it? Meanwhile it'd be best to tell the police what ye saw in Bethnal Green, the O'Rourke lad visiting there."

I hugged her, and once she'd finished the last of her ironing and put it away, we set off together to Huntley Street hoping Hamish would be able to help, if he'd finished cutting up his greens.

"No, Janey, I've no idea where he lives." Hamish looked a wee cross to be asked. "I thought we'd agreed; there's no proof Hoskins had anything to do with O'Rourke's murder, and to accuse him without would bring no end of trouble."

"I could find out without asking him direct," I said, but with little idea how. I paced the student's study and was aware of Verity's eyes darting about the room taking in all the strange items I'd become familiar with. She looked now at Hamish, and their eyes met fleeting but I could tell what they were both thinking. They thought me mad, and I had no way to prove them wrong. I stood by the window and down below me the early evening street was busy. The servant at number nineteen was flirting with a coachman. I took a sharp breath and when I spoke couldna' suppress the triumph in my voice.

"We can ask Hoskin's woman, her at number nineteen. She'll know where he lives, for sure." I hardly waited to see their reaction, but hurried down the stairs and away across the street.

The coachman was mounting his box as I arrived, the cheeky maid giving him a wave and, puckering red-painted lips, she blew him a kiss. He flicked his whip and with a laugh drove away at speed.

"Hoskins out of favour?" I asked her in a low voice. "He'd no' be too pleased to see ye flirt with another." Her face paled for no more than a moment then she shrugged defiantly.

"Don't know what ye mean. I ain't answerable to 'im."

"That's all right then." I wasted no time, blurting out, "Where does he sleep these days?" Seeing her eyes narrow, I said "I've to see him urgent. The Master needs something from him and doesna' have his address."

She thought for a moment but must ha' decided it was safe enough to tell me.

"Down off Giltspur Street. 'E 'as rooms up by the Fortune of War. Why would he want to see you, or 'elp your Master? 'E's not a servant to no one now."

"'Tis a business matter – he'll understand." I'd heard then speak indoors of the Fortune of War and knew it to be a den of thieves and murderers. I hoped my voice didna' give away my fear and I sounded sure of mysel', and was pleased at her change in tone.

"I'm going there with a pie as it 'appens, so I'll show you the way." No, she clearly didna' trust me there alone.

"Aye, thank'ee." I panicked then, thinking I shouldha' let someone at home know where I was going, and when she went indoors to fetch the pie I turned to look up at the window where Hamish and Verity had been standing not a few minutes since. I could see nothing of them, jest a glimmer of light on the glass, brighter now since I'd washed it. I had to wait but a moment longer before the girl came out, her covered pie in a basket.

"This way," she said, and strode out in the direction of the College. I hurried to catch up with her, trying to appear carefree. I asked, friendly, for her name

"I've seen ye around here, but I fear we've no' been introduced. I'm Janet, Janet Brown."

"I'm Maggie. I've seen ye, working on the step there." She smiled, like she shared the drudgery and understood my situation. Though I canna' say I'd seen her working too hard.

"Aye well, it gets me out o' the house and away from the Master." Mebbe if I built a feeling, sisterly with her, against those who held power over us, she would help me in my quest. She was quiet though, and her long legs strode out, with me having to scuttle along to keep abreast of her, and I was panting too much to talk by the time we'd reached Giltspur Street.

"That's St. Sepulchre's" she said suddenly, pointing

to a great church casting a shadow over the street. "And there's St. Bartholomew's 'ospital. Hoskins, he earns well there and lives close by for the purpose. Just there, look."

A great building, with the sign of a public house hanging outside, gave a glow of warmth to the fading light of the street. The sign showed a ship, sails full with the wind.

"That's the Fortune of War," said Maggie. "It's where a lot of business gets done, know what I mean?" She winked and moved to a doorway in a wall, long ago painted and now peeling, jest to the left of the inn. She raised a hand and gave a firm bang on the knocker. The house was run down, hardly worthy of the name, being but one floor tall, patched in the roof and with a boarded up window.

"Why is that lass wi' ye?" Hoskins was no' pleased to see me and growled at Maggie.

"She 'as some business to put your way, or so she says." Maggie arched her brow, and I had a sudden dread of where I'd got mysel'. "I brought ye a pie, Jeremiah, fresh baked and full of beef. Will ye keep me on the step then?" Maggie pushed her way past me and past Hoskins, comfortable enough in his presence. She looked over her shoulder at me, urging me on, and I entered the house, careful to avoid Hoskins' as I passed him.

We skirted a pile of boxes in the narrow hallway and walked through to the back o' the building, coming to a halt in a grubby kitchen.

"Here, shall I cut ye a slice my dear?" Maggie put her pie on the table and cast around for a knife. Hoskins obliged, picking up a long blade from the dresser, and a plate laid by ready for his supper. He toyed a moment with the knife, letting it glint in his hand long enough for me to appreciate it, before handing it to Maggie.

"I won't lie," she said with a laugh, "I didn't bake it meself. But the cook won't miss it. If she does, I'll just tell 'er the Master's son was 'ungry and must 'ave took it. If she tells on 'im and 'e gets a thrashing it'll serve the brat right." She laughed loud then and Hoskins joined in, giving her a squeeze and a wet kiss on the cheek.

While Maggie cut into the pie, Hoskins smile disappeared. Eyeing me all the while, he poured some beer from a bottle and slurped it out of a tankard.

"What's this business matter ye have, lassie? Yon fellah, Knox, is he after a subject to be working on? Large or small, eh?"

Maggie was studying me over her own tankard now, sharp dark eyes not missing a thing. My brain rushed to find something to say, and I decided the Master was best left out o' this mess.

"'Tis for the students really, I'll not lie. A, eh, set of teeth. Not too rotten mind." What was I doing? "How much?"

He was frowning. "Well, for three guineas I could provide a set of teeth, but if ye want the whole jaw, that'll be five." Seeing my surprise, he rushed to defend his prices. "Teeth are in great demand ye know."

"Aye, well, I'll tell 'em. Ye have plenty of stock here do you?" I looked around, praying inside that I'd no' see anything, yet wanting to know for sure if he was murdering folk and stacking 'em there. I found my eyes lingering over a huge laundry basket in the corner of the room. It was the sister of a group of such baskets on the step of St. Bartholomew's.

"I don't keep anything here, I'm no fool. If you have the money for a firm order, I'll take half now and the rest on delivery."

"I'll need to check with the lads," I said and, seeing his impatience, I cleared my throat. "Of course, if he were still with us, young Rory O'Rourke would ha' come to ask ye. But someone slit his throat." There was no' as much as a flicker on Hoskins' face, but I noticed Maggie look sharp at him. "Can't say we miss the laddie though," I tried another approach, "for he was a pest to us all. I woulda' slit it mysel' afore too long," my laugh fell flat. I shuffled my feet, deciding mebbe I should leave for this was a foolish journey and I was wishing I'd waited for Verity to come with me.

"I'll walk ye back 'ome," offered Maggie then. "With so many dangerous men about it'll be safer to walk together, for you'll not want your throat cut will ye?"

Maggie wrapped her shawl about her and gave Hoskins a close hug. He bent his head to her lips and I'll swear she whispered something more than a farewell for the sly looks between them. I was fearful then and pleased to be on my way home.

As we moved back to the passage, Hoskins suddenly announced it might be better to use the back door in case there were Peelers about.

"There'll be drunks coming out o' the inn at this time as well. The scullery door will take ye out by the back of the inn and be less public, so to speak."

I had no choice as Maggie was behind me and edging me into a small scullery. Hoskins opened the door and I stepped out into the yard with Maggie by my side. I turned my head but briefly to bid my farewell and was pleased to see him smile politely and begin to close the door behind me. Turning away, I suddenly felt my arms held in a strong grip and a sack was pulled over my head. I tried to scream as something was tied around me, and then, when I struggled, a blow brought darkness and the hard cobblestones crashing into my knees.

20

I FACE FEAR AND DANGER

I felt sick when I came to my senses. The air was musty and there was something scratching at my face. I jerked and tried to sit up, but my hands and feet were tied. Someone pulled the bag off my head and the light stabbed at my eyes. I was inside a building, a brick wall next to me and a candle burned not more than two feet away and wavered about. I looked into the eyes of Aldo and gasped.

"What are you doing here? Help untie me, there's a good lad."

Aldo was nervous, his hands shaking, but he did as he was bid, put down his candle and loosed the knots which bound me. He passed me a cup of water and I was pleased to drink it, even though the taste was brackish and warm.

"Where is this place," I asked. "Is this part of Hoskin's house?"

He shook his head and asked what I was doing coming to a place like this. "'Tisn't a place for 'spectable women. We're in the cellar of the inn. Don't worry," he added, "him's not likely to come back 'til dawn."

"Him? Hoskins?"

"No," his chest swelled with pride, knowing what I did not. "'Mister Black."

"Be still, laddie," I hoped my voice didna' betray my terror. "I canna' be sitting here all night. I'm away home and if ye've any sense you'll come with me. Verity has been worried about ye." At that I saw his eyes sadden. "She'd be pleased to have ye back at the vicarage."

"I'm needed 'ere'" he said. "I got an important job. I'm a good lad is what Mister Black says."

I was losing patience now and shook him. "What do you know of Mister Black? Did ye see 'im when you went to Bethnal Green?" I tried to sound calm. "Is that where business is done?"

"Mister Hare. 'E's the one Mister Black supplies for making stiff 'uns." He laughed then and I caught his arm and jerked him still. Hare! And Mister Black was to come at dawn. Did that mean I was to be a stiff 'un then?

It was late, the middle of the night I supposed, for all was quiet. Aldo had been instructed to be my gaoler, but he left me untied when he locked the door between the cellar and the kitchens of the inn. I caught sight as he left of a great cauldron and some hanging birds. I prowled for a while in the candlelight 'til it flickered to its end. Around me were great flour bags like those I'd seen in the yard of Black's cottage, with old clothes, or rags, and there were shoes and belts, and dozens of beer and wine bottles. I sat then in misery for a wee while thinking I must surely die, and these were the relics of past prisoners. Why hadna' I taken one o' the Master's knives? I had naught here to defend mysel'. The damp of the cellar floor bit into me and I got up to move about again. It was then I noticed, like a slow dawning, the light was not altogether gone. Some slight rays of moonlight showed through slats at the other end of the room, and I went to explore where it came in. Part of the cellar must be above ground, and there was a hatch for emptying fuel straight into the building. It was made of wood, some of the slats rotten, but with a stout plank on the outside holding it down. The roots of a tree were growing through the wall beside it where the plaster and lath was broken. The place smelt of soil and something that had leaked from the privy I should think. I pushed and couldna' shift the hatch an inch, and was near to giving up. I didna' know the inn, or whether my dungeon was close to the street, or in the yard? I waited a few minutes and decided I'd no choice but to try and force mysel' out, for I feared for my life.

It was quiet outside, no drunken revelling or passing folk, though I listened close, and if there had been I wouldna' have dared to call out, lest they be in league with my captors. Standing on a crate, I used a stout buckle from among the hoard around me to pick and scratch at the end of one of the laths and had it free in no time. I wiggled it like a rotten tooth and, with a sudden and terrible crack it broke loose. I waited, my own teeth clenched, expecting someone to come and catch me in my folly. All was still. I worked on the lath next to the first and it broke free too, along with a lump of wall from next to it, leaving a space big enough for me to climb through.

I scrambled out, not caring who saw me then so keen I was to get away. I snagged my dress on the broken lath, but dragged myself free and crawled to the shadows of the inn's main wall. The cellar it seemed was on the side of the inn around the corner from Hoskin's house, and I could see the wide open road ahead of me. I ran, like I was chased by devils and left the dark towering inn behind me.

It took me nigh on an hour to get home I think, for I took wrong turns and lost mysel' among the narrow lanes behind Saint Paul's, and then again near the Bailey, before hurrying on, I know not where, tears in my eyes blurring my sight. It was fully dark now and only with the help of the moon did I recognize Southampton Row at last, passed the Institute, closed and silent, and ran as fast as my sapping strength allowed to Huntley Street.

Not knowing if the whole household was abed, I crept upstairs but as I passed the Master's room the door flew open and he emerged, in night cap and dressing gown, and before he could say a word I broke into a sobbing that silenced anything he might ha' said.

"What the devil!" He stood for a moment observing me then took me gently by the shoulders and into the grand drawing room. He poured a glass of brandy and having sat me down he handed it to me.

I looked down at my skirt, filthy and with a great tear from hem to knee. I was dirty as an urchin, and with a throbbing head too where I'd been clouted earlier in the evening. I gulped my brandy and choked.

It didna' take a few minutes before Hamish and Ewan appeared, and even Carlo came downstairs in a nightshirt and stockings. Hamish hovered close, like a mother hen, and fondled my hand in his.

"Here lad, out of the way now, let me look at the lass." The Master's voice was stern, but he was gentle as he dabbed at my head with witch-hazel, then my face, where I had bruises but know not how I came by them. He sent Ewan down to the consulting room for potions and he was back in a moment, then set about mixing something in a glass.

I steadied myself to tell my tale. "I was right, though, to suspect Hoskins of helping with murder if he didna' do it himsel'," I said. "They would ha' killed me, and with those clothes in the cellar, bloodied and...." My voice cracked and I felt tears come. Hamish threw down the bloodied rag he'd been twisting in his hands, and took me in his arms, soothing and stroking me; my hair, my back; his fingers found and gently touched my eyes, my lips. With the softest of caresses, he kissed me. 'Twas like a butterfly had landed on my face, and yet there was such passion burning inside him it frightened me. He said naught, but must ha' known how much I yearned for him at that moment.

The Master sat quiet as I told them about the cellar and what I'd seen, and it was only when I spoke the name Hare that his head jerked up.

"William Hare! That rogue! He's a devil, or has the reputation of one. Dealing in bodies is legal enough, just, but there's no-one more likely to hasten folk on their way. He'd slit your throat without a thought! If Hoskins is working for him he'd best take care for Hare will kill him without blinking if he double crosses him." He stood and paced about a bit, then scratched his head. "The police will be keen to investigate this cellar and the Bethnal Green house. It sounds as though there's enough stolen property to hang them if it can be proved they're responsible. But Hoskins is a canny swine and can talk himself out of worse trouble." He asked me then, "Janet, who is this Italian boy you spoke of, Aldo? What part does he play in all this?"

"He's an innocent child, Sir; that I'd swear. He untied me and left me to escape. Hoskins was the one who held me prisoner and he's been getting Aldo to do odd jobs for him, but he's too wee to do anything much."

"He might be able to provide information to the police," muttered the doctor, "which could help end their murderous business. I'll speak to the fellah from Scotland Yard when it's fully light, and suggest he talk to the lad."

"Oh, Janey, we were so worried for you. Verity was in tears and sure you were murdered."

Hamish brought some soup and soft rolls from Carlo and sat with me while I ate. We didna' speak much, but his eyes studied me close, to ensure I finished every last drop of broth. When I was done, he took the tray and placed it on the floor.

Meanwhile, the Master mixed me a potion and then I was sent off to bed.

I must ha' slept, for it was only moments I lay there staring at the ceiling in my room, feeling every bone in my body ache and my head throbbing with pain. A lump was forming, the size of an egg, and I touched it gingerly. But the Master's draught must ha' taken effect, and I was soothed enough to sleep for a while. When I opened my eyes daylight streamed in through the window. There was no sign of Doctor Knox when I stirred, and Hamish was gone already to another of his examinations. It was the middle of the morning. I thought to stay home and mebbe help Carlo for I'd no fancy to go out, wanting only to hide away and keep safe. Ewan was hovering in the kitchen checking on me, the patient, and I was growing wearisome of the attention when Verity arrived at the house.

"I had a visit from Aldo this very morning," she told us. The three of us were sitting in the kitchen eating Carlo's pastries, and drinking strong fresh tea made special with lemon and herbs.

"'E was keeping out o' the way of 'oskins 'e said, owing to 'aving upset 'im. Someone else was coming to visit 'em and the lad didn't want to 'ang about." She reached out and brushed my face with her hand. "That's a fine bruise coming up there. You was clouted a good 'un then?"

"Aye, Verity. I don't know who I'm more fearful of, Hoskins or the mysterious Mr Hare. It seems he's the Master now and runs a fine ol' gang of body snatchers." I shivered though it was warm in the kitchen.

"Where is Black in all this?" asked Verity.

I wondered if Hoskins was using him or working for him as well as Hare. My head was still dizzy with what had passed.

Verity said "Black will find himself in trouble if he gets in the way of this Hare, if he is setting himself up in competition in the bodysnatching business."

I told her then that he had angered the Master when he and Hoskins stole a body from him. "Well it must ha' been the pair of them, working together." I told her about poor Master Jakes and his heart and she shuddered. I wondered if the competition was what had killed O'Rourke, and what part young Aldo played in the filthy business.

All these questions and the only one I knew the answer to was where Black lived, the house in Bethnal Green where O'Rourke had visited before he disappeared. Would Black have any reason to kill him? If he had, surely the body would have been sold on at King's College or somewhere he wasn't known, not jest left for the polis to find? No, Hoskins was my suspect and now I knew he was evil enough to be working with Hare it made me more certain than ever.

21

MUCH DANGER AND DEATH

When Hamish returned from that day's examination, he seemed a wee bit more light-hearted but when he saw me, bruised and mebbe still quieter than is usual for me, his face clouded, and he came and sat by me. He reassured me with a gentle kiss and his hand brushed my unruly hair off my face. He didna' linger as Carlo came bustling by with a brace of fowl, fresh off a man as shoots out in the countryside beyond Hampstead but told me then that the Master had returned, and they'd already spoke together in his study.

"He met with the police and they're going to arrest Hoskins," he said. "They may not be able to prove murder, but he kept you a prisoner against your will, and that's a grave enough crime to hold him." He fiddled with a thread come loose from his cuff. "He spoke of Black, too. He's of interest to Mister Grey and his Master's it seems. They are a strange breed of policemen, wearing civilian clothes. I asked about that, and the Master didn't know. He thinks they are government spies, but Mister Grey says they are some new breed of detectors...."

"Spying on Mister Black, or on all of us? Mebbe they still think we are Chartists?"

Hamish nodded, uncertain but suspicious. These were strange times, and who knew what the government would do. Spying on the people wasna' too hard to believe.

The next day, I felt strong enough to venture out and visit Verity, it being her day off, and we decided to go shopping and take the air. Samuel was in the kitchen mending a chair, but he put aside his work and insisted on driving us in the dog cart.

"There be rogues out there and I want to keep my eye on you both. The Master and Mistress being away a few days they won't be missing the cart or calling on us for anything."

"Oh, Samuel, there's no need, I'm sure; but thank'ee all the same." Verity gave him a wee peck on the cheek and shook her head as he hurried outside to get the horse ready. Mysel', I was mighty relieved to have a man's protection and a cart to rush us home away from any danger, even if Hoskins should be safe out of my way in a cell by now.

We wandered for nigh on an hour, slowly driving round the wider streets of Covent Garden, seeing the grand shops from afar and I was fidgeting to get down and walk. Verity must ha' felt the same for she called out to Samuel to stop the cart outside the Flowerpot Inn to allow us to stretch our legs. He could wait in the cart and watch us from there.

"You can run to our rescue if you see anyone attack us," she said. "Or go and 'ave yerself a pint and we'll be back afore ye know it."

Samuel didna' need too much encouragement and went to get his ale, and the two of us slipped across the road to a draper's shop and lingered amongst ribbons and bows 'til we'd had our fill. We walked among the flower sellers, a shop selling hats and one with a hamper of exotic foods piled high. Verity was pointing out the pineapple balanced on top and the great figs from the east, when Samuel came to join us, with three steaming pies wrapped in a rag cradled in his hat. He held it out to us and, hungry by now, we took one each. They were mainly empty mind, apart from a few fatty bits of something and a lot of gravy, but they filled a gap. Samuel agreed to follow us in his cart as Verity and I wanted to walk, for the weather had brightened and I hoped my mood would too, in time.

I ignored the low wolf-whistle of a street vendor selling tobacco and turned my attention to a row of fine shops where, in one of them an 'Astronomical Musical Clock' had caught my eye. I studied it and its ornate written label through the glass window. It was a fine object of carved metal, yellow like gold, and might have been indeed, for there was a small black boy in a turban standing guard by it. There were painted figurines, some with arms and legs moving even as I watched them. I breathed and the window misted before my eyes. Verity was as smitten as I and together we marvelled at the goods inside.

"'Pinchbeck, Maker of Musical Automata'," she read aloud from the sign above the door. I pressed my nose against the window and the small boy pressed his nose the same, so if there was no glass we would have touched. He grinned at me, but a shout from further back in the store made him jump up and retreat back to his watch-post. A short man in a patterned shiny brocade coat and tight white breeches cuffed the lad and glared at me through the glass. I stood back, deciding if I ever had enough money, I'd make a point not to shop there, poked out my tongue and was about to turn away when I saw him, reflected in the glass of the window.

Black was coming out of a house with a barber's pole over the door, jest across the way, and I ducked into a doorway lest he saw me though, I told mysel' there was no reason to be afeared. His hat was pulled down over half his face and he hunched his shoulders before turning away.

"What is it, Janet?" Verity looked about, alarmed by my gasp, before she too stepped into the shadows.

"'Tis Mister Black; he's jest over there. Come let's go inside here lest he see us."

A man jostled my elbow as he left the shop, untied his flea ridden nag and moved a cart away jest as Black turned and spat into the gutter. It was not him. I saw that straight away. 'Twas jest another man. He rubbed his face and I saw blood had stained his cheek. I recovered myself, feeling daft. He was some innocent who'd been to see the tooth puller by the look of him and had no interest in me at all.

We went into the shop and made a show of sniffing about amongst some spices and I thought I'd have to remember this place and tell Carlo of it when I got home. I was feeling a mite foolish, to run at the sight of Black, or anyone who reminded me of him, and I'd likely upset Verity in my panic. I was jumpy, that's all. I gave her hand a squeeze and we bought a bag of dates between us and left the shop chewing on their juicy succulence. The man with the toothache was nowhere to be seen now; the sun was still shining and enough of its light was making its way between the buildings so we could see we'd almost reached the last of the row of shops. It was near the middle of the afternoon and I for one was tired enough.

A full week went by, with nothing of note happening in Huntley Street. Hamish had been studying hard and when, after his last examination, he got home and threw his books aside and he and Ewan went drinking they didna' come back 'til noon the next day. The Master was angry and said he expected more of Hamish and how he should set an example to Ewan, for he was still a lad and easy led astray. I heard him shouting and threatening to withhold his reference, but I knew he'd never do that for he loved Hamish like a son most o' the time. They were but a year apart in age, the two lads, but now

Hamish was near a full-grown doctor, and it hurt his pride to be told off so.

I took mysel' off for a walk and left them to their dinner and sore heads, carrying in my pocket a list of spices from Carlo. He was too busy to go himsel' but asked me to visit the shop I'd been in with Verity. I swung my basket as I strode out, the breeze blowing my skirts and hair, but enough sun to warm still. With Hoskins rotting in gaol, the autumn day so grand and now a chance to buy some more dates, I walked with a light heart.

I'd walked a goodly way after buying my spices, and was chewing on another date, spitting the stone into the gutter as I crossed the main thoroughfare at the Aldwych before turning into Fleet Street under the great Temple Bar. This was where traitor's heads used to be spiked, so Verity had said. I shuddered and then cheered myself with the thought of Hoskins' head stuck up there. The smell of the prison and the river Fleet being foul I hurried on, passing Saint Dunstan's church, when I heard steps close behind me and turned, too late, squeaking with pain as my arm was taken in a grip strong as my mangle.

"Your Master wouldna' be pleased to see you wandering alone again," hissed Black. "The streets are no' safe for some young women."

"'Tis my afternoon off and I'll go where I please," I told him, trying to keep my voice steady.

"I don't take kindly to being accused of things; people coming to ma home and causing trouble. Maybe you should come back there with me now and satisfy your nosy wee mind."

"No, thank'ee." I tried to twist free and a man passing by paused and looked at us. He must ha' decided I was an errant wife or servant, for he shook his head and walked quickly on, leaving me to what he thought was my just chastisement.

I struggled for a moment longer then saw the knife in his hand, hid by his sleeve but glinting like the eye of a serpent in its cave.

"Walk."

I walked, slow and unyielding in front of him, gripped still and rigid with fear. We passed the smart houses of Johnson's Court, the Old Cock public house and the premises of the London Wine Company where the Master kept an account, then finally turned into Ludgate Hill. I stopped for a moment, hoping to catch my breath and brought Black and his knife sharp against my back. He swore and pushed me on. In a corner across the way from Saint Paul's Churchyard, a group of men took my attention. One, tall and well-built, was standing with another fellah, a countryman by his dress, and a third man, the one who had passed us a while back and looked at me so disapproving, was standing now with his arms demonstrating to the other two. The rustic started forward as we approached keeping his distance and whistling as he looked about him. He stopped in a doorway and fiddled with the buckle on his shoe, allowing us to pass him. The tall man stood his ground, watching us. All this I saw through sly eyes, sideways, without turning my head. At first, I thought he was a down at heel type, with his old checker cloth suit and black woollen cap, but his finger was hooked in a watch chain and his shoes looked stout. He could have been a cabman. There was something familiar about him, but even as I stared, trying to call for help with my eyes, he turned, smartish, and looked away. If I'd any doubts they vanished now, for I recognized him as Mister Grey, the detecting policeman, even without his fine clothes.

I was pleased to have him watching Black as he'd promised, but I didna' care for him looking away, leaving me in danger. He had seen me though and must be hiding his interest from Black. That was it. I hoped the rustic was good at keeping up with his quarry, if indeed he was following behind us. Mister Grey crossed the road, for all he'd lost interest in us, and stood in the doorway of a public house, the name of which I canna' recall.

Black pushed me on, and we walked for some way, silently. I don't recall every twist and turn we made, but we went through a gap between some tall buildings and turned towards Swan Lane Pier, and he pointed with his knife-hand to some stone steps leading up to a doorway facing the river. Two boats were tied up on the quay below, loaded high with building materials, great sacks and a vat of something steaming warmly in the cool of the late afternoon. He pushed me then against a wall, knocking the breath from me.

"You know where we are?" he asked, his face split into a cold grin.

I shook my head, for I was too out of breath to speak, and fear had a hold of my tongue.

"'Tis the Temple, where the lawyers study their arts." He laughed and I remember the stink of his breath, the sound of seabirds screeching and the chime of a clock somewhere near at hand. No man was near, and the knife Black held to my throat jest pierced the skin, for a small trickle of my life blood flowed free and ran down towards my breast. I felt my belly tighten and tears filled my eyes.

A lad, with his group of friends, passed by on the other side of the courtyard and called out some lewd thing to us, for all we were some loving couple dallying there. I tensed to call out, but the knife grazed my skin again under my shawl, jest below my ear.

"No, lassie. We don't want anyone to spoil our walk. Come." He pushed me further away from the road, through a maze of buildings, some ancient and hung with the heads of dragons and goblins looking down on me, others with new brick and here and there a gas lamp for when the darkness came.

As we rounded a corner and nearly crashed into a pair of gowned be-wigged gents, I wrenched my arm free and made to run. There were steep steps there, and I tumbled down them, and right behind me was Black. I tried to stand and found mysel' sinkin' into mud, near the river's edge, up past my ankle.

"It's alright gents, I have her!" I heard him call, and an arm wound itself round my waist. Black hissed into my ear to be still. My basket with Carlo's herbs had spilled its precious load as it flew from my clasp, so now as he turned me, I could use my free hand to strike out.

My blow must have caught him by surprise, and off-balance, and from the wince of his face I'd mebbe caused him to prick himsel'. He swore and, jest for a moment, his hold on me was lost. I put all my weight into another shove that had him tumbling down onto his back into the mud with me atop him.

The muck squelched as we fought, the slime suckin' and draggin' at us. My limbs were heavy, and it was impossible to move after a brief and breathless tangle and, from the hoots of a filthy child come to watch, we must ha' looked a sight. A shout rang out and Black looked up towards the steps. He loosed his hold enough from my wrist for me to twist it and take from him the short shiny blade.

I stabbed him then. It was not a moment I regret, for I was angry and hurtin' and fightin' for my life. I stabbed him again. The knife was slippery and when I saw the blood gush from his chest I stabbed him again, the blade snagging against his shoulder bone. He gasped and drew up his legs and I felt his belly tense against mine as I pushed mysel' up. His eyes were wide and there came a gurgling in his throat, a wheezin', creakin' breath that was his last.

A hand grasped my arm, holding me tight, and when I turned, I found mysel' looking into the eyes of Mister Grey. Weak then, either from my struggle with Black or from the horror of what I'd done, and with my blood pounding in my head, I began shiverin' and shakin' violently, and didna' resist as Mister Grey pulled me to my feet. I welcomed the weight and warmth of his coat as he placed it around my shoulders.

"Well, I'll be damned," he said, so quiet I hardly heard him.

I don't know how I got back to the path, but I suppose he carried me part of the way, and I canna' recall much of what happened in the next few minutes. I'd begun to shake with cold and was deafened by the shrieks of the crowd growing thicker around us. With sickness welling up inside me, I remember I was grateful when he offered me a flask of brandy to sup from.

As I tipped up the vessel and let the liquor flow into my throat, burning its way down, I heard Mister Grey curse. He pulled a wooden rattle from his pocket and swung it round his head in an arc; the sound it made was deafening. The crowd cheered as he jumped down the steps and abandoned me.

Down on the quayside jest beyond the mud, a movement at the edge of my sight; some filthy thing was crawling. Black was no' dead but breathed still and was sliding away towards the moored boats and the buildings around the pier. Mister Grey was hurrying toward him, fast as the mud would allow him, and came abreast of him where the steps led up to a wee building standing alone by the water's edge. Black was on his feet, lashing out and, no! Mister Grey was caught off-guard and stumbled.

All this while the crowd was roarin', but not one soul went to his aid. The rattle was meant to call his polis friends, but where were they? I stood and peered about, then lifted the hem of my sodden skirt and squelched my way over towards where the two men were grappling still.

Black had Mister Grey by the throat, shoved against the wall and was dashing his head against the bricks. How so much strength from one near dead? Out of the corner of my eye I saw a group of blue-clad men enter the quay, some distance away still. I couldna' wait for them, starting forward up the steps towards the fray.

The struggle was no' over. Black, for all that his own blood was flowing, was grappling still with the polisman who, his face as grey as his name, was wriggling still. Despite his wound the rogue was strong, and he had his left hand tight around the throat of Mister Grey, while his right, claspin' once again the thin steel dagger, pointed it but inches from his face. Although Mister Grey had him by the knife wrist, he was being crushed against the wall and had no space to move or to take the blade. He must ha' done something to make Black drop it, for it clattered to the ground nearly at my feet, and it was but a heartbeat til I moved to snatch it up. Black's foot lashed out, and my weapon bounced away down the steps. Once again, I felt my blood pound in my head and my heart roared in anger. I lunged forward, hitting out with my fists and swearing with words unused since my days on Edinburgh's streets. Black buckled under my crazed assault.

I recall his pale face turned towards me, then the twitch of his shoulder as Mister Grey broke free from him and heaved him round to face the wall. Black struggled but must ha' been greatly weakened by his wounds, as he gasped and spluttered a deal of blood forth from his mouth. Even then he made a final attempt to break free, but it took only a moment for the polisman to finish the fight, gathering both his wits and his strength. I don't know how exactly it happened, for in a moment Black was falling over the parapet. Mebbe he'd struggled loose and threw himself aside. There was no great splash of water, jest a wee plopping sound, for he had landed in the open vat on board the boat moored jest below, and even as we watched he sank slowly into the grey slurry it held.

"If he's not dead already he soon will be," gasped Mister Grey and then, seeing my confusion he explained. "Quicklime; caustic stuff, for use on the new bridge over there." He pointed along the river to where the great London Bridge was half-finished. "It'll burn the skin off him before the builders find him."

I shivered violently. It was no' because I was sad for Black, but mebbe overwhelmed that I was still alive. Else it was the wind off the Thames and the cooling air as the sun slipped down.

Mister Grey eyed me close, then barked a short laugh and told me I was a brave girl. I'd expected him to put me in chains and arrest me for stabbing a man, but he didna'.

He turned serious then, helping me to the bottom of the stairs, for my belly was a wee bit queasy and I staggered 'til he took my elbow and supported me. He sat me down and from his pocket pulled out the rattle again. The noise was alarming for all it was expected. I put my hands over my ears. He left me for a moment and approached the river wall. He looked over at the boat below, mebbe to check Black was really gone then, with a firm nod, he turned back to me. There was a commotion along the quayside and a group of men crowded towards us, among them at last the rustic I'd seen earlier and three tall police constables their hats towering above the rest. Other men, mebbe local tradesmen come to answer the call for assistance and decent to a man, now the fight was over, rallied round and brought a horse and cart to take us to Scotland Yard.

I took another swig of the brandy, and the warming liquid revived me enough to stop the shivering, nearly, and with a quick pat on my knee Mister Grey picked up the reins and off we set at a brisk trot.

22

ALL IS EXPLAINED, AND JUSTICE DONE

The building they called Scotland Yard was no' in Scotland, so we were there in but a few minutes. It was no' more than a big house in Whitehall Place, dark and quiet, high black windows looking out in the evening gloom. Once inside, I sat in a warm room, a fire burning in the grate, waiting while Mister Grey spoke with his superior. At last, the two of them came in and stood for a moment in the doorway. The other, taller even than Mister Grey, was introduced to me as Inspector Neale. He sat down behind a big desk and stared at me; no doubt curious at what muddy creature I might be.

"Well, seems to me you've had a narrow escape young Miss. Grey has told me all that has happened and given me some of the background to this sad case. It would seem harsh to charge ye with anything, especially as you helped Grey here, so....eh, might be best if ye went home and had a good rest. We have your address should we need it, but I can't see this matter going to court at all." I couldna' make out whether he was a kindly man or jest wanted to see me gone, for by now the lights were being lit along the road outside.

Mister Grey himself drove me home in the grocer's cart, and I hoped he wouldna' have to go all the way back to return it that night. He was quiet, no' having much to say, but shot me worried glances from time to time. He walked me up to the front door and I was surprised and relieved when it was Hamish who opened to his knock.

"Janey! Thank God! The Master will be relieved to see you," he said, "As am I. What adventure have ye been on tonight?"

The Master came out of his study then and ushered me inside, Mister Grey and Hamish following behind. Once again Mister Grey explained all that had happened, and the others sat open-mouthed and, for once, silent.

"And what was this place Black was taking her to?" asked the Master.

"Our constables will be investigating that now, Doctor All I can say is it's a good thing for him that he died tonight for he'd have swung for sure. Given what we found at both his cottage and at Hoskins' house, and given what that rogue has confessed in custody, we know the man calling himself Black was guilty of even more vile crimes."

"What did you find?" I asked, my voice croaking.

He was no' quick in answering, mebbe thinking was it wise to say anything to me. But then he sighed, wiped some dust off his trousers and looking in the fire he said,

"The body of a young boy. He's laid out at Bow

Street now, but he was in an outhouse, a privy, at the back of Hoskin's place in Giltspur Street. He wasn't long dead. No idea who he is, of course. Another poor wretch they were going to sell on no doubt. But he'd been murdered for sure......."

I dunno what else he said for I felt mysel' slipping down in a black wave, the sound of his voice fading to nothing.

I woke lying on the examining bed in the Master's consulting room, with Hamish rubbing my hands and calling my name. The sharp smell of salts under my nose had me gasp and come to. It couldna' be true. Was it possible it was some other boy? Would Hoskins have killed the wee laddie, Aldo? Why? Because he'd let me escape? I couldna' bear it if that were the truth of it, and I cried then, 'til Hamish took me in his arms and held me, crooning and whispering to me, telling me all would be well, and we would know more soon. But I knew. In my heart, I knew. Poor wee Aldo!

The Master fussed over me in his quiet way, when I saw him later in his study. His eyes watched me close all the while, to see if I was strong enough to hear what he had to say. Mister Grey had gone, and Hamish sat me in a chair and stood behind me, a silent guard.

"Well, lass, this is all a big shock. Black has turned out a greater rogue than we thought. Hoskins, I'm not so surprised about. Hamish tells me you knew a lad who accompanied him sometimes and you think this dead boy may be him? Grey would be grateful if you could take a look and identify him – if you're strong enough?"

"I could do that, Sir." Hamish was quick to jump in.

"No, Hamish." I took his hand and squeezed it. "Thank'ee, but I saw him more than you and would know the laddie straight away if it's him. Verity knew him best of course, and she'll be right torn apart when she hears." I couldn't bear the thought of telling her until I was certain, and didna' want her to have to look at the body. I would go.

Hamish came with me in the morning, after a night of restless dream-ridden sleep, and Carlo came too, muttering in his foreign tongue and tutting.

"I might know him," he insisted. "If there is a likeness in him maybe I will know his family. If I can help him, well, we are from the same homeland..." he wiped a tear then and fetched his coat.

The three of us set off, the men walking quiet and strong by my side, to the low building in Bow Street where the dead were kept. Carlo had never met the laddie as far as I know, but his tears flowed like it was a brother he was to identify, not some wee street boy.

We were left to wait for a few minutes while there was much discussion in whispers between the guardians of the crypt and the polisman who took us in, and then we were shown into a small room where the body had been hastily brought in and laid on a table. It looked like it was an office for there were books and papers moved roughly from the desk and piled on the floor nearby.

"They couldn't have ye go in the charnal house with all the other, eh... It's better in here I suppose..." Hamish muttered.

Aldo was laid out under a grubby sheet. It was him. I knew him straight away. His wee pale face, the eyes closed now like he was sleeping. The sheet had slipped down enough to show the edge of a vicious slash across his neck, though the polisman hitched it back up with an apology. I felt my bile rise, and gripped Hamish's arm tight enough for him to wince.

"Aye, 'tis Aldo." I didna' ken his family name, nor where he lived or if there was another living soul who would miss him. Carlo burst into tears and was helped outside by the polisman.

I touched the cold cheek and would ha' whispered a farewell, but my mouth was dry and my throat so tight I couldna' make a sound.

We left Aldo, with Hamish slipping a few coins to the warder towards a decent funeral, then turned towards home, but then I stopped Hamish and said,

"What about Verity?"

He sighed and with Carlo following us, blowing his nose into a great kerchief and crossing himself as Papists do, we walked to the Vicarage and down the steps to the kitchen.

There was a great weeping when we told Verity, and Samuel held her close and comforted her as best he could. We didna' stay, for there was no strength in me now, and after a brief hug we left her be.

"I'll tell you all that happened when we next meet," I promised her. "And there's much to tell and, oh, Verity..." I jest shrugged and shook my head, no' knowing where I would start. She patted my shoulder and retreated once more into Samuel's arms.

The walk home was took in near silence, and once we were safe back the Master gave me a draught and sent me to my bed.

I slept for nigh on two days, Hamish said, awaking eventually and finding him pacing my room.

"I thought you were never to wake," he said, trying to smile but with a grave face about him.

"Mister Grey is here again, with his Master, Neale. They are in the study with Doctor Knox, and all is mystery and drinking of tea."

I rose and washed, even now finding Thames mud in the creases of my body. I dressed and went down to the kitchen. Carlo fussed and cooked me eggs, and I ate them with a hunk of buttered bread and fresh tea, surprised at my appetite. Only then did the Master send for me and I went upstairs with Hamish close behind.

I don't know what I was expecting; to be arrested, sent back to Scotland or jest dismissed and thrown onto the streets, but not what was said that morning.

"He had been using the name Black since leaving Scotland," Mister Neale told us. "Hare should have hanged along with Burke, but the Sheriff was worried he'd not testify unless he was given his freedom. There was little evidence against either of them for any of the killings in Edinburgh saving the last one, and the courts are getting more and more demanding when it comes to that. The people wanted to know about all the other dead and how it had happened, and Hare provided details aplenty."

"But you had been watching him here, in London?" The Master asked. "Why?"

"Hare was on parole; one slip and we were under orders to arrest him. I'd not much interest in him, to tell the truth, til your student came to see me. Master O'Rourke. He was keen on finding the man and pestered us for months on and off to find out where he lived. He heard you were here Sir and was biding his time as a student. He was out for revenge."

"And you told him where he might find him?" There was shock in Hamish's question.

"No, not in so many words...." Neal looked uncomfortable and he flicked his eyes towards Mister Grey.

The gentleman stood leaning against the wall by the side of the fireplace. He was smoking and tapped his pipe against the hearth before clearing his throat.

"O'Rourke hadn't told us his full story. I had it out of him the last time I saw him. He'd been gambling early this year in some den in Seven Dials and met with Hoskins, who apparently was bragging about working for the famous Doctor Knox. It was then that the lad came to you Sir and sought a position. He thought he'd find more information from you on the false identity Hare was using. He'd a suspicion you and he were in league, Sir." He laughed then, a nervous apologetic laugh, and re-lit his pipe. "We assume it was through Hoskins that Hare was sent to seek out your lad here, Hamish, to get an introduction, using his new identity. He and Hoskins go back a long way and had known each other in Edinburgh. Black as he was known to you all, carried on doing what he'd done in Scotland, selling on bodies and occasionally producing a few of his own when times were hard."

"So, Hoskins knew who Black was?" Hamish was angry at the thought, no doubt fearing himself guilty of bringing a wolf to our door.

"Undoubtedly," Neal said. "They seem to have worked hand in hand, especially after Hoskins was dismissed from your service."

The Master was sitting silently staring at the square of carpet in front of him. He'd been fooled, that was for sure, jest as he'd been fooled in Edinburgh. Lost in his work and not knowing where his bodies were from, or how they'd been killed. I felt my heart beating faster, wondering all the time if Hare had recognized me as soon as he'd come to the house disguised as Mr Black, and why I'd nae suspected who he was at all. I'd barely glanced at him in the courtroom, and in London he was jest a man in a cloak and hat creeping in the shadows most of the time...

"So, what was Hare to O'Rourke?" Hamish was asking. "Was he responsible for the death of the lad's father?"

"Oh, yes!" Mister Grey was animated, sucking on his pipe he explained that "O'Rourke's mother gave him her name, as she was never married to his father. They lived in Ireland and the lad had known him as a fine gentleman, with a smart uniform in the local militia, marching about at the weekend. Quite the hero! After hard times befell him, he went to work on the canal building in Scotland. He was William Burke. "

"*The* Burke?" The Master was white now, whether with shock or rage or both I canna say. For mysel' I couldna' speak. O'Rourke had told us much of that himsel', jest not his father's name.

"Indeed!" said Neale. "So, he sought you out, Sir. Once he heard you were in London. He'd been to Edinburgh and got nowhere with his enquiries other than learning of his father being hanged, and for a monstrous crime too, and that Hare had been freed with a new identity. He apparently wanted to get his revenge on everyone concerned in corrupting his father. He blamed Hare and also yourself, Sir, for what Burke became. The Sheriff's men warned him off after he made a nuisance of himself up there. Then he came down here and started on us!"

I'd wanted my revenge too. I'd come to London wanting to kill Knox, but instead had fallen under his spell and now, why, I looked across the room at him and felt so very different. I had naught much but a liking of the man. Pride even, in a strange way that I was working for him. He had shown me he was a good man, even kindly. But O'Rourke? How would he have felt, in the house of the man his father had been dissected by? I shivered. What would he have been looking for in the Master's study? Some proof he was in league with Hare, something he could use to prove the Master a devil too? How had he felt in those lectures, watching the Master at work. I shuddered to think what went through the laddie's mind.

"Did Hare kill O'Rourke?" The Master had stirred and spoke quiet. "How would he have known the lad was onto him?"

"He went to visit him," I said, "In Bethnal Green."

"Yes, Hoskins would have told him where to find Hare." Neal was certain then. "There was no love lost between them, it seems. These body snatchers are always squabbling over their finds, buying and selling and cheating on each other. Hoskins owed Hare money we think, or the other way round. Who knows, rogues all of them. Maybe Hoskins wanted the lad O'Rourke to go round and kill Hare for him - would have been useful to him after all."

"And when O'Rourke challenged Hare, the lad was killed." The Master said, shaking his head sadly.

"That is most likely what happened, yes." Mister Grey sucked on his pipe. "We found a few items of his at Hare's cottage. "A crucifix, I recall. We might not have been able to prove anything, mind. But you say the lad visited him? You know that do you?"

"Oh, aye," I nodded and thought back to that day. "When the lads took me to Bethnal Green and we, eh..." I saw a look between the Master and Hamish. "I followed O'Rourke a wee way and saw him go into the cottage. We didna' see him after that...." I remembered the heavy hamper being carried out of the cottage and my worst suspicions were right, for that was the body of O'Rourke being taken away.

"You didn't need to tell them that," Hamish reproached me later on, when we were alone in the kitchen, and I was washing the dishes.

"I'm sorry, I hadna' realised it would get you in trouble with the Master. He wasna' so pleased then, on you taking me along to the workhouse and picking up bodies with ye?" I gave him a wee grin, the first time I'd smiled in days.

He gave me a wee hug, and I turned and kissed him. I sighed then, and asked him, "When do you leave us?"

"I'm only going along the road, to Doctor Wakley's. He's so busy with his work in Parliament and with his more important patients and wants some help with the others. Doctor Knox wants me some of the time still, so I'll be back and forth."

I was relieved, I'd no' be losing him completely. "And where will ye sleep at nights, Doctor?" I asked.

"Wherever the bed is most comfortable," he laughed.

I frowned, knowing that would no' be upstairs with Ewan snoring one side and Carlo the other in his wee room.

"I will be back, for there is a bed I miss already. If I am welcome in it?"

I stood staring out o' the window for a moment then said, softly with no' meaning to hurt him,

"I think mebbe you will want more than that, laddie." Whatever happened to him now he was a full made Doctor, always welcome to a place in my heart. But he would be wantin' a respectable wife, and to keep a place in society, and I wouldna' want to risk spoiling his chances. And if truth be told, I was makin' plans too. So far, things had turned out well enough. I kissed Hamish again, lightly on the cheek, sisterly, and made my peace with him. Justice had been done. The dead were avenged and those of us left alive could move on.

The polis, they were grateful to me for my stabbing

Hare, and slowing him down. It seems I was almost a hero; Mister Grey had said as much. And though the Master had grunted at that, I was to stay on in Huntley Street, for he had made it clear he wouldna' want me to leave.

And so, the next months passed. More students came and went; Ewan was becoming more studious, his new spectacles making it easier for him to read his books. The Master was pleased with him and no doubt he too would make a good doctor one day. I continued my afternoons off with walks about the town with Verity 'til, in the winter, she announced her Samuel had asked her to marry him. So, they were all leaving, moving on; but what of me? I do believe the Master looked at me now with a different eye, mebbe seeing me as more than jest a servant with an unbridled tongue. He found more work for me helpin' with his patients and puttin' them at their ease, something I think the womenfolk at least were glad of. I had saved my wages, when the Master remembered to give me any, and bought a great piece of cloth from the haberdasher's shop in Covent Garden. Verity spent hours making it into a coat for me, when she wasna' stitching things for her wedding box, as we sat together in the Vicarage kitchen. She stitched and I read, for I had taken up with the Institute and started goin' to lectures, leastways those women were allowed in, and the Master approved of.

"You've come a long way, Janet," Verity said,

without lifting her eyes from her stitches. "I remember you not so long ago far too busy with mischief to read a book properly."

"Why, Verity!" I cried, "Mischief!" We laughed together but there was sadness too for all we had been through.

"No, really, Janet. Wiv all this learnin' and 'elping the Doctor as you do, well, won't be long afore you are running that household properly."

I wasna' sure what she meant by that – that it was no' run properly now? But she was looking at me in her sideways way and smiling and I gave a laugh. "Aye and will have maids under me too before long!" Jest as Hamish had long ago predicted.

MORE FROM SERENADE PUBLISHING

Brigadier Station Series

By Sarah Williams:

The Brothers of Brigadier Station

The Sky over Brigadier Station

The Legacies of Brigadier Station

Christmas at Brigadier Station (An Outback Christmas
Novella)

The Outback Governess (A Sweet Outback Novella)

Heart of the Hinterland Series

By Sarah Williams:

The Dairy Farmer's Daughter

Their Perfect Blend

Beyond the Barre

A Dying Second Sun

by Peter A. Dowse

Winner Winner Chicken Dinner

by Sarah Jackson

A New Page

by Aimee MacRae

Middle Women

By Jack Garrety

Mim and Wiggy's Grand Adventure

By Jay McKenzie

For more information visit:

www.serenadepublishing.com

ABOUT THE AUTHOR

I was born in North London and after leaving school worked very briefly for a high street bank before joining the local library service. I was in my happy place surrounded by books and worked there for over twenty five years, the last fifteen or so in the Local History Archive. I've always been fascinated by social history, and studied for a History degree as an external student of London University. Later

I studied for a Science degree with the Open University, choosing subjects my Arts background had ignored – biology, genetics, and criminology. A fantastic learning experience which gained me a 2:1 - in my forties!

After a stint at the turn of the Millenium at University College, London as a Personal Assistant to a professor, I moved to be an Administrator at Birkbeck College, London, working with post graduate science courses and supporting academics and research staff in the laboratories. I was lucky enough to do a creative writing course while I was there and was inspired to write a novel!

I left work in 2010 to take on caring responsibilities and a year later moved with my husband to a rural village in West Norfolk, UK. I've been actively involved in the local community – helping save pubs seems to be a theme! -supporting a Local History project and an orchard and loving the country life!

I completed my first novel, Janet, Resurrection, in Lockdown and have started a second, continuing the life of Janet Brown. I enjoy the odd writing competition and spend a lot of time working in my garden, baking for village events, and playing table tennis with the village ladies team.

Visit my website at: mhaustinfictionwriter.com

HISTORICAL NOTES

The book starts at the hanging of William Burke and continues with his public dissection – well-documented facts. It is also true that he was hanged after William Hare, his partner in crime, gave evidence against him of some seventeen murders in return for his own freedom and a change of name. Hare was put on a mail coach leaving Edinburgh at midnight, heading for Carlisle. What happened afterwards is unknown. In my book I have Hare ending up in London. This is entirely feasible. The new University College London had recently opened (1826) and he would have found a market for his skills in its Medical School or working for any of the surrounding private anatomy schools. His end is uncertain though rumour has it he was murdered and thrown in a vat of lime... Janet Brown and Mary Paterson were two prostitutes mentioned in the trial of Burke and Hare. Mary was murdered and sold to the medical school as I have written. She was recognized by medical students who had seen her alive and well weeks before.

Janet had left her at Hare's boarding house and gone home, returning later to look for her, again as I have written. History records her but only as wandering the streets of Edinburgh hunting, in vain, for her friend. I have given her a new role, totally imaginary, along with ambitions for a better life.

Robert Knox, surgeon, was disgraced and out of favour for a time but did continue to work and teach in Edinburgh for some years, and it was only in 1847, years after the Burke and Hare scandal, he left for London. He ended his days living in Hackney. He had various medical roles and his last position was at the Royal Marsden Hospital. Anything I have written about him relies on imagination, and an author's licence to invent.

George Birkbeck opened a Mechanics Institute in 1823 for the education of working men. His vision of enabling social mobility through education was revolutionary. Ordinary workers were able to improve themselves, and also supply the skilled workforce needed in a new steam age. His ethos is carried on to this day as Birkbeck College, part of the University of London.

Thomas Wakley, surgeon, Member of Parliament, and founder of the medical journal the Lancet, was a champion of social reform. He campaigned against incompetence and nepotism and a better regulated examination system for doctors. I give him a twinkle in his eye and a dash of flair which he may already have had, but which I would expect of him.

Sir Astley Cooper, an eminent surgeon who had various run-ins with Wakley over the years and won a court case against him, as I describe. He worked at Guys

Hospital and Kings College, a more conservative, Establishment-run, university than University College. He is famous for his daring if often deadly operations and for treating King George IV for some time. He was present when the king died. His autopsy report, like everything else he said and did, was contested by Wakley.

Other characters in this book, my medical students, Verity and Samuel, the horrible Hoskins and Carlo the chef are all completely fictional. The Italian boy, whom I have named Aldo and to whom I have given a brief life of sorts, is based upon a real boy found dead in London at about this time. His life and death, and so much of what was happening in the medical underworld at that time, is described by Sarah Wise in her book The Italian Boy. I owe her a debt of gratitude for her work and how it fed my imagination. Sarah, like me, was a student at Birkbeck College.

Janet's world was one where the old and new clashed, the role of the church was being challenged and men of science were exploring via legal and illegal means animal and human bodies. The 1832 Anatomy Act will go on to make it much easier for bodies to be found as the workhouses filled with the desperate and powerless and added to those from the gallows.

But in all this crowded and unsavoury society there were seeds sown to improve people's lives. Political reform is on the horizon, after the draconian clampdowns following the French Revolution. Even women like Janet are allowed to attend some of the lectures given at Birkbeck College, and University College London, the first secular University in Britain, would soon admit them too. Janet is more optimistic for the future than her real-life namesake, but I make no apologies for that.

The title of this book, Resurrection, refers in part to the new life Janet creates for herself in London, but also to the term used by many to describe the work of those who dug up the recently buried dead and gave them a new role – the Resurrectionists.

ACKNOWLEDGMENTS

I would like to acknowledge the amazing help and support I have had over the several years it took to complete this book. Firstly to the Norwich based National Centre for Writing who, with the Arts Council run competitions for new writers. I was lucky enough to win a prize and have my work read and critiqued by a professional, Lesley McDowell, who saw potential in me. And to my publisher Sarah Williams of Serenade Publishing who boosted my self-belief further by saying she loved my work and wanted to publish it!

Thanks go too, to my fellow students on a Birkbeck writing course with whom many hours of discussion (and several glasses of wine) helped me thrash out what I wanted to write about. I'd like to mention particularly Sandra Lawrence, Moshe Elias, Neil Heathcote and Hilary McCollum.

To my good friends Rachel Pugh, Chris Lawrence, Sue Hatfield and Sue Ferguson who have encouraged my scribbling over the years, my gratitude. Most recent thanks to Jim McNeill who has helped me craft a website, something I've never had the courage to attempt before. He is an incredibly patient man! Final and greatest thanks go to my beloved husband Alan who has put up with me talking about my writing for ages, lived with my books and papers strewn about, driven me to writer's events, and had a little hut built in the garden so I can scribble in my ideal peaceful setting.

www.ingramcontent.com/pod-product-compliance
Lightning Source LLC
Chambersburg PA
CBHW030512120726
47904CB00005B/1433